THAT BOY FROM
NAZARETH

THAT BOY FROM NAZARETH
The Coming of Age of Jesus of Nazareth

Joel Gordonson

RUDI PUBLISHING

Copyright © 2015 by Joel Gordonson
All rights reserved

Published in the United States by Rudi Publishing

Hardcover ISBN 978-0-945213-40-6
Paperback ISBN 978-0-945213-50-5
E Book ISBN 978-0-945213-42-0

Library of Congress Control Number: 2014956850

All rights reserved. No part of this publication may be reproduced, distributed, or transmitted in any form or by any means, including photocopying, recording, or other electronic or mechanical methods, without the prior written permission of the publisher, except in the case of brief quotations embodied in critical reviews and certain other noncommercial uses permitted by copyright law.
For permission requests, email the publisher, at terri@rudipublishing.com
with subject line "Attention: Permissions Coordinator."

Cover design by Gillian Kirkpatrick
Book design by Terri A. Boekhoff

*To the memory of my Laura,
whose love, forgiveness, sacrifice, and death
showed me how happiness becomes sadness
and taught me how tragedy can lead to triumph.*

Contents

Acknowledgments *ix*

Prologue *xiii*

1 Commander of the Garrison *1*

2 The Manger *9*

3 Home *21*

4 The Well *35*

5 The Carpenter *47*

6 The Rabbi *57*

7 Demons *73*

8 The Map *87*

9 Magic *99*

10 The Sadducee *117*

11 The Pharisee *129*

12 The Sea of Galilee   *145*

13 The Prophecy   *159*

14 Temptation   *177*

15 The Pilgrimage   *191*

16 The Tetrarch   *213*

17 The Temple   *229*

18 Missing   *257*

19 Revelations   *289*

20 The Plots   *305*

21 Sins   *319*

22 Miracles   *333*

23 The First Supper   *345*

About the Author   *353*

Acknowledgments

In mysterious and unforeseeable ways, I was given the plan, the tools, and the people to create *That Boy from Nazareth*. Those people included many friends, personal and professional, who provided support through unlimited and innumerable contributions. To them I say, "Thanks be unto you!" But in particular, my inexpressible and deepest gratitude must go to Terri Boekhoff and Eugene Schwartz whose remarkable intellects, dedicated belief in this book, and two distinguished lifetimes of publishing experience made the book a reality. Finally, heartfelt thanks are for Jeanette who was there for me at the beginning and remained through it all.

*Thank God for what He reveals,
and thank God for what He conceals.*

Alfred Edersheim
(1825-1889)

So when they had performed all things according to the law of the Lord, they returned to Galilee, to their own city, Nazareth. And the Child grew and became strong in spirit, filled with wisdom; and the grace of God was upon Him.

His parents went to Jerusalem every year at the Feast of the Passover. And when He was twelve years old, they went up to Jerusalem according to the custom of the feast. When they had finished the days, as they returned, the Boy Jesus lingered behind in Jerusalem. And Joseph and His mother did not know it; but supposing Him to have been in the company, they went a day's journey, and sought Him among their relatives and acquaintances. So when they did not find Him, they returned to Jerusalem, seeking Him.

Now so it was that after three days they found Him in the temple, sitting in the midst of the teachers, both listening to them and asking them questions. And all who heard Him were astonished at His understanding and answers. So when they saw Him, they were amazed; and His mother said to Him, "Son, why have You done this to us? Look, Your father and I have sought You anxiously." And He said to them, "Why did you seek Me? Did you not know that I must be about My Father's business?" But they did not understand the statement which He spoke to them.

Then He went down with them and came to Nazareth, and was subject to them, but His mother kept all these things in her heart. And Jesus increased in wisdom and stature, and in favor with God and men.

The Gospel According to Luke
Chapter 2, Verses 39–52

Chapter 1

COMMANDER OF THE GARRISON

"Palestine is a puzzle. The questions for you are how much blood are you willing to shed to solve it—and whose blood will it be."

A hot morning sun above Galilee glanced off the golden helmet of Pontius Pilate as he contemplated his answers to the puzzle. The large red plume on his helmet and the red cloak slung back over his shoulders indicated his rank as the recently appointed commander of the Roman garrison in Nazareth. A bead of sweat trailed down his neck, picking up speed until it raced under the breastplate armor covering his chest.

Pilate looked over at Flavius Petro, the retiring commander of the garrison. Followed by a soldier armed with a spear, they wandered through the shops and stalls of the crowded Nazarene market place. It was unusual in these dangerous times to see officers of their high rank wandering through the market, especially guarded by only a single soldier. But Flavius specifically chose this common setting to introduce Pilate to the difficult situation the new young commander would be inheriting. He wanted Pilate to experience the deceptively simple place and people before describing the reality of their complex history and politics.

"I worry about you, my young friend," Flavius continued as he and Pilate strolled through the market place. "I doubt you fully understand what you are getting into here in Galilee."

Glancing around, he also doubted whether Pilate had noticed that they already were being followed.

To his surprise, Pilate found that he enjoyed the walk among the merchants who hawked their wares in the busy market. Stopping under the awning at the entrance to the Wine Seller Shikkor's shop, Pilate helped himself to a long swallow from a jug of fine wine that a moment earlier had been for sale. The Commanders and their guard sauntered on, ignoring the Wine Seller Shikkor's muffled complaint about their lack of payment and the large man's mutterings about Rome stealing their land and everything in it. Pilate took a perverse pleasure from people's polite smiles which a few steps later turned into silent and hateful glares that he could feel on his back.

Flavius was curious about his young successor whose remarkable reputation had resulted in a rapid rise to the rank of commander. Virtually overnight, the officer became renowned throughout the Roman army. It was unprecedented that a man this young would command a garrison. Flavius asked him straight out how he came to his rank.

"A lot of bloodshed and, as in any battle, a little luck," answered Pilate.

"My legion was sent far to the east of the Empire at the Black Sea where the local tribes were mounting an active rebellion. I was leading a cavalry detachment on a long patrol through territory where we weren't expecting any hostile encounters.

"We rode onto a sheltered peninsula that reached out into the Black Sea to water the horses, when we stumbled into a large encampment of rebels. The rebels were caught completely by surprise. It turns out we had cornered the main force of the rebellion with all its leaders and their families.

"With nowhere to flee and their families in peril, the rebels had no choice but to fight to the death. We suddenly found ourselves fighting as if we were defending Rome itself. But with the advantage of being on horseback and catching the rebels off guard, the battle turned in our favor surprisingly fast."

Flavius gave him a suspicious look.

"It is said that no prisoners were taken and no lives spared. Is that true?"

"It started and ended quickly," Pilate replied vaguely. "We managed, with luck and through no choice of our own, to completely destroy the rebellion in a single battle."

Flavius knew the rest of the story. The Roman generals and the Emperor were surprised and pleased at the news of Pilate's victory. They had expected a long and bloody war in the rebels' territory. As word of the extraordinary victory spread throughout Rome and the Empire, the young officer quickly became legendary with a reputation as the man who could suppress rebellions in short order through ruthless cunning. The Emperor desperately needed such a man in Galilee. So Pilate was dispatched with a quick promotion and a legion of soldiers to command the newly fortified garrison in Nazareth upon Flavius's retirement.

Pilate was pleased with his orders, but also felt the pressure of his new reputation and responsibilities. While Palestine was perhaps not an ideal posting for a Roman officer whose ambitions lay more with generals in Rome than among Jews in the hills of Galilee, the Roman garrison outside of Nazareth was quickly acquiring strategic military importance. Palestine was the important land bridge between the Roman province of Syria in the north and Egypt which Rome also ruled in the south. Galilee was in the center of Palestine, and Nazareth was in the heart of Galilee.

Flavius was as old and tired as Pilate was young and ambitious. In his long service to Caesar and the Roman Empire, he had stood on the smooth marble of the Roman Senate, the drifting snow in Gaul, the searing sands of Egypt and the harsh salt from the Dead Sea. Now, he no longer worried whether the plumes of his helmet were a bit ragged or that his red cloak was slightly faded. Yet his sword was always sharp as was his punishment of any soldier who shirked his duty. And his men were intensely loyal, for Flavius knew no fear.

"Make no mistake, Pilate. You are in the middle of another rebellion with all the rebels and their families around you. But you won't be stumbling across any rebel army camped in a single place. The rebels are everywhere, and yet are nowhere that you can find them.

"See those boys standing over there?" Flavius pointed at several older boys standing on the edge of the market. "For a few coins, they deliver messages for people in Nazareth. I've even used them a few times. I'd wager that those boys know more about the Jewish rebels than Herod's secret police, if they're not rebels themselves."

"Certainly we are not turning the wooden stockade in Nazareth into a stone walled garrison because of Jewish boys," scoffed Pilate.

"The rebels are everywhere but cannot be found hiding among the people because many of the rebels are the people without any way for us to identify them. That's the main reason the situation in Galilee has only become worse," replied Flavius after another cautious look over his shoulder.

"There are active rebel forces like those led by a nasty animal named Judah who attacked a palace not an hour's walk from here in Sepphoris. They seized money and weapons that were used very effectively to terrorize the region. But there are also many other splinter groups like the Sicarii."

"I've heard of these assassins and their hidden daggers," said Pilate.

"They are more than just assassins," warned Flavius. "They will come out of nowhere to slit your throat just to taste blood as much as to free their country."

"But the Roman Empire has occupied Palestine for almost seventy years," observed Pilate. "How can Galilee in the middle of Palestine still be filled with uncontrolled rebels?"

"Unfortunately, that answer will have to come later," said Flavius as his hand cautiously moved to the handle of his sword.

Suddenly, Pilate's helmet was yanked off his head into the air above. The move jerked his eyes upward to see a slight boy sitting on the edge of the awning where it attached to a building. The boy was holding the helmet by its feather plumes with a happy smile as if he had just found a new toy.

"Welcome to Nazareth," he said pleasantly before he launched the helmet high into the air. He rolled off the awning on to the ground and disappeared into the market crowd just as the spear of Pilate's guard ripped through the awning where he had been crouching.

Pilate and Flavius swiftly drew their swords and instinctively balanced to defend against an attacker. Instead they saw Pilate's helmet land in the hands of a plump teenage boy with pimples over his face. Completely surprised by this engagement with an enemy unlike any he had encountered before, Pilate hesitated until the boy turned and started lumbering away as fast as he could with Pilate's helmet held high in triumph.

"Seize him!" Pilate loudly ordered his guard. The soldier started running after the plodding boy, expecting to make quick work of him, when he abruptly handed the helmet to another boy with long hair down his back coming full speed right by him back in the direction of Pilate. Before the soldier and the astonished Pilate could stop and reverse direction, the boy with the helmet tucked under his arm had already raced past them.

"Get the fat one!" Pilate barked at the guard. Pilate himself turned to chase the fleet-footed boy with the long hair.

The soldier turned and started to run back after the large boy, but was tripped by another boy who then disappeared into the crowd. By the time the soldier regained his feet, he was unable to pursue or even see a trace of the large lad or his pimples. The guard returned to Flavius's side where the two of them lost sight of Pilate.

"These boys are harmless," observed Flavius dismissively after watching the action with mild amusement and thinking Pilate was foolish to give chase. "I'm going back to the garrison. Wait here for the commander to return or find him if you can," he ordered the soldier. Feeling rather undignified chasing boys with his spear, the guard was only too happy to obey Flavius's first order.

Pilate was in hot pursuit. The long haired boy deftly dodged around people bunched between the market stalls. When the boy stumbled on some loose rocks, Pilate, who had always been a good runner, began gaining on him. Just as Pilate thought he might catch the boy in a few more strides, the helmet was handed off to yet another boy in a striped tunic who ran straight across their path.

As quickly as he grabbed the helmet, the boy tucked it into his belly and rolled under a donkey cart at the end of a long pathway formed by market stalls on both sides. He bounced to his feet and began running down the back side of the market stalls on the left.

Pilate could not get through the stalls between him and the boy in the striped tunic, so he continued the chase by running down the center walkway between the two rows of stalls. Pilate began to draw even and started looking ahead for an opening in the stalls to get at the boy in the striped tunic. Suddenly the boy stopped dead in his tracks. Pilate skidded to a stop and watched him throw the helmet high above Pilate's head across both rows of stalls.

The helmet fell into the waiting hands of a taller boy behind the stalls on the right. The tall one took a only few quick strides and also came to a complete stop. Pilate again saw his helmet being thrown back over his head and the stalls on the left once more. There it was caught by a very short boy who resumed the sprint behind the stalls on that side.

Pilate, now drenched in sweat, renewed the chase. He could see that he was nearing the end of the row of stalls. Although the shorter boy was difficult to see, Pilate quickly estimated where he would likely reach the end of the row and prepared to make a move through the stalls to intercept the boy and nab the helmet. With six great strides he reached the spot and spun left to make his charge.

But no one was there except a surprised old man selling jars of olive oil whose eyes could not leave the tip of Pilate's sword. Pilate stood for a brief moment breathing heavily, his eyes hunting for the boy. It was then that he first heard the laughter of the stall vendors and their customers. With his anger rising at the thought that the new Roman commander was becoming a laughing stock to the locals, he suddenly realized that they were not laughing at him.

Their eyes were turned to the end of the row of stalls where there stood a donkey looking a bit puzzled by the red plumed helmet of a Roman commander sitting on its head. One ear stuck out on the side of the helmet which put it at a rakish angle that made the sight of the donkey even more ridiculous.

Pilate wiped the streaming sweat from his matted hair out of his eyes. With gritted teeth, he started walking, his sword pointed, towards the animal. He was not sure of what he was going to do with the donkey, but he knew it would not be pretty. Before Pilate even had taken two steps, a hand reached out of the crowd and gave the donkey a sharp slap on its rump. The startled donkey took off down a short passageway between two buildings at the end of the market.

Pilate had no desire to carry on the chase, but he preferred even less to remain standing there embarrassed among the amused crowd. He started down the passageway at a much more fatigued pace.

As the donkey reached the end of the passage, it stopped. Pilate watched in disbelief as yet another boy snatched the helmet off the donkey's head and shooed the animal away down a connected passageway. The boy did not move. He just stood there holding the helmet in front of him.

"How many boys are there?" the exasperated Pilate wondered. Wary of another tricky maneuver, he looked about cautiously as he began to step closer.

The boy remained motionless as Pilate slowly came within four, then three and then two sword lengths from him. He was close enough that even in the dim light of the passageway Pilate could see that he was a good looking lad with curly black hair and matching jet black eyes.

Just as Pilate was about to lunge, the boy in one quick motion kneeled down and sent the helmet spinning through Pilate's spread legs. Sparks flew off the spinning helmet as it struck the cobblestones between his feet.

Pilate whirled around. There, inexplicably standing behind him, was the very same boy with the same black eyes under the same curly black hair, smiling and holding the helmet as before. Pilate was baffled. How had the boy moved behind him? For an instant Pilate wondered if it was magic or he might be going mad.

With a roar of rage, he threw himself after the boy. In his anger, Pilate no longer knew what he sought, the boy or the helmet. He was not stopping now until he had captured or conquered something.

The curly haired boy had only to spin around and take a couple quick steps back into the sunshine of the market where he flipped the helmet in the air to his right as he ducked in the opposite direction. Pilate hurled himself around the corner after his helmet.

The helmet was being carried away by a tall, handsome older boy with a thin beard who ducked into another passageway. Pilate's anger drove him on, but he was out of wind and slowing quickly. The older boy had already put several paces between them when Pilate followed him around the corner.

Pilate stopped when he saw the older boy standing against a wall at the end of the passage. He did not move. Pilate thought there was fear in the boy's eyes. "He's cornered," Pilate suspected. But as Pilate moved towards him, he unexpectedly disappeared to the right. With one last great effort, Pilate flew around the corner at a dead run.

Around the turn, two more boys sitting on the ground gripped the opposite ends of a rope lying across the opening at the edge of the market square. At the sight of Pilate, they pulled the rope taut a few inches off the ground in an instant of perfectly synchronized timing.

As Pilate's foot caught the rope, he catapulted through the air with his sword flying like a freed bird. He landed face first with a mushy thud among a frightened flock of bleating sheep in a mud filled pen surrounded by a crowd of men who had been bidding on them. Their surprised silence was quickly broken by laughter when one of the bidders immediately offered "two shekels for that runt of the flock who can't keep his feet."

Pilate, struggling to breathe, pulled his face out of the mud. He wiped some of the muck from his eyes and looked up straight into blinding sunlight. A figure leaned over him, blocking the sun and easing his pained squint. Pilate could barely make out the silhouette of a boy's head framed by a halo of sun behind the soft curls of his hair.

With both hands, the boy gently set Pilate's helmet down on the commander's red cloak thrown in the mud around his shoulders.

"Forgive them," the boy said quietly, "for they know not what they do."

Suddenly a woman's hand grabbed the boy's arm and pulled him up to his feet and away from the Roman. The blazing sun again seared Pilate's eyes.

"Yeshua!" the woman hissed into the boy's ear in Hebrew. "You get home this very instant—run!"

Chapter 2

THE MANGER

The small old barn looked like it was about to collapse. It was so old that no one could even remember when it was built. The shepherd who had built it died long ago. But he had constructed the barn and its manger with loving hands and had built it to last. So it never quite fell down.

People took little notice of the decrepit looking barn anymore though it remained a serviceable shelter for a few head of livestock. But someone had taken notice of the old barn when others did not. A group of older boys often slipped in and out like shadows.

Inside, the gaps in the timbers and mortar let in shafts of light that lit up particles of dust dancing about in the breaths of air that entered with the light. It was cool, dark and quiet, like the inner sanctum of a temple.

Bartholomew sat on a pile of straw on the floor of the barn next to the manger, still out of breath and sweating. As overweight as he was, Bartholomew was not used to running so much. The sweat made his pimples sting, but he did not notice. He was too excited.

"That was unbelievable, Judas, how you snatched the helmet. I thought you were done for when the soldier ripped the awning with his spear. But after that, the whole plan went perfectly," he spoke rapidly with a happy smile as he tried to catch his breath.

"And those two were amazing!" he went on energetically. Bartholomew and Judas looked with admiration and pride at James and John. The brothers were truly extraordinary. To the human eye, they were perfectly identical. No one, not even their parents, could find a difference between the twins with their curly dark hair and dark eyes.

The sight of sparks coming off the soldier's helmet when it hit the stones beneath his feet still thrilled the twins. But like the other boys sitting around the manger, they now felt uneasy with an unspoken sense of how foolish and truly dangerous their prank might have been. They all knew Roman soldiers were not to be trifled with. These were trained warriors who were proud of their Legion, who killed prisoners rather than captured them, and who had crucified over two thousand rebels not long before. The boys finally realized that they may have put their lives in great peril. It was not likely that the new commander of the garrison would leave this "welcome" to Nazareth unanswered, even if it was at the hands of fun-loving boys.

Each of the boys in the barn silently reviewed his part of the plan to guess at how much trouble he might be in if they were caught. Judas sat there frowning while Andrew in his striped tunic looked at Matthew and Philip. They all wondered whether the Roman officer would recognize their faces from tossing the helmet back and forth as they ran through the market stalls. Simon was almost certain that when he ran right at the two Roman soldiers, they had seen his face. As if he knew what everyone was thinking, Simon shook his head of long hair and declared defiantly, "I would run at a whole legion of Romans if I could."

The barn door opened and three more boys slipped in. With a laugh, they all took exaggerated bows as if they were at the Coliseum in Rome before the Emperor himself. Once he rose from his bow, Peter, with the beginnings of his first beard, stood taller than the other boys as he slapped them on the back and complimented them all. He was still proud of his final feint and flee move that led the new garrison commander around the corner to his muddy initiation to Nazareth. The other two, Thaddeus and Jim, immediately became busy untying the sections of brown rope they had used into shorter pieces that were carefully returned, one to each boy who tied his rope as a belt at the waist of his tunic.

Suddenly the boys went silent at the sound of hooves outside. After a tense moment, the barn door banged open and sun lit up the corner of the barn. Before anyone could move to escape, a shadow blocked the door. They froze in their places.

In sauntered the old donkey looking for a bit of fodder. Instead he got a relieved groan of recognition from the boys. A bit startled at first, the donkey sensed the friendship of the familiar figures and even joined in with a loud bray.

Right behind him entered another familiar figure who announced, "I bet you boys doubted we were coming back." Thomas scratched the ears of the appreciative donkey and led him to his stall by the manger.

The donkey had been given to the boys by Joseph the carpenter, with the admonition that they must take good care of him because he had earned some rest and retirement by traveling from Galilee to Egypt and back. Joseph told them that in the donkey's life he had carried loads more precious than they could imagine. The boys joked that the old donkey must have carried gold or jewels for some wealthy priest, so they named him Jewels and gave him the same care and affection as if he were a stallion in the Roman cavalry. Jewels soon became more interested in the grain with which Thomas had rewarded him.

In the strange mixture of excitement and concern that filled the barn, Peter looked around and realized for the first time that someone was still missing.

"Where's Jesus?" he asked with a worried look.

"He's in big trouble," answered Thaddeus. "His mother was in the market and was there when he gave the Roman soldier his helmet back. She made him go right home."

Judas spoke up. "He shouldn't have given the soldier his helmet anyway. Doesn't he know why we took it in the first place?"

"Why did we take the helmet in the first place?" asked Bartholomew.

"Not to give it back, that's for sure," said Judas.

"We took it because he's a Roman soldier and he's not supposed to be in our country," declared Simon.

"Oh Simon, you're just saying that because that's what you hear from the Warriors of the Wilderness," responded Thomas. "Besides, how does stealing a Roman soldier's helmet get him out of Palestine and back to Rome anyway?"

When no one answered, Peter finally spoke up. "No one thing will drive the Romans out. It will be many small wounds that ultimately kill the Roman beast in our land. That's why we deliver messages."

"I thought we deliver messages to make money," observed Matthew.

"We do," Peter responded. "But every message we deliver for the Romans or Sadducees or Pharisees, we remember, and what we remember we tell the Warriors of the Wilderness, and what the Warriors know about the Romans and their friends will help give them the chance to cut the Roman beast again and again until it must leave or die."

"And the whole time we take their money for taking their secrets," Judas noted smugly.

Andrew asked, "Hey Judas, how much money do we have now?"

Judas reached into the manger and pulled out from beneath the hay a pouch that jingled with coins. With the coins was a piece of parchment that Judas unrolled and studied a few moments until he announced the total proceeds of their services. It was not a small amount, particularly for twelve boys from poor working families in Nazareth. They were prospering because the politicians, businessmen, secret lovers and gossipers in Nazareth knew no better means than these twelve boys to have messages delivered quickly, reliably and confidentially.

Especially confidentially. What better way for a clay tablet, a piece of parchment, or a few spoken words to be delivered with discretion than to have them carried by a fleet-footed illiterate boy who for a silver coin could be counted on to say nothing of it to anyone? As long as the sun was up, there was always such a boy standing at the north corner of the market square wearing the distinctive brown rope belt of an Apostle messenger tied at the waist of his tunic, ready to receive any summons from a slave for his master, a worker for his employer, or a maidservant for her mistress.

The boys with the brown rope belts were known to all in Nazareth as the "Apostles", the Greek word for messengers. What was not known to all was that the Apostles in fact could read very well, and not only

Aramaic, their native tongue, but also Hebrew, Latin, Greek and several other languages from that part of the world. The Rabbi Zacharias made them learn to read the languages in which all important documents were written. Living in Nazareth and its market taught them the rest.

What was known only to a very few was the other service provided by the Apostles. The written messages that were delivered, they read. The messages they read and heard, they remembered, and the messages they retained in their remarkable memories were told to the Warriors of the Wilderness.

Twice a day each Apostle would report to Peter and Judas. Each of them would give Judas the money he had received for their deliveries, and then recite to Peter word for word from memory the contents of messages that seemed to have any possible importance. Peter, at the end of each afternoon, would divert from his deliveries into a dark passageway on the northern edge of Nazareth where he would start singing a song taught to every boy as a child. As he walked, somewhere along the passage a door would open, but never the same door twice in a row. Sometimes no door would open, and Peter walked on singing his song until he returned to the road leading back to the market.

When a door did open, Peter would slip in and recite to the person in the room the contents of all the important messages recently delivered. Often there were several people who would listen to the messages. Sometimes they were women from the town, sometimes older men whom he did not know. But sometimes there were the thrilling moments when the door would be opened by one of the Apostles' heroes, one of the young and strong Warriors of the Wilderness who had sworn that someday their swords would drive the Romans from the land.

Their friend Jesus did not deliver messages since he worked long hours for his father as a carpenter. Still, Jesus always seemed to have some idea of everything that was going on. Maybe not all the detail in the messages, but always some idea. It was so natural, no one really thought anything of it.

Thomas watched Judas as he put a large number of coins back into the pouch after recounting the total. "Do you think this is a safe place to keep all that money? It's only a manger in an old barn."

"Who would think to look here anyway, for us or our money?" Judas responded. "No one uses this dirty old barn anymore."

"How did we end up using the barn as a hideout in the first place?" asked Matthew.

"Jesus found it," Judas responded. "He said a barn and a manger is the last place where people would expect to find anything important."

No one replied. It made sense to them and after all, it made sense to Jesus. Judas slid the bag of silver coins back under the hay in the manger.

After a moment, Peter stood. "I have to go," he said.

"Where to?" asked his brother Andrew.

"I promised Mother I'd go to the well and fetch water for her this afternoon."

"I'll go with you," announced Andrew.

Philip spoke up, "I have to go to the well too."

"Me too," James and John said in unison.

"Where are Thaddeus and Jim?" asked Matthew.

"They just slipped out a moment ago," answered Bartholomew.

Simon, Matthew, Judas and Thomas glanced at one another and darted out the door as quickly as they could in the direction of the well after Thaddeus and Jim.

Bartholomew and Jewels watched them all head out towards the well. In the sudden quiet of the dusty barn, the two looked at each other for a moment until Jewels' head went down into the manger for another mouthful of grain. Bartholomew, feeling a little hungry, looked at the donkey with envy, and then decided he too would wander down to the well.

***

Flavius was trying hard not to show his amusement as Pontius Pilate paced in front of him with fuming fury.

"Boys! I was humiliated by a bunch of boys! I won't tolerate this sort of thing. They will be punished. The entire Roman Empire is embarrassed by such an incident."

"No one in Rome knows anything about what happened to you." The old soldier tried to placate the young man's anger. "I would not worry about the matter."

"That's because it wasn't you with a face full of mud being laughed at by a bunch of sheep herders," Pilate replied.

"You should be grateful it was mud and laughter, and not blood and screams," said Flavius. "We just found the bodies of two more of our men who were ambushed by rebels last night."

Pilate's jaws clenched in anger. "We have had Roman forces here for seventy years, and the Herodian family has ruled with the Caesar's blessing for almost as long. How can the situation still be so out of control?"

"You have to understand," replied Flavius, "that almost ninety years before the Romans took over Palestine, the tribes of Israel had a healthy taste of independence with their own Jewish dynasty established by the great military victory of the Maccabee warriors.

"Alexandra-Salome was their Queen. But following her death, her two opposing sons each requested help from Rome to seize the crown, and the Roman general Gaius Pompeius was only too happy to pick one as an excuse to defeat the Maccabees, take possession of Jerusalem for Rome and end Jewish independence.

"After the Imperial Army took Palestine," Flavius explained to Pilate, "Rome tried to control its conquered territories by installing local rulers who were to govern while remaining loyal to Rome. Even after twenty years of bloody uprisings by Jewish rebels, Caesar Augustus turned the Jewish governor of Galilee, Herod the Great, into the King of Judea and all Jews.

"Now, Herod would not have been my first choice. He was a half-Jew that would jump scared at a cat's shadow. The good thing for Rome was that he didn't lose a minute's sleep from shedding Jewish blood to protect his throne under the Empire. But his idea of suppressing rebels who killed innocent people was mainly to marry a Jewish princess and spend his whole treasury on rebuilding the Temple in Jerusalem. For a while Herod believed he could win the hearts of the Jewish people through great and generous sovereign acts."

"In other words, winning their hearts by spending their money," Pilate offered.

"Exactly," answered Flavius. "But of course that didn't stop the violence from the Jewish rebels. In fact, it only made the rebellion worse. By the time he got around to killing some rebel zealots and confiscating the wealth of rich Jews in Jerusalem to pay off his debts, Herod was scared of anything that moved.

"He was even convinced that a newborn baby in Bethlehem was part of a movement to replace him as King of the Jews. So our brave and mighty Herod defended the Empire by murdering every male child under the age of two in that city to be certain an infant was no threat to his throne.

"As if the slaughter of babies wasn't bad enough," Flavius continued, "Herod managed to anger the Jews even more by trying to cover up his blood bath. He sent his secret police into the Holy Temple in Jerusalem to destroy part of the registry of Jews maintained by the priests. The Jews didn't take too kindly to Herod erasing the names of hundreds of Jewish babies after killing them. Can't say as I blame them."

"He was one seriously frightened and frightening coward," Pilate concluded.

Flavius nodded as he picked out a sweet fig from the bowl in front of him. "Neither the Jews nor the Romans liked or trusted him at that point."

"Then how did we end up with his son Herod Antipas ruling Galilee?" Pilate asked. "I understand he's every bit as bad as his father."

"That's a good story," replied Flavius. "After ruling for forty years, Herod the Great was still too frightened of losing his crown to name his successor. So his wives started plotting for each of their sons to succeed him, and one son went so far as to plot against Herod himself."

Flavius took a bite of the fig.

"Here's the best part," he added with a smile and a full mouth. "To prove to the Jews he should be their King, Herod strictly followed the laws of Moses, including the restriction against eating pig. But when he found out about the family plots for his throne, His Highness executed his mother, his first wife and three of his sons, including one who tried to poison him."

Flavius's smile grew bigger. "Do you know what Caesar Augustus himself said when he heard what Herod had done? He said 'I would rather be one of Herod's pigs than one of Herod's sons.'"

Laughter erupted out of Flavius.

"But in the end, the coward got what he deserved," Flavius observed. "He had some sickness that gave him a gut full of excruciating pain for months. I suppose it should be no surprise that around the same time he managed to arrange the current mess you are inheriting in Galilee.

"All hell was breaking loose from the rebels who were sensing Herod's weakness. So he decides first to make his oldest son Archelaus the King of the Jews. But then for reasons no one understood—maybe he was in need of a good fart," Flavius chortled, "our Herod the Great changed his will seven times until he finally decided to divide Palestine up among three of his sons and not have a King of the Jews.

"Archelaus was to rule Samaria and Judea including Jerusalem in the south, while his brother Philip was given most of the northern regions of Palestine. The third son Herod Antipas was to rule Galilee in the center of Palestine and Perea across the Jordan River to the East.

"Now having Palestine ruled by the three Herodians who were all as worthless as their father, and leaving the Jews without a King, made as much sense as not eating pig—it seemed like a good idea at some point, but now nobody really understands why.

"When the three of them presented themselves to Caesar Augustus in Rome to obtain his approval of their claims, Herod Antipas without much brotherly love argued that he ought to inherit the whole kingdom and be made King of the Jews. He's a fox, that one, and smarter than his two brothers. But he didn't get the crown. Caesar confirmed the division among the three of them."

Flavius grinned at Pilate.

"But the randy young Herod Antipas did get a saucy little consolation prize. He fell in love with his half-brother Philip's wife, Herodias. And she figured if anyone was going to become King of the Jews, it was going to be Herod Antipas rather than her mild-mannered husband Philip. So Herod Antipas divorced his wife who was the daughter of Aretas, King of the Nabateans in the south, and married the willing Herodias.

"But here's the interesting little twist—Herodias was the granddaughter of Herod the Great and the wife he murdered. So when Herod Antipas married Herodias, he married his sister-in-law who is also his niece.

"And now King Aretas, who was none too happy about his former son-in-law running his daughter out of her palace in the middle of the night for a new wife, is preparing his army to thrash Herod Antipas soundly.

"Have you got all this, Pilate?" Flavius asked him. "Because you might find yourself fighting Jewish rebels at the same time you are in the middle of a war among Herod's army, the Nabateans, and Philip so that Herod can continue romping around with his scheming little Herodias."

Pilate shook his head in disbelief. "That's quite a family. How do you suppose they figure out the seating at family dinners?"

Flavius laughed. He was pleased that Pilate could find some humor in the serious situation. That attitude might help keep the new commander sane while dealing with it all.

"When the three Herodians took over," Flavius went on, "Rome's foreign policy of governing through our Jewish brothers was working so well that we would have done better to give the Jewish rebels a paid holiday and hand them the keys to Palestine when they returned.

"That's when the palace in Sepphoris was taken by the Jewish rebels. The Roman governor of Syria had to come in with a couple of Legions for a counterattack. He didn't worry about Moses' law and eating pig. He destroyed the palace by fire, sold its inhabitants as slaves, crucified two thousand rebels for good measure, and exiled Archelaus to the snows of Gaul. Now that's Roman foreign policy."

"It should be," said Pilate, "but things aren't any better now."

"That's because Rome didn't get rid of the whole Herod clan once and for all when we had the chance," Flavius answered. "Galilee, including your new garrison and hordes of hidden Jewish rebels, is still under the rule of Herod Antipas."

"And what is Herod Antipas doing to bring control over the Jewish rebels?" Pilate asked. He did not give Flavius a chance to answer. "Just like his father, he's trying to become King of the Jews by building more palaces instead of killing Jewish rebels who would like to kill him."

Flavius tried to offer some hope. "Well, Pilate, soon you may have the opportunity to explain to Herod Antipas that building palaces for himself and temples for Jewish priests, who do nothing but kiss the Caesar's arse and count their tax money, does not make Galilee more secure for Rome."

"I look forward to it!" Pilate's hand tightened around the handle of his sword. His mind was no longer on Flavius's briefing. If he could use soldiers with merciless dispatch to bring this Jewish rabble under control, the Emperor surely would express generous gratitude for his service. Archelaus had been replaced by direct Roman rule. Could Herod Antipas be next? Pilate was mentally surveying the options for maneuvering Herod Antipas out of Galilee and Philip out of the northern regions, and then moving Rome, and more specifically Pilate himself, into a secure seat of direct power over all of Palestine.

There was little doubt in his mind that control over Galilee and Palestine would have to be accomplished by the Roman army with swords for submission and crosses for crucifixions. "And crucifixions," Pilate concluded confidently, "should give a Roman commander in Galilee all the bloodshed and luck that he needs."

Chapter 3

HOME

"You are my beloved son, Jesus, with whom I am *not* at all pleased. Just what did you think you were doing with those troublemaker friends of yours?"

"I was just—" Jesus tried to answer his mother's question, but Mary did not give him the chance.

"Do you have any idea what those Roman soldiers would have done to you if you were caught? And stealing the helmet of the new commander of the Roman garrison! Did you think you were going to be best friends after you handed him his helmet when he was face down in sheep dung? Don't you remember those hundreds of crosses outside of Nazareth?"

Jesus winced at these words as two of his brothers got up and left the room quickly. They knew what was coming next. Only his two sisters Rachel and Rebecca and his brother Jude remained in the main room of their small home.

"Do I have to remind you who you are and where you come from?"

Jesus looked down and took a deep breath. He knew now that he was going to be there a while.

"You were born the son of Joseph, who is the son of Heli, who was the son of Matthat. He was the son of Levi, who was the son of Melchi, who was the son of Janna."

"Yes, Mother, I know and I'm very sorry that—"

Mary would not hear him. "And Janna was also the son of a Joseph, who was the son of Mattathiah, and he the son of Amos who was son of Nahum who was the son of Esli."

At this point Jesus' sisters started silently mouthing the names as Mary continued through them. "Naggai was his son, and his son was Maath who was also son of a Mattathiah. He was the son of Semei, who was also the son of a Joseph who was the son of Judah. Before him was Joannas and Rheas and Zerubbabel..."

Jesus knew all his forebears by heart, so before long his mind started wandering as his Mother carried on with the long list of his lineage. He thought of how much his Mother loved him and that he loved her despite the fact she sometimes gave her love in strange ways and heavy doses with all the family prayers and celebrations of the Sabbath and holidays, and always with the full recitation of every one of his endless ancestors.

"... who was the son of Shealtiel, who was the son of Neri who was begat of Mechi and Addi before him..."

And his family, Jesus loved every one of them as if each was the most important person in his life. His father Joseph expressed his love for all of them through hard work and the time he spent with each of them all by themselves. Joseph lived his life as a husband dedicated to his wife, a father dedicated to his children, a working man dedicated to those who hired him, and a man of faith dedicated to his God. He rarely told them how to live their lives. He just tried to live a good life and let them watch.

"Then Cosam was the son of Elmodam who was the son of Er who was born of Eliezer and he of Jorim..."

It was a challenge oftentimes for Jesus and all his brothers and sisters to live together and yet live their individual lives in their humble home. Jesus and his three brothers shared a small room and bed which was not easy in the best of times. And now his Mother had just told them she was with child again which she was sure would be another boy. As the oldest, Jesus was often responsible for the daily affairs and disputes of his brothers Jamie, Jude, and little Joses. But with Jude, it was especially difficult.

Jude was one of those people who were said to have "demons." Some people with demons had fits, some behaved oddly, and some had ticks and twitches. Jude's demons seemed to keep him in his own isolated world after the age of two when he stopped listening and talking to or looking at any other person. Now most of the time he would just sit on his blanket in the corner of the main room, rocking back and forth and incessantly smoothing out the lap of his tunic. But then the demons would possess him to act in a wild and violent way. When the demons took possession, usually no one except Mary could even touch him without him breaking into a great rage in which he would hit or bite anyone who came near him. In the worst times, even Mary had been hurt trying to calm Jude, and Joseph had to wrestle him down to prevent him from hurting himself or the family.

Jesus did not know how to be a loving brother to Jude until one day after a particularly violent and angry outbreak of Jude's demons, Joseph explained to Jesus that the hardest but best kind of love was the love given without receiving any love or reward in return. That love, Joseph said, was pure.

After that, Jesus decided he somehow would find a way to love his brother Jude as he did his other brothers. He started simply by kneeling as near to Jude as he could for as long as possible without upsetting him. That changed things. Not only did Jesus look at his brother differently, but Jude started letting Jesus briefly sit close to him without acting up, and sometimes even permitted Jesus to rest his hand on Jude's shoulder to calm Jude when he became agitated. Eventually, Jesus could sit right next to him and after a few minutes touch him softly on his cheek without any anger or reaction from Jude.

Mary's voice came back to him, "...the son of Matthat who came from the great line of Levi, and Simeon and Judah who followed from the houses of Joseph, Jonan, Leiakim and..."

Jesus tried hard not to smile when he noticed that his sisters were silently saying the numerous names of his ancestors as Mary recited them sternly. It was remarkable that they too could remember all of their names in order, though the two of them had heard Mary lecture Jesus with those many names innumerable times. But it was truly extraordinary that Rebecca could mouth the names silently because she had not been able to speak or hear since a life-threatening sickness as a small child. Seeing Rebecca always made Jesus want to smile, for Rebecca seemed to be smiling all the time. Jesus believed she smiled not because things made her happy, but instead because she knew that by smiling she could make things happy in the first place.

Rebecca's lips moved with Mary's, ". . . who was the son of Melea, who was the son of Menan, who was the son of Mattathah . . ." When Rebecca lost her speech and hearing, she with Jesus slowly learned to speak and hear again. Not with her voice and ears, but with her hands and eyes. Jesus taught her to watch closely people's lips, faces and bodies to understand what they were communicating in ways far beyond what her ears used to perceive. Then the two of them came up with hand signals to speak to one another. They could communicate with a momentary gesture all sorts of complex thoughts that would have taken far longer for them to speak.

". . . who was the son of Nathan, who was the son of David—King David."

His Mother would always pause for effect after she reached David in her recitation of Jesus' lineage. The pause worked. Jesus would always feel a tingle of excitement at the thought that he was an actual descendant of the greatest King in the history of the tribes of Israel. He would imagine himself a great prince and heir to the Kingdom which he would rule with a firm and wise hand while defending the land as a great warrior against attacking invaders. But then he would see the reality of the small room around him and wonder how the relatives of the greatest king the Jewish people had ever known could be living such a simple life in a Galilean town far from Jerusalem.

Yet Jesus loved Nazareth. He loved how it sat in the low hills that let its people look out for miles over the plains of Galilee below. From the hills Jesus could see the orchards of olive and fig trees, the vineyards climbing and descending the rolling hills, the herds of goats, sheep, cattle and oxen meandering among the rocks, and the far off fields of golden grain.

Nazareth was an exciting place for a twelve-year-old boy. The town was not as large as the nearby cities of Sepphoris and Tiberias, the new city that Galilee's ruler Herod Antipas was building. But Nazareth, sitting in the middle of Palestine's land of plenty, was quickly becoming bigger and busier by the day as a crossroad of commerce. The crops and livestock in the distance eventually made their way into the town where they turned into a beehive of commercial activity. The bakeries turned out daily smells that would make morning stomachs growl. The grape and olive presses worked from dawn until dusk after the harvests arrived. The weavers' looms hummed as their hands moved in mysterious patterns that magically turned out cloth with all types of designs. The picklers would place the olives in urns and jars filled with their strong smelling, carefully mixed concoctions which they sealed before sending them off to strange places faraway.

The potters' wheels spun while their hands turned the wet clay into graceful plates, bowls and urns. The tent makers would make movable shelters while the leather workers would tan hides for the makers of sandals and saddles. The blacksmiths would bear the heat of their fires under the Galilean sun to hammer out metal with their strong arms. That metal went to many people for many purposes from needles and fishhooks to horseshoes and swords. Artisans produced things of beauty and enjoyment such as jewelry, tiles, stone carvings, and toys.

Eventually everything and everyone found their way to the market in the center of the town. Although the population of Nazareth was mostly Jewish, the sellers and buyers in the market created an ever-changing mix of people and cultures. The stalls, tents and buildings always seemed busy with crowds of people looking to purchase their daily staples and special items for their pleasure. Each week brought a new stall or tent with wares never before seen in Galilee. Every day one would see new and different people for the first time. People tall and short, thin to fat, loud and silent, beautiful to ugly, friendly and mysterious, with exotic skin, eyes, beards, clothes, would all trade with each other in the market even though their tribes or people might be hostile to one another.

There was also great interest and entertainment in the new messiahs that appeared regularly to preach near the market. All of Palestine seemed to be looking for a messiah to improve some aspect of their difficult world. So each new messiah brought a message and promise of different things to come—the end of the world, the coming of God, the return of Moses, freedom from Rome, relief from hunger and poverty. The list and combination of promises were endless. Their message could be loving or hateful, persuasive or commanding, whispered or shouted, eloquent or incomprehensible. They could be well-dressed radical priests celebrated in their own synagogues or wild-looking men half naked and unwashed from living in the desert. The new messiahs the people seemed to like best were the ones who claimed to do miracles, which inevitably ended up being some sort of magic trick to get the attention of the crowd.

The market had a special music all its own in the many languages spoken as people, merchandise and money came and went. The common language of Nazareth was Aramaic and the Jews also spoke their Hebrew. But when friends talked, deals were struck, complaints were raised or arguments arose, one would also hear Greek, Phrygian, Phoenician, Moabite, Edomite, Ammonite, and occasionally a new language called Arabic.

"Before him was Jesse who was son of Obed who was the son of Boaz who was born of Salmon who was conceived from Nahshon . . ." Jesus sighed at the ancestral names still coming from his mother and thought about the people he had seen that day in the market.

In Nazareth there were people with money and people without. But by far, most were poor. There were those to whom fortune had not been kind, the crippled, the blind, the beggars, those with demons in their heads, and the diseased, especially the lepers who were shunned and feared by all. But even the basic working men—the tradesmen, laborers, farmers and shepherds—lived a peasant's life. Most Nazarenes said they were unhappy because the Romans occupied their land, but Jesus wondered whether their unhappiness in fact came from the fear and uncertainty of not being able to feed and clothe themselves and their families.

While the poor had a difficult life, it was far better than that of the slaves. Some were born slaves, some became slaves as punishment for a crime or their inability to pay their debts, and some were kidnapped and forced to remain slaves or be killed. Some wore rags and went hungry. Some were slaves to wealthy landowners or priests who fed and clothed them well. But they all lacked for one thing: their freedom. Jesus was always greatly saddened when he saw the slaves in the market, and especially when he saw the uncertainty or fear in their eyes after they had been sold to a new master.

The richest people were the Pharisees. The Pharisees were a closely connected fraternity that was involved, despite their small numbers, in the political and religious control of every city and village in Palestine. In Nazareth, the Pharisees held every one of the twenty-three positions as elders on the Sanhedrin, the local council with authority over municipal matters and the governance of the synagogue.

One could always tell a Pharisee in public from his clothes and his conduct to others. His elegant attire included no fewer than eighteen pieces of carefully arranged clothing of distinctive material, cut and colors. The outer jacket was the finest white and purple embroidered garment with broad borders edged in blue fringe and with a fashionable wide silk sash around the waist. Under the jacket, an inner garment went down to the heels but was carefully cut not to touch the ground. His hair and beard were trimmed and perfumed, and his head dress was a pointed turban curiously wound so that the ends hung gracefully behind. He would often wear a seal ring and bracelets of gold or ivory on his right wrist.

Even more conspicuous than a Pharisee's clothing was his behavior in public. First and foremost, he would avoid wherever possible physical contact with others, especially foreigners. They were considered unclean even to look at, let alone to touch. Second were his demonstrative devotions in public places. When the time for his prayers arrived, a Pharisee would stop on street corners or the middle of the road, prominently position his body and clothes, place his feet together and bend over so far every vertebrae in his body was stretched to the limit. The longer the prayer and the more benedictions, the more likely the Pharisee would be heard by God. If he thought his displays were being silently mocked by passersby, he did not care. A Pharisee was devoted to his brotherhood of Pharisees without fear of consequences.

"Amminadab was the son of Ram who was the son of Hezron who was the son of Perez…" Mary's voice carried on with a relentless rhythm.

Then there was the building going on in every direction one looked. The carpenters, the stone masons, the laborers, all seemed be hurrying from one construction site to another. There was the garrison in Nazareth growing for the increasing arrivals of Roman troops, the great palace that Herod Antipas decided to construct in nearby Sephoris, and the buildings and houses for the new people who seemed to be moving to the town every day. But the town's tradesmen and materials also went farther to Tiberius where Herod Antipas was building a great new city of Roman design as a tribute to the Empire that gave him his power.

"And then the great Patriarchs—Judah and his son Jacob, and his son Issac, and his son Abraham."

Jesus wondered how the "great Patriarchs" in his family history compared to his Rabbi Zacharias who was like a patriarch of their synagogue in Nazareth. Jesus had been taught by Zacharias for as long as he could remember. He loved talking with Zacharias and hearing his lessons. They talked about everything: the wisdom of the Torah, the stories and history of the Jewish people, life in Nazareth, Jesus' problems and fears, his friends the Apostles who were also taught by Zacharias, and anything else that came to their minds.

For the last several weeks, however, their conversations were all about preparation for Jesus' first trip to the Temple in Jerusalem for the Feast of the Passover. Mary and Joseph made the three-day journey to Jerusalem every year for the Feast where Jews gathered from throughout Palestine to celebrate God's passing over the homes where there was the blood of a spring lamb on the doorpost and sparing the first-born children in these homes from the plague that fell on Egypt for enslaving Israel. Mary and Joseph would leave the children behind with Zacharias's wife Elizabeth. But now that Jesus had turned twelve, he too would travel to Jerusalem with his parents to see the Temple and celebrate the Passover.

Jesus' first trip to the Temple in Jerusalem would be more special than usual, however, and demanded much time and work with Zacharias. The High Priest of the Temple had declared that this year's celebration of the Feast of the Passover would involve two boys about to come of age, chosen from selected synagogues throughout Palestine, who would read a passage from the laws of Moses or the books of the Prophets and give a testimony before the Priests of the Temple about the meaning of their verses in their lives. Jesus did not know whether he was filled with more pride or more fear at the chance to read from the scrolls before the High Priest.

"And Terah, Nahor, Serug, Reti, Peleg, Eber, and Shelah . . ."

Mary's husband Joseph came through the door looking hot, dusty and tired after a long day's work. Ordinarily when he returned home at the end of the day, he as head of the household would give each child a blessing. But when he heard Mary punctuating the names of his father's fathers yet again, he entered and turned around in one motion, and with a sympathetic glance at Jesus, went right back out to join his other sons who stood safely in the shade outside.

". . . who was the son of Caiman, who was the son of Arphaxad, who was the son of Shem, who was the son of Noah who saved mankind and the beasts of the earth from the Great Flood, who was the son of Lamech, who was the son of the ancient and venerable Methuselah . . ."

Jesus thought again about the encounter with the new Roman commander. The Roman soldiers had been in Nazareth his whole life and a long time before that. He felt the hatred of the local people towards the Romans, and had seen firsthand the harsh cruelty they showed the Jewish rebels with the beatings, imprisonment and crucifixions of any suspected men. But so far Jesus and his family and friends had not been subjected to any mistreatment from a Roman.

The truth was that his family was doing well under Roman occupation. At one time, no Jewish tradesman dared do work for the foreign invaders. But men needed work, and the Romans were hiring, so people now generally looked aside when Romans put Jewish men to work. Joseph and Jesus were employed most of the time doing special carpentry and stone work in the expansion of the Roman garrison. When Joseph talked with the Romans, they spoke to him in a business-like way with no other purpose than to get a job done right. They paid Joseph well for his work every Friday before sunset as he requested. As a working tradesman, Joseph could not want for better.

But there was genuine hatred of the Romans by most Jews in Palestine. They were taught as children that the Romans were invaders who had stolen both the land from the Jewish people and the power to have their own king instead of Herod who ruled only because the Roman soldiers maintained his power and tolerated his abuse of his own people.

In addition to the hatred of Romans was the hatred of taxes. Palestine was a Roman province, and therefore the Emperor believed all that was in Palestine belonged to Rome. So the Romans created a tax system that was systematically relentless and cruel. Rome sold the right to collect taxes to companies so that the Emperor had a guaranteed supply of money. Then the companies, to whom the Emperor had farmed out his power to tax, hired tax collectors and acquired great wealth in the process.

The first step of ensuring collection of all possible taxes was a census taken by Quirinius, the governor of Syria, to establish the number of people and their income and property. Women had to pay tax starting at the age of twelve and men at the age of fourteen. They paid two principal taxes, the ground tax and the poll tax. The ground tax was on property, and the poll taxes were on everything above the ground. These taxes included tax on one's income, on all that was bought and sold in the towns, on all imports and exports, and on the use of public highways, seaports, bridges, and entrances to cities.

The great wealth amassed by the tax collectors was increased further with their additional unforgiving schemes. They would increase the taxes by establishing false high values on property and income. Then they would loan money with extremely high rates of interest to persons unable to pay the inflated taxes. The taxpayer would think he was in a better situation by not owing taxes. But if he could not pay the debt and the high fees for borrowing the money, he was seized by the throat in public and dragged off to prison or sold along with his wife and children as slaves.

". . . and then Enoch who was the son of Jared who was the son of Mahalalel who was born of Caiman . . ."

When Jesus heard the name of Enoch, he refocused on the moment as he knew Mary would soon finish the list of his forebears. His sisters also knew that the end of the list was near and started moving to their chores for preparation of the evening meal since Joseph had returned home. He and his sons would be quite hungry by now.

". . . who was the son of Enosh, who was the son of Seth, who was," Mary paused, "—the son—" She inserted as always an extra long pause to impress Jesus with the last name, as if he did not know whose name was coming. "—of Adam."

Jesus braced himself for the final lesson and punishment. This moment was always the most interesting part of Mary's lectures so his brothers and Joseph carefully timed their entrance back into the house to see how Mary would end the session. Jesus never knew what was coming, but he knew Mary always did. She could come up with a scolding so withering it could make a Roman soldier cringe, sometimes she would just tell Jesus that he had shamed all of his family, alive and dead, and sometimes she would come up with a punishment that seemed to make no sense and would leave everyone completely puzzled.

"Your conduct with those troublemaker friends of yours brought great shame upon your name, your family and all of your ancestors." When his brothers heard this, they were disappointed. It was the usual stuff.

"Your actions today were dangerous. Extremely dangerous! Don't you ever do anything to a Roman soldier that could anger him. Do you hear me?"

"Yes, Mother," Jesus answered.

His brothers now thought this could be getting better, for Mary clearly was not through.

"If you continue to act like a trouble maker, especially like that no good Peter friend of yours—" his brothers leaned forward. It was coming now. When she mentioned Peter, the punishment was always worse than usual. "—I will never, ever, be able to arrange a betrothal between you and someone respectable like Susanna, that lovely young daughter of the Wine Seller Shikkor."

A groan of disappointment came from Jamie and Joses. Bethrothal? They wanted some sort of humiliation, house arrest or horrid house chores like only Mary could conceive. But then they thought of the Wine Seller Shikkor's daughter and a sour look came over their faces. Even Joseph had a look of concern at Mary's statement.

"Oh, Mother, not her," said Jesus with a slight look of panic in his eyes.

"Why not?" responded Mary. "She's such a nice girl. You could do much worse, you know. And she has such beautiful skin."

But Mother, she—she—" Jesus struggled to say something to save himself and not get in even more trouble. "She has such a great deal of beautiful skin."

His brothers nodded in agreement. A moment ago they could not wait for his punishment. Now they feared for their brother.

"I learned to love your Father. You can learn to love her," Mary answered sharply.

Joseph did not like at all where this discussion was going, so he tried to intercede gently.

"Mary, it's getting time for the evening prayers and meal. We don't have to decide anything right now."

"So you didn't talk to the Wine Seller Shikkor yet, did you?" she asked with a menacing look.

"Only for a moment, my sweet."

"Well, do it before your son ends up a criminal."

"Yes, my pet."

Mary sighed deeply, burdened by the never-ending frustration caused by the men of her family.

"Mother," said Rachel, "we need more water from the well."

Jesus jumped up. "Mother, I am truly sorry if I upset you. I will stay out of trouble in the future, I promise. Let me go to the well for you. It will be my punishment and privilege."

"All right then." She looked at him with a loving frown. She obviously had forgiven him and could not hide it. "But take your brother Joses." Jesus was once again her pride and joy.

"And you stay away from that girl from Magdala!" she warned him as he picked up two water urns and a smaller jug for his little brother to carry. "She is nothing but trash."

"But Mother, she has done nothing wrong, and she's my friend."

"You keep your distance from her, young man. Do you hear me?"

He hadn't. He was already out the door, with the water jugs and his little brother in hand, heading hastily for the well.

Chapter 4

THE WELL

She was the most stunningly beautiful girl Jesus had ever seen. And Peter had ever seen. And Matthew, and James and John, and all the other Apostles. And for that matter, every other man in Nazareth who could find a reason to be at the well when she fetched water there twice a day.

She and her mother had moved recently to Nazareth from Magdala for unknown and rather mysterious reasons. Her name was Mary, so being from Magdala she was known as Mary Magdalene. But because Mary was such a common name in Galilee, her family and friends called her by her nickname, Maggie.

Her beauty was the perfection of which all men dreamed. A thick braid of long hair as black and shiny as a raven's wing fell down to the small of her back. Although carefully braided in the style of a young woman in Palestine, a lock of her hair would often break free and fall over her eyes and make her look as if she was shyly peaking out at the world.

Maggie looked at the world through striking silver blue eyes framed by the long graceful curves of her dark eyebrows and the smooth olive skin of her high cheek bones. When spoken to, she would look down at first, and then slowly look up with those intense blue eyes in a way that made a person her captive—unable to move, unable to look away.

Her nose and ears were small and delicate. Underneath them the line of her jaw that joined the graceful curve of her chin suggested strength in her beauty. Her full soft lips formed a natural little pout that could disappear instantly into a dazzling smile.

She stood the height of a man's shoulder. Her figure underneath her robes suggested a full feminine softness, but she moved and spoke with a spirit that dared to be tamed. The beauty of what one could see of this young woman's body left no doubt in the beholder that the parts of her body which could not be seen were equally perfect. What the eye and the imagination did to men who looked at Maggie was unlike anything they had ever felt within themselves before.

The well in Nazareth was the sole source of precious water for the town's residents. It was fed by some shallow springs that collected water from the hills around the town. The well was dug hundreds of years before, and was deepened and improved with the passage of time and the growth of the town. Some small pools were built around the well for washing and to make access to the water easier. Because a large number of people would gather at times around this life sustaining place, an open area with cooling shade trees grew around the well and pools which made them as pleasant as they were important.

The well served as a natural gathering point for the conversations of anyone seeking to quench their thirst in the Galilean heat and especially of the women and girls who traditionally drew water twice a day for use at home. It was at the well where the women could confidentially exchange complaints about their husbands and gossip about each other, and the girls could talk about boys, clothes and the mysteries of life and love they yearned to experience.

But ever since Maggie moved to Nazareth and started going to the well to draw water, men and boys alike were happy all of a sudden to help with this daily household chore. Even Roman soldiers on patrol started to stop at the well in Nazareth to drink instead of returning to the garrison where water from its well was quite good and cool. Not surprisingly, the women and girls of Nazareth started resenting Maggie for the loss of their traditional preserve for exchanging confidences and for the diverted attention of their menfolk. Because none of this attention was of her intended doing, she thought their attitude was unfair, and so she resented them in return.

Jesus tried to get his little brother to walk as quickly as he could as they headed to the well. Timing was critical for getting in the line at the well for one's turn to draw water. These days, when a man or boy arrived at the well, he did not immediately get into the line. He found other things that appeared important enough to deal with on the edge of the market or the buildings nearby. Then when Maggie came around the corner and walked the fifty paces to the well, a badly disguised rush of males with urns, jugs and sheeps bladders headed to the line with carefully calibrated haste to end up ahead of the others and right next to her in the line.

But today Jesus feared he would be too late arriving at the well for any strategic advantage in lining up. Today of all days it was critically important that Jesus have a good chance to talk with Maggie. Maggie received and responded to so much attention, that one day you could talk to her and feel like she thought you were the man of her life, and the next day she could ignore you as if the two of you had never spoken before. She drove every man and boy who sought her out crazy from her fleeting and uncertain recognition. But Jesus had spoken with her a day earlier, and she had called him by name twice and even given him her soul-melting smile. He just had to talk to her today so that he could say and do something to make her remember him again now and hopefully forever.

Jesus tried to hurry little Joses along by taking his brother's water jug along with the two he was already carrying, but that only seemed to slow them down more as he tried to juggle all three jugs while answering his little brother's "why" questions about a thousand things along the way. Peter, he was afraid, would already be there in line next to her by the time Jesus could get to the well.

Just as Jesus and Joses began to pick up some speed towards the well, they ran into Bartholomew who started walking with them. With his substantial bulk, Bartholomew did not move very fast and walked even slower than Jesus' little brother.

"Are you headed to the well?" Bartholomew asked.

Jesus resisted every temptation to say something sarcastic as he struggled to carry the three empty water urns.

"Yeah, but we are in kind of a hurry."

"That's all right. I don't mind," he said without picking up his pace at all.

"But we are in kind of a hurry, Bartholomew," Jesus repeated while trying to walk faster to make his point.

"I know. I heard you." Bartholomew sort of leaned forward in his stride which did nothing to increase his speed. Jesus sighed in frustration but eased back to Bartholomew's pace.

Bartholomew was excited to talk to Jesus about their Roman helmet adventure, but when he looked at his companion, he could tell something was wrong.

"You don't look very happy, Jesus."

"I just found out my mother is arranging a betrothal for me."

"Well you must have known that your parents would soon be making arrangements for a betrothal for you," Bartholomew responded. "You're the age when most families arrange for a marriage in a couple years. Your parents must think it could be a good arrangement for your family and another."

"I suppose, but I didn't think my wife would ever be the Wine Seller Shikkor's daughter Susanna."

Bartholomew stopped suddenly as a look of surprise flashed across his face. He looked down and started forward again to stay alongside Jesus and Joses.

"Susanna's not so bad. She could be a good wife for someone—for you, I mean," Bartholomew corrected himself.

"She's a very nice person," Jesus agreed. "I'm just not sure I ever thought I'd marry someone that—that nice." Jesus chose his words carefully.

Bartholomew's pace seemed to slow again.

"I don't think my parents will ever be able to arrange a marriage for me," Bartholomew concluded glumly.

"I don't know why you say that," answered Jesus.

"Jesus, you're not blind like Lazarus. Look at me! I'm fat and have pimples. Who would agree to marry this?"

Jesus did not want to agree with this likely truth, but neither did he want to lie to Bartholomew.

"Well I'm sure some women like big men or there wouldn't be big men. And the pimples might just go away some day."

Bartholomew was making an effort in his mind to be convinced of Jesus' words as they turned the corner and came upon a man sitting on the ground begging from the passersby.

"Alms for the blind. Please help a crippled man who cannot see." The beggar had got the attention of a man and was working him hard for some charity in the form of hard cold coins. It was late in the day and the beggar still did not have enough to buy food and wine. Jesus' face took on a small frown as he veered over to the blind man.

"Good afternoon, Lazarus," Jesus greeted him while also giving a nod and pleasant smile to the man about to show him some generosity.

"Why good afternoon, young Jesus," said the beggar who recognized Jesus' voice. He stared ahead without blinking.

Jesus set the urns down, reached into a small pouch inside his tunic and took out a coin. With a distinct "cling" sound, Jesus flicked the coin high in the air above the beggar, quickly picked up the urns and started walking off.

Lazarus instinctively reached out and snatched the coin from the air.

"Lazarus has the best eyesight in Nazareth," whispered Jesus to Bartholomew.

"Why you're not blind!" accused the now unsympathetic man. Lazarus looked at the coin and then up at the man. The man turned to leave with an irritated look from the realization that he had almost been fooled into giving money to a charlatan.

Lazarus thought quickly and glancing at Jesus walking away shouted, "It's a miracle! I can see! Thank you, young man. Thanks be unto you!"

The man looked down at Lazarus and then stared down the passage after Jesus in complete amazement. As Jesus turned the corner, the man excitedly pointed at him to the people standing and passing nearby.

"Did you see that? It was a miracle! That boy healed a blind man."

The crowd buzzed with excited questions and marveled at this young miracle worker. "He's just a boy, but he gave the blind man sight!" exclaimed the man.

Lazarus immediately shifted his strategy to a desperate attempt to take advantage of this new financial opportunity. He implored the crowd, "Sir, Madam, some alms for a crippled man who is —who is now very nearsighted."

"Let us find the boy who does miracles," cried someone in the crowd as they all hurried in the direction Jesus had left.

"Dammit, Jesus!' muttered Lazarus after the crowd of people moved off and left him sitting there alone. Then he remembered the coin from Jesus and gave it a long look. With a shrug and a smile at having been cleverly done in by his young friend, he slipped the coin into his pouch, stood up, stretched and headed down the passage with a day's wage in his pocket and a spring in his step.

***

At the well, Maggie appeared around the corner with her friend Susanna, the daughter of the Wine Seller Shikkor. The area around the well instantly looked as if someone had dropped honey on an ant hill. Maggie and Susanna each carried a water jug as they walked towards the well. Or at least Susanna did. Maggie had not walked two steps towards the well when five boys surrounded her and each demanded that they should carry that enormously heavy empty jug so that Maggie would not hurt herself. Each of them tried to grab the water jug before the other. It was a wonder the jug did not fall and break. Susanna stumbled as the boys jostled her to get at Maggie's jug.

Susanna frowned at their insensitive treatment, but she had grown used to it. She had befriended Maggie when Maggie had first moved to Nazareth from Magdala. While she and Maggie were now best of friends and shared all their feelings, Susanna often felt that she became as invisible as a ghost whenever the two went out together. At the well, in the market, at the synagogue, everyone's eyes were on Maggie, and no one ever looked at Susanna, even though with her size there was a great deal to see.

But while Susanna missed getting any attention and sometimes felt sorry for herself, she often felt sorry for Maggie as well. Although men appeared to be paying attention to Maggie, Susanna could see that it was actually themselves they were flattering and that it was also the other men they were trying to impress and dominate. Susanna could tell that no one ever saw Maggie as the good person Susanna had learned she was. When men fawned over her and women scorned her, all they saw was Maggie's beauty, and not Maggie.

Peter was strategically positioned. Taller than the rest and with his long arms, he was able to wrest Maggie's water jug away from the other boys.

"Here, Maggie. Let me carry that for you," he said to her although still unable to look at her while trying to pry the hands of the other boys off the water jug.

Maggie tried to thank Peter. She was pleased that he had got hold of her jug because she thought he was one of the better-looking boys in Nazareth. But before she could speak to him, at least another half dozen men and boys surrounded her, each with an offering of desert flowers or fragrant herbs, perfumed water, sweets made of dried figs and honey, or bracelets from the market. Maggie walked as quickly as possible through the group offering their gifts, graciously but quickly accepting them so she could make her way to the line waiting to draw water at the well.

"Oh, that's very nice, thank you—Oh, I couldn't possibly take that, it must be very expensive—Isn't that lovely, I must make room for this in our small house."

Then she walked past the well down the line of men jostling for position to draw water next to her. The few women who had been in line had left since the line was hardly moving. Grumbling at the men standing in the unmoving line and at Maggie who was not even there yet, they had figured out that the line would be going nowhere until Maggie's water jug was full and being carried to her house by a willing volunteer. Each and every man and boy in line graciously offered Maggie and her empty water jug, now carried proudly by Peter, a spot in front of them.

She stopped when a young Pharisee dressed in particularly fine robes paraded up to the front of the line and said, "Maggie, you must take this spot in the line so you don't have to stand long in the sun." Maggie looked down the long line of eager faces waiting to offer their places when she passed them.

"Why thank you, Nicodemus," she said giving the young man a sweet smile and delicately brushing her head scarf back so that the bangs of her black hair shone in the sun. She looked at the long line of men and boys behind her giving them the same smile as an apology for her good fortune and their failed opportunity.

"Please may I let my friend Susanna join me as she and I have come together to fetch water for our families?"

"Of course," said Nicodemus not even looking at Susanna as he waived away the boy at the front of the line to make room for Maggie. The boy took the silent order and moved aside quickly for the important Pharisee who sat on the local Sanhedrin. Peter tried to step into the spot in the line with Maggie, but the Pharisee moved between Peter and Maggie with his back to Peter blocking any view of her.

"You look lovely today, Maggie. I am very pleased to see you." He spoke to her in a tone of voice that sought not only to engage her attention, but also to let the men and boys around them know that no one should dare attempt to intrude on her conversation with this young yet influential man of rank and wealth.

"Why thank you, Nicodemus. You are very kind to say so." Maggie looked up at him shyly.

With that look, the Pharisee became a slave to her blue eyes. He could list from memory the names of most taxpayers on Nazareth's tax rolls. He could calculate sums of long columns of tax payments almost instantly. With one word, he could put fear into the heart of any person who owed taxes to the Pharisees. But after the glance from Maggie's eyes into his, he could not get a single word to come out of his mouth.

After a moment's awkward silence, Maggie spoke again. "There are so many kind people in Nazareth," she said, nodding down at the gifts she held in her arms. "Since I moved here, people have been so nice to me, like Peter here."

She turned back to Peter and gave him a smile that made him almost drop her water jug. Nicodemus started to scowl at Peter, but then Maggie turned back to Nicodemus with that same smile and struck him speechless once again.

"Why, Peter, I do believe the sun will go down soon and I need to get water back to my mother. Would you be so kind as to fill up my jug for her?"

Peter lunged past Nicodemus for the rope tied to the bucket on the edge of the well, quickly lowered it into the well and pulled it back up repeatedly to fill Maggie's water jug. While Peter worked eagerly, Maggie gave little glances and smiles to the men and boys straining to get a look at her from the line behind.

When Peter finished and the jug was full, Maggie turned to the Pharisee.

"Thank you again, Nicodemus, for giving me a spot in the line. I feel guilty jumping in front of all these fine young men." She turned and beamed a smile at the line of men and boys behind her. "I hope no one minded too much."

Every head in the line behind vigorously shook an emphatic "No" as Susanna finished filling her water jug. When Maggie, Peter and Susanna started moving away, Nicodemus finally found his tongue.

"Will I see you at synagogue on the Sabbath?" he called after her. "I am reading from the Torah."

"You may just," she called back over her shoulder as she walked towards the passageway that led to her home. Then she turned and said in a low voice to Susanna, "Unless I can think of something else unpleasant to do."

The two of them giggled, but then Susanna said to her in a warning tone, "Now Maggie, don't you do anything to upset Nicodemus. He can make life very difficult for anyone who makes him cross."

Just as Susanna, Maggie and Peter with the full water jug began to turn into the passageway, Jesus hurriedly stumbled around the corner in front of them, clumsily trying to control his three water jugs and little brother. Maggie stopped and was about to say hello to Jesus, when a crowd of people a short distance behind him distracted her attention with their loud talk of a miracle. Jesus looked over his shoulder at the crowd. But when he turned back, Maggie had walked on past him, and Susanna was standing there looking down at him with a big smile.

"Hello, Jesus," Susanna said in a very friendly voice. She remembered her father's instructions to be as nice as possible to Jesus whenever she saw him.

"Hello, Susanna," he answered with a forced smile. His smile transformed into a frown as Peter walked by holding the full water jug and trying to catch up with Maggie. Peter gave Jesus a proud smile of victory, as Bartholomew, staring at Susanna, clumsily bumped into Jesus and knocked the three water jugs from his grasp onto the ground. Bartholomew stepped past him next to Susanna.

"Hello, Susanna," Bartholomew mumbled shyly. "That water jug looks awfully heavy. May I carry it for you?"

"Why yes it is, Bartholomew. Thank you very much." With a look of genuine appreciation, she handed the full jug to him with one hand as they walked off behind Maggie and Peter.

The sun was now starting to set as Jesus slowly gathered up the jugs, filled them from the well, and then struggled to pick them up and find his little brother. Although the sun was just sliding under hills in the horizon, his world already seemed dark as midnight. He was in trouble with his Mother. Maggie was much more interested in Peter than in him. And he was looking at living a life married to a woman who surely would end up twice his size.

"Come along, Joses," he said without enthusiasm as he started down the street toward their home. "We are late for prayers and supper."

Suddenly, three men stepped menacingly close in front of them and stopped them in their tracks. Jesus' head jerked up as tried to make out their faces in the fading light.

"Hello, Cousin," one of the men said to Jesus. It was not a friendly greeting.

"Hello, J.B."

Jesus now recognized him as well as the other men. At his cousin's side were two vinedressers who worked tending the vines in a vineyard far outside of Nazareth. They were known to be dangerous men who enjoyed causing fear in people, even the vineyard owners who employed them.

J.B. turned to them and said, "Why don't you two help with these water jugs and take young Joses here home to his parents so I can have a word with my cousin."

Before J.B. was done speaking and Jesus could say a word, the two men took the jugs from Jesus and one of them scooped up Joses in his arm. Joses looked anxiously over the man's shoulder back at Jesus as they strode swiftly away down the darkening street.

"What do you want, J.B.?" Jesus asked.

"A little favor, that's all," J.B. answered, glancing around to be sure they were alone.

J.B. was not even two years older than Jesus, but he seemed much older. While Jesus was at the stage of youth known as the *naar* in which he was "shaking himself free," J.B. had already ripened into a *bachur*, a young warrior. Jesus had not seen his cousin in the last year since overhearing Mary and Joseph talking about a heated argument between J.B. and J.B.'s father that almost had come to blows. After that, J.B. disappeared from Nazareth.

He had changed. His black hair had grown long and was uncombed. He wore a curious camel's hair shirt over his lean hard body and a unique leather belt around his waist. With an unkempt dark beard growing down from below his dark eyes, he looked more like a bandit than the son of respectable parents.

"What kind of favor do you want?" asked Jesus. He had no idea what J.B.'s answer would be, but was apprehensive nonetheless.

J.B.'s voice had not changed. It had an intensity which reflected the passion that always filled his words.

"I need you to draw me a picture."

"A picture? I don't understand, J.B."

"It's quite simple," he answered as he grabbed Jesus' hand and thrust a clay tablet into it. Jesus examined the clay tablet with a puzzled look. It was about the size and thickness of his hand.

"You work most days with your father doing carpentry and stone work in the Roman garrison. All you have to do is scratch onto this tablet a map of the garrison, its main passages, and the location of the rooms where the weapons are kept and the commander's quarters.

"Simple for a capable person like you, Cousin," J.B. concluded as if the matter were done.

Jesus held out the clay tablet to hand it back to him.

"I don't think so, J.B. I could get caught, and I think I'm already in trouble with the Romans."

"Good! So am I. We have nothing to lose."

"But J.B., if they think I am a rebel zealot, they could kill me."

J.B.'s eyes narrowed to a glare.

"And if we think you're *not* a rebel zealot," J.B. paused, "*we* could kill you."

He pulled up the sleeve of his camel's hair shirt to show Jesus a dagger held against his forearm by a leather strap. He started backing away slowly, his intense unblinking eyes fixed on Jesus.

"I will return for the tablet before the Sabbath. Sleep well—Cousin."

With one more step back, he disappeared into the dark of the Nazarene night.

Chapter 5

THE CARPENTER

Jesus was having the nightmare yet again. It was always the same complete dream before he would wake up drenched in sweat, every muscle painfully clenched.

In the dream he is three years old, holding his father Joseph's hand in the hot, crowded market. He is happily licking from his finger some sweet honey from an old farmer with no teeth who is laughing with Joseph.

The tall crowd surrounding him suddenly starts jostling and pushing to look at something passing by the market. He loses the grip of his father's hand as he is bumped and spun around. Feeling panicked, he turns to find Joseph's hand. Instead he sees the awful sight of a rebel, dirty, bleeding and struggling under the weight of the cross the condemned man is dragging to the site of his crucifixion.

The criminal stumbles under the weight of the cross which falls with a loud thud right in front of the badly frightened Jesus. He turns his blood-streaked face towards the boy, and his glazed eyes widen as he looks directly into the face of the horrified child.

In a raspy voice, he implores Jesus, "Save me . . . Save me!" as his trembling hand reaches out to touch Jesus' face.

Just as his bloodied fingers are about to touch Jesus' cheek, another hand grabs the criminal's wrist away from the little boy's face. It is Joseph who then lifts Jesus up into the safety of his arms, with the comforting whisper, "Jesus, it's me, your father. It's all right, Jesus."

Jesus bolted awake, tense and sweating, a hand on his shoulder.

"Jesus, it's me. It's all right, Jesus." Joseph's quiet voice immediately calmed Jesus without waking his brothers sleeping around him in the soft light of the dawn.

"Come, Jesus," Joseph whispered after a moment. "It's time to go to work."

Jesus breathed deeply with relief. Lately the nightmare was more frequent and even more intense, and he was glad it was over. Wiping the sleep and sweat from his eyes, he climbed carefully over his brothers.

Mary had a small fire going to warm some breakfast. They prayed their thanks and quickly ate their food in silence. No one else was awake except for Jude who was rocking back and forth fiercely, murmuring and staring without seeing at the wall immediately in front of him.

Jesus and Joseph picked up the wooden boxes that held their tools. Heading for the door, Joseph paused and stroked Jude's hair. Jude let out a sharp whine, knocked Joseph's hand away, and resumed rocking with even greater agitation. With a sad and pained look, Joseph walked through the door into the early morning sun light.

Joseph was respected by everyone in Nazareth—when they weren't laughing at him behind his back.

He was a carpenter and stone mason. Skilled tradesmen were well regarded in the Jewish community, and Joseph was respected more than most for his reliability, his honesty and the quality of his work. Almost every fine home in Nazareth had some sturdy construction or elaborate carvings and lattice work of olive wood, sycamore or cedar done by Joseph's hand. And he charged his customers a reasonable price, even the Romans. As the wisdom of the rabbis stated, "there is nothing more poor and nothing more rich than a trade."

But then there was his oldest son Jesus. When the two of them walked by, the smiles and smirks would follow as soon as they had passed.

Everyone in Nazareth knew young Mary when she got engaged to a man from Bethlehem named Joseph. He was rumored to come from a good family. There was even a report that his family was descended from King David, although many doubted it at first when they found out that he was just a carpenter and again once they laid eyes on him.

Before they were married, it became obvious that Mary was pregnant. After they had traveled to his home town of Bethlehem to register for the Roman census, they did not return. Mary's relatives found out that a child had been born, and that the three of them had gone to Egypt of all places. All of Nazareth assumed that because their shame was so great, they moved to a faraway land that had no love for Jews.

They eventually returned to Nazareth with their son, and the suspicions only grew worse. It took only one look at Joseph and Jesus.

Joseph could not be called a handsome man. He was short with a slight build. Although strong, he looked less like a carpenter and more like someone built to ride donkeys in a caravan. He had a dark complexion, a large nose, thinning kinky black hair, and squinty eyes.

Jesus, on the other hand, was handsome. His large soft brown eyes matched the thick auburn hair that fell in gentle waves to the top of the shoulders of his well-proportioned body.

Father and son? There were many reasons to doubt it. But people held their tongues, at least until the two of them had passed out of earshot.

For all their snide comments at Joseph's expense, everyone in Nazareth considered Joseph a good man. He was a loving father to his many children and a caring husband to Mary, which many agreed might not be the easiest of jobs.

He was also a dedicated member of the synagogue in Nazareth. Every year he was part of the caravan of worshippers from the synagogue who faithfully made the three-day journey on foot with the local Rabbi Zacharias to the Temple in Jerusalem for the Passover festival. While Joseph was not a particularly learned man, he and Rabbi Zacharias were very close. They often could be seen conversing quietly and earnestly for long periods of time. No one could quite figure out what a carpenter with a checkered past and a distinguished rabbi could be talking about so intently during their long walks or their meetings in the cool shade under the olive trees just outside of Nazareth.

Even the Romans respected and relied on Joseph. For years they had maintained a small and unimportant military garrison in Nazareth, but now that the Jewish insurgency had returned to Galilee with violent acts of outright rebellion, Joseph was kept busy building a fortification with space for the increased numbers of Roman soldiers, weapons and horses arriving monthly.

Joseph felt very uncomfortable when he first worked on the beams and stonework for the solid new walls surrounding the garrison. At one time it was against religious law to work on any project that was part of foreign rule or heathen worship. But the law finally gave way to men's need for work to feed their families and pay their ever-increasing taxes. With all their hatred of the Romans, many men worked as labor for the construction of the garrison. If the Romans had to be there, one might as well take their money.

His good work and ideas for the construction of the garrison came to the attention of Flavius who immediately appreciated Joseph's natural understanding of the military functions and needs of the garrison. As the garrison began turning from a collection of tents surrounded by a wooden stockade into a stone fortress with substantial rooms and passages, Flavius came to rely upon Joseph to conceive the design for the garrison's additions and oversee their construction.

So Joseph, the humble tradesman whose people laughed at him behind his back, was respected and relied upon by the most powerful man in Nazareth for the town's biggest building project that could become the key to protecting the Roman province. And with that came long hours at work and a sufficient wage to support his growing family.

Joseph and Jesus lugged their tool boxes through the guardhouse at the gate of the garrison. The two guards gave them a glance in the early morning light. Because the workmen's familiar daily entrance was no longer a cause for any interruption of the guards' morning conversation, one of the guards simply waved them through the gate.

"It will be a busy day, Jesus," said Joseph in a businesslike manner as he walked briskly across the parade ground past the guardhouse. They stepped aside and lowered their eyes as some soldiers came out of the corridor into which they were headed.

"We must work quickly this morning to finish the quarters for the new garrison commander Pontius Pilate. He's been here a week and will take over command soon. So Flavius has asked me to complete the commander's rooms before Flavius leaves for Rome."

Joseph listed from memory and without hesitation the items to be completed by Jesus in the commander's quarters even though the two of them had not worked on the site since the week before.

"Then this afternoon we will have to hurry to complete the tiles and finish work on the baths. Pilate has said he wants the finest and deepest Roman baths outside of Rome. So he has now ordered that one bath be deeper than a tall man, which is taking twice the tiles that we had planned. I don't know that we will be able to finish before you must leave to meet with the Rabbi, but he is coming to inspect the baths today. Pilate is a demanding man with little patience, so it must be done."

They worked most of the day in quiet concentration. When they started working on the Roman baths in the afternoon, Jesus placed the tiles along the floor and walls of the deep Roman bath while Joseph worked on the intricate mosaic designs and difficult corners. Joseph's hands moved deftly as they placed the tiles precisely into position and smoothed grout on the wall of the bath. Not a man of many words, Joseph preferred to speak little when he was focused on his work. Occasionally he would stop to survey Jesus' work and make suggestions or compliment what Jesus had done. Towards the late afternoon, he spoke to Jesus without taking his eyes from the tiles before him.

"Your Mother told me what she saw at the market yesterday. Now you tell me what happened."

Jesus explained that Simon had convinced the Apostles that they should do something like the Warriors of the Wilderness to let the Romans know they are not welcome in Nazareth. They had noticed that the new commander of the garrison was taking walks through the market and had come up with the idea of stealing his helmet. Jesus described the intricate plot the Apostles had developed and how it had gone just as it had been planned.

Joseph showed no emotion in response to Jesus' description of the events in the market, but was at once horrified at the danger created by the boys' scheme and yet secretly impressed at the cleverness and courage in its execution. He stopped working and turned to Jesus.

"What was your role in this plan?" he asked in a serious voice.

"I was to follow alongside all the action, and help if something went wrong in the helmet chase."

"How is it then," Joseph asked, "that you ended up giving Pilate his helmet?"

"No one had thought about what to do with the helmet afterwards. Peter ran by the sheep pen and handed it to me when I came around the corner, and then he just kept on running.

"When I saw the commander lying in the mud, I realized that we might really be in trouble. So I thought I would give him back his helmet to try to get us out of trouble, or at least some of it."

Joseph frowned. "Did he see your face?"

"I don't think so. His face and eyes were covered with mud. I'm not even sure he heard me because of the noise from the sheep and the people laughing. I ran off after Mother told me to go right home.

"Father," Jesus looked at Joseph earnestly, "I was trying to do the right thing."

Joseph said nothing for a long moment. Then he spoke softly and slowly to Jesus.

"Jesus, being part of a plan to steal a soldier's helmet is not doing the right thing.

"I know you tried to make good of a bad situation. But you jeopardized your own safety, if not your life. You jeopardized my work for the Romans and from that the safety and happiness of our whole family.

"You did a good thing in the situation, Jesus. But it may not have been the right thing considering all else."

Jesus knew there was truth in what Joseph was saying. But he was confused and uncertain about how he was to know in any single moment the circumstances that made an action right or wrong.

"And your mother was right," Joseph continued. "You must not do anything to anger Roman soldiers."

Joseph looked around and lowered his voice.

"You understand, Jesus, that you know things no Roman soldier must find out."

At these words, Jesus cautiously glanced about as well.

"Yes, Father," Jesus answered. He realized even more how his attempt to help the situation by returning the helmet had risked doing unmentionable and irreversible harm.

Joseph looked him hard in the eyes.

"Jesus, this is more serious than you know."

"I know how serious it is, Father."

"I'm afraid you don't, Son. At least not entirely."

Joseph set down the tiles he was holding. He wiped the grout from his hands with a rag and handed it to Jesus.

"It's time for you to go to your lesson with the Rabbi. You don't have many lessons left before we go to the Temple in Jerusalem for the Feast of the Passover."

Jesus felt another short shot of fear, this time at the prospect of his having to recite before the priests of the Temple a passage from the books of Moses or the Prophets. The rabbi kept giving him so many verses to read and memorize instead of giving him just one on which to focus as the rabbi had done for Judas for his preparation for the Temple. He didn't know how many he could still remember or how many more he was capable of remembering. He wished he could just stay there in the garrison working on the Roman bath where he knew precisely what was needed to finish the tasks he had been given.

"Go on, Jesus," Joseph gently ordered when Jesus lingered over his tool box. "Judas will be waiting for you outside the garrison gate by now."

Jesus walked down the passageway to the parade ground where he saw the partially finished rooms that were to be the quarters for the garrison commander. Reaching into the shirt of his tunic, his fingers felt the smooth surface of the clay tablet held in place by his cloth belt.

As he moved on down the long corridor and turned the corner, he slowed when ahead of him several Roman soldiers finished carrying into a large room a number of spears bound together. After the soldiers had locked the door to the room and moved on, Jesus continued down the passage until he came to the door. He paused before the door and looked at it as if he could see through it. Carefully he drew the clay tablet out of his tunic, then hastily jammed it back into his tunic and started walking again. Eventually he entered the sunlight of the parade ground outside and headed for the main garrison gate beyond the guardhouse.

Jesus did not recognize the two soldiers standing guard at the gate. They were recent arrivals for whom a young Jewish worker carrying a tool box was still a new sight. Jesus could not breathe as their eyes followed him closely through the gate.

* * *

Back at the main Roman bath, Joseph was wiping down the last of the tiles carefully placed at the corners of its deep bottom where he had put extra grout between the tiles to eliminate any risk of leaks. He felt very pleased at completing the baths as he had never before worked on such a project. Construction of these modern, state of the art baths, let alone baths of such size and depth, was not something that a carpenter in Nazareth ordinarily had the chance to do. The scale and beauty of the project along with the technical challenges of the structural support and plumbing were accomplishments of which he was rightfully proud.

Joseph heard voices above him. Down in the corner of the bath he could not see who it was, but then he recognized the voices of Flavius and Pilate. They stopped speaking midsentence as they reached the edge of the bath. Their eyes slowly took in all the detail of the tiles until they noticed Joseph stand up below.

"Joseph!" Flavius sounded slightly displeased. "You may have to redo this whole bath. If the Emperor were to hear about this bath, he would be so jealous that my life could be at great risk."

He looked down at Joseph and gave him a broad smile of congratulations. Joseph smiled back and nodded with satisfaction.

"Come up here and let's have a word."

It took a moment for Joseph to walk to the ladder at the other end of the bath, climb out and walk back to where the two commanders stood. Flavius held out his hand to Joseph.

"The baths are truly beautiful, Joseph. Beyond anything I imagined. You have done well."

Joseph tried to wipe off his hands with the rags he was still holding.

"I have grout all over my hands, sir. I can't shake your hand," he said apologetically.

"Shake my hand, Joseph!" Flavius commanded in a friendly voice. With a simple "Thank you," Flavius looked Joseph in the eye as their hands grasped each other firmly. Pilate coldly scrutinized the carpenter and remained silent.

"Now I am afraid I must punish you for your good work with a demand for more," Flavius announced with an official tone.

"I have received a message from Chuza, Herod's chief servant, who has indicated that Herod Antipas may be visiting Nazareth before long. Herod has requested that we put him up in the garrison since the construction of his palace in Sepphoris is a year behind schedule and they have just broken ground and started construction."

"I am aware of that delay, sir," Joseph replied, "since they have told me I am to work on the construction of the palace. It is a large and difficult project, I fear."

"Not surprising," Flavius responded. "Herod Antipas is a difficult man with a large opinion of himself.

"I suspect the reason he asks to stay in the garrison, which is hardly a place for the Ruler of Galilee to lay his head, has less to do with his palace construction and more to do with being sure that Jewish rebels don't remove his head from the rest of his body."

Joseph was a bit surprised Flavius would say such things to him in Pilate's presence.

"At any rate," Flavius continued, "we will need you to complete some of the rooms near the weapons storage for him and his servants and guards. How quickly can you turn a fort for soldiers into a palace for a ruler, Joseph?"

Before Joseph could answer, a soldier burst into the baths.

"Sir, Jewish rebels attacked a supply train carrying weapons from Sepphoris. Twenty soldiers were killed, and the weapons have been taken," he announced breathlessly.

Joseph saw the anger flare up in Pilate's face. Flavius ordered the soldier to have his chief officers meet with them immediately.

"Yes, Sir!" the soldier saluted and turned to leave.

"And one more thing," Pilate stopped the officer who quickly returned to attention.

"Order the daily patrols to look out for older boys in the town. If any of them does anything suspicious, arrest them and bring them directly to me."

Pilate spun on his heel and marched through the door of the baths followed by Flavius. Joseph stood there unmoving, trying to control his fear for his son, his family and the life in Nazareth the carpenter had constructed so carefully.

Chapter 6

THE RABBI

It is never too late in life to have dreams.

As the Rabbi Zacharias sat in the synagogue waiting for Jesus and Judas to arrive for their lessons, he stroked his long white beard and contemplated how this message had been God's first of two important lessons for him and his wife Elizabeth.

Zacharias had been an old man looking towards the final period of his life when he was told most unexpectedly that in fact his life was just about to begin. He had long been a devout and humble priest at the Temple in Jerusalem. He had chosen not to be ambitious like many of the elite Temple priests living in luxury. Instead he had valued his service at the Temple over the grand lifestyle available to Temple priests, and had cherished his life with Elizabeth outside of Jerusalem in the small village of Ein Kerem. After long and dedicated service at the Temple, he had been thinking much more about the last stage of his career and enjoying his remaining days with Elizabeth.

Although they had served God faithfully and followed the Laws of Moses, Zacharias and his wife lived with personal sadness and the shame in their society from not being able to have children. Not only did it pain them that their marriage did not lead to the love of a family, Zacharias was disappointed as a devoted servant of God who sought to do His will. He knew from experience and history that when God wanted something done on earth that was truly important, a baby was born. But now they were older, and they expected to rely only on their love for each other in their marriage to sustain them in their last years.

Then one day everything changed.

That day had already begun as an extraordinary day for Zacharias. At first, it had started as usual before the break of day when the priests of the Temple on duty for the week would divide in half to inspect the Temple before dawn. One group headed eastwards with a torch while the other circled westwards until they met to announce that "It is well! All is well!" Then they moved to the Hall of Polished Stones to cast the first of several lots to determine their duties at the daily service for the burning of incense on the Golden Altar before the Holy Place.

To draw lots, the priests stood in a circle around the presiding priest who chose one of the priests in the circle and removed the cloth covering his head. Then on a signal from the presiding priest, each of them held up one or more fingers just as the presiding priest called out a number. He then counted their fingers starting with the bare-headed priest until he reached the number named. That priest was selected as the one on whom the lot had fallen.

The first lot chose those priests who begin the cleansing of the altar and prepare its fires after washing their hands and feet by laying the right hand on the right foot and the left hand on the left foot. They scraped the burnt coals and unburned sacrifices from the previous evening, and laid fresh wood on the altar, taking care that it was not from an olive tree or a vine.

Next the priests assembled once more for the second lot. The priest on whom the lot fell was responsible, along with the twelve priests standing next to him, for slaying and offering the sacrificial lamb and cleansing the Altar of Incense. After the sacrificial lamb had been bound by its feet and its head laid towards the south and its face turned to the west while the sacrificing priests stood on the east side, the elders who carried the keys to the Temple ordered the opening of the Temple gates. As the heavy doors slowly swung open, the priests blew three blasts on their silver trumpets to announce to the worshipers that the morning sacrifice was about to be offered. At that same moment, the great gates that led into the Holy Place itself were opened for the priests who were to cleanse the altar of the incense, trim and relight the candles and refill all the burning lamps.

After the blood of the sacrificial lamb had been sprinkled around the corners of the altar and then poured around its base, the priests assembled for the third time in the Hall of Polished Stones for the solemn ceremony in which the final lots were drawn. First prayers were said, and the Ten Commandments were recited. The third lot was then cast for the most important selection of the day, the priest who would have the one opportunity in his service at the Temple to burn the incense and offer up the prayers in the Holy Place.

With mounting excitement, Zacharias watched the count of the third lot come to a stop at him. Today, after years of patient hope, he had been chosen for the greatest service a priest could perform in the daily ministry, the burning of the incense on the Golden Altar within the Holy Place. For the first and for the only time in his life, this honor would fall on him.

Zacharias nervously put on his special robes for the ceremony and reviewed the long prayers and blessings he would be reciting during the service. When it was time for the service to begin, Zacharias and his two designated assistants approached the altar where the lamb had been sacrificed as a burnt offering. One of the assistants filled a silver vessel with incense while the other placed burning coals from the altar into a golden bowl. Next they moved from the Court of Priests to the Holy Place. Along the way they struck a loud instrument to summon the priests and Levites to their places in the service and the people who were waiting to attend.

The two priests who had previously prepared the altar and candles ceremoniously climbed the steps to the Holy Place followed by Zacharias and his two assistants. The first two priests removed the vessels they had left behind, bowed after a prayer and withdrew. Next Zacharias's assistants carefully spread the coals and arranged the incense on the altar before leaving Zacharias alone in the Holy Place.

Zacharias heard the announcement to all assembled that "the time of incense has come." At that point, the entire multitude gathered outside withdrew from the inner court and fell to their knees with their hands spread in silent prayer. He had heard the quiet at this point in the service thousands of times. But standing alone at the Golden Altar before the Holy Place, Zacharias had never in his life experienced anything like the reverence of the deep silence that surrounded him in the vast Temple on that day.

He laid the incense upon the burning coals on the altar and watched in awe as a visible cloud of smoke and an invisible cloud of odors rose up to the Lord in Heaven above. Asking God's forgiveness for his indulgence, he said a personal prayer of thanks for this special experience and for all the blessings that God had bestowed upon him and his wife in their long lives. He savored the silence as long as he dared before he was to return to the priests and people to offer the long prayers and blessings they were awaiting followed by the music of instruments and singing at the end of the service.

As he turned to leave, Zacharias was startled by the figure of a stranger standing on the right side of the altar. His heart raced from the shock of this unexpected and improper intrusion on his solitude and the holy silence.

"Do not be afraid," the stranger told Zacharias. Then he spoke the last words Zacharias expected from anyone.

He told Zacharias that Elizabeth would bear him a son.

At this preposterous statement, Zacharias's first thought was to call for the Temple guards. But before he could do anything, the stranger proceeded to tell him matter of factly in detail that his son would be named John, that even in his mother's womb he would be filled with the Holy Spirit, that he would be great in the sight of the Lord and many would rejoice at his birth, and that he would drink neither strong drink nor wine.

Astonished by this bizarre message on the most personal and painful subject in his life, Zacharias stood there not quite knowing what to do or say. The stranger went on.

"Your son John will turn many of the children of Israel to the Lord their God. He will also go before Him in the spirit and power of the

Prophet Elijah to turn the hearts of the fathers to the children and the disobedient to the wisdom of the just, to make ready a people prepared for the Lord."

These last words struck Zacharias, "... make ready a people prepared for the Lord." They were from a prophecy in the Torah about a prophet who would come before the Promised Messiah. He did not call for the Temple guard quite yet.

"Who are you and how can you expect me to believe this?" Zacharias asked the stranger. "I am an old man. My wife has never been able to have children."

The stranger paused and answered, "I am the angel Gabriel who stands in the presence of God. I was sent by Him to speak to you and bring you these glad tidings."

Zacharias's eyebrows rose at this announcement. It was time to call for the guard he decided.

"All right then, if I must," the stranger sounded slightly irritated as if he had heard Zacharias's thought. "You will be mute, and unable to speak until the day these things take place, because you did not believe my words which will be fulfilled in their own time. Go ahead—try to call the guard, and then see if you believe me."

Zacharias opened his mouth to call for the Temple guard, and nothing came out. His throat was tight, his voice gone. He looked over to the stranger. The stranger had vanished.

Outside, the worshippers and priests were getting restless and wondered what was keeping the priest at the altar. It was time for his prayers and blessing before the music and end of the ceremony. Suddenly Zacharias stumbled out of the Holy Place with a glazed look in his eyes. He staggered and began beckoning to the crowd since he could not speak. Seeing Zacharias in distress, his assistants hurried up to him. The priests took Zacharias's arm and helped the struggling rabbi down the steps while the worshippers slowly dispersed with looks of dismay and concern.

After the stranger's visit, Zacharias's life quickly unraveled. Without a voice, he could no longer fulfill his duties as a priest in the Temple.

When the other rabbis and the High Priest read his notes to them on tablets that included ramblings about a visitation by an angel and prophecies of a coming messiah, they became concerned about his mental condition. The last straw came when the old rabbi claimed that the angel said Elizabeth would bear him a son. After that statement, pressure from some Temple priests was put on the High Priest to bring Zacharias before the Great Sanhedrin of the Tribes of Israel which ruled on all final legal disputes and governed the priests in the Temple. They would render a legal determination of whether Zacharias should be disqualified as unfit to serve in the priesthood.

The Great Sanhedrin held its proceedings in the Temple's Chamber of the Hewn Stones. In this large and solemn chamber, the Great Sanhedrin would hear testimony about a priest's conduct and statements, and listen to his defense. If a priest was found to be disqualified, he was clothed and veiled in black, and was escorted from the Temple. If he was not disqualified, the priest was not only allowed to continue to serve in the Temple, he was dressed and veiled in white and a great feast was held with blessings placed upon him by his brother priests.

Zacharias sat alone in his silence as the presiding member of the Great Sandhedrin, a wise and learned scribe who had known Zacharias for many years, announced that the hearing was to determine whether Zacharias should be disqualified from serving as a Priest of the Temple. They next listened to the statements of the priests and worshippers who had seen him at the service of the Hour of Incense. Then Zacharias's written statements were read to the members of the Great Sanhedrin. In Zacharias's own words written earlier to the High Priest, those now sitting in judgment heard about the stranger at the altar, his announcement about being an angel, Elizabeth's bearing a son, and then the angel striking Zacharias mute.

When the readings were finished, the head of the Great Sanhedrin turned to Zacharias and asked, "Zacharias, who will be speaking for you in this hearing?"

Zacharias shook his head.

"Are you saying that no one will be speaking on your behalf?"

He nodded in response.

The presiding member was surprised. He did not want this respected priest and his longtime friend disqualified by silence. It could be a simple matter for Zacharias to say simply that he had not been well and was now restored except for the temporary loss of his voice. On that basis the Great Sanhedrin could find that he was not disqualified for the Priesthood.

He leaned forward and asked, "Have you no witnesses or statements to offer on your behalf?"

Zacharias paused and then took a piece of parchment from the table before him. Once he finished writing, he handed the parchment to a scribe who took it up to the presiding member. After a glance at Zacharias's statement, a sad look came over his face. The presiding member handed the parchment back to the scribe.

"Read it to the members sitting in judgment," he ordered. The scribe held up the parchment and cleared his throat.

"The statements you have heard are true. God is my witness!"

"Zacharias," the presiding member asked, "do you have anything further?"

Zacharias shook his head. The hearing was over. All that was left was the quick decision.

But the decision did not come quickly. It was several hours before the Great Sanhedrin returned to the Chamber of Hewn Stones to render its verdict. The presiding member told Zacharias and all the priests in the chamber to rise for the decision. Once the priests stood and everyone else grew quiet, the presiding member spoke.

"Zacharias, after due consideration of the evidence and circumstances placed before us, we find that you are no longer able to serve as a priest of the Temple."

Zacharias bowed his head in disappointment as murmurs filled the chamber. The presiding member raised his hand for silence.

"However," he continued, "we do not find that you are disqualified from the priesthood."

Confused looks passed among the priests and scribes.

"In light of your long and faithful service to God and to this Temple, and the respect the Great Sanhedrin has had for you these many years, we find that it would not be fitting for you to wear the black robes and veil of disqualification. However, it is the considered holding of the Great Sanhedrin that because of your unfortunate inability to speak, it is time for you to retire and for your service at the Temple to end.

"There will be no feast for your return, Zacharias. But we leave you with God's blessings."

* * *

For weeks afterward, these words burned in Zacharias's ears. Then his deep depression from forced retirement and his inability to speak became even worse.

Elizabeth announced to him that she was going to have a baby. She had not told him about her pregnancy for five months to spare him another burden in his difficult period. However, her condition could no longer be concealed. At any other time in his long life, this news would have been the most joyous message for which he could ever hope. But now, he could not talk, he had no position in a synagogue or means to support a family, his fellow rabbis thought that he had demons in his head, and the fact that Elizabeth was actually pregnant forced him to acknowledge the unsettling fact that had ruined his life and threatened his sanity. He had been visited by an angel.

That situation eventually led to Zacharias' understanding of the second lesson God had given him. After God's first lesson that "it is never too late in life to have dreams," His second lesson for Zacharias was, "Those dreams are never realized as one plans or expects."

While Zacharias was struggling with these developments, Elizabeth's cousin Mary came to visit from Nazareth. Six months into her pregnancy, Elizabeth eagerly welcomed Mary's arrival. Zacharias was troubled, bored, and could not talk. He tried to be supportive but frankly was not able to be very comforting or empathetic as Elizabeth experienced difficult changes in her body and temperament. So Elizabeth's spirits were lifted by Mary's visit and having another woman with whom to share her feelings and concerns.

Zacharias was pleased to have Mary around to keep Elizabeth company, that is, until one evening over supper. As they were reaching the end of the meal, Elizabeth and Mary were talking about little things and working hard to keep their conversation to subjects and questions to which Zacharias, without his voice, could simply shake his head yes or no. They felt sorry for him and knew that he must be frustrated with his inability to speak. Zacharias, however, was beginning to appreciate the fact that he was no longer expected to say anything. As a rabbi, a teacher and a husband, he was always expected to say the right thing on all matters at every occasion. Now, while he certainly wished to have his voice back, he often enjoyed the fact that he was relieved of any pressure or responsibility to do anything other than look thoughtful and nod his head as if he were pondering the words he had heard. If a question were posed to him directly that he did not want to answer, he simply would point to his silent lips and shrug his shoulders in apology for his inability to answer. It was a freedom he had never before experienced in life.

Mary grew quiet after they finished eating. She looked at Elizabeth and Zacharias with hesitation in her eyes.

Noticing her look, Elizabeth asked, "Mary, is something wrong?"

Mary felt both fearful and relieved as she confided to them that she had been visited by an angel named Gabriel. She then recounted a fantastical story of how the angel told Mary that she, while still a virgin, would nevertheless conceive a son to be named Jesus who would be called the Son of God.

A flood of fear and emotions filled Zacharias when her announcement of the angel's visitation brought back the sense of unreality that had destroyed his life. It took all his control not to run from the room.

Mary told them that when she naturally questioned this message in her mind, the angel said to her, "This news may be difficult to believe, but its truth can be confirmed by a visit to your cousin Elizabeth. She is older and unable to have children, yet you will find that she is now six months with child. Go see her and prove to yourself that my message to you is indeed true."

Mary, like Zacharias, was unsettled by this strange visitor and his incredible message. So she made the three-day journey from Nazareth to the village outside of Jerusalem as soon as possible only to learn the remarkable news that Elizabeth was six months pregnant. Now that Mary had confirmed the angel's message, she was moved to share it with Elizabeth and Zacharias.

Elizabeth took Mary's hands into hers and looked into Mary's eyes.

"Mary, I have to tell you that when you arrived and walked through that door, I felt my baby leap inside me. I thought it was just my happiness at seeing you, but now I believe it was much more.

"I am lucky to have this baby. But you, Mary, are truly blessed among women. And the baby you will bear will be blessed as well."

Tears filled the eyes of the two women as they together felt that special moment in which their whole lives were given purpose and meaning. They spoke quietly for a few minutes as Mary poured out her feelings of thanks and her excitement for all that her son could become.

Zacharias sat and watched in his silence. He was terrified. He believed in God's great power, but could not bring himself to believe all that he was seeing and hearing. Visitations by an angel— being struck dumb—surreal predictions of barren women and virgins bearing children—and now the revelation of a complete plan that his son was to be a prophet for Mary's son who was to be the Promised Messiah. All of it was beyond belief, but some of it was actually happening. Zacharias could bear no more of this blurred reality. To the women's surprise, he stood up abruptly and left the house.

***

Joy returned to the lives of Zacharias and Elizabeth with the birth of their son. The newborn baby completely filled their hearts and lives, and also used up every bit of energy they had. They were not young people any more. Meeting the demands of the baby all day and all night was not as easy as it might have been years earlier. There was no time for thoughts of angels or prophecies. They were too busy and tired happily bearing the burdens of caring for a newborn.

Eight days after the birth of the baby boy, he was to be given his name and circumcised according to Jewish law and tradition. However, Elizabeth made an additional request. She asked that after the naming and before the circumcision, the baby go through the ritual called the *Tvilah*. This ritual under Jewish law involved the act of being washed in a small pool of natural waters called a *Mikvah* for symbolic cleansing and spiritual purity. Elizabeth's request was out of the ordinary for a newborn baby, and such a ceremony had never been done before in the Temple in Jerusalem. But she made it clear to Zacharias that she would have it no other way.

Zacharias felt uncomfortable about the ceremony that had been planned. Tradition called for the baby to be named after his father or a family member, but Zacharias kept hearing in his head the statement of the stranger at the altar who had announced to him that the baby would be named John. But there were no men in Zacharias' family with that name. Zacharias felt uneasy that there already was much talk about the unusual circumstances of the birth of this baby to the older couple as well as his silence and the loss of his position in the Temple. It would be even more out of the ordinary and much noticed for Zacharias and Elizabeth to pick out such a name.

Then there was the *Tvilah*. Elizabeth's insistence on the baby's cleansing in the purified water of the *Mikvah* was a new practice that was becoming more popular and even had its own new name. It was called a baptism. The priest who was to preside over the naming and the circumcision, a young priest named Caiaphas, had frowned his disapproval when Elizabeth had told him of her desire to combine a baptism into the ceremony. Many of the priests of the Temple in Jerusalem considered baptism to be a fad which distracted attention from the traditional circumcision ceremony, and Zacharias, who had been a rather traditional rabbi, was inclined to agree. But Zacharias did not have the voice and the priest did not have the nerve to deny Elizabeth whose mind was clearly made up about what she wanted for her baby. And that included the new ceremony of baptism.

The final thing that made Zacharias uneasy was that priest who would officiate at the ceremony. Caiaphas was a young ambitious rabbi who had become a priest at the Temple in Jerusalem at a relatively early age. It may have been coincidence, but the timing of his appointment closely followed by his marriage to the daughter of Annas, the High Priest of the Temple. He was associated with the Sadducees, an affluent sect of Jewish priests who held high positions in the management of the Temple and in government. Zacharias had suspicions that Caiaphas, for his own political advancement, had been among the priests who urged that Zacharias be retired and removed from the Temple so that another rabbi would take Zacharias' place and be indebted to Caiaphas.

The day of the ceremony arrived. The chamber in the Temple that held the *Mikvah* was filled to capacity with the many friends of Zacharias and Elizabeth as well as numerous priests and scribes from the Temple who were former colleagues of Zacharias. They all had many reasons to be there. The first of course was the occasion to celebrate the birth of the child to the couple they loved and respected. But beyond that, they were drawn by the unusual circumstances surrounding the event. Most of those packed into the room had not seen the older couple since their unlikely pregnancy. Many men joked about what could cause the newly found virility in an old man like Zacharias, and many women secretly wondered about the same thing. It was also the first time for most of them to see Zacharias after he had lost both his voice and his position in the Temple. And then there was the new baptism ceremony that many had heard about but never seen. There was much curiosity about how Caiaphas would react to conducting in the Temple of Jerusalem this new rite of purification that people were requesting with more frequency. It undoubtedly was going to be an interesting occasion.

The priest began the ceremony with time-honored traditions, readings from the Torah and several prayers for the newborn baby and his family. Then the time came for Caiaphas to bestow the child with his name. Elizabeth and Zacharias brought the child up to Caiaphas.

He raised his hand and announced in a loud voice for all to hear, "We are given this child from the Lord our God to the People of Israel to be called by the name Zacharias after his father."

Elizabeth looked up quickly. She did not know whether the High Priest had not been told that the traditional name of the baby's father would not be given to the child or whether he had decided on his own that the traditional name would be given according to custom. But she did not hesitate and spoke up.

"No, Rabbi. He is to be called John."

At Elizabeth's interruption, murmurs ran through the crowd of worshippers. Zacharias looked over at Elizabeth with a look of great discomfort and then up to the priest. Caiaphas was taken aback at the interruption and felt very foolish that he appeared not to know the baby's name at its announcement in the Temple ceremony.

In an irritated voice, he spoke directly at Elizabeth. "But there is no one among your relatives who is called by this name."

"The baby is to be called John, Rabbi," she answered in a quiet but firm voice.

Caiaphas in his great embarrassment decided he'd had enough of this woman with her sacrilegious and inappropriate request for a baptism and now this outrageous indignity. His ceremony, in the holy Temple of Jerusalem of all places, was being made a mockery. He turned to Zacharias.

"What would you, his father, have him called?"

The worshippers looked on in a horrified silence. Had Caiaphas in his irritation forgotten that Zacharias could not speak? What could Zacharias do in his silence? And what should he do even if he could speak, disagree with the priest or his own wife?

Zacharias looked at Caiaphas, at the anxious faces of his many friends and family, and then at Elizabeth. He indicated to a young rabbi assisting the Priest that he wanted something on which to write. A piece of parchment was quickly brought to him. During a brief uncomfortable silence, he wrote on the parchment and handed it back to the young rabbi.

The young man read the message. With a worried look over at Zacharias, up at Caiaphas and finally out at the roomful of waiting worshippers, his eyes went back down to the parchment to read aloud Zacharias's words.

"His name is John."

Pandemonium broke out in the Temple as everyone began speaking at once. Caiaphas exclaimed to the young rabbi, "It can't be so." The scribes and rabbis raised their voices at one another as a new question of Jewish law gave them the chance to challenge each other's authority. "There is no tradition for this," argued one; "Any name chosen by a child's parents is right and good," answered another. The men and women among the worshippers all took sides arguing loudly for Elizabeth, Zacharias or Caiaphas. The baby starting crying as the noise startled him from slumber in his mother's arms.

Suddenly a loud, commanding voice filled the room.

"HIS NAME IS JOHN!"

Everyone immediately fell silent and turned to see who had spoken.

There stood Zacharias with a look of anger that quickly turned to a look of surprise at the sound of his long lost voice. He carefully cleared his throat, turned to Caiaphas and repeated in a respectful voice, "Rabbi, his name is John."

The priest was still so embarrassed and angry that it was lost on him that Zacharias was now speaking after nine months of silence.

"I will not baptize this child in this Temple! I don't care what his name is."

Zacharias stepped up to Caiaphas and looked him directly in the eye. After a tense moment, he turned around and looked at the worshippers.

"Is there anyone in this Temple who believes there is a reason why this baby should not receive God's blessing?"

No one spoke.

After another pause, Zacharias asked all of them, "Is there anyone here who believes there is a reason why this baby deserves not to be cleansed and made pure by the waters of the *Mikvah*?"

Not a sound was heard. Zacharias turned back to Caiaphas.

"Rabbi, blessed is the Lord God of Israel, for He has visited and redeemed His people.

"As He told us through the mouths of His holy prophets, we have been saved from our enemies and from the hand of all who hate us so that we may perform the mercy promised by our fathers, and also that we may remember God's holy covenant which grants that we, being delivered from the hand of our enemies, might serve Him in holiness and righteousness—without fear."

Zacharias turned to Elizabeth and looked down at his son asleep once again in her arms. Everyone in the room could feel the love of the father for his son. He spoke to the baby.

"And you, my child, will be called the prophet of the Highest. For you will go before the face of the Lord to prepare His ways to give knowledge of salvation to His people by the remission of their sins through the tender mercy of our God with which the Dayspring from on high has visited us. Give light to those who sit in darkness and the shadow of death to guide our feet into the way of peace."

Zacharias looked up at all the people before him, but spoke to Caiaphas.

"Rabbi, bless and purify this baby and his spirit. I ask you to baptize him with the waters of the *Mikvah* and circumcise him on this day in accordance with the Laws of Moses."

Caiaphas felt all eyes on him. He stepped forward and took the tiny baby from Elizabeth's arms. Holding the infant, he said a prayer of blessing on the life of the boy and held the child just above the water in the *Mikvah*. Caiaphas said another prayer before carefully reaching into the water with a cupped hand and pouring the water gently on the baby's head.

Awakened by the cool water, the infant started waving his arms about and splashed water on himself and Caiaphas. The priest looked up in surprise. The worshippers once again tensed and waited for Caiaphas's reaction. He wiped the water from his face, looked down at the baby, and, to everyone's astonishment, laughed out loud.

"This baby doesn't need me to baptize him," he announced to the worshipers. "He can do it himself. He is John the Baptizer!"

The story was told repeatedly throughout Jerusalem for weeks after about how a newborn baby had taken the name of John and then baptized a priest in the Temple. The baby in the story came to be known as John the Baptizer after the words of the priest. But at some point when family and friends picked up the new baby and told yet again the story of "John the Baptizer" for everyone's enjoyment, someone shortened his nickname to J.B. The name stuck.

* * *

As these memories ran through Zacharias' mind while he waited for Jesus and Judas to arrive for their lessons, he thought hard about his life and the two lessons God had given to him. His dreams had not come as expected or planned. His son J.B. as a very young man was not the prophet the angel had foretold. And the Priests of the Temple in Jerusalem may have been done with Zacharias more than thirteen years ago, but Zacharias was not done with them. It was not too late in life for Zacharias to dream.

Chapter 7

DEMONS

"You're late!" he snapped at Jesus.

Judas was waiting for Jesus outside the garrison gate. Although he was much smaller than Jesus, he walked quickly ahead towards the synagogue.

"Sorry," said Jesus. "My father and I had to finish up a project."

"It doesn't matter. I just got here myself," Judas replied. "We had a lot of messages to deliver today."

"So I'm not late," thought Jesus. He felt his usual irritation at Judas as he caught up with him.

"Is something special going on?" Jesus asked.

"There were a bunch of messages about some new messiah," Judas answered. "I guess he healed some blind man in front of a crowd, and then disappeared. So now everyone is trying to find him."

"Are you sure it wasn't some trick?" Jesus asked. "These new messiahs always seem to be conjuring up some fake magic to get people's attention."

Judas gave him an annoyed look. "How do I know? I wasn't there."

"Sorry," Jesus apologized again. It was another of those odd moments he often had with Judas.

Judas Iscariot was Jesus' best friend. And then he wasn't. And then he was. The situation always seemed to be changing for no apparent reason. Judas was supportive with one breath, and critical with the next. One minute he was happy for you, and the next he was jealous of you. He would do you a favor and then do something hurtful. His friendship was always a coin with two sides.

While their friendship was frustrating for Jesus, he thought of Judas's mother and father and was not surprised. When Jesus was at Judas's home, his parents were always going on about how they loved one another and gave each other hugs and kisses. But in an instant they would get angry with one another over the smallest thing.

They did the same thing to Judas. It seemed they were always being extra nice to Judas, complementing him and buying him presents, but then they would scold and criticize him over some little thing that seemed harmless. Once Judas had come to Jesus' home with an ugly welt on the side of his face. Shortly after, his parents came by looking for him and acting overly affectionate. Jesus could tell that Judas was uncertain about what to do before he left with his parents to go home.

Jesus tried to change the subject to make their conversation friendly again.

"Were there any messages about what happened to the Roman soldier's helmet? What did the other Apostles think about what happened?"

"We met at the manger afterwards, and everyone felt pretty good," Judas smiled at Jesus like they were successful comrades in arms, "although later on it seemed a little scarier than when it was happening. But I haven't heard anything else about it."

Then Judas gave Jesus a critical look.

"Just why did you give the helmet back to the soldier anyway? That was dumb. We had just taken it from him."

Jesus once again felt foolish and frustrated. This was the second time that afternoon his well-intentioned action had been viewed as a mistake.

"I was surprised when Peter handed it to me," Jesus replied, "and I didn't know what to do. I guess I just did something I hoped would make the situation better for all of us."

"Well, some of the Apostles were not too happy about it."

"Who was unhappy?" asked Jesus.

"Simon, Matthew I think, and maybe Peter, although all he thinks about now is Maggie."

Jesus' concern about what the Apostles were thinking quickly shifted to Peter's interest in Maggie.

"What's Peter thinking about Maggie?"

"Probably the same as all of us. If we could arrange a marriage, it would be with her and would happen tonight."

Suddenly Jesus and Judas had to jump to one side of the street as a dozen Roman soldiers on horses galloped by dangerously close to the scattering people.

"It must be true," said Judas.

"What's that?" Jesus asked.

"I heard in the market that rebels killed a lot of Roman soldiers between here and Sepphoris."

"That's the third time in three weeks that Roman soldiers have been killed by rebels," remarked Jesus. "Do you think the Warriors of the Wilderness were involved?"

"I know the Warriors of the Wilderness were involved."

"How do you know that?" Jesus asked.

"I am an Apostle. We messengers hear and know a lot of things," Judas stated proudly. "I also know that someone important is coming to Nazareth soon because of all the trouble with the rebels."

"Who?" Jesus wondered.

"That I don't know yet. But some sort of advance preparations at the garrison have been requested," Judas replied. Jesus was surprised by this news as he was usually aware of most of the activity in the garrison from working with his father.

Soon they arrived at the synagogue where Zacharias sat deep in thought. Jesus and Judas stood quietly for a moment waiting for Zacharias to notice them.

Although most of the people living in Nazareth were Jewish, the Nazarene synagogue was very modest. It was an unexceptional building that stood on the edge of the town without anything distinctive to make it stand out. Most members of the synagogue were not wealthy. Its roof could not cover all its worshippers. But there was a spacious courtyard area that was covered for worship on the Sabbath by a large tent newly made each year by the tentmaker who belonged to the synagogue.

Zacharias loved this synagogue even though it was not a grand place of worship like the Temple in Jerusalem where he had served most of his life. He had taken the position as its rabbi when it had been offered by Mary's father who had been head of the local Sanhedrin, and he and Elizabeth had moved to Nazareth not long after their son had been born and his voice had returned. Mary was quite insistent with her father after the synagogue's previous rabbi died that Zacharias be offered the job. She wanted him, and him alone, to be responsible for the formal education of her soon-to-be-born son. Her father finally gave in and convinced the other elders on the Sanhedrin to give Zacharias the position despite the rumors about his strange behavior in Jerusalem.

In Zacharias's view, the synagogue in Nazareth was a greater place of worship than the Temple in Jerusalem. While it did not have mighty walls and a golden gate, or large chambers, white marble, or ornate holy altars, it had what a synagogue required most. The synagogue had worshippers who believed in and served their God regardless of the surroundings.

And the synagogue had a beautiful Torah. The worshippers of the synagogue did not have much money, but they had each given a remarkable amount of their meager savings for the purchase of an exceptional Torah with beautiful writing on highest quality parchment rolled onto two golden rods with purple cords that tied bells to the tops of each of them.

But best of all, the synagogue had its children. The recent growth in Nazareth from the military and economic activity in Galilee resulted in more families worshiping at the synagogue. It was not a surprise that with the additional families in the synagogue came the presence of more children. But what was surprising perhaps was how much the children loved the old rabbi. Zacharias had a tender nature about him that made the children feel safe. The children also had a natural sense that Zacharias was honest with them, so they trusted him. Zacharias was also a good teacher. With all these things coming together under the small roof of the humble synagogue, its largest and busiest activity became its school.

From the school's collection of children, Zacharias found his "Apostles." They were remarkable boys. Of all the children taught by Zacharias in his many years as a rabbi, these boys in this one place and time all stood out with their amazing memories and extraordinary facility for picking up languages. Twelve of them came from families in the town who had migrated to Nazareth for a number of reasons, but mostly for jobs and the economic opportunities to live a better life than they had in their own villages. In addition to the twelve was Jesus, the son of his good friends Joseph and Mary. So when Zacharias suggested that he hold special lessons for their sons, everyone gladly gave their consent and made sure the boys attended the additional sessions with the Rabbi.

One day Zacharias in his lesson had been teaching the boys about the ancient prophets and had taught them the word "Apostle" from the Greek word "apostolos" used to describe the prophets as "messengers." Later when he learned that the enterprising boys had started to deliver messages for money, he chuckled to himself when he heard that they had started calling themselves the Apostles.

After a few minutes in which Zacharias did not move, Jesus began to grow concerned that the old man might fall asleep, which he sometimes did during their lessons. Judas, on the other hand, was hoping the rabbi would fall asleep so they could slip out without having to sit through another tedious lesson. Zacharias finally looked up, slightly surprised to see them.

"Ah, boys, you're here finally. We have much work to do as our time to prepare for the Feast at the Temple is growing short.

"I don't have to remind you that you both are very lucky. The High Priest of the Temple in Jerusalem has directed that for this celebration of the Feast, two boys from certain synagogues in Palestine, including ours in Nazareth, will each read a passage from the Laws of Moses in the Torah or from the Books of the Prophets, and then tell the priests of Temple what meaning those verses hold for his life. It is a great honor that you two have been chosen from the synagogue in Nazareth. But you will be before the High Priest and all the priests of the Temple, so your words must be perfect.

"Now, from where in the Torah does it come that the boys of your age will be in the celebration of the Feast? Jesus, do you know the verse?"

"Yes, Rabbi," Jesus answered. "'And Isaac the child of Abraham grew and was weaned, and Abraham made a great feast on the day that Isaac was weaned.'"

"Very good, Jesus.

"This ceremony represents the moment when you are no longer a child. You are at the age where you now take a vow of personal responsibility for your obligations under the laws of Moses and the traditions of the Jewish faith. Then you are able to participate in all areas of life in our Jewish community, including the arrangement of marriage and the responsibilities of family."

Jesus' brow furrowed slightly as he imagined himself years from now standing in the shadow of Susanna and several large children towering above him.

Judas asked, "Rabbi, is the Temple in Jerusalem as beautiful as they say? Is it true that the gates and the roof of the Temple are made of gold?"

"Yes, the Temple is very beautiful, Judas. But wait to see it with your own eyes. They will tell you where the true beauty of the Temple lies," Zacharias replied.

"All right, Judas. Read for me the verse that you have been studying."

Judas read his verse flawlessly. Jesus was not surprised. Judas had worked on that verse for weeks.

"Have you given more thought to what you will say to the priests of the Temple about the meaning of that verse to you?" Zacharias asked.

"Yes, Rabbi," he answered.

"Well then, tell the meaning of your verse, Judas."

Judas paused, and said, "This verse is important to the children of Israel because God has given this message to us in the words of the prophets."

"That is very good, Judas," Zacharias acknowledged. "Go on."

"That's all I have, Rabbi," Judas replied.

The corners of Zacharias's mouth turned to a slight frown under his long white beard.

"I suspect, Judas, that your statement is something the High Priest may have figured out already. Why don't you take this piece of parchment and see if you can add some further insights to your thoughts."

"Yes, Rabbi," Judas responded. He took the parchment eagerly since it was always special for the boys to have the opportunity to write on the valuable paper.

Zacharias turned to Jesus.

"Jesus, have you memorized the verses I gave you in our last lesson?"

"Yes, Rabbi.

"And do you understand their meaning?"

"I think I do Rabbi, but sometimes the meaning is not always clear from the words at first. Sometimes the words seem to be about something until I repeat them and think about them a while, and then I realize that the verse is talking about something else entirely different."

"Yes, my son. There are many descriptions for a verse that has a different meaning than its words. The first verse you memorized from our last lesson is called a parable. It is a story about one thing that gives a lesson about something else."

"Like the story about Lot's wife who turned into a pillar of salt when she looked back at the destruction of Sodom and Gomorrah?" Jesus suggested.

"Exactly," answered Zacharias.

Jesus was surprised when Zacharias did not ask him to recite the verses he had memorized from the previous lesson. Instead the Rabbi handed him a piece of parchment with three new verses written on it.

"Read these verses to me, Jesus, and then commit them to memory before our next lesson."

Jesus felt a nervous knot in the bottom of his stomach. More verses! He could not even count how many he had memorized in his preparation for the celebration of the Feast, let alone be sure he could remember them if one turned out to be the verse he would read and speak about before the High Priest.

"From the Book of Isaiah," he began reading.
> *Listen to me, you islands;*
> > *hear this, you distant nations:*
>
> *Before I was born the Lord called me;*
> > *from my birth he has made mention of my name.*

"Very good, Jesus," said Zacharias. "Now the next one."
"From the Book of Proverbs," Jesus read,
> *The Lord brought me forth as the first of his works,*
> > *before his deeds of old;*
>
> *I was formed long ages ago,*
> > *at the very beginning, when the world came to be.*

"And the last one please."
Jesus read on. "From the Psalms of David,
> *In the beginning you laid the foundations of the earth,*
> > *and the heavens are the work of your hands.*
>
> *They will perish, but you remain;*
> > *they will all wear out like a garment.*
>
> *Like clothing you will change them*
> > *and they will be discarded.*
>
> *But you remain the same,*
> > *and your years will never end.*

"Do you know what these verses are talking about, Jesus?" Zacharias asked.

"No, Rabbi, I don't," he answered.

"They are about the Promised Messiah."

"Rabbi," Jesus interrupted, "What verse will I be reading before the High Priest? Judas has been working on his verse for weeks, but you have given me so many verses and I still don't know which one I will have to speak about."

"It is not yet clear, Jesus, which passage is to be yours," Zacharias answered. "So it is important that we find that special verse and its message and then prepare it for the Temple celebration."

Jesus was unsure what that answer meant and still was worried that he would not be able to prepare his verse and testimony to perfection.

"Study those verses now so that you can recite them from memory," Zacharias told him, "and give thought to their message about the Messiah and how you would describe it in your own words."

As the boys huddled over their parchment, Zacharias thought about Judas's question about the Temple. It was indeed beautiful. He had cherished every moment among the white walls, porticos, courtyards and altars of the ancient Temple that Herod the Great had remodeled so magnificently. It had been the spectacular setting for the precious memories, hallowed thoughts and wide-reaching hopes of his life until the High Priest and the other priests of the Temple convinced the Great Sandhedrin to take it from him.

Now Zacharias would be returning to take it back. To the priests of the Temple, Jerusalem in Judea was the only place where real learning and piety were cultivated. The saying among rabbis was that "Judea is grain, Galilee straw, and beyond Jordan chaff." But he would return to show them the work of a truly dedicated rabbi and the product of a great teacher. He would be the rabbi who established a standard of excellence in the Temple that he knew the other priests could not meet. When that was done, in their hearts the Temple would be his, not theirs.

He knew he would never again be a priest serving at the Temple's holy altars. The words of the Great Sanhedrin stilled echoed in his mind: "There will be no feast for your return, Zacharias. But we leave you with God's blessings." With the appearance in the Temple of a boy from the synagogue in Nazareth, he intended to show all the Temple priests God's ultimate blessing that had been given to him. He had that boy from Nazareth. He did not need a feast.

For the moment, however, there was another concern on Zacharias's mind. Earlier in the day a man from the synagogue remarked to Zacharias that he had seen J.B. on a street near the edge of town. It had been a year since Zacharias had seen his son. He and Elizabeth wanted so badly to see him again. But fear filled his heart. Why had J.B. returned to Nazareth?

Zacharias pictured his son in his mind. J.B. was handsome and strong, loved by all who met him, and a good student of the Torah. How he wished J.B. were there studying verses alongside Jesus and Judas. Zacharias in his dreams had hoped that J.B. and Jesus would grow up together to become great rabbis and leaders of the Temple.

J.B. had a passion for whatever he did. His enthusiasm and boundless energy meant that whatever his interest or project, it engulfed him entirely. He never took on anything half heartedly. For J.B., it was all or nothing.

This strength of character in J.B., that once gave Zacharias such hope for J.B.'s future, now gave Zacharias great concern. J.B.'s passions no longer were directed at the Torah or the Temple, or even his family or friends. They were directed against the Roman occupiers of Palestine.

At some point, Zacharias suspected that J.B. had become involved with the rebel zealots. He was not at all sure he wanted to know how. But he could not forbid J.B. His son had become a man, albeit young and impetuous. And besides, Zacharias knew it would not have done any good.

Zacharias at first did not know whether J.B.'s passion had resulted in his becoming one of the Warriors of the Wilderness or just a supporter of their cause. Either way, Zacharias knew it could come to no good for J.B. The Warriors of the Wilderness had been active and taken Roman lives in other parts of the country before becoming active in Galilee. Their violent actions had resulted in the rebels' being summarily executed when they were captured. Even Jews suspected of aiding the Warriors of the Wilderness had been killed without hesitation by the Romans. They were lucky. Those not so lucky were tortured and crucified, hanging on the cross for days. In the end, they begged for the death that had turned from their greatest fear into a comforting friend.

Then Zacharias asked J.B. whether he was a Warrior of the Wilderness, and J.B. forthrightly admitted he was. Zacharias knew it was futile, but the rabbi talked about the obvious danger and appealed to J.B. to think about what it would do to his mother if something were to happen. J.B. not only refused to reconsider his involvement with the rebels, he began to speak heatedly about how their cause was so important and necessary, that he would give his life if he had to. That was more important, he said, than anything his mother felt. When Zacharias heard this, he became angry, and they argued loudly, until Zacharias heard the one word he dreaded most.

"Sicarii."

Zacharias would not stand for this. He raised his hand in anger to strike J.B.

J.B. did not move, and glared at his father without any fear. Zacharias stopped. He was ashamed at his action and lowered his hand. J.B. looked at him another moment, and then turned and walked out the door.

J.B. simply disappeared after their argument. Now, after a year, he apparently was back in Nazareth, and Zacharias yearned to see him. "But why is he here?" Zacharias wondered.

Zacharias looked back up at Jesus and Judas studying intently the words on their sheets of parchment. Suddenly, Jesus' sister Rebecca burst through the door of the synagogue. The three of them looked up in surprise. With an anxious look, she gestured some hand signs to Jesus.

"How long?" Jesus asked her out loud. Rebecca held up five fingers.

"Rabbi, forgive me. I must go quickly." Jesus hurried toward the door with Rebecca right behind.

"Is something wrong, my son?" Zacharias asked with a concerned look.

All Zacharias heard Jesus say over his shoulder as he stepped swiftly through the door was, "Demons."

***

Earlier, Mary and Joseph in the main room of their home struggled unsuccessfully to calm Jude. Joseph arrived from work just after Jude started wailing loudly and banging his head against the wall. When Mary tried to stop him, he knocked her down with one arm as easily as if he were a strong man instead of an eight-year-old boy. He then started throwing his body heavily on the floor and rolling around.

Rachel ran from the house crying followed by Jamie who was pale with fright as he pulled Joses by the hand outside with him. Rebecca did not leave. She crouched in the corner wanting, but unable, to help. Mary saw her, got her attention, pointed to the door and carefully mouthed two words.

"Jesus—synagogue."

Without any hesitation, Rebecca ran out the door.

Jude's eyes were wild looking and a white froth started collecting at the corners of his mouth. When Joseph tried to grab Jude to hold him down, he dodged Joseph's grasp and started flinging his body about the room to avoid Joseph. He knocked over the table and sent plates crashing to the floor. Then he ran across the room and with a scream threw his body into the shelves of pots and pans next to the fireplace.

Joseph again lunged at Jude and tried to tackle him. Jude easily avoided Joseph's outstretched arms and ran to the opposite wall. His eyes and mouth opened wide. After a momentary silence, an eerie, howling laugh came from deep within him. A shiver ran though Joseph at the sound. It was a noise unlike any he had heard out of a human being.

Jude, Mary, and Joseph all stood still breathing heavily. Jude's eyes rolled about while his throat made a gurgling sound as drool dripped off his chin. His fists kept clenching and unclenching rapidly.

Suddenly Jude sprinted for the door. Joseph instinctively dived to block him. With a sickening crack, their heads collided knocking them both to the floor. Joseph was dazed and struggled to raise himself up on his arms. Mary tried to run to him, but Jude leaped up between her and Joseph. Jude threw his head back and began to let out a long, unearthly scream.

The frightening sound stopped abruptly in Jude's throat as Jesus stepped through the door. Out of breath from running, Jesus looked at Jude and took a step toward him. Jude scurried to the darkest corner of the room where he turned and hissed at Jesus like a snarling animal. Mary ran to Joseph's side. He winced as she touched the large bump swelling on his forehead.

Jesus stood completely still facing Jude, not taking his eyes off his brother.

"Mother—Father, are you all right?" he asked in a quiet voice.

"Yes," they both answered.

Jesus started taking small steps toward Jude, so slowly that Joseph and Mary barely noticed he was moving. Jude continued to breathe heavily with a low growling sound as his eyes darted around the room. Jesus' eyes stayed unblinking on Jude.

Jude's head snapped up as he realized Jesus had moved several steps closer. With a roar, he leaped into the air and landed right in front of Jesus, his face so close to Jesus that spittle flew on Jesus' face.

Jesus did not move or even blink. In a low voice as steady as his stare into Jude's eyes, he said, "Be quiet, and come out of him."

Jude shook his head about like a lion and once again roared into Jesus' face. Jesus stayed motionless. When Jude stopped, Jesus, still looking into his eyes, repeated in the same voice, "Be quiet, and come out of him."

Before Jude could respond, Jesus' hands came up quickly to Jude's ribs with his palms on both sides of Jude's chest. With a sharp intake of breath, Jude stood motionless. Mary and Joseph looked on intently—helplessness, fear and hope in their eyes.

Jesus steadily pressed the palms of his hands more firmly against Jude's ribs. Jude's breathing started to slow, and the gurgling stopped. After a few moments, Jesus moved closer and very slowly placed his arms around Jude until he held him in a brotherly embrace. Jesus gradually applied more pressure as Jude's body became more slack. Their eyes closed together as Jesus eventually eased the pressure from his arms.

"Be quiet and come out of him," Jesus whispered into Jude's ear one last time.

At these words, Jude fell limp into Jesus' arms. Jesus carefully kneeled and laid him down on the floor as Mary came over and covered him with her shawl. Jesus' shoulders dropped from exhaustion. He looked at Mary with tired eyes he could barely keep open.

"Mother, I think I'll sleep now. It has been a difficult day."

"Of course, Jesus," she answered.

But instead of walking to the door of the room where he and his brothers slept, he kneeled down there on the floor and laid next to Jude.

"Jesus," Mary spoke to him softly. "Thank you. I'm sorry you had to do that again."

Joseph doubted that Jesus had even heard her as he laid a blanket over his sleeping sons. Jesus' hand came out from under the blanket and rested against Jude's cheek.

Chapter 8

THE MAP

Pilate had made up his mind.

After seventy years of festering rebellion in Palestine, bold action was called for. The rebels were not only a continuing problem for Rome and the army, they were becoming more powerful and popular as time passed. Pilate needed a strategy that would stop the rebels' momentum, and at the same time would send a signal to the people that Palestine was Roman and the Romans were in control.

Pilate also felt pressure to do something that would magnify his reputation in Rome as the commander who could crush a rebellion with a single blow. He realized now he was not likely to be as lucky in Galilee as he was at the Black Sea. Herod's army and the Romans did not know who and where all the rebels' leaders and forces were, let alone have the capability to eliminate them all at once. They had small organizations and supporters throughout the villages and countryside. Many were nothing more than brigands or bandits, and others were respectable citizens who either supported or joined the fighters as needed. The rebel forces were hidden and small, but they were organized and effective. Even with luck, Pilate could not eliminate the Jewish rebellion with a single battle or a wave of crucifixions.

Pilate, however, had concluded that there was one surprising weak point he could attack that would change the battle against the rebels and get the attention of Rome. That unlikely target was Rome's very own ruling ally, the Herodian family. The Emperor had given Palestine to the Herodians to control for Rome, and they had failed. Pilate would remove Herod Antipas as the ruler of Galilee and the most prominent leader of the Jews, and then his quiet brother Philip. In their place, Pilate, with the help of his reputation and political support in Rome along with the Roman troops under his command, would become Governor and ruler of all Palestine.

"An interesting idea, but it will never work," observed Flavius.

Pilate had decided to confide to Flavius his plan to remove Herod Antipas despite the risk of revealing that he was thinking of committing treason against Rome's appointed Jewish leaders in Palestine. However, Flavius was a man who, despite his pointed views on foreign policy, was trustworthy and would keep his counsel confidential. And Flavius in the two weeks since Pilate's arrival, seemed as if he could not care less about what happened to Palestine after his departure.

Today was the day that Flavius was officially turning over command of the garrison to Pilate and leaving to return to Rome. This was their last private meeting before Flavius would mount his horse and ride away from his long service to Caesar to a small house north of Rome that he had not seen in fifteen years. That house and its garden were to be his last garrison in which he intended to defend himself as long as possible from the aching in his joints and from any of the Emperor's gods who might decide it was time for him to leave this earth.

"Why wouldn't it work?" Pilate asked with some surprise. Pilate had been certain that Flavius, with his disdain for the Herodians, would have supported a plan to get rid of Herod Antipas and Philip.

"Well first of all, it was a Roman emperor who put the Herodians in place to govern Palestine. If you try to take them out completely, you'll be going against the longstanding policy of the emperor. That may lose you support in Rome. And Herod is not without friends there as well. They will become your enemies.

"And remember," Flavius continued, "Herod has his own army, even though it could not fight off a crowd of angry old women. The last thing you want is to have to fight his army for control of Palestine as well as the rebel zealots.

"If you remove him and replace him with a Roman government, the rebellion will only get worse. Herod may be more than happy to kill off anyone who is a threat to his throne, whether they are Jewish or not. But as far as the people are concerned, he's at least half Jewish, and he has let his people worship in the Jewish faith. Take him out and replace him with a Roman governor, and you'll only be throwing more wood on the fire of a peoples' rebellion."

"But we did exactly that with his brother Archelaus in Judea," responded Pilate.

"Yes, and look what happened. We drove the rebels out of one part of Palestine and they just moved their main operations to Galilee and other areas. You take out Herod in Galilee to control the rebels, they simply will move somewhere else and still be a problem to Rome.

"Taking out the Herodians and replacing them as governor of all Palestine won't change anything and would just make you more enemies here and in Rome," Flavius concluded.

Pilate was not ready to give up. "But nothing will change if we don't remove Herod, and I will fail in my mission and look like a fool if I don't bring order to Galilee."

Flavius thought for a moment. "A Jewish ruler has been in place from the Herodian family for some seventy years. From that time and the previous Jewish rule of Queen Alexandra-Salome, the Jews have come to believe they have some kind of right to a Jewish leader. So if you're going to get rid of Herod and Philip and give Palestine a new ruler, you had better plan on replacing them with a new King of the Jews whom you and Rome can control."

"But there's no other family or person in Palestine who is known to all the people that could be a royal leader, is there?" Pilate asked. He was frustrated with the problems in his plan, but he could tell that Flavius was now thinking hard.

"There's really been only one person outside the Herodian family who has presented a threat to their rule that they have taken seriously," Flavius offered.

"Who is that?" Pilate was now hopeful.

"Don't know actually," answered Flavius.

"What do you mean?" asked Pilate. He was frustrated once again.

"It was that baby in Bethlehem who Herod the Great was sure would become the next King of the Jews. Remember, that threat caused him to exterminate all the male infants in the city. Something about it must have been real for him to take such drastic action."

Flavius went on. "I don't know what family the infant came from or who was promoting the quest for the baby to be made King of the Jews twelve years ago, but it must have been a real movement for Herod to feel so threatened."

Pilate was intrigued, if only because he knew of no better options for a Jewish king than this baby from Bethlehem.

"Do you think the baby was killed in Herod's massacre?" wondered Pilate.

"It's possible I suppose. But Herod kept looking for him for a few years after that. He had his army searching for some wealthy men who had been in contact with the infant's family. Maybe they were the power behind the plot to make the baby king," Flavius speculated.

There was a knock on the door followed by one of their guards.

"Sir, two of our scouts were found killed in the hills next to the road from Tiberius," he reported. "Stabbed in the back."

Anger rose once again in Pilate's face. Flavius, in his last hours as commander of the garrison, could only feel a deep sadness.

"Call my officers to meet with us here immediately," ordered Pilate. Flavius did not take offense at Pilate's premature assumption of power. In fact, he felt relieved to give Pilate his responsibility for a response to the killings. He could order his men to do many things, but he knew he could not command anyone to bring those two dead soldiers back to life.

"Damn those rebel cowards!" cursed Pilate after the soldier exited. The two of them sat in silence for a moment. Flavius finally spoke.

"You know, Pilate, I think you may be right after all. It's time we do have a new King of the Jews to rule all of Palestine with Rome's help. The Emperor won't object to a replacement for Herod if he is convinced that a new King will be popular with the people and completely under Rome's control."

Pilate felt encouraged by Flavius's change of heart. "Well the Jews are always talking about the coming of a new Messiah. Maybe it's time we gave them one, Flavius."

"No," Flavius replied. "It's time *you* gave them one."

Pilate was buoyed by Flavius' encouragement.

"But how do I begin to find a baby from Bethlehem after twelve years?"

"Ask the Sadducees," answered Flavius as he rose to leave. "They keep track of every Jew in Palestine to keep tax money coming into their coffers, and they're always interested in doing favors for the Emperor."

"Which of the Sadducees do I contact?" Pilate asked quickly before Flavius reached the door.

Flavius paused and thought for a moment.

"Use a Jewish priest from the Temple in Jerusalem named Caiaphas. He's been very helpful to us recently. I'm sure he would be happy to help you find a new King of the Jews who would make him the next High Priest of the Temple."

Pilate's mind was spinning with plans after Flavius left the room. He was no longer thinking of just Herod, the Sadducee priest, and the baby from Bethlehem. His mind was on to how his future control of Palestine could expand to the Roman legions in Syria in the north and even the legions in Egypt in the south. With that many legions under his command, he would have as much military power as the Emperor himself. And then . . . . He smiled inwardly. That plan would have to wait for another time.

First, he must find the boy from Bethlehem.

***

Outside next to the parade ground, Joseph and Jesus saw soldiers rushing about. A number of soldiers returned from patrol carrying the bloody bodies of the two scouts. Joseph and Jesus paused only briefly before carrying their tool boxes as quickly as possible down the passageway to the Roman baths. They had not worked at the garrison in a day and a half. Joseph could see that Jesus had been too tired to do any work, and Joseph still had a throbbing headache underneath the ugly purple bruise on his forehead. Now they had to hurry since they could not work after sunset tomorrow when the Sabbath started.

"First we'll fill the deep bath with water to make sure everything works, and then do as much as we can to finish the living quarters for Herod," Joseph instructed.

"Herod's living quarters, Father?" Jesus asked.

"Yes, son. He will be visiting Nazareth and will be staying at the garrison. So we have to finish the rooms next to the weapons storage for him and his servants."

Jesus started thinking excitedly about how his work would be done for the ruler of Galilee. He was also eager to tell Judas and the Apostles that he knew who the important visitor coming to Nazareth was. He struggled a bit under the weight of his tool box to keep up with Joseph's brisk pace. He felt exhausted, but that would be no excuse if their work was not done before the start of the Sabbath.

"The Sabbath!" thought Jesus suddenly. He looked down into his tool box where the clay tablet sat beside his tools and nervously remembered the glare of J.B.'s eyes and the glint of his dagger.

They walked into the large room with the Roman baths. Joseph climbed down the ladder into the deepest bath and carefully inspected the tiles and grout that had been sealed to prevent any water from leaking. When he was satisfied with the work he saw, he instructed Jesus to be prepared for his command to turn the wheel that would let the water flow from a heated cistern into the bath while he watched for any problems as it filled.

"If I see something," he told Jesus, "I will call for you to turn the wheel again to shut off the flow of water. You must do it quickly if I call to you. Do you understand?"

Jesus nodded and was only too happy to walk a safe distance away from the deep bath to the wheel that controlled the water. He did not like deep water. Growing up in the dry hills of Galilee, he never really had the opportunity to learn to swim. Only once in his life had he seen a body of water in which he could swim. When Jesus was a small boy, Joseph had taken the family on a trip to see the Sea of Galilee and had coaxed Jesus out into the water to play. But while he was laughing as Joseph bounced him up and down in the cool water, he tried to take a breath when his head went under and took in water instead. A panic seized him as he felt for the first time a frightening sense that he could die. From that time on as a child, Jesus would not go close to the well with his mother as she fetched water. Even now when he filled water jugs from the well, he would avoid looking at the dark water below.

After Joseph's command, Jesus turned the wheel and the water began to rise in the Roman bath. Joseph, who had stripped off most of his clothing, sloshed and scurried around looking for any possible problems with the sealed tiles. He finally had to reach for the ladder and climb out before the water level went over his head. Once he was out of the bath, he raced around its edges looking for any problems within sight. When the water reached the maximum depth, he called to Jesus to turn the wheel to stop the flow.

Joseph giggled like a child as water ran from his flattened hair into his eyes and down his body onto the floor.

"Everything worked! It's perfect! Jesus, come look."

Jesus had never seen his father so giddy with happiness. He was relieved when the thrilled Joseph did not notice that Jesus just smiled and gave a wave of congratulations without moving any nearer to the bath. After a few more minutes of satisfied looks at the bath and irrepressible smiles of pride, Joseph resumed a businesslike manner.

"All right, so far so good," he said. "But now I must make sure it drains well and there are no problems with the tiles after being wet."

"Jesus, you go on to Herod's living quarters and start the tasks there. We are running late. I'll be along as soon as I can."

Jesus picked up his tool box and walked through a couple passages until he reached the entrance to Pilate's personal quarters. He turned the corner and started walking down a long passage which ran inside the outer stone wall of the garrison that he and a crew of stonemasons had built under Joseph's supervision. There were no openings for natural light in the passage so torches in iron holders bolted to the wall burned along the walkway.

Halfway down the passage, Jesus stopped where two torches sat closer together burning side by side. He set down his tool box and studied the two torches for a moment. Then he took measured steps which he counted carefully until he came to the door. It led to the weapons storage where he had seen the Roman soldiers carry in the spears before locking it. He said out loud to himself the number of steps he had taken.

He continued down the passage counting his paces until he came to the next door. This door was the entrance to the quarters on which they were working to ready them for Herod and his servants. Once again he said out loud the number of additional steps he had taken. Then he walked to the end of the passage and noted the number of steps he took to reach the corner.

Jesus walked back to his tool box under the two torches and paused before looking both directions down the long passage. Then he picked up the clay tablet lying among the tools. After a short while, he tucked the clay tablet into the shirt of his tunic where it was held snuggly in place by the cloth belt tied around his waist. He finally picked up the tool box, walked down to the entrance to Herod's quarters, and went inside to start work on the tasks that Joseph had given him.

A while later Joseph joined Jesus. He did not say much about the baths, only that the drainage had worked well and the sealed tiles remained sound. Joseph helped Jesus smooth plaster onto the rough walls to be whitewashed. But Jesus knew he was extremely pleased about the Roman baths for Jesus had never before heard him hum songs as he worked.

"It's about time for you to go see the rabbi for your lessons," Joseph eventually announced.

"Yes, Father," Jesus answered as he rose to begin putting away his tools and wiping off his hands. Mixing and applying plaster that afternoon had been dirty work.

When Jesus picked up his tool box to leave, Joseph spoke to him firmly.

"Jesus, as you leave, go directly to the gate, keep your head down and don't speak to anyone or do anything to draw attention to yourself. Do you understand?"

"Yes, Father," he answered. But as soon as he left the room and turned down the passage, he stopped and felt for the clay tablet secure in his tunic under his belt. He swallowed hard and started walking towards the parade ground and the gatehouse.

There seemed to be more activity among the soldiers than normal. Jesus picked up his pace and tried to stay out of anyone's sight as best he could without looking suspicious. When he walked out into the sunlight of the parade ground, a few groups of soldiers were standing about dressed in full uniform and armed with spears, swords and shields.

He could not help but walk in front of one of the groups of soldiers as he headed directly across the parade ground towards the gatehouse. They were talking casually but stopped and looked down at him as he walked by them. Jesus' breath stopped in his chest. The gatehouse seemed miles away.

Out of the corner of his eye, he saw another group of soldiers walking quickly toward him. He veered away slightly and tried to walk faster. Then he noticed the spears of several other soldiers approaching him from the other direction. He needed air but could not breathe.

Jesus stumbled slightly, but it felt as if he were being spun around out of control. More soldiers were approaching. He tried unsuccessfully again to breathe. He could hear their spears clatter against their shields.

Jesus' mind was suddenly filled with his nightmare vision of the bloodied face of the condemned rebel who had fallen under the weight of his cross. He even thought he heard the thud of the criminal's cross falling next to him.

More soldiers moved towards Jesus. He felt like he was in the middle of an attack by an entire Legion. His throat choked for air.

"Save me!" the raspy voice of the vision pleaded in Jesus' ears. Jesus' mind could see only the vision's bloody fingers reaching for his face.

Jesus' tool box dropped from his hands as he reeled into the side of a soldier. He felt a hand roughly grasp the shirt of his tunic and squeezed his eyes closed as he felt himself being lifted up and dragged away.

When he opened his eyes, Jesus saw the inside of the gatehouse. Outside he saw the parade ground filled with soldiers.

"What do you think you're doing here, Jew boy?" said a guard who shook him by the shoulder. The clay tablet fell out of his tunic and clattered to the floor.

"Here, what's this?" said another guard who picked up the tablet. He turned it over and examined each side with a suspicious look.

Jesus stood still and said nothing.

The soldier stepped up to him, grabbed his tunic and shook Jesus violently.

"I asked you, boy, what is this?" he shouted in Jesus face.

"It's a clay tablet, sir," Jesus answered.

"I know it's a clay tablet, you worthless piece of dirt." The guard raised his fist. Jesus braced himself for a blow. "Why do you have it on you in your shirt?"

"My teacher the rabbi thinks I should know how to read and write."

The two soldiers looked at each other and burst out laughing.

"He's filthy as a pig, and he wants to learn to read and write." The soldier looked scornfully at Jesus. Jesus wiped his face and realized it was very dirty from the day's work.

The other soldier sneered. "Jew boy, why don't you learn to eat pig first, and then you can learn to read."

They laughed again, but stopped short as Flavius stepped through the door to the guard house. The soldiers snapped to attention with a salute of "Hail Caesar."

"What is so funny, soldier?" Flavius asked sternly.

"Sir, we found this Jew boy stumbling about the parade ground, and he just announced to us that he's going to learn to read and write like a regular rabbi."

The other soldier started to chuckle again, but stopped short when Flavius raised his hand for silence. Flavius walked up to Jesus and looked down at him. Jesus felt Flavius's eyes studying him closely.

"Who are you, boy?"

"I'm the son of Joseph, the carpenter who works in the garrison."

"See, sir," said one of the soldiers with a weak laugh. "I told you—"

Flavius silenced him with a withering look. The soldier snapped back to attention.

"I know his father very well," Flavius announced to the soldiers while continuing to examine the boy whose eyes stayed fixed on the floor before him.

"And I fully expect that this boy will end up reading and writing better than the both of you since you spend most of your time stuffing your faces with the pig this boy will not deign to eat."

"Yes, Sir! Hail Caesar!" they saluted loudly once again as Flavius turned on his heel to leave.

"Go home, son," Flavius said over his shoulder as he strode out the door. "And learn how to read and write."

Jesus bolted for the door on Flavius's command, snatching the clay tablet from the hand of the rigid soldier as he scurried out of the gatehouse.

Out on the parade ground, Pilate paused to watch the boy run out of the gatehouse. The new garrison commander stood in full regalia with a long red cloak, a gilded bronze breastplate and shin guards with ornate metal work, and his ceremonial helmet with tall red plumes. Once the boy was out of sight through the gate, Pilate walked a few paces to the spot where Flavius would turn over command of the Roman garrison in Nazareth. Before him, every soldier from the garrison stood at attention in two long lines leading to the gate. They had not been ordered to do so. In fact, Flavius had requested that no traditional ceremony occur when the command passed at his departure for Rome. The soldiers appeared of their own accord and stood respectfully at strict attention with their weapons raised in salute.

Flavius appeared with his horse which he led between the lines of soldiers until he reached Pilate at the gate. Two soldiers walking their horses followed behind Flavius to accompany him on his long journey. They would not have been going with him except that Pilate had commanded it over Flavius's objections.

He stood by his horse and faced Pilate. The two spoke quietly so that no one else could hear.

"Pilate, I wish you success in your new command. I leave you with two final thoughts.

"In any of your decisions and actions, remember this about the Jews. They have known hope in their faith in their God, their homeland, their families and their independence. They will sacrifice all they must to defend these things. If you threaten their hopes in these matters, you will know no greater enemy.

"And do not forget, my friend, that Palestine is a puzzle, and you will have to decide whether to solve it with someone's blood. Your decision could well put the name Pontius Pilate on the lips of those who tell the tale of this place for thousands of years."

Flavius looked into Pilate's eyes for a long moment, and then turned and mounted his horse.

"The Garrison of Nazareth is under your command, Pontius Pilate," announced Flavius officially.

"I accept your command, Flavius Petro," responded Pilate. He already felt a strong sense of regret that he never again would have the benefit of Flavius's advice.

Pilate struck his fist hard on his breast plate above his heart. "Hail Caesar," he saluted to Flavius.

"Ah yes—I'd almost forgotten about Caesar," Flavius sighed. For a moment his mind seemed to wander far away. Then he spurred his horse and galloped through the gate away from the garrison.

Chapter 9

MAGIC

"A camel go through the eye of a needle? This I've got to see!"

Lazarus jumped up from the street where he had been begging as a cripple and headed for the market with Simon and a few of the Apostles. The boys told Lazarus about the magician who had been proclaiming that today he would perform feats of magic including passing a camel through the eye of a needle.

The streets leading to the market began to fill with people who had heard of the magician. The magician, who had arrived with his servant in Nazareth a few days earlier, was in the market every day telling people about the great magic he would show them. Word spread quickly. He planned the place and time for his magic well. It was a busy day in the market just before the Sabbath, and it was one of the days each month in which slaves were bought and sold in an area near the place where his magic would be performed.

Mary's children begged her to go see the magician. Joseph was busy working at the garrison, and Jesus was not at home. So Rachael, Jamie, Rebecca and little Joses asked their mother if she would take them to the market to see the magic.

"No, you can't go to the market to see some foolish false prophet," she told them. "You have chores to do, and someone has to watch Jude."

Rebecca looked like she might cry, and the other three groaned with disappointment. They immediately started promising her that their chores would be done before the end of the day and that they would be fine to go by themselves if they had to.

Rachel spoke up. "Mother, Jamie and I can take Rebecca and Joses right to the market and right back home as soon as the magician is done. We'll be all right, won't we, Jamie?"

"Yes, Mother. We'll hold their hands the whole time," he added.

Mary frowned and thought of pickpockets, beggars, soldiers, new messiahs and all the strangers that seemed to be appearing in Nazareth these days. But she looked at those four eager faces and thought about how they were good children who worked hard and had been through a lot lately with Jude and with Joseph's being gone a great deal at his work.

"All right, you can go, and I'll stay with Jude," she said. "But Rachel, you and Jamie are responsible for the little ones. And Rebecca and Joses, you do what Rachel and Jamie tell you. Don't talk to any strangers and come right home when the magician is done. Do you understand?"

"Yes, Mother," they said in unison with Rebecca's wave as they scampered out the door.

"And remember, it's not real. It's just magic," she called out behind them.

"Not real . . . just magic." She thought about her words and her life, and smiled.

Jesus, Peter and Bartholomew were walking down the street headed towards the market for the magician's show. They had timed it just right so that they were following Maggie and Susanna who also were headed for the market. But unfortunately the Pharisee Nicodemus had already intercepted the girls and was accompanying them.

Out of the blue, Bartholomew suddenly announced, "I've got to get rid of these pimples!"

Peter and Jesus gave him a puzzled look.

"What?" they both asked together.

"I'll never be betrothed as long as I have these spots all over my face," he said.

Peter laughed. Jesus looked like he was thinking hard as they arrived at the place where the magician's stage had been set up. People were gathering and getting settled on the ground.

"There's a cure for that, you know," Jesus said to Bartholomew as they sat down.

"For my pimples?" Bartholomew looked surprised.

"Oh, yes," said Jesus with a firm nod.

"What is it?"

"Well, first you have to get some salt from the Dead Sea. Then every morning mix it with water warmed by the rising sun and splash it on your face. After that you dry off your face, but only with a cloth woven by the wife of a rabbi. Then you must do the same thing in the evening with warm water heated by the sun before it sets."

"Where did you hear that?" asked Bartholomew.

"I don't remember exactly," Jesus answered. "Maybe I saw it somewhere in the Laws of Moses that Zacharias made me read."

Peter snorted. "I don't believe it. Sounds like something a rabbi's wife would say just to sell the cloth she's woven."

"Yeah, it sounds like an old wives' tale," agreed Bartholomew. "Besides, where could you even find Dead Sea salt and a cloth woven by a rabbi's wife?"

Bartholomew tried to sound skeptical but looked at Jesus hoping to hear an answer.

"The Dead Sea salt is not a problem," replied Jesus. "The bald merchant from Perea sells it in his stall at the corner of the market where the Apostles wait for messages. And the Rabbi Zacharias's wife Elizabeth weaves cloth to give to the poor all the time."

Bartholomew was quiet for a few moments as people kept crowding in close to them.

"Save my seat," said Bartholomew as he stood up unexpectedly and started stepping over the people sitting around them.

"I don't know if we can. You'd better stay here," Peter called to him. Jesus and Peter watched him head in the direction of the salt seller's stall in the market.

"Does that salt and cloth really work?" Peter asked Jesus.

"I don't really know," Jesus answered. "But the rabbi says we should never underestimate what can happen when someone truly believes in something. It can be pretty powerful."

The area around the magician's stage was getting crowded. Many of the vendors stood on the edge of the gathering where they still could keep an eye on their deserted stalls. The Wine Seller Shikkor, like many other shopkeepers, closed his doors temporarily so that he could see the magic. No messages were being delivered since all the Apostles were scattered among the spectators. Even Zacharias strolled down to the market from the synagogue. The only people in the market who were not excited by the event, Jesus noticed, were the forlorn-looking slaves waiting to be sold.

The magician's stage was oddly shaped, a circular platform about eight paces across and the height of a man's knee. Around it were tall poles anchored in the ground at regular intervals.

Once the area was completely filled with people, an old man with a long white beard down to his knees stepped up onto the round stage. He wore a long coat of many bright colors in stripes that ran from the ground up to a pointed hood that covered his head and face. All one could see of his face was the beard and the light of his eyes that shone in the darkness under his hood. The crowd grew quiet as he raised his arms covered in wide sleeves that hid most of his hands. He spoke loudly and slowly with an unusual accent.

"I am Balthazar. I am from far, far away in the East. I study among the stars. I am an astrologer, an astronomer. I am a Magi," he raised his hands high above his shoulders like a rabbi about to pray, "and I—do—MAGIC!"

As he shouted this last word, he brought his hands together with a loud clap that sent sparks and a cloud of smoke up from his hands into the air above him. The crowd cried out in surprise and awe. They had never before seen a man produce fire and smoke from his hands. Applause broke out. Balthazar took a deep bow, the tip of his hood almost touching the ground.

Zacharias, who had just wandered into the market, stood at the back of the crowd. When the sparks and smoke shot out from the magician's hands, Zacharias only smiled. He leaned forward to hear what the magician would say next.

"My fine friends of Nazareth in Galilee, I have come here to show you special and wondrous works and to see the great wonders of your town that I have heard of from afar.

"My magic is for all of you," he announced. "But let us have all the children sit here in front so they can behold the mysteries of the universe that are about to unfold."

The youngsters started moving through the crowd and sitting on the ground right in front of the magician standing on the platform.

That's right," encouraged Balthazar. "All children, tall and small, come up close and behold my magic with your eyes." He pointed at some of the Apostles and with a gesture urged them to sit down in front of the stage. Peter, Matthew, James and John, Thomas, Judas and the others sat down along with Jesus so they would have a clear view of the magician. When Jesus saw Rachel, he waved at his brothers and sisters to come sit next to him.

"Come! Come!" Balthazar called for them to hurry as he watched closely the excited young people settle in. Once everyone was in place, he looked back up at the audience.

"But forgive me. I am being a rude guest. I must bear gifts for you my hosts. Tell me what you would like."

"Rain!" called out one of the farmers. The crowd laughed.

"Ah, yes, rain," said Balthazar. "A common request these days. I will do that magic when I next come to Nazareth if you still need it. But in the meantime, let my magic give you some of the beauty that rain bestows."

He lifted his arm up in the air and pulled the sleeve back to show his bare arm down to the elbow. When he lowered his arm and the sleeve fell back down around his hand, he reached into the sleeve with his other hand, paused and pulled out a bunch of beautiful desert flowers still on their branches.

The onlookers applauded once again. This show looked like it might have real magic, unlike all those fake messiahs who attempted to get people's attention with tricks that a child could see through.

"Who would like these?" Balthazar asked. His eyes scanned the crowd and stopped when they came to Maggie.

"You there, young lady, come up here."

Maggie stepped forward and up on to the stage. She smiled shyly at the magician and the audience. Balthazar seemed to lose his words for a moment, but quickly composed himself and announced, "Beautiful flowers for a beautiful young lady."

Balthazar handed her the flowers. The men in the crowd clapped even more loudly than they had for the magic trick. Most of the women remained still.

"Now, young lady, I want you to do something for me." Balthazar pulled from his pocket a piece of rope the length of his arm. "Please look at this rope and tell me if it is in one piece. Go ahead, pull on it if you like."

Maggie took the rope and examined it closely. She gave it little tug and handed it back.

"Is this a solid piece of rope?" he asked her.

"Yes, it is."

"Are you sure?"

"I'm sure."

"Very good. Now you stand right there for a moment and watch closely while I fold the rope in half."

He took a step back, held the ends of the rope in each hand and folded it in half. With the loose ends in one hand and the folded end in the other hand, he gave the rope a couple hard tugs. Then he let go of the loose ends and held up his hand with the loop of the folded end sticking up just above the back of his hand.

"Now I need another assistant," announced Balthazar. "Is there anyone in the audience who has a sharp knife?"

A young man stepped up on the stage. Jesus, who had been watching Maggie more than the magician, looked over at the young man. He recognized him as one of the vinedressers who had been with J.B. the night he was given the clay tablet for a map of the garrison.

"Good afternoon, young man," greeted the magician. "And do you have a sharp knife?"

The young man looked Maggie up and down with a lurid smile.

Then in one swift motion, a dagger appeared out of the sleeve of the man's tunic and stopped close to the magician's face. Balthazar leaned his head back.

"I guess you do have a sharp knife," he said with an uncomfortable laugh. "Now, carefully cut through the loop of rope in my hand. And please don't cut off any fingers, I need them for my next magic trick."

The people chuckled and then watched closely as the man slipped the blade of the dagger into the loop of the rope and sliced through it effortlessly.

"Very good. Thank you, sir. And thank you, young lady," Balthazar said to them. As the two of them stepped off the stage, everyone in the audience could see the vinedresser leering at Maggie.

The magician smoothly folded up the two pieces of rope into his hands. Then, with a quick move, he held up his hands and moved them apart. Between his hands was a single long piece of rope pulled taut. The cut rope had been magically repaired.

His growing admirers applauded his magic. The Apostles clapped as loudly as they could. They particularly liked the trick with a rope like the belts that were the trademark of the messengers. When the crowd quieted down, the magician looked across the gathering to the edge of the market where some Roman soldiers stood together.

"Now I need a special volunteer." Looking over at the soldiers, he said, "Centurion, would you mind coming up here to give me some assistance?"

The leader of the group of soldiers clearly did not want to go on the stage, but the other soldiers teased and pushed him forward until he relented, walked over to the stage and stepped up next to Balthazar.

"You know, soldier," said Balthazar pointing to the plumes on his helmet, "with those feathers in your hat, you're almost as pretty as the young lady who was up here earlier."

The crowd laughed with approval of the magician's jest at the Roman's expense. The other soldiers laughed even louder than the rest of the crowd. Although the centurion smiled, everyone could tell he was not happy about the remark.

Balthazar's servant next to the stage handed him a tall narrow urn that came up to the waist of the soldier. After he set the urn down between them, Balthazar asked the centurion, "Sir, first would you look into this urn and tell us whether you see anything in it."

"There's nothing in there," announced the soldier after peering down into the urn.

"Very well," said Balthazar. "Now, would you happen to have a coin that I could borrow?"

The centurion reached into a small leather pouch tied to his belt, pulled out a silver denarius coin and handed it to the magician. Balthazar looked at the coin and then held it up for all to see.

"I see, sir, that this coin has the image of Caesar on one side. Is that correct?"

"That's correct," answered the soldier.

Balthazar held the coin high in the air and again pulled his sleeve back so that his bare arm, hand and fingers holding the coin were showing. With his bare arm, he reached deep down into the urn. While his arm was in the urn, he tapped the coin on the inside several times. Then keeping his sleeve up, the magician pulled his bare arm out of the urn and held it up so that everyone could see that his hand was empty and the coin was still in the urn.

He turned back to the centurion and let his sleeve down. "Now, soldier, you may not realize it, but you have a magic sword. Would you be so kind as to take it out and wave it over the top of the urn three times as the audience and I count. Ready everyone?"

The centurion took the sword from its scabbard and held it above the urn.

"One," said everyone at the direction of the magician as the soldier passed the sword over the opening of the urn.

"Two," counted the crowd as the soldier waved the sword over the urn again.

"And . . . ," Balthazar prompted the crowd.

"Three!" they answered enthusiastically when the soldier did a final pass with his sword.

"Thank you, centurion," said Balthazar. "You can put your sword away now."

"And by the way, don't ever take it out again," he jested with partial seriousness. His fans again sounded their approval until the magician raised his hand for silence.

"Now let us behold the true power of your sword."

Balthazar put his hands on each side of the urn and raised it as high as he could. Then he slowly tilted the urn until it was completely upside down and no coin fell out. The crowd clapped in appreciation. Balthazar set the urn back down quickly and raised his hand again for silence.

"Whenever you draw and wave your sword, my friend, it makes money disappear." Balthazar looked at the soldier seriously, and then turned with a smile to the audience. "But we cannot let a little magic deprive this soldier of his hard-earned wages."

The magician reached up behind the soldier's ear and appeared to pull out the silver coin which he held up in his fingers for the audience to see. They cheered once again as the soldier, looking surprised, raised his hand to his ear. Balthazar showed the coin to the soldier.

"And does this coin have Caesar's image on it?"

"Yes it does."

"Then let us render unto Caesar that which is Caesar's," said Balthazar as he handed the coin back to the centurion.

The assembly clapped in appreciation. But a few rumblings could be heard throughout the crowd. Rendering unto Caesar was just what most of them had done with the recent payment of taxes, and they were not at all happy about it.

Balthazar walked to the front of the stage and lowered his head so that his face disappeared under his hood. When the audience went silent with expectation, his head raised and his piercing eyes looked out at them.

"And now, for one and all, it is time for great magic." He paused dramatically. "I will now pass a camel—through the eye of a needle!"

Everyone stirred with excitement and shifted for the best possible view of the whole stage. The children all leaned forward. Rebecca and

Joses were so excited they both grabbed the sleeves of Jesus' tunic.

Balthazar stood motionless for a moment to heighten the crowd's anticipation before clapping his hands in the air and striding to the edge of the stage where his servant held what looked like a wall made of palm branches tied together. The magician and his servant lifted the wall of palm branches up onto the round stage and secured it firmly in place by jamming two rocks the size of a man's head on either side of its bottom corners. The wall now sat firmly upright about head high across the entire width of the circular stage. It looked solid except for a small thin opening in the middle about the shape of a man's finger.

The magician turned back to the centurion. "Sir, I have one more favor to ask. This is a solid wall of palm branches. But I would like you to examine it closely and test the wall so that everyone out there can see that the wall will not move and there are no holes to crawl through."

The soldier carefully inspected the wall left to right and top to bottom. Then he lightly pushed on the palm branches at several places with his hands. The wall did not move.

"Now tell us, sir," said the magician, "Can this wall be quickly moved with ease?"

"Not really," he answered.

"Are there any holes or spaces in this wall for anyone or anything to step through?"

"Yes there is," said the centurion to everyone's surprise. "There's a little slit right here in the middle."

The soldier looked very pleased at his cleverness. Balthazar stepped over and looked directly at the small space in the wall.

"Why indeed there is!" he exclaimed. "I'll just have to do something about that."

He held his arm in the air, pulled back his sleeve and again reached behind the soldier's ear. When his hand came back, his fingers held a large needle like those used by the tentmakers. Everyone laughed once more at the puzzled soldier touching his ear.

Balthazar held the needle up for the audience to examine. The needle was the length of his fingers. The eye of the needle was an opening about the size of a small fingernail. Then he stepped over and pierced a leaf of a palm branch with the needle so that its eye hung in the small opening in the wall.

"Soldier," Bathazar turned to the centurion, "you have been a great help. You are dismissed!"

He turned to the audience. "Let's thank him for his service, at least just this once." As the centurion stepped down from the stage, the thought occurred to Zacharias that this might be the only time in the history of Palestine that a crowd of Jews gave appreciative applause to a Roman soldier.

"And now, people of Nazareth—" The crowd went quiet. "A camel—through the eye—of a needle."

Balthazar pointed to the side of the audience where his servant led a camel by its reins. A red cloth with gold fringe covered its hump. Matching red and gold tassels with tinkling bells hanging from its neck swayed as the servant walked the camel around for everyone to see. Circling back, the servant had the camel step up carefully onto the rear of the round stage where its head barely looked over the wall of palm branches at the audience.

The servant then handed Balthazar one end of a long folded cloth curtain which he and the magician deftly unfolded and hung on the tall poles surrounding the circular stage. When they finished, the view of the stage from the back and sides was blocked.

"My friends," Balthazar addressed the crowd. "You have seen a real camel, and you have seen a real needle in this solid wall of palm leaves." On cue, his servant pointed at the camel and then the needle in the wall.

"Now you will see, by the powers of great magic, this camel and my servant, pass through the eye of that needle!"

The servant moved to the side of the camel behind the wall while Balthazar walked across the front of the round stage to secure the curtain to completely block the audience's last view of the platform.

Stepping off the stage in front of the curtain, Balthazar asked the crowd, "Are you ready?"

The audience shouted "Yes" and then went completely still.

Balthazar called out to his man behind the curtain, "Are you and the camel ready, my good and faithful servant?"

"We are," he answered so that all could hear.

Balthazar paused, and spoke firmly and slowly. "Then I command you, with all the powers of my magic, to pass with the camel through the eye of a needle!"

The audience held its breath as they heard the camel's hooves stomping on the stage floor. Their eyes were fixed on the curtain.

Everything went dead still until they heard the tinkling of the camel's bells and the magician quickly stepped back to the stage to pull away the curtain.

The audience gasped in amazement. There stood the servant and the camel facing the audience in front of the wall as if they each had magically passed forward through the eye of the needle.

The crowd burst into deafening shouts and applause. When Balthazar stepped next to the camel, everyone came to their feet cheering. The magician and his servant both walked over to the wall and shook it to show the audience that it was still solid and immovable. Then Balthazar reached over and took the needle from the wall. He stepped to the front of the camel and with a flourish held the tiny eye of the needle in front of its large nose. The crowd cheered loudly once again.

The servant shook his head and looked to the audience as if he still could not believe what had just happened to him. But what astonished the servant was how simple it all was. Balthazar called it the "half circle trick." All they did was put up a curtain, then turn the secretly movable round stage in a half circle so the back of the stage with the camel was now in front, and finally turn the camel around in a half circle to face the audience.

While Balthazar had been speaking, the servant was moving behind the curtain with speedy precision. He gave the camel a pat, reached under the floor of the circular stage and pulled out a block of wood that was holding the stage firmly in place. He lowered one knee to the stage floor, put his other foot on the ground and gave a firm push. The round stage floor began turning smoothly and silently like a chariot wheel lying on its side. With one more push of his leg, the stage ended with the camel's rump and the back of the wall facing the curtain in front. He reached below the front of the stage with the wooden block and locked the stage in position just before he heard Balthazar ask if he was ready and called out "We are" in response. When the magician finished the command to pass through the eye of the needle, the servant was already standing next to the camel with its reins in hand and started turning the camel around in front of the needle to face the audience. Then all he did was shake the camel's bells to signal Balthazar to pull back the curtain.

"But these people," thought the servant, "really believe that we actually went through the small eye of that needle. That's the real magic going on here," he concluded as he smiled and waved at the crowd.

Balthazar stepped forward and once again bowed until his hood almost touched the floor of the stage. He took repeated bows to show his appreciation. Each time he rose up, he took care to look directly at the faces of the children and smile at each of them. When the noise finally started to die down, Balthazar raised his hands for silence.

"Thank you, All of you are very kind.

"I live for my magic and give it to you freely. I would do it for nothing. But alas, my servant and my camel must eat and drink."

His servant jumped off the stage with a basket in his hands and started moving toward the adults in the crowd.

"So I must ask that if you can, please give my servant and my camel your kind gifts of thanks for the power of magic so that they do not go hungry and so the magic can continue."

As people began to throw coins in the basket, Balthazar went on. "Now I know you may not be rich, especially since you just paid your taxes."

Another rumbling of unhappiness went through the crowd. This time a few angry shouts were heard as well. The Pharisee Nicodemus felt uncomfortable and for once tried to avoid being seen.

"But remember," continued Balthazar, "being rich will not help you enter the kingdom of heaven. It is easier for a camel to go through the eye of a needle than for the rich to enter the kingdom of God.

"So please be generous to my servant and camel. Thank you. Thank you very much."

Balthazar stepped off the stage and went over to where the children were gathered. They were thrilled as he smiled at them and patted them on their heads. He asked their names and talked to them. When he reached Jesus and his brothers and sisters, Rebecca gave him such a sweet smile that he reached behind her ear and pulled out a brightly colored glass bead which he gave to her.

Eventually the crowd began to disperse. The magician watched everyone carefully as if he was looking for someone. Finally he gave instructions to his servant to take apart the stage and gathered up the reins of his camel.

"Hello, Balthazar. Still trying to move the stars around in the sky these days?"

The magician turned around at the sound of a familiar voice.

"Well hello, Zacharias. I gave up on that trick years ago. But I can still make coins stick to old honey at the bottom of an urn," he smiled. "Are you still doing the Lord's work."

"I am," Zacharias responded.

"What are you doing in Nazareth?" asked Balthazar.

"I'm the rabbi at the synagogue here. I came out of retirement from the Temple in Jerusalem when I was offered this position. And what, may I ask, brought you and your magic to Nazareth?"

"I seek the Promised Messiah," he answered.

Zacharias looked at him with surprise. "In Nazareth, Balthazar? This is an odd place to search for the Chosen One, don't you think?"

"Zacharias, I have followed a long trail for many years, and it has brought me to Nazareth. I know I am in the right place for what I seek."

Balthazar sounded certain, and Zacharias wondered why.

"I thought you found the Promised Messiah as a baby in Bethlehem many years ago."

"I truly believe that I did," replied Balthazar. "And he was in Bethlehem, of that I'm certain. But when I went again to worship him, he was gone. I wanted—No, Zacharias—I needed to be in the presence of the Promised Messiah. He will be the Savior of our People. So I began to seek him once again. But this time there was no star in the East to guide me.

"I spoke with many people until I learned from some shepherds that his parents had taken him to Egypt, which was fortunate since Herod murdered every baby boy in Bethlehem while searching for him. So I followed their trail to Egypt where I sought them in every Jewish community through which I passed. I'm certain I came close to finding them several times, for several people had seen and even given shelter to a young couple with a small baby traveling from Palestine on a donkey.

"But after years of unsuccessful searching in Egypt, I returned to Jerusalem. I thought that the Promised Messiah must surely return one day to the Holy Temple in Jerusalem to claim his throne and lead his people.

"I waited for years in Jerusalem, and it came to nothing. But then the answer came to me. I found the key to my search."

"And what was that?" asked Zacharias.

"The census," Balthazar answered.

"The what?"

"The Roman census ordered by Caesar Augustus when Quirinius was governor of Syria. Everyone was ordered to go to the city of their family's lineage to register in order to be taxed. Remember? That's when we found the baby, the Promised Messiah, in Bethlehem."

"I'm sorry, Balthazar," Zacharias interrupted, "but I'm not following you."

Balthazar explained, "I went through the entire census registration for the city of Bethlehem looking for a couple with a newly born baby. It took a while, but I finally found them.

"The father who had to register in Bethlehem, the city of David, was a descendant of David. His name was Joseph, and he listed their home as Nazareth. That's why I'm here."

"I am afraid it's not that simple, Balthazar," said Zacharias. "You won't be surprised to hear that there are many men with that name in Nazareth, let alone the area around here in Galilee where almost every family has a Joseph."

"I know that," replied Balthazar. "And that's the problem I've found. But remember, it's not Joseph I'm looking for. I'm looking for his son, the Promised Messiah.

"By now he's twelve years old. If he is the Chosen One and is here in Nazareth, he certainly must stand out as an exceptional boy. And, Zacharias, I think I may have found that boy from Nazareth."

"Who is he?" Zacharias asked quickly.

"I've only been here a few days, but I've already heard of a boy who just healed a blind man. I don't know his name yet, but I will see every boy in Nazareth before I am through."

"And that's why you announced for days in the market your magic show so that every boy in Nazareth would come to see you," concluded Zacharias.

"Exactly," Balthazar replied. "And so that I would see every boy in Nazareth."

"Did you see your exceptional boy? Did you find the Chosen One?" asked Zacharias.

"If I did, I didn't recognize him," he answered sadly. "But Zacharias, you must know most of the boys in Nazareth." Balthazar looked at him hopefully.

"Balthazar, if the Promised Messiah was in Nazareth, I'm sure I would already know who he is."

"I suppose so." Balthazar was disappointed. The day had not gone as he had hoped. "I'll just have to keep looking. I've come this far, and I have the feeling that once again I am close."

With a friendly goodbye and a promise to meet again, Balthazar pulled the reins of his camel and walked wearily over to the stage to help his servant.

Zacharias, like most of the magician's audience, was thirsty after the show and headed towards the well for a cool drink under the shade trees. As he drew near, he could see and hear some commotion among the people gathered near the well.

Up by the pools around the well, heated words were being exchanged. The vinedresser who had cut the rope in the magic trick could not get

Maggie out of his mind. When he saw her by the well drinking with Susanna and Nicodemus, he walked up to her and shoved Nicodemus aside.

"Hey, Beautiful, forget this sissy boy and let's you and me go someplace quiet."

He put his arm around her waist and tried to steer her away. She could smell wine on his breath.

"Let me go," she ordered as she tried to pry his arm off her.

"Leave her alone!" said Nicodemus.

The vinedresser sneered at him. Nicodemus started to step forward when a tight grip on his arm held him back.

"I wouldn't do that if I were you, Pharisee."

Nicodemus turned and saw the other vinedresser who flashed his dagger in front of Nicodemus.

Maggie's sandals slipped against the ground as she resisted when the vinedresser pulled her toward him. Suddenly, a small figure flew out of the crowd and pushed him away from Maggie. He staggered slightly and turned with an angry look.

There stood Judas with his fists clenched. The vinedresser looked at him and then over at his companion next to Nicodemus. With a laugh, he waved over his friend and walked right up to Judas. They picked him up, carried him struggling over to the pools and tossed him in with a big splash.

The crowd had now gathered around. The vinedresser growled at them, "What are you looking at?"

He turned around for Maggie. There standing between him and the girl was Jesus.

"Move aside, pretty boy," he snarled at Jesus as he walked towards him.

"Leave her alone and go back to your vineyard," said Jesus.

At these words, the vinedresser rushed at Jesus. Just as the vinedresser was about to tackle him, Jesus turned sideways, stepped one leg forward between the vinedresser's legs, turned his back to the vinedresser and bent over so that the vinedresser flipped over Jesus' waist and landed hard on the ground.

Jesus stood up and saw the other vinedresser running at him. A flash of light reflected off the blade of a dagger as Jesus fell gracefully to the ground on his back and stuck his foot up into the chest of the vinedresser. With the force of his rush and the thrust of Jesus' foot into his chest, the vinedresser flew into the air and did a complete somersault before landing with a crushing thud on top of the other vinedresser. They both staggered to their feet, and pointed their daggers at Jesus.

"Enough!" a loud voice ordered. Zacharias stepped between Jesus and the vinedressers.

"Stop this fighting and put away your weapons." Zacharias turned to the crowd. "The rest of you go to your homes and your businesses. There is nothing more to see here."

Seeing the angry looks that surrounded them, the vinedressers slid their daggers under their sleeves and slunk off in silence. Susanna put her arm around Maggie and led her off towards her home. Judas stood there sopping wet and gave Jesus a puzzling angry look. Jesus looked around for his brothers and sisters when he saw Peter, Andrew, Simon and Bartholomew.

The four Apostles were surrounded by the Roman soldiers who had watched the magic show and were being led off toward the garrison by the centurion for whom they had applauded only moments earlier.

Chapter 10

THE SADDUCEE

Caiaphas was very intrigued, slightly nervous and dead tired.

He had made the three-day journey between Jerusalem and Nazareth in two days. When Caiaphas received the request from the new commander of the garrison in Nazareth to meet with him immediately, the priest summoned two Temple guards as a precaution against bandits and left before the sun had reached midday. The commander's message sounded more like an order than a request.

Caiaphas had no idea why the commander would summon him for a meeting with such urgency. But the priest knew two things for certain. First, the Romans had taken possession of the robes and vestments of the High Priest of the Temple and kept them under guard in a stone chamber in the Temple. It was the Romans' less than subtle way of reminding the Jews that the High Priest of the Temple would be chosen by the Roman authorities. The second thing he knew for certain was that when significant opportunities appeared, one should take immediate advantage of them.

That knowledge explained how he came to be married and a priest of the Temple in Jerusalem. As one of many young rabbis in Jerusalem, he had served the Lord in the obscurity of a small synagogue until one day when he went to the Holy Temple to pray outside the Court of the Priests and dream of being a priest standing before the sacred altar inside. When he opened his eyes after praying, he saw a young woman staring at him. She was not particularly attractive.

But he smiled at her, and they began talking.

It was not long before he learned of her desperate situation. She was the oldest daughter of Annas, the High Priest of the Temple. Three attempts had been made by her father to arrange for her to marry a rabbi, and none of them had been successful. Now she was growing older, her prospects were getting slim, and her father refused to arrange marriages for her younger sisters while she remained unmarried.

Caiaphas seized his opportunity. In short order, he declared his love for her, asked Annas for permission to marry, and suggested to Annas that he would be far better prepared to be a good provider for her if he were a priest of the Temple in Jerusalem. Just as Caiaphas had calculated, Annas was feeling even more pressure for his oldest daughter to marry than she was. Caiaphas was soon married after a generous dowry was hastily fixed, and he became the youngest rabbi ever to be raised to the distinguished position as a priest of the Temple in Jerusalem. Following the marriage, he proved to be an able assistant and confidant to the High Priest, and in the process met every important Roman in Palestine.

Now he was in Nazareth to seize the unexpected opportunity to meet the new Roman commander of the garrison that was planned to be a major military installation in Palestine. Although tired and dirty from the journey, Caiaphas sent one of his guards to the garrison to let the commander know that he had arrived and would be available to meet with the commander immediately. Caiaphas headed to the well to wash before going to the garrison. While he refreshed himself, he became curious about the loud cheering and applause coming from the market place. A woman at the well told him of a magic show in the market just as his guard returned from the garrison with the message that the commander would see him right away.

When he arrived at the garrison, Caiaphas was escorted from the guardhouse directly to Pilate's offices. Pilate rose from a long table where he had been studying maps of the region.

"Rabbi, thank you for coming on such short notice. Welcome to our humble camp here in Nazareth. I apologize for the inconvenience and discomfort you must have suffered."

Pilate shook Caiaphas's hand and waved him to a seat at the end of the long table.

"It was nothing, Commander. It's always a pleasure to meet with an officer of the emperor. How can I be of assistance?"

"Rabbi, you may be aware that the rebel zealots have been creating more trouble in Galilee lately, and Roman soldiers now are frequently being attacked and killed."

"Most unfortunate, Commander," said Caiaphas.

"It's not just unfortunate, Rabbi." Pilate slammed his fist on the table. "It's war!" he shouted.

The startled priest did not know what to say. Pilate resumed a calm demeanor. He had made his first planned impression on the priest.

"And it's a difficult war, Rabbi, more so than usual."

"Commander," replied Caiaphas, "the Roman army and, by your reputation, you yourself are excellent at fighting difficult wars."

"Rabbi, in Galilee the enemy is hidden everywhere, in homes, farms, shops, even synagogues." Pilate gave Caiaphas a warning look that made him uncomfortable. "The enemy is often indistinguishable from our friends. Consequently, we are taking steps to identify and find anyone of importance who can be influential in helping either the rebels or the Emperor."

"There should be no doubt from our actions, Commander, that we Sadducees are loyal subjects of the Emperor who will do anything in our power to preserve the Emperor's position in Palestine," Caiaphas responded.

"So I am told," replied Pilate. "That is why we seek your help in identifying someone who once was on the verge of having influence and power in Palestine and whose whereabouts are now unknown."

"Tell me who it is you seek, and we will find him for you," Caiaphas assured Pilate.

"Twelve years ago, Herod the Great took extreme measures to locate and if possible kill a baby boy in Bethlehem whom he believed would be the next King of the Jews. With that power and influence even as a baby, that child is a person of interest to us. If he is still alive, the boy could be either a significant threat or a strategic supporter of the Emperor here in Palestine." Pilate's voice grew firm. "We must find that boy from Bethlehem. I cannot emphasize enough the importance of this mission. And we need the help of the Sadducees."

A look of surprise came over Caiaphas's face.

"That's odd," remarked Caiaphas. "You're the second person who has been looking for the boy from Bethlehem recently."

Now it was Pilate who was surprised. "Who is the other person?"

"My father-in-law, Annas the High Priest, told me not long ago that there was an eccentric old man going about Jerusalem and the Temple seeking any information he could find about the baby from Bethlehem.

"From what I heard," Caiaphas added," it should not be hard for you to find the boy."

"Why is that?"

"I was told that the old man managed to locate the boy's whereabouts. He's supposed to be living right here in Nazareth."

Pilate could hardly believe his good luck. He tried not to show his excitement at the Sadducee's news.

"Can you provide any more information on the boy's identity?" he asked.

"I have some sources here in Nazareth. I can make inquiries and report back to you."

"How quickly can you get back to me?" Pilate sounded anxious.

"I can start today and continue tomorrow. Then I must return to Jerusalem to prepare for the upcoming ceremonies for the Feast of the Passover," answered Caiaphas.

Pilate rose from his chair. "Excellent, Rabbi. I look forward to your report tomorrow."

They shook hands once again, and Caiaphas headed towards the door.

"Oh, and Rabbi," Pilate stopped him. "If your information brings me the boy, I am sure the Emperor will be very grateful."

"Thank you, Commander. I seek only to serve God and the Emperor,"

Caiaphas answered before bowing out the door.

"As well as your own holy robes," muttered Pilate.

Pilate immediately called in his chief officers who were waiting outside for their meeting to plan operations for dealing with the rebel zealots. The officers sat in a line on one side of the long table across from Pilate who sat alone facing them. They were not long into their discussions when a soldier entered the room and stood at attention.

"Yes?" Pilate addressed him looking up.

"Sir, we have the boys. You asked to be notified immediately."

"Thank you," he replied with a satisfied look. "Bring them here now."

The officers glanced at one another with questioning looks, trying to figure out what this interruption was about. The soldier gestured through the door and two guards armed with spears marched four boys into the room.

They were an odd-looking collection. A fat boy looking very frightened stood on the left next to a shorter boy with very long hair who wore a sneer on his face. Next to them were two boys who looked like they could be brothers. One wore a brightly striped tunic. The other, with a scraggly start of a beard, was taller and looked to be a bit older. Neither of them showed any expression on his face.

Pilate studied them for a moment, and then carried on talking to his officers.

"I'd like to turn next to another important item. Herod has communicated with me that he wishes to visit Nazareth to see the progress on the fortification of the garrison. He will be coming in on the road from Tiberius where he will be inspecting construction on his new city.

"Also he will be staying here in the garrison. I am having rooms prepared for him in the west wing next to the weapons storage."

Pilate paused. "We have a problem with the scheduling, however."

"His visit is to occur during the celebration of the Jewish Feast of the Passover in Jerusalem. We have reports of possible rebel activity around Jerusalem planned to coincide with the celebration. In order to prevent any violence or rioting the rebels might be organizing, I am planning to take most of our troops from the garrison to Jerusalem in order to deter or respond to any actions by the rebels."

The officers looked at one another with concern on their faces.

"But, sir," one of the officers spoke up. "Won't that leave the garrison somewhat vulnerable? There has been much more violent activity from the rebels around Galilee than around Jerusalem."

"That is a risk," acknowledged Pilate. "But Herod will have his own guard, and new reinforcements from Syria are scheduled to arrive here shortly after the Feast. There may be a brief window of vulnerability in the garrison right after Herod arrives, but it should be temporary."

Each of the officers sitting across from Pilate had one image in his mind. It was the picture of twenty dead Roman soldiers being carried into the garrison a few days earlier.

"Decimus, you will remain at the garrison with four units. Petillius, you are in charge of preparing the rest of the troops for the journey to Jerusalem. We will be leaving the day before Herod arrives."

The officers looked shocked at what they had just heard.

"Sir," Decimus replied. "That leaves barely thirty soldiers to guard the garrison and Herod. And meaning no disrespect, Sir, I don't think Herod's guards on a good day could protect him from a kitten."

"That is my decision," Pilate answered firmly. "Oh and Decimus, you'll give Herod as much ceremony as you can when he shows up, won't you? Thank you, gentlemen. You're dismissed."

The officers stood in unison and saluted. Unhappy looks of concern and disbelief were still on their faces as they filed out of the room. Pilate rose from the table and turned to the boys.

"Marcus," he said to his aide standing next to the door, "bring me my helmet."

The aide stepped outside for a moment, and returned with the red plumed helmet which he handed to Pilate. Pilate held it up in front of his eyes, turning it around and examining it carefully before he set in on the table.

Next he slowly drew his sword out of its scabbard with a smooth scraping sound and carefully laid it next to the helmet, its tip pointing at the boys. Their eyes were wide when he looked up at them sternly.

"Have any of you boys ever touched this helmet?"

"No, sir," they answered together, but with a slight hesitation by Bartholomew.

"I see," said Pilate after a pause. He reached out and casually stroked the blade of his sword with his fingertips.

He looked back at them and asked more sharply, "Do you know anything about the rebel zealots in Nazareth?"

"No, sir," they all answered.

"Are you sure?" Pilate asked. "It would not be a good thing for you if I found out you were lying."

With a "Yes, sir," and a variety of nods, the boys answered as affirmatively as they could.

Pilate gave them another long look before returning to his study of the maps on the table. After a moment without showing any further interest in the boys, he dismissively ordered, "Let them go." The guards pushed the boys out of the room with a rough shove from the shafts of their spears.

Once he was alone, Pilate leaned back with a thoughtful look. He stood up after a moment, picked up his sword and with an affectionate look slid it back into its scabbard.

"I won't be needing this now," he thought. "Herod will be taken care of by the blade of a rebel, and I will be far away in Jerusalem commanding my troops when it happens. After that, I will come back with my army to restore order for the Roman Empire.

"All I will need then is my new King of the Jews. I need to find that boy from Nazareth."

* * *

Caiaphas hurried toward the synagogue on the edge of Nazareth. When he arrived, he found Zacharias deep in prayer and did not wait for him to finish.

"Peace and blessings be upon you, Rabbi," he interrupted.

Zacharias opened his eyes and was surprised to see Caiaphas flanked by two Temple guards. He had not seen or spoken to the priest in over thirteen years since the day of J.B.'s baptism and circumcision.

"Caiaphas, blessings be upon you as well. Welcome to this house of the Lord and may you enjoy its protection."

Zacharias tried not to show either his surprise or concern at Caiaphas's appearance on the heels of Balthazar. Between learning of Balthazar's mission and facing the dagger blades of the vinedressers, the old man was feeling like the day already had been too much for him. Now, long-buried emotions from his last days in the Temple in Jerusalem were welling up inside.

"My friend, you look well," said Caiaphas. "The fresh air and bounty of Nazareth have kept you healthy."

"It is the love of God and my family that I have to thank," he answered.

"How are your wife Elizabeth and your son? Forgive me. I've forgotten his name," Caiaphas lied.

"They are well, thank you. You are far from the Temple in Jerusalem, Caiaphas. Why are we blessed with such a visit?"

"I come on a worthy mission. The ceremony of the Feast of Passover will be very special this year with the appearance of boys from the synagogues throughout Palestine. The High Priest has asked me to visit as many as possible to check on their preparation," he lied again.

"Please thank your father-in-law for his concern," responded Zacharias. "I can report that I will be bringing two boys to the Temple who are well prepared and will do our synagogue honor at the celebration of the Feast."

"Very good. I am not at all surprised, Rabbi," replied Caiaphas. "Do you teach many boys in the synagogue?"

"We have many boys and girls who are taught inside these walls," answered Zacharias. "It is the great privilege and pleasure of my service here."

Caiaphas was exhausted from his journey and eager to bring good news to Pilate. He decided to speak his mind plainly to Zacharias.

"Zacharias, there is one more important reason for my visit. We are checking not only on the boys who will participate in the celebration of the Feast. We are looking also for a special boy. As was said by the prophet Micah:

> *But you, Bethlehem, in the land of Judah,*
> *are by no means least among the rulers of Judah;*
> *for out of you will come a ruler*
> *who will shepherd my people Israel.*

"We think, Zacharias, that the shepherd of the people Israel may be the baby born in Bethlehem twelve years ago for whom Herod the Great shed the blood of babes to kill.

"It is more important than I can say that we find this boy. Do you know of any boy in Nazareth who might be that boy, Zacharias?"

Zacharias slowly bowed his head and then looked up at Caiaphas.

"Rabbi, you fill my heart with joy that the Promised Messiah may be among us. But why would you think that I, a rabbi in this humble synagogue, would know the boy who is the Chosen One?"

"I am asking every rabbi I know who might have any chance of knowing the name of that boy," Caiaphas responded. "If he is here, Zacharias, we must find that boy."

"You do me honor with your question, Rabbi," answered Zacharias. "But I have known many exceptional boys. I am an old rabbi in a humble synagogue. How is one like me to know the Promised Messiah before he is announced?"

Caiaphas felt fatigued and frustrated. "Let your mind rest on it, my friend. And if your memory suggests anything that might help us find the Shepherd and Savior of our people, let me know immediately. May I count on you for that, Zacharias?"

"I will do for you as you would do for me, Rabbi," answered the old man.

After blessings and an embrace, Caiaphas started to leave when he stopped and turned to Zacharias.

"One last thing, Rabbi," he said. "I need to see an acquaintance of mine in Nazareth, a Pharisee named Nicodemus. Can you tell me where I might find him tomorrow?"

Zacharias directed him to a large house in one of the finer areas of the town. After Caiaphas finally departed, Zacharias sat down. He did not know which he needed more, rest or prayer.

* * *

As soon as Peter and the other three Apostles were shoved through the gate of the garrison on to the road, they had gone to the barn and talked about what they heard in the garrison.

"Don't say anything about what we heard to anyone," ordered Peter. "This is information that should be given to the Warriors of the Wilderness and no one else. Understood?"

They agreed, and Peter raced out the door. The sun was setting behind the Galilean hills as Peter hurried towards the edge of town. He eventually reached the familiar dark street where he turned the corner and began singing the song he had learned as a child. Walking slowly as he sang, he passed a door that creaked open. Peter peered in but could not see anything in the dark. He cautiously stepped through the doorway. Suddenly the door slammed behind him, and he felt the blade of a dagger on his neck.

"Take it easy!" a voice ordered. "It's Peter."

Peter felt the pressure of the blade ease off. A lamp was lit to reveal several people in the room. He turned and saw one of the vinedressers holding the dagger that had been at his throat. Then he saw J.B. standing in the back of the room along with several other Warriors of the Wilderness who surrounded a man with a long black beard streaked with gray. He was wearing a black turban of a rural tribe in the desert wilderness.

Peter realized then that this was the leader of the Warriors of the Wilderness. No one knew his name. The Romans, Herod's secret police and the people of Palestine knew him only as the Black Turban.

"I have important information from the Romans," said Peter. He told them the precise details of Pilate's briefing on Herod's arrival at the garrison when most of the troops would be in Jerusalem. The Black Turban listened carefully without speaking. When Peter was done, everyone in the room waited for the Black Turban to speak. He stroked his beard for a few long moments.

"What were you doing in the garrison?" he finally asked.

Peter told him all about the prank with the commander's helmet and even his theory that the Romans had singled out the four of them since Pilate had got a good look at Peter's face with the beginnings of his first beard and could easily recognize Andrew by his brightly colored tunic, Simon by his long hair, and Bartholomew by his large size and bad complexion.

The Black Turban then asked him many detailed questions about the briefing and the information. Peter realized the leader was suspicious and was trying to find holes in his story. Eventually the Black Turban stopped asking questions. Everyone turned to see what their leader would do.

The Black Turban walked up to Peter, his dark eyes peering directly into Peter's. His face was so close Peter could smell his foul breath. He slowly reached up and slid a small dagger with a short blade from under the back of his turban. With a flick of his wrist, he put a painful knick in the bottom of Peter's chin.

"Go home," he ordered Peter. "And say nothing of this to anyone. Do you understand?"

"Yes, sir," answered Peter. He felt blood start to run down his neck as he turned and hurried out the door.

After a moment, the Black Turban broke the silence.

"Who is that boy?" he asked.

"He is the son of a man from Bethsaida who fishes the Sea of Galilee. He lives in Nazareth with his mother and brother to help sell the fish that his father catches and salts," answered a woman who was from Nazareth.

"Can he be trusted?"

"I believe so," the woman replied. "He has been a reliable source of valuable information for some time."

The Black Turban stroked his beard in silence for a long while. Then he stood up and looked around the room into the eyes of each person.

"If what the boy says is true, this is our moment. Now is our time to strike!

"Herod will die by our hand, but where no one expects: inside the Romans' fortress. Let the people think that Herod's blood is on the hands of the Romans."

The Black Turban turned his dark hooded eyes towards J.B.

"Do you have the map from the boy who knows the garrison?"

"Not yet," answered J.B.

"Get it!" he ordered.

Chapter 11

THE PHARISEE

"There are two kinds of money problems," thought Nicodemus. "Not enough, and too much."

At that particular moment, he had the problem he preferred, too much money. He had just finished counting the money that the tax collectors had turned over to the Pharisees the week before. The sum was surprisingly good from all the commercial activity, building and newcomers in Nazareth.

What's more, the Pharisees had managed to shift into their own bags of coins some of the tax money belonging to Herod and the Sadducees. A few strokes of Nicodemus's stylus in the right places on the tablets of the tax collectors, and they would never know. He did not feel particularly guilty. He had caught them stealing the Pharisees' tax money many times. Now he was mainly worried about reviewing the registry of taxpayers to determine who had failed to pay their taxes. After that, the next round of unpleasant work by the tax collectors would commence. In the meantime, the bags of coins from the vendors and shopkeepers in the market, the tradesmen and laborers in the town, and the farmers who had managed to sell off some of their crop harvests had to be safely secured and distributed to the coin counters of the tax collectors.

"I don't really love money," Nicodemus concluded. "I love what it can buy."

But the one thing he truly wished he could buy, he was not able to purchase outright. And that was Maggie. The practical side of him regretted that she was not a slave. Then the matter could be arranged and resolved quite readily. But Nicodemus did not want another slave. He wanted a wife.

He and his father had always been too busy handling tax money to worry about arranging a marriage. His mother died when he was quite young, so his father's activities and interests as the official overseeing tax money for the Pharisees in Galilee defined his life from that point on. When his father's heart seized up and the man died unexpectedly, Nicodemus took over his father's position without a second thought from anyone.

Then Nicodemus saw Maggie the day she moved to Nazareth. After that, the blue of her eyes became more beautiful to him than the gold of his coins. He had managed several encounters with her. But there were always other men around to prevent him from saying anything other than superficial pleasantries. When it came to women, he was not good at much more than that. He needed the chance to talk with her in a situation where he could tell her comfortably what he wanted.

Trying to meet Maggie at the well was difficult and far from ideal, but it was the only place and opportunity for someone like him to speak to her without her mother's arranging something. And her mother had no idea yet who Nicodemus was. He put his money problem aside for the time being, and headed for the well.

Nicodemus arrived at the well and cursed his bad luck. Maggie was already there sitting with her friend Susanna and surrounded by several men and boys. She appeared to be talking and laughing with one boy in particular. The boy was a good-looking lad, but still a boy. Nicodemus paid him no attention as he interrupted their conversation.

"Good morning, Maggie. You look well, today," Nicodemus said to her.

Maggie turned from Jesus to look at Nicodemus. "Why, good morning, Nicodemus. You look very well too."

Nicodemus smiled and handed her a beautiful bracelet that he had his servant pick out at the market.

"I found this lovely bracelet and thought that you were the only person lovely enough to wear it."

The eyes of the men and boys standing around grew wide as she slid the bracelet onto her wrist. Susanna gave a slight gasp when she saw it. It looked very expensive.

"Why thank you, Nicodemus. It's beautiful!" said Maggie as she held up her wrist to admire the bracelet. She gave Nicodemus an appreciative look.

Jesus felt devastated. He had maneuvered successfully to have an actual conversation of a few sentences with Maggie, and had even managed to make her laugh. He was feeling elated, until the Pharisee came along and impressed Maggie with a bracelet that would take a half-year's wages from his father for him to buy.

Maggie's attention was now fully on Nicodemus. "You really shouldn't have done this, you know," she said to him.

"Oh, it was nothing," he answered. "Maggie, I was wondering if after the service at the synagogue where I'll be reading from the Torah, you and your mother would like to—"

"Maggie!" They were interrupted by a boisterous greeting from a figure that had burst through the group surrounding her.

"Peter!" she greeted him with a smile that made every male there envious. Peter stopped up short, and his smile went away when he saw Nicodemus standing there giving him an angry look.

"How wonderful to see you," she said. Her hand with the bracelet reached back to flip her braid of thick black hair over the front of her shoulder.

The young man and the teenager stood awkwardly looking at each other for a moment. Maggie stood up to break the tension.

"Well, I must go home now. Won't you come with me, Susanna?" she said to her friend. "It was so nice to see all of you."

The two of them walked off as the men and boys headed their separate ways. After a safe distance, Susanna looked at Maggie.

"So which one do you really like, Maggie?" asked Susanna.

"What do you mean?"

"Well, Jesus is such a nice person and good looking. And Nicodemus, he's mature and has so much money. And Peter, he is gorgeous and so much fun. So which one do you like the most?"

"I don't like any of them, because they don't really like me."

"What?" Susanna could not believe what Maggie had just said. "They're all in love with you."

Susanna was surprised when Maggie gave her an angry look.

"They don't love me. They are just looking to use me for their own purposes and pleasure. That's what men do.

"Men don't love, Susanna. When men want something from a woman, they just take it if they can. But if they can't just take something they want, then they try to get it another way and call it love." She sounded bitter. "So I do the same thing. When I want something badly enough from a man, I'll call it love and get it."

"Do you really believe that?" Susanna asked her.

"That's how love worked in Magdala." A dark look crossed Maggie's face. "So we moved here. And I'm sure love hurts in Nazareth too."

They walked on without saying anything more. Susanna could tell Maggie truly believed what she had said about love, or at least wanted very much to believe it.

* * *

Nicodemus returned home feeling frustrated and cross. Another opportunity to speak with Maggie had gone nowhere. He decided, however, that his bad mood might be good for sorting out plans for those who had failed to pay their taxes. Nicodemus enjoyed not only identifying those who hoped they might slip past the tax collector's attention, he also took great pleasure in creating ways he could have the tax collectors surprise and intimidate the guilty person into paying immediately. For him, the unpleasant process had become a game with a gold prize at the end. He sat down and started to unroll a large scroll with the names and accounts of Nazareth's taxpayers when a slave entered the room and bowed.

"Master, there is a rabbi here to see you. He says his name is Caiaphas and that it's very important you meet with him."

"Caiaphas?" He was surprised to hear the name. "Seat him in the garden and tell him I'll join him shortly. And bring us some wine and figs."

Nicodemus had met Caiaphas in Jerusalem during meetings between the Pharisees and the Sadducees to negotiate how tax revenues would be divided between them. As usual, the Pharisees joined with Herod and the Sadducees sided with the Romans in wanting the lion's share of the money. Caiaphas had been there representing the High Priest of the Temple, and Nicodemus had been assisting his father. For the most part, the Sadducees and Pharisees did not get along well. But the two young men had dined together several times to fill their evenings and had enjoyed each other's company. Yet Nicodemus could think of nothing from their conversations that would lead to an important meeting.

Caiaphas rose from a bench as Nicodemus entered the garden.

"Caiaphas!" Nicodemus greeted him.

"Nicodemus, my good friend!" They shook hands warmly. "I have decided that I want to spend the rest of the day sitting in your beautiful garden doing nothing but listening to the birds sing and feeling the sun on my face. It is a beautiful place," Caiaphas complimented. "You live well, my friend."

Nicodemus looked about at his father's garden. He had never really paid much attention to it.

"Thank you, Caiaphas. You are welcome to hear the birds and feel the sun. That I can afford."

They laughed and sat down on two benches facing each other. A slave arrived with glasses of wine and a bowl of fresh figs.

"So, Caiaphas," Nicodemus addressed him, "you must be here because the Sadducees once again want all the Pharisees' money. Am I right?"

Caiaphas smiled. "No, Nicodemus. I am seeking something that will cost you nothing. Just some information."

"Information from me? Then maybe it will cost you," Nicodemus jokingly replied.

Caiaphas smiled again and then grew serious.

"I don't quite know how to ask this, Nicodemus. We are looking for someone from Nazareth, and could use your help to find him. But we don't actually know who he is."

Nicodemus gave him a puzzled look. "Your search sounds difficult, Rabbi."

"Well, we sort of know who he is, or rather, who he was," Caiaphas responded. "We just don't know his name. So we thought your list of taxpayers in Nazareth might help us identify the boy."

"A boy?" Nicodemus asked. "Caiaphas, as much as I wish it were otherwise, boys in Nazareth don't pay taxes."

"I know, Nicodemus. But you must know pretty much everyone in Nazareth, and we thought you might be aware of whether anyone had a son who is known to be—well, a rather exceptional boy."

From the look on Nicodemus's face, Caiaphas could tell that he was not being taken seriously.

"Look, I know this must sound odd to you, Nicodemus. But it's very important. We are seeking such a boy from Nazareth for the Romans who have told us that we must find him."

"Caiaphas, why ever would the Romans be concerned with a boy from Nazareth?"

Caiaphas eyed the ground for a moment and then looked directly at Nicodemus.

"For the same reason that Herod the Great was concerned about him and sought him when he was a baby from Bethlehem."

Nicodemus leaned back and gave Caiaphas a look of disbelief.

"Are you saying the Romans are looking for a boy from Nazareth because they think he could be King of the Jews?"

"That's right, Nicodemus. And that's why it's critically important that you help us find him."

Nicodemus thought for a moment.

"I'm afraid, Caiaphas, that unless he had an exceptional tax debt, I would not know an exceptional boy from Nazareth. I'm sorry that I can't be of any help."

With a disappointed look, Caiaphas rose and shook Nicodemus's hand. "I understand," he said. "But if you learn anything that might help our search, would you please let me know as soon as you can?"

"Of course," answered Nicodemus. "Have a safe journey back to Jerusalem."

As soon as Caiaphas left the house, Nicodemus called for his slave.

"Go fetch one of the messenger boys from the market and bring him to me at once," he ordered. He did not want any of his servants, slaves or anyone other than a Pharisee to read the message he was about to send.

Nicodemus sat back down on the garden bench and thought about his extraordinary meeting. "So the Romans and the Sadducees are looking for a boy from Nazareth to be the King of the Jews. I wonder what Herod Antipas would think about that."

The sun's light hit Nicodemus in the eyes as it moved from behind a cloud. Irritated by the sun's intrusion, he raised his hand to block it from his eyes and stood up to head back to his work. The frightened birds fluttered from the garden into the sky.

Nicodemus returned to his scroll and tried to work. But his mind kept returning to Caiaphas's remarkable disclosure, and questions kept leaping into his mind. A new king of the Jews? And a boy, at that. How did the baby born in Bethlehem far south in Judea end up in Nazareth? How would the Romans and Sadducees find the boy from Nazareth? What were they planning to do with Herod?

He had just finished writing his message on a piece of parchment and was folding it up when his slave returned with the messenger. When Nicodemus looked up, there stood Peter. Both males bristled at the sight of each other.

"What are you doing here?" Nicodemus demanded to know.

"I was brought here to deliver a message."

Nicodemus did not like the idea of Peter's delivering his message, but time was short. Then a thought came to him.

"Do you have many friends here in Nazareth?" he asked Peter.

"Yes, sir," Peter answered.

"Are any of your friends particularly talented or exceptional boys?"

Peter looked puzzled at the question. Nicodemus gave up on his hunch, and moved back to business.

"I have a message here that is very important. I want you to take it immediately to Samaias. He is President of the Sanhedrin and the leader of the Pharisees in Nazareth. Do you know where he lives?"

"Yes. We often deliver messages there."

Nicodemus unfolded the message and showed it to Peter. "Can you read this message?"

Peter squinted at the parchment. The message was upside down.

"The rabbi taught me some Hebrew, but these don't look like Hebrew letters."

"All right," Nicodemus refolded the message. "Deliver this directly and show it to no one else. Do you understand?"

Peter nodded as Nicodemus handed him several coins that were worth much more than the usual charge for delivering a message.

"Go!" ordered Nicodemus. "And quickly!"

Once Peter reached the street outside and turned the corner, he stopped, unfolded the parchment and read the message.

> Urgent! Meet at my home at sunset with the Pharisee council. Romans and Sadducees are looking for a boy in Nazareth who is to be made King of the Jews. We must advise Herod and find him first.

Peter hurried on down the street, but not to deliver the message. He first headed straight to the dark street on the edge of town where he started singing his song until a door was opened to him.

***

Outside the synagogue, Jesus met Judas for their next lesson to prepare for the Temple in Jerusalem. Judas did not speak to Jesus and would not look at him.

"What's wrong, Judas?" he asked when he saw that Judas was very upset.

"You made me look like a fool! That's what's wrong."

Jesus looked at him with surprise. "I made you look like a fool? When?"

"You made me look bad after those asses threw me into the waters at the well."

"But Judas," answered Jesus, "they were trying to hurt you, and I didn't have time to think about anything when they came at me."

"I don't care. You made me look like an idiot right in front of everyone in Nazareth!" Judas said angrily.

Jesus did not know what to say. Once again he was confused and frustrated because he had tried to do the right thing and the consequences were not at all what he intended. Jesus followed as Judas turned his back on him and walked into the synagogue.

As usual, Zacharias had Judas recite his verse and asked him more about the meaning of its message. Then the rabbi turned to Jesus and told him there were several more verses that he wanted Jesus to learn.

Jesus took the sheet of parchment from Zacharias on which he had written the verses. He started to read them out loud, but wasn't really thinking about what he was reading.

He was angry. Angry at himself for trying to help Judas and failing. Angry at Judas for being angry at him. Angry at Zacharias for giving him more verses to learn and not telling him what verse he would be reading at the Temple in Jerusalem. Angry because he was sure he would make a fool of himself in front of the High Priest. Angry that every man in Nazareth wanted Maggie. Angry at Jude's demons. Angry that Rebecca could not hear or speak. Angry that tomorrow was the Sabbath and he would have to face J.B. All at once, he was angry about everything he had to deal with when none of it had been his doing. So angry he did not even hear the words he was reading.

A shoot will come up from the stump of Jesse;
from his roots a Branch will bear fruit.
The Spirit of the Lord will rest on him—
the Spirit of wisdom and of understanding,
the Spirit of counsel and of might,
the Spirit of the knowledge and fear of the Lord.

He will not judge by what he sees with his eyes,
or decide by what he hears with his ears;
but with righteousness he will judge the needy,
with justice he will give decisions for the poor of the earth.
He will strike the earth with the rod of his mouth;
with the breath of his lips he will slay the wicked.
Righteousness will be his belt
and faithfulness the sash around his waist.

Jesus finished reading.

"Those words are from the Prophet Isaiah," noted Zacharias. "He mentions Jesse. Isn't Jesse one of your forefathers, Jesus?"

Zacharias's question brought Jesus' attention back to his lesson.

"Yes, Rabbi. He is." Jesus could hear his mother's voice listing Jesse in his long line of ancestors.

"I want to you memorize those verses for next week, Jesus. But first I want to talk to you boys about questions the priests of the Temple may ask you after you have read your verses and talked about their meaning."

Jesus' stomach tightened at the thought of being asked questions about his verse when he did not even know yet what his verse was. He was still upset.

"You must recognize, boys, that there are different types of questions. First, there are questions that simply ask for a piece of information or fact that you know. For example, if the High Priest were to ask which of God's commandments requires that you love the Lord your God with all your heart and with all your soul and with all your mind, you would simply answer, 'The first Commandment.'

"Next, there are questions that make you not only recall such facts, but also to think about and explain them. For example, the High Priest might ask you, 'Does the commandment to love the Lord your God mean that you should love anyone else?'

"And if the High Priest asked you that question, Jesus, how would you answer that?"

"It means that we should also 'Love your neighbor as yourself.' Just as you taught us, Rabbi," Jesus answered.

"Yes I did," Zacharias nodded. "But the point is that you had to think about the answer, and connect the message and meaning of the answer to the question.

"Now, there's a third kind of question, which can be very dangerous. It is sort of a trick question that forces you to give an answer that you don't want to give.

"For example, what if I asked you, 'Are you as bad a boy as everyone says you are?' You don't want to say 'Yes' because you would be admitting that you are bad when you are not. But if you say 'No.' you are still admitting that everyone says you are a bad boy." The question forces you to answer in a way that harms you.

"Now I will teach you what you can do when you are asked such a dangerous question. I will give you three responses. Imagine that they are arrows that you have in your quiver, and when you are attacked by a trick question, you can pull any of them out to shoot it down before it harms you.

"The first arrow is shot right at the question to kill it. If someone asked you 'Are you as bad a boy as everyone says you are,' you attack the question by saying 'Not everyone says I am a bad boy, and no, I am not.' There you have attacked the question so you don't have to answer it or you can answer without harm.

"The second arrow attacks the question by responding with a greater authority. For example, if someone were to ask you whether it is all right to steal back from a thief something he has stolen from another, if you say 'yes,' you are admitting that you yourself would steal and break the commandments, but if you say 'no,' you are condoning the thief's stealing. So instead, you attack the question by citing a higher law and answering, 'The Lord's commandment tells us Thou Shalt Not Steal, whether from a thief or another. If I were to steal from a thief, then under the law of God I would be no better than him.'

"Do you understand so far?"

"Yes, Rabbi," they answered. They were concentrating closely.

"The last arrow in your quiver is to be used when the other two arrows will not work or when the trick question is asked from a desire to do you great harm. In this situation, you must shoot your last arrow to attack the person who has asked you the trick question.

"For example, if the question 'Are you as bad a boy as everyone says you are,' was intended to do you much harm by a great enemy, you could attack the questioner by saying, 'You are a hypocrite to ask me such a question as you yourself are considered bad by everyone and you know that I am not.'

"With these three arrows, you can defend against any trick question that would do you harm by your answer."

The two boys were thinking hard about the lesson Zacharias had just taught them.

Eventually Jesus asked, "Rabbi, may I ask a question?"

"Of course, Jesus."

"It's about the slaves, Rabbi."

"The slaves, Jesus?"

"Yes, Rabbi. If they are not protected by being Roman citizens, people are forced to become slaves because their skin is different, or because they have no money to pay their debts. No one chooses his skin or wants to be in debt, so why is it that they are made to be slaves?

"Well, Jesus, you know, don't you, that there have always been slaves?"

"But Rabbi, just because there have always been slaves doesn't mean there must always be slaves. And should you not 'Love your neighbor as yourself' even if he is a slave? Surely you, as a rabbi, do not want men to disobey the commandments by making other men slaves when they themselves would not want to be slaves, would you, Rabbi?"

Zacharias did not have an answer for Jesus. He realized that he had just been shot by three arrows.

"Jesus, there's one more verse I would like you to learn. I haven't written it down, but if I say it, can you remember it?"

"I'll try, Rabbi."

Zacharias recited,
> *He made my mouth like a sharpened sword,*
> *in the shadow of his hand he hid me;*
> *he made me into a polished arrow*
> *and concealed me in his quiver.*

"That's also from the Prophet Isaiah, Rabbi," said Jesus.

"Yes it is, my son," Zacharias smiled. "Yes it is."

"It is time to go to the Temple in Jerusalem," the Rabbi thought happily. "We are ready."

The three of them looked up as someone stepped through the door. There stood Nicodemus.

"Forgive me for interrupting, Rabbi," said Nicodemus. "May I speak with you alone for a moment? It's rather important."

"Of course, Nicodemus. Boys, that will be all today. Tomorrow is the Sabbath. Our next lesson will be two days after. All right? I'll see you then." Nicodemus waited for the boys to leave. After he watched them depart through the door, Nicodemus turned to Zacharias.

"Rabbi, I'd like to ask you about a boy from Nazareth...."

* * *

Outside the synagogue, Judas and Jesus started walking towards their homes.

"Are you nervous about the Temple?" Jesus asked Judas.

"Sort of," answered Judas. "But I know my verse and I know pretty much what I am going to say about it."

Judas's confidence caused Jesus to feel even more worried. Suddenly Judas stopped. Jesus looked over and saw him staring straight ahead with a frightened look on his face. There stood the two vinedressers with evil grins on their faces.

Without hesitation, Judas spun around and ran as fast as he could. Jesus watched him start running and quickly looked back at the vinedressers. He was about to follow Judas, when J.B. stepped out of a doorway and stood next to the vinedressers.

"Hello again, Cousin," said J.B. Jesus did not answer.

"Sorry I haven't seen you," J.B. tried to sound pleasant. "I've been busy preparing for the Sabbath. Have you been preparing for the Sabbath, Jesus? It's tomorrow you know."

Jesus remained silent.

"I believe you were going to give me something for the Sabbath, weren't you, Jesus?"

"I don't have anything for you," Jesus answered.

The vinedressers lunged at Jesus and pinned him against a wall. J.B. stepped up to Jesus with his face close.

"Give me the map on the clay tablet!" he demanded.

"You don't need one," Jesus replied.

All three of them answered instantly with daggers pointed at Jesus.

"Let me kill him now!" said one of the vinedressers as the tip of his dagger pressed against Jesus' throat.

"Wait!" ordered J.B.

"You don't need a map," Jesus repeated. "The entrance to the garrison that you want won't be on any map," he said quickly.

J.B. drew his dagger blade back. "Take away your blade," he told the vinedresser. With a look of disappointment, the vinedresser pulled his dagger off Jesus' neck.

"What are you saying?" J.B. asked Jesus.

"On the back wall of the garrison that has no gate, there are torches at even spaces along the top. Except that in the middle of the wall, there are two torches that are closer together than the others. Your entrance to the garrison is there."

"Go on," J.B. told him.

"Below those torches there is a foundation stone on the ground about as wide as a man's arm is long. The two corners at the top have been chipped away. If you put your hands into the spaces at the corners, you will find that you can grab the stone firmly. If you grab the corners of the stone and pull, the stone will roll away from the wall. There will be an entrance to a passageway inside."

"You're lying!" growled the vinedresser who moved his dagger back up against Jesus' throat. "One man can't move a stone large enough to be a foundation stone in a wall that large."

Jesus tried to lean away, but could not move.

"He can if the stone has been hollowed out and is resting on smooth round tree branches," Jesus said, his voice tight from the blade pressed against his throat.

J.B. grabbed the vinedresser's arm firmly and pulled the dagger away.

"And just who, good Cousin, would hollow out a foundation stone?"

"My father and I. We worked late for two weeks and hollowed out the stone from the top down while the guards were at their supper. One strong man can easily open the secret entrance by himself."

"Well done, Cousin! There's more to you and your father than I ever would have thought."

"But what about the weapon rooms and the quarters of the Roman commander?" the vinedresser asked angrily. "We need that map!" He wanted badly to put his knife back against Jesus' throat.

"You don't need a map," replied Jesus. "It's simple. Once you go through the secret entrance, you'll find the weapons stored down the corridor to the left in the room around the corner where the passage turns right. And the commander's quarters are down the corridor to the right around the corner where the passage turns left."

Jesus continued. He wanted to finish, get out of there and never see J.B. and the vinedressers again.

"When you're through the entrance and in the passage, you will find there are also two torches close together above the secret entrance so that it can be located quickly to get out. At the bottom of the foundation stone, the two bottom corners have been chipped away so that the stone can be grabbed from the inside and pulled back into place or pushed to roll open."

"This is too good to believe. He's making this up," accused the vinedresser. "He's lying to save his skin."

"I am not lying," Jesus responded. "And besides, I couldn't make up this: My father placed the entrance to the rooms so that the guards at either end stand where they can't see down the passage where the secret entrance comes in. I couldn't make that up."

J.B. looked at Jesus closely for a moment.

"Brilliant!" he exclaimed. "Let him go."

J.B. and the vinedressers started striding away leaving Jesus standing against the wall.

"Cousin," J.B. called over his shoulder, "I think you and I may have a great future together."

Chapter 12

THE SEA OF GALILEE

"A fishing trip?" asked Jesus. He did not like the idea much.

"That's right," said James and John together. "And all the Apostles are going," added James.

"So you must come too," concluded John.

The trip had all been worked out. James and John were going to visit their father Zebedee who was a fisherman on the Sea of Galilee. Their father lived in Capernaum, a picturesque town on the north shore of the Sea of Galilee, but the brothers lived with their mother in Nazareth because their parents had not lived together for some time. So every few months the twins would go spend time with him. Peter and Andrew's father Jonah, also a fisherman from nearby Bethsaida, was coming to Nazareth to deliver dried and salted fish. He would take all the boys back with him and then return them four days later when he had to make another delivery to Nazareth. It was a chance for the men and boys to take a short break together, fish for fun, and relax.

The timing happened to be convenient for everyone, even Jesus, Mary and Joseph. Joseph did not need Jesus' help since he was spending a few days working on plans for the next building projects at the garrison and the long-delayed palace for Herod. In fact, Mary and Joseph seemed almost relieved that Jesus would be leaving Nazareth for a while. Jesus assumed that because they were busy with preparations for the journey to Jerusalem and getting everything ready for his brothers and sisters to stay with the Rabbi's wife Elizabeth while they were away, it was easier for them to have one less child to worry about.

Even Zacharias had told Jesus and Judas to go and have fun despite the fact that there was not much time left for lessons before the celebration of the Feast at the Temple in Jerusalem. The rabbi, after much thought, had finally given Jesus his verse to read before the High Priest. Because it was one that Jesus had already committed to memory and knew well, there had been no difficulty preparing the message that Jesus would give on its meaning.

There really was only one problem for Jesus in accompanying the Apostles to the Sea of Galilee. That was the sea itself. He had not seen the beautiful expanse of blue water since the trip with his family as a very young boy. And his memory of the Sea was not the beautiful blue of its water. Rather it was the sense of fear and panic from being helpless and unable to breathe. He planned to stay on the shore to fish with a line and intended to stay away from the boats that the boys' fathers took far out in the sea to fish with their nets.

The journey from Nazareth to Capernaum took most of a day. Peter and Andrew's father did not push on as if he were traveling for business. He stopped occasionally to let the boys rest and play as they traveled the greater part of their journey across the plains and hills of Galilee to the middle of the Sea on its western shore. From there they would turn north and follow the shoreline to the top of the Sea where Capernaum and Bethsaida sat near one another.

Their small caravan walked for the most part, but sometimes rode on the backs of the donkeys that had carried the cargo of salted fish to Nazareth. Happily traveling among the pack of donkeys was Jewels. It worked out well to have him carry some of their light load of rucksacks and sleeping rolls. The old donkey enjoyed being on the open road once again.

The day's journey gave the boys many opportunities to talk. They told Jonah about the magician and insisted that they had seen with their own eyes a camel and man step through the eye of a needle. Judas and Jesus shared their excitement about seeing Jerusalem for the first time and being part of the celebration of the Feast at the Temple. They all told funny stories from delivering messages and watching people in the market place. And of course they talked about Maggie and teased one another about who had the biggest crush on her.

During one of their rest stops near a small spring, Jesus took Jewels a short distance away to graze briefly on some grass growing at the base of a large mound. As the pleased donkey started pulling at the grass, Jesus heard someone talking on the other side of the mound. He recognized the voices of Peter and his father.

He thought he heard Jonah ask a question and then heard Peter describing a man with a long black and gray beard.

"Did he wear a black turban?" asked Jonah.

After Peter confirmed it, Jonah said, "He's evil, that one. But he makes things happen."

Following a short pause, Jonah asked, "Does he know about that boy from Nazareth?"

Jesus felt uncomfortable eavesdropping on their conversation, so he led Jewels back to where the boys were resting by the spring. A while later, Peter and Jonah returned to the group, and they all started the last good stretch of walking before reaching the Sea. Eventually their caravan started climbing through breaks between some low mountains until they came to a ridge where the land dropped away.

There was the Sea of Galilee. The large expanse of bright blue water was surrounded by a ribbon of green along its edges in front of the sand-colored mountains rising behind into the light blue sky. At first the boys did not say a word. Their gazes turned as far as they could from left to right, and they still could not see the whole lake. Then they broke out in shouts of triumph as they started the trek downward to the town on the shore below.

"That is Magdala," Jonah told them. Every one of the Apostles immediately thought of Maggie and wondered if all the girls in her home town would be as beautiful. After reaching Magdala, they turned to the north and followed the shore. The strip of green along the shoreline gradually widened into a plain filled with beautiful fields.

Jonah told them all about the Sea of Galilee as they walked. The

Sea, he explained, was shaped like an oval that was wider at the top and thinner at the bottom. Some said its shape was like a harp, which is why the locals often called it the Sea of Kinnereth after the Hebrew word for the musical instrument. It was the largest lake in Galilee. It took a man more than a half day to travel its length north to south and just over half that to cross its width east to west at its widest.

Its water was clean and sweet. The water came mostly from the Jordan River which flowed into the north end of the lake and out the south. The Sea was formed from the river's flow by low hills on the west that sloped down towards the water and by a high mountain wall on the east. In most places it was too deep for a man to swim to the bottom. Many believed that the water even had healing powers, so the sick and the lame came from far away to bathe in it.

Nature and man flourished in and around the lake. Thick woods surrounded much of the lake, but fruit trees and fields in the shore plains yielded rich harvests throughout the year. Peter's father spoke proudly of the many harbors that were being built and creating new towns on the sea's coastline. However, the greatest bounty from the Sea of Galilee was its fish. Many fishermen would cast their nets and almost always filled their boats with the Coracin fish that could be eaten fresh or preserved with salt or oil. Jonah said there were now over two hundred boats that were sending fish throughout Palestine and the Roman Empire.

But for all its beauty and bounty, the Sea of Galilee could bring sudden and frequent terror.

"It happens to any fisherman who is on the sea when the Devil flies over," Jonah told them. "When the Devil flies over and his breath turns the warm air cold, the calm water suddenly turns into furious waves that destroy strong boats and drown able men with ease."

The boys listened wide eyed.

"Then, when the Devil is pleased with what he has taken, he passes on, and like that," Jonah snapped his fingers, "the sea is calm again."

With the smooth lake resting before them, it was hard for the boys to believe the tale. But each of them had a picture in his mind of the Devil flying over the sea looking for helpless, unsuspecting boats.

The happy caravan finally arrived in Capernaum where Zebedee greeted them all and then hugged his sons James and John. The eerily identical twins played their usual trick on him with each pretending to be the other until he, and everyone else, was completely confused. Capernaum was a pleasant town. Its low houses built with black basalt rocks between wood timbers were attractive sitting under green shade trees.

Tired from their long journey, they soon split up to eat and sleep, half the boys staying with Zebedee in Capernaum, and the other half going with Peter and Andrew to their home in nearby Bethsaida. Matthew made sure he stayed the night in Capernaum.

"I love this place. I would really like to live here," he announced to the others.

The next morning the boys were up early eager to try their hand at catching fish. Peter, Andrew, James and John helped their fathers give them all fishing lines and show them how to tie on the hooks with the right knot. Next they taught them how to fasten on the line a pebble that would help sink the hook down to where fish would be swimming. Then they gave them different kinds of bait they could put on the hooks to try to lure the fish. Finally, the men patiently explained the art of choosing the right combination of bait for the type of fishing spot and how to toss the line, feel for the fish and bring the fish in once it had taken the bait and was hooked.

The Apostles were not equally blessed with fishing skills. Peter, Andrew, James and John showed them all the good spots for fishing along the shore. Some of the boys spread out near the reeds and marshy areas where larger numbers of smaller fish hid. Others fished off rocky bluffs where the water below was deeper and bigger fish might be swimming. The four sons of the fishermen soon started catching fish but then gave it up to help the boys who were still struggling to prepare their lines with hooks and bait. Some of the others were quick to start fishing but could not quite get the hang of throwing their lines to the right spots and keeping their hooks where the fish might find them.

Bartholomew was the first novice fisherman to catch a fish. He held up a small silver and black Coracin fish with pride for all to admire. The other new fishermen tossed their lines once more with renewed hope. Then Bartholomew caught another, and the other boys started to wonder whether they were doing something wrong. There was a wave of movement as boys changed locations, put on new bait and began recasting their lines. Each of them waited and worried about his luck.

Eventually the other boys started to catch fish. Thaddeus and Simon were next. They compared their catches and argued about which of the small fish was bigger. The others soon began to bring in their prizes when Philip and Jimmy and then Matthew, who had been silently counting everyone's catch, caught their first fish. Thomas was beginning to doubt whether he would ever catch a fish when his line went taut, and he clumsily dragged a fish out of the water. Jesus luckily caught a small one near the shallows even though he was not close enough to the water to cast his line far. At the end of the day, everyone had something to show for his efforts except Judas who was the only Apostle who had not caught a fish.

The following day the group set off for a day of fishing at a special spot followed by a night of sleeping under the stars. Their destination was an isolated and solitary location known as The Place of Seven Springs. It was a distant walk so the fathers decided to get there by sailing their fishing boats. The boat trip would make it easier to carry their gear and food, and would give the boys the experience of being out in the sea in a fishing boat. The boys divided up between the two boats at the harbor in Capernaum. James and John went with Zebedee in his boat, and Peter and Andrew went in their father's boat.

Jesus looked doubtfully at Zebedee's boat before he climbed in with extra care not to look down into the water. He did not want to be out in the water at all, let alone in a boat that looked like it could swamp easily. The boat was like most of the commercial fishing boats on the Sea of Galilee. It had a single mast for a square sail and three oars on each side. Although it seemed sturdy enough, what Jesus did not like was its shallow draft and how the sides of the boat were low to the water. That made it easier to drag nets filled with fish over the sides of the boat, but it also made it easier for the boat to take on water. When Bartholomew stepped into the boat, Jesus thought the sea water was already coming over the side as he grabbed the edge of the boat as tightly as he could. He wished Bartholomew had been in the other boat.

Everything went well at first. The other boys rowed the boat out of the harbor into the sea where a light wind filled the sail that Zebedee hoisted up the mast. Rowing looked like fun, but Jesus preferred to sit near the stern with a firm grip on the side of the boat. Feeling the warm sun and breeze on his face, Jesus almost started to relax when the other boat drew alongside. Peter and Andrew led its crew in an attack of splashing with their oars and hands. The crew in Zebedee's boat responded by splashing back. The boat rocked back and forth as the water fight ensued. Jesus held on in horror as he watched the water edge closer and closer to spilling over into the boat. After a while the conflict faded. But then Andrew gave them another splash that sent the battle to even greater heights of wet fury. Jesus closed his eyes and tried not to scream at them to stop.

Finally the battle died down. The boys in Zebedee's boat, however, saw how Jesus was frightened and started teasing unmercifully by rocking the boat back and forth to torment him. Looking very pale and slightly sick, Jesus told them to "Stop it!" in a voice that was so serious, they quit immediately and left him alone. They had never seen Jesus show any temper like that before.

The boats sailed on pleasantly. The sun warmed the air, and the sea was calm. Zebedee gave the tiller and sail to his sons and started drinking from his wineskin. He was enjoying the rare luxury of being on his boat without having to haul nets about and worrying about the price he would get for his catch. The last thing he saw before he started to snore was the other boat about a stone's throw away drifting in another direction.

"Father!" John's voice woke Zebedee from a deep sleep. He felt a strong cold wind on his face and looked up to see John struggling with the sail. Stumbling to his feet in the rocking boat, he ordered James to turn the tiller to head the boat into the wind. Spray from the rising waves stung the frightened faces of the silent boys. He stepped between them to get to the ropes flapping from the sail like serpents flying through the air.

James managed to turn the boat into the wind so that the sail quit snapping about long enough for Zebedee and John to grab hold of the ropes. As they tied down the sail, Zebedee looked for the other boat. It was nowhere in sight. Zebedee climbed back through the boys to the stern where he took the tiller from James.

Jesus sat as still and rigid as a stone statue, his face as gray as the storm clouds above. His hands gripped the side of the boat so tightly he did not even feel the splinters piercing his palms when the boat lurched between the waves.

Everything moved in slow motion before Jesus' fearful eyes. He saw James and John looking back and forth between the sail and their father fighting to control the tiller. Bartholomew lay on the bottom rolling back and forth with his eyes squeezed shut. Judas and Matthew held on to each other. He watched the waves smash against the sides of the boat sending arching sprays of sea water over them, suspended in the air for a timeless instant, before drenching them.

With all the terror Jesus was feeling inside, he was hit with another panicked fear that if he looked into the sky, he would see the Devil flying over and be taken by him. He tried to force his eyes to close, but they would not. He saw everything before him—Zebedee shouting to his sons at the sail, the crashing waves, the rising and falling of the boat—moving slowly before him without any sound. Terrified that he would look up to see the Devil himself, he rose to his knees and looked instead over the edge of the boat into the terror of the sea. His body tensed as he saw the grayish green water churning below his eyes.

Jesus' eyes grew wide as there in the sea he saw the dirty face of the criminal below the fallen cross from his recurring nightmare. Jesus felt a choking feeling in his throat. The bloody fingers of the criminal appeared before Jesus' face and reached out towards him.

"Save me! Save me, Jesus!"

Jesus saw the criminal's parched lips move but heard Judas's voice speaking the words. The vision disappeared when he felt a hand grab his tunic just as he vomited violently into the sea.

When his body stopped retching and he was finally able to breathe, Jesus sensed the sun's warmth on his back and realized the waves no longer were pounding against the boat. He looked up to see Judas next to him and the others watching the storm clouds move off as quickly as they had descended upon the boat.

"There's the other boat already docked," said Zebedee pointing at the shore. Except for being soaking wet, he looked as if nothing out of the ordinary had happened. He called to John to trim the sail as he turned the tiller so the boat swung about in the direction of their destination.

They reached the shore wet and relieved. At first the boys did not say much. But before long Judas and Bartholomew were telling the Apostles from the other boat how they had seen the Devil fly over the boat during the storm. Zebedee smiled at Jonah and asked the boys to help unload the boat. The other boys spread out their bedding to dry in the sun before going off to explore and fish. Jesus stood quietly on the shore for a moment before disappearing into the trees around their campground.

Later in the day when the sun started lowering on the horizon, James and John became concerned about Jesus. They had never seen Jesus so frightened, and no one had seen him all afternoon. The two searched for a while when they saw him sitting quietly in a small grove of trees with his head bowed. Once they found him, they decided to leave him alone.

Judas, however, was worried about something else. After two days of fishing, he still had not caught a single fish. The other Apostles did not tease him or even mention it. Most of them knew it could have been one of them just as easily. But for Judas, no one's saying anything only made it worse. The fact that he knew that they knew he had not done the same as the others was eating at his insides.

Though the daylight was fading, Judas kept casting his line out into the water. The other boys headed back to the camp except for Peter who stayed nearby hoping it would make Judas feel better. But the two of them sitting there alone only frustrated Judas more.

"You know, Judas, I don't think the light is good enough now for the fish to see the bait," Peter finally told him.

"I don't care," Judas replied. With a stubborn look, he cast his line again and mumbled something about "stupid fish."

"You should cast your line over by that rock," said a voice behind them.

They turned around to see Jesus pointing at a large rock that stuck out into the water near one of the Seven Springs.

"I don't think so, Jesus," said Peter. "Fish don't usually gather where the spring waters go into the sea."

Judas immediately pulled in his line and cast it over by the rock. Peter became irritated. It was now starting to get dark, and he was getting hungry. He was done being patient with novice fishermen. Suddenly Judas's line went taut.

"Ouch!" he cried. The pull was so strong that the line hurt his fingers.

Peter looked in surprise at the dark water and squinted to make out the size of the silver and black Coracin fish. But the fish did not behave like a Coracin. Instead of zig zagging back and forth in short spurts, it ran straight out from them taking Judas's line with him. Peter started helping Judas by telling him when to let out line quickly and when to draw the fish in gently whenever the line went slightly slack. It stayed under the surface so they still could not see it. After a while, Judas was able to bring the fish back in near the rock where it unexpectedly began to swim left to right in sudden bursts.

Suddenly, the fish leaped high out of the water.

"Pull hard!" shouted Peter. Judas yanked on his line and pulled the fish's head and body around in the air in a graceful spin. The move set the hook firmly in the fish's mouth which enabled Judas to start bringing it in with less resistance. Once the fish reached the shallows, Peter waded in and was able to grab it.

The fish was unlike any Peter had seen before. Even in the fading light he could see that it did not have the silver and black markings of a Coracin. It was more of a bronze colored fish and was as long as his forearm. Even as Judas held the fish in the air proudly, it kept up its struggle. Peter took the line from Judas and examined the fish closely.

"What kind of fish is it?" Judas asked Peter.

"I'm not sure," he answered. There was a look of envy in his eyes as they went up and down the length of the fish's body.

"Let's go show it to the others!" The excited Judas headed towards the campground.

"You go ahead," Peter told them. He looked over at the rock. "I'll be there in a little bit," he said as he pulled out his fishing line, picked out a pebble and started tying on a hook.

Judas looked back at Peter as he and Jesus were walking away.

"Doesn't he want to show the fish to his father?" asked Judas.

"When he shows a fish like that to his father," answered Jesus, "he'll want it to be Peter's fish."

Peter sat in the growing darkness, waiting to feel for something on his line. There was not enough light to see his line in the water. He knew there was no real hope of catching a fish now like the one Judas caught. But he stayed where he was, staring into the black water.

"A fish," he thought. "I'm sitting here doing nothing but hoping to catch a stupid fish."

Then the sobering realization flashed across his mind like a bolt of lightning.

"I am going to spend the rest of my life doing nothing but hoping to catch fish."

He could hear his father's words before he went to stay with his mother in Nazareth. "Just because you are leaving the sea and living in the town for a while, don't get any ideas about not coming back," he warned Peter. "Your grandfather and his father were fishermen. My father was a fisherman, and I am a fisherman. You, Peter, are a fisherman. How can it be otherwise?"

Sitting in the dark, hoping for a special fish like that Judas had caught through dumb luck, he knew in his heart he would not find happiness from just a boatful of fish. He stood up, threw his line into the water, and swore to himself then and there that he would not be known in life simply by his nets full of fish.

But if not by his nets and fish, then what?

"Am I just a fisherman?" he asked himself. "And how can it be otherwise?"

He ached for an answer.

*　*　*

It was dark when Peter returned later to the campground without any fish. A large fire lit up the trees around the shore where they had made camp. Zebedee, James and John were busy cleaning fish to cook over the fire. Andrew and Jonah were laying out the rest of the food. Jonah noticed that Zebedee had brought only three loaves of bread and wondered whether that would be enough for fifteen hungry people, but there was plenty of fish, fruit and nuts to go around.

Several of the boys were throwing rocks at the sea while they waited. Matthew and Thomas were arguing about something. Simon kept tossing pebbles at Bartholomew and looking away as if he had not done it when Bartholomew turned to look for the culprit. Thaddeus and Philip had made a contest out of punching each other on the arm. Peter sat near the fire deep in thought, stroking his thin beard. The smell of fish cooking on the fire soon made them all think of one thing only.

"Supper!" called Zebedee as the boys scrambled to line up for the food. He put a couple fish on the plate held out by each boy who then grabbed fruit and nuts before stepping over to Jesus who broke off a piece of bread from the loaves and put it on their plates.

Sitting around the fire, fifteen men, young and old, ate with a will. Tales of great feats of fishing and survival at sea were recounted, and much laughter at their foolishness and embarrassment erupted from their full mouths. They went back often for the plenty of fish they had caught and cooked, and for the sweet figs and meaty nuts. Jesus kept tearing off hunks of bread for the hungry adventurers who asked for more. The men, who had been drinking from their wineskin, started passing it around for the boys to have a taste.

Almost as if there had been a signal, they all stopped eating about the same time with a large sigh of satisfaction. Plates were piled up behind them and fingers were licked as the boys stretched out, bellies full, around the warm roaring fire. Clean up could wait until morning. The men took the wineskin and walked off a short distance where they talked in earnest.

"What are they talking about?" Matthew asked Andrew.

"Around here, fishermen talk about two things," Andrew answered. "First it's always the prices paid for their fish. When they don't get enough for their catch, then they have to catch more fish which only makes the price go down more since there are so many fish being sold.

"And there's always talk of the Romans and the rebels. Always talk of taxes and trouble," he concluded.

They grew quiet for a while as the food in their bellies and the warmth of the fire took over.

"Have you ever been drunk?" Peter asked them after he looked over at the two fathers tipping back their wineskin.

"No," they all admitted.

"Neither have I," said Peter. "But it must feel good. The Roman soldiers get drunk all the time. There are always people who are drunk in the market. And I've even seen the Warriors of the Wilderness drinking together."

He thought for a moment. "Maybe we should get drunk."

"I'm not sure getting drunk feels so good," Thomas responded. "Haven't you seen the soldiers vomiting in the alley afterwards? Besides, where would you get enough wine for all of us to drink?"

Peter thought of the Wine Seller Shikkor's shop.

"I don't know. We could figure out something," he said.

Simon spoke up. "I wish the Apostles could figure out something special to do like the Warriors of the Wilderness. I just don't know what a small group like us could do."

"I don't think being a small group prevents us from doing something special," said Jesus.

"We could be sort of like a mustard seed. When it's sown on the ground, it's smaller than all the other seeds that are planted. But after it's sown, it grows to be larger than all the other herbs and shoots out large branches big enough for birds to nest in its shade."

They each considered Jesus' words for a moment.

Then Peter asked, "Hey, have any of you heard of a new boy who has moved to Nazareth?"

"Like who?" James asked.

"I don't know. But someone who is not just any ordinary guy."

None of them had. Peter seemed puzzled as he looked around at each of the Apostles.

The talk broke down into smaller conversations around the fire. Thaddeus was making fun of Philip's voice that was cracking when he talked. A few of them starting giggling about something. Some of the others were content to lie there quietly staring at the fire. Simon stroked his fingers through his long hair. Judas was holding up his fish and admiring its bronze color in the firelight.

Bartholomew was rubbing his cheek lightly. Jesus who was lying next to him noticed that there were now only red blotches where many of the pimples had been.

"When is your betrothal to Susanna going to be arranged?" Bartholomew asked Jesus.

"I don't know. My parents haven't said anything. Father has been so busy I don't think he's even talked with the Wine Seller Shikkor about it."

Bartholomew frowned at the fire. After a while, they all started getting sleepy and a few grabbed their bedrolls while some just laid their heads on their arms right there on the sand in the warmth of the fire. They were full, warm, tired and happy. Most of them were already asleep when someone spoke the last words of the day.

"I am stuffed! Who brought all that bread? It was really good."

Judas glanced over at Jesus just before he closed his eyes and started dreaming about his special fish.

Jesus lay there on his back, staring up at the stars.

Chapter 13

THE PROPHECY

"I don't know what's going to happen," Jesus said to Bartholomew.

Jesus was walking to the shop of the Wine Seller Shikkor, when he was joined by Peter and Bartholomew who were also headed towards the market after delivering some messages. Bartholomew had asked Jesus once again about whether a betrothal was going be arranged between him and Susanna.

Mary ordinarily did not have Jesus buy wine for the family. She asked Jesus to check on whether the Wine Seller Shikkor had any special wine that she might buy Joseph for his birthday which was coming soon.

"Is that really why you want me to go to the Wine Seller Shikkor, Mother?" Jesus asked with a skeptical smile.

"You just go, young man," she ordered.

Jesus, Peter and Bartholomew arrived at the shop of the Wine Seller Shikkor.

"Why do you have to stop here?" Bartholomew asked Jesus.

"My mother sent me to ask about some wine for my father, but she doesn't really want wine. She wants me to talk to Susanna because she still wants to arrange a betrothal."

Neither Jesus nor Bartholomew looked very happy as they stepped through the door of the wine shop. The Wine Seller Shikkor looked up and smiled when saw Jesus.

"Good morning, Jesus." His smile went away when he saw Jesus' companions.

He called over his shoulder into the back room, "Susanna, would you come out and help here please. We have a customer."

Susanna came through the door. She paused when she saw the three boys. Her father waved at her to come into the room.

"Go help Jesus, Susanna. He is here shopping for his mother."

She walked over to the boys and smiled at Jesus. "Is there something I can help you with?"

"My mother would like to find a special wine for my father's birthday," he answered.

"Let me show you some of the wine that has just come in from the vineyards in the plains of Sharon," Susanna offered as she steered them over to some urns in the corner. Bartholomew followed closely. Peter started wandering about the room.

Jesus looked at the different jugs and urns and listened to Suzanna's description of the grapes and the vineyards from which the wines had come. Occasionally he would look up at her as she talked and tried to appear interested. Bartholomew never took his eyes off her. When she finished showing Jesus the wines in the corner, she looked down at Bartholomew. Their eyes connected. She smiled at him as he blushed at her attention.

The Wine Seller Shikkor hurried over to them. "Do you see anything your father might like?" he asked.

"Perhaps," answered Jesus. "I will tell my mother about these nice wines and she will decide on one of them, I'm sure."

"Well, you must come back after the Sabbath. We have some more new wines arriving in a few days."

Jesus thanked the Wine Seller Shikkor and headed to the door where he stopped and looked back.

"Are you coming?" Jesus asked Bartholomew and Peter. Peter stood near some wine jugs next to the wall and was examining closely the window above them.

"What?" Bartholomew asked, turning his gaze away from Susanna's eyes. "Oh, yeah," he answered when he saw Peter and Jesus leaving. The Wine Seller Shikkor gave his daughter a stern look as

Bartholomew followed them out.

They reached the edge of the market and went their separate ways. Jesus headed for the synagogue for his final lesson with the Rabbi before leaving for Jerusalem. Bartholomew went to the Apostles' spot in the market to wait for more messages, and Peter headed north to deliver a special message.

When Peter reached the dark street on the edge of Nazareth, he began singing his childhood song. He had almost reached the end of the passage and was thinking no door would open to him that day, when the last door before the corner opened slightly just after he had taken a step past it. There was no sound or movement behind the door. Peter stood still for a moment. When nothing happened, he stepped back and slowly pushed open the door. The room behind was completely dark, so he leaned his head forward to look in.

Peter jumped as a dagger blade flashed in front of his eyes from behind the door. The hand holding the dagger waved him into the room. Peter nervously stepped inside and squinted into the dark.

Behind the door was a larger room than Peter had ever been in before when reporting his messages to the Warriors of the Wilderness. As his eyes adjusted, he also saw more people than usual gathered at the end of the long room. A hand grabbed his arm and led him into the middle of the room. Peter stood there uncomfortably for a moment until a group of the Warriors stepped aside. Sitting behind them was the Black Turban stroking his beard. At the sight of the Black Turban, Peter's hand reached up and touched the scab on his chin.

The Black Turban watched Peter in silence for a few moments. It seemed to Peter as if the man's dark eyes could see everything about him. Every part of his body and mind and soul seemed exposed under the man's evil stare. He felt utterly naked.

"Why are you here?" he asked Peter. Peter hated the strange sound of his voice.

"I have information from messages delivered among the Pharisees," Peter answered.

"What is this information?"

"We have read two messages from the Pharisees' leader here in Nazareth. The first message said they have not been able to find the boy from Nazareth they are seeking and are looking for additional ways of identifying him. The second message ordered a Pharisee to deliver to Herod the news about the boy in Nazareth who is to be the Romans' King of the Jews so that Herod will be grateful to the Pharisees even if they cannot find the boy."

The Black Turban considered the news from Peter. No one around him said a word. The longer he remained silent, the more nervous Peter became. Eventually, he asked Peter another question.

"Do you know the boy in Nazareth that the Romans, Sadducees and Pharisees are seeking?"

"No, sir."

His eyes stared unblinking at Peter.

"You're lying!" he accused Peter.

Peter said nothing. He did not know what to say and was too scared to speak.

"If you will not tell us who he is, we might as well cut your tongue out now since it does us no good," the leader said. His hand reached up and touched the black folds of his turban where Peter knew a dagger was hidden.

Peter forced himself to swallow. "I know of no boy in Nazareth who is to be King of the Jews," Peter managed to croak from his dry throat.

"You had better be right, because you will die if you're lying.

"Take him out," the Black Turban ordered one of the vinedressers. The vinedresser grabbed Peter's arm and led him to the door where he was pushed roughly out into the street.

The Black Turban stroked his beard and addressed the Warriors assembled in the room.

"Our original mission remains our highest priority. Herod must be killed behind the Roman walls when he arrives at the garrison while it is poorly guarded. And the mission must be carried out before the Romans have declared the boy as a popular new king of the people."

The rebels around him nodded their agreement.

"J.B, come before me," the Black Turban ordered.

J.B. stepped forward from the back of the large group of Warriors and stood before their leader.

"Show me your dagger," he ordered J.B.

J.B. drew his dagger from his sleeve and held up its blade with the tip pointed to the ceiling.

I have chosen you for the honor of completing the mission to assassinate Herod. Your dagger has yet to taste blood, and you know the secret entrance to the Roman garrison. You will receive our instructions and then you will become a great hero to your people."

J.B. bowed his head before the leader.

The Black Turban turned to the assembled Warriors of the Wilderness. With a scowl on his face, he addressed them.

"We cannot rid ourselves of one ruler who is under the control of the Romans only to have him replaced by a boy king who is a puppet in the hands of the Romans. It is critical that we find the boy from Nazareth before the others have proclaimed him king for their control. When we find him, we will make sure there will be no boy king for the Jews. The Jewish people shall be ruled by a greater power than one man alone.

"The Romans, Sadducees and Pharisees have been unable to locate him here in Nazareth. This means the boy must be hidden somewhere in the town for safekeeping and is difficult to find. But it also means we still have an opportunity to find him first.

"If the boy has been chosen by the Romans to be a king who will be popular with the people of all Palestine, he must not be a common boy. There must be someone in Nazareth who would know which Jewish leaders would protect and promote such a boy. He cannot remain hidden forever."

With an increasingly irritated look, the leader continued to stroke his beard as he waited for a response from the people around him.

"Is there no one here who can save our rule of the Jewish people by finding a boy in this town?" His voice grew louder with anger.

No one answered. They started shifting about nervously until J.B., who was still standing before the leader, finally spoke.

"I know the one person who knows every Jewish family and every boy in Nazareth. I believe if the boy is here, he would know who the boy is."

An evil smile came from below the black turban.

"And who is that person?"

"My father," answered J.B.

"Very good, J.B. Let us find our second target and find him fast."

* * *

Zacharias had no idea that he was now of importance to the rebel zealots and that two of them at that very moment were speeding towards the synagogue. His attention there was devoted to Judas and Jesus at their last lesson before the journey to Jerusalem. Judas once again read the verse he had worked on for so long and his message on its application to his life. Jesus then read his verse, but Zacharias made him think of new comments he could make on the meaning of the verse. Changing what he planned to say once more with so little time before the celebration of the Feast made him nervous.

After the lesson was finished, Zacharias told them again about the beautiful Temple in Jerusalem. Then he gave them a final blessing and sent them home excited about the journey ahead.

Jesus paused at the door before leaving and turned back to Zacharias. He did not see the two figures move into the shadow next to the door.

"Rabbi, may I ask you about something?"

"Of course, my son. What is it?"

"I am very confused about something, Rabbi. Things keep happening that are—well, they're sort of different."

"What do you mean by 'different,' Jesus?"

"I don't know how to describe it exactly. I just sort of do some things that seem different—things no one else does."

"Tell me about these things," said Zacharias.

"Well, Rebecca cannot hear or speak, yet I can talk with her when no one else can understand us.

"And when Jude has demons now, I can make him calm by pressing my hands against his chest and can make the demons go away just by telling them to leave."

Zacharias's face showed no reaction.

"Then at the well after the magician's show, remember the vinedressers who came at me? One of them even had a knife. I didn't want anyone to get hurt and I didn't mean to hurt them. But everything happened so fast, and I just knew what to do even though I'd never done anything like that before."

"I remember that very well, Jesus," said Zacharias.

"When I went to the Sea of Galilee, Rabbi, something else like that happened.

"Judas had not caught a single fish in two days. I was not feeling well and had spent some time by myself, when I came down to the sea where Judas was still trying to catch a fish with Peter. When I saw that he was not catching anything, I told him to cast his line near a rock. And when he did, he caught a fish so big that Peter was envious."

"What made you tell him to cast his line there?" asked Zacharias.

"That's the thing. I don't know what made me tell him that," answered Jesus. "I just knew.

"I thought that maybe I just had a lucky hunch, but then something happened at supper that couldn't be just luck. Something that I could not explain and that finally made me want to talk with you, Rabbi."

"Go on, my son," said Zacharias. "What was it?"

"We were all very hungry after a long day of sailing and fishing, and we were having a meal of fish and fruit and bread. I was given the task of breaking off a piece of bread and putting it on each plate with the fish. But I was concerned that there would not be enough bread to feed everyone because there were only three loaves that were not very large.

"Everyone was so hungry that no one said a prayer of thanks and blessing for the meal, so I said a little silent blessing on every piece of bread that I broke off the loaves and placed on the plates.

"As I kept breaking bread from the loaves, Rabbi, there was always enough. At first I was sort of surprised and just kept breaking off bread to put on the plates. But then it was really strange how there was always more bread, so I tried not to think about it. I don't know how it happened or where it came from, but every time someone came for more bread, it was there when I broke it from the loaf. Even when everyone came back several times for more, we never ran out of bread."

Zacharias could see that Jesus felt very uneasy.

"I don't know what doing all those things means, Rabbi. I can't explain how I am able to do them all. And I don't like being different like that."

Jesus watched the Rabbi close his eyes and take a deep breath.

"Is this the time?" Zacharias was asking himself. "What am I to reveal?" Little did Jesus suspect that Zacharias at that very moment was himself hoping to find a special power to answer Jesus' question.

"Jesus, you must understand first that everyone is given certain talents and powers that are to be used for the glory of God and for the benefit of all as well as those close to you."

"Yes, Rabbi. But these powers seem different and special. They're unlike anything I have seen my friends or anyone else do."

"Everyone's powers are special in the eyes of God, my son.

"Do you remember the story of Job?" Zacharias asked. "He was the man who had everything, a wonderful family, great wealth and many friends. And God let Satan take everything from him, even his health, to test his faith. Job knew firsthand the power of what God can give and what God can take away.

"Job said,
> *I will teach you about the power of God;*
> *the ways of the Almighty I will not conceal.*

"Jesus, maybe God is teaching you about His power and is not concealing His ways. You know He has done that to many others.

"You say you have a special power to speak with your sister Rebecca. But the Prophet Isaiah talked of such powers when he said that,
> *Then will the eyes of the blind be opened*
> *and the ears of the deaf unstopped.*

Then will the lame leap like a deer,
and the mute tongue shout for joy.

"You can tame Jude's demons, but the prophet Samuel told the story of how your own forefather David would be summoned when King Saul was taken with an evil spirit. The young David would simply take up his lyre and play, and the evil spirit would leave Saul.

"You knew what to do with the vinedressers' attack even though you had never done anything like that before. But how exceptional was that?

"King Solomon noted that 'the race is not to the swift, nor the battle to the strong.' And his father King David sang in his psalm that the Lord told us to 'sit at my right hand until I make your enemies a footstool for your feet.' That's what the Lord did with the vinedressers, Jesus.

"As for Judas's fish and your loaves of bread, remember when the Israelites grumbled to Moses about food during their exodus through the desert? The Lord told Moses that they would eat meat, and be filled with bread. That evening quail came and covered the camp, and in the morning there was a layer of dew on the ground around the camp that became the bread of manna the Lord gave them to eat.

"Yes, Jesus, you have special powers, as have others before you, and as does everyone now. But consider them next to God's.

"He spreads out the northern skies over empty space; he suspends the earth over nothing. He wraps up the waters in his clouds, yet the clouds do not burst under their weight. He covers the face of the full moon, spreading his clouds over it. He marks out the horizon on the face of the waters for a boundary between light and darkness. The pillars of the heavens quake at his rebuke. By his power he churned up the sea. By his breath the skies became fair. And these are but the outer fringe of his works; how faint the whisper we hear of him! Who then can understand the thunder of his power?

"Jesus, these were the thoughts of Job, who was given everything and who had everything taken away by God. He saw the full might of God's power on men, and yet understood that God's power was even greater still.

"So you should consider your powers not by how great or special they seem, but by how you have used them.

"When you want to understand how special your powers are, look at how Job judged one's use of power:

> *How you have helped the powerless!*
> *How you have saved the arm that is feeble!*
> *What advice you have offered to one without wisdom!*
> *And what great insight you have displayed!*

"If your use of your powers shows love for all, tolerance for those who are different and intend no harm to others, forgiveness for those who have offended you, and sacrifice for a good greater than your own personal gain, then your powers are indeed special."

Jesus thought of the cool metal of the commander's helmet in his hands and also remembered the anger on Judas's wet face at the well when his efforts to do good seemed to go wrong.

"But Rabbi, what do you do if you use your power to help people but your help ends up doing things you never intended? Is it wise to avoid using your power to help if you don't know what could happen?"

"Jesus, important things never go as you intend or expect them to happen. If you acted only when you knew exactly what would happen, you could never do anything.

"When you act, be sure you do no greater harm than you see, and then take action out of love of others and not for your own gain. It will be those acts that will define who and what you are, rather than what you own or what other people think about you. And your acts will become part of a wisdom greater than any one of us can ever understand."

The two of them sat quietly for a few moments thinking about what each of them had told the other.

"Jesus, you should be heading home. It will soon be dark and your parents will be wondering where you are," said Zacharias finally.

"We have no more time for lessons before we leave for Jerusalem. But we have a three-day journey that will give us plenty of opportunity to prepare you finally for the Feast at the Temple."

"Thank you, Rabbi," said Jesus. As usual, he felt much calmer after hearing the rabbi's words.

"You're welcome, my son," answered Zacharias.

Once Jesus went out of the synagogue, Zacharias felt great relief and said a brief prayer of thanks. He rose and turned to go gather his things before going home to Elizabeth.

A short cry of fright came out of him as he was startled by a figure standing in the shadows next to the altar. His body tensed from a wave of old fears.

"Hello, Father," said a voice. J.B. stepped out of the shadow to where Zacharias could see him.

At the sight of each other, both men felt an unsettling rush of deep love, restrained anger and their dread of this uncertain encounter.

"How is Mother?"

"What do you care? You haven't seen her in over a year."

J.B. felt a pang of regret, but his face remained impassive. His mind returned to his mission where he felt less vulnerable.

"Rabbi," J.B. now addressed Zacharias formally, "we are looking for a boy from Nazareth. You teach all the boys of Nazareth. You must know him."

This time it was Zacharias whose face showed nothing despite the emotional reaction inside of him.

"Who are 'we' and why are you looking for a boy?" asked Zacharias. His voice had no hint of willingness to cooperate.

"There are men who would have this boy become King of the Jews so that they can rule the Jewish people through him. But God alone should be King of the Jews. I belong to a group of men and women that will not let unworthy men or this boy take God's place as king of our people and land."

Zacharias gave him a sharp look. "You belong to a group of people who murder like cowards."

J.B. took a threatening step toward Zacharias.

"Rabbi, would you have the Romans remain in Palestine forever, killing innocent men and women, choosing our leaders and priests for us, and taking every last coin we earn so the Emperor can have his circuses in Rome? Are we cowards for wanting to stop that?

"And would you always have the Sadducees lick the bottoms of Roman sandals so they can charge money to worship and sacrifice in the Temple, or the Pharisees tax the happiness out of every man's life so they can count their money as a hobby?

"It is the people who continue to let that happen who are the cowards, Rabbi. God will remain our king, and not a boy from Nazareth used by those men."

"I know that our king is God," replied Zacharias. "But have you ever stopped to consider that our king might be both God and Man?"

The Black Turban stepped out of the shadows.

"Don't give us your theological contradictions, Rabbi." His strange voice and presence sent a chill through the air in the synagogue. "Give me the name of the boy from Nazareth who could become the King of Roman Rule and Human Greed."

Zacharias saw the anger in their eyes and knew they would stop at nothing to find the boy.

"I don't know where you would get the idea that such a boy would be in Nazareth. The King of the Jews would not be in a Galilean town, would he? What can he rule from here? The market place? You people are fools."

"Where would he be then?" the Black Turban demanded.

"Where do you think a king of the Jews would be?" Zacharias tried to avoid giving an answer. He knew immediately that he had made a mistake.

"Of course!" exclaimed J.B. to the Black Turban as the answer came to him. "In his capital! No one can find the boy in Nazareth because he would have to be in Jerusalem to become king."

The Black Turban's cloak swirled around as he turned to hurry out the door. J.B. started to follow, but then paused and turned back to Zacharias.

"Think of me what you will, Father. But tell Mother I love her."

For an instant, Zacharias saw in J.B.'s eyes the look of the son he loved.

"No, J.B. If you love her, you must tell her yourself."

The angry look returned to J.B.'s face as he left the synagogue. Zacharias stepped outside and watched them stride down the street.

"What have I done?" the anguished Rabbi asked himself. The old man started walking as quickly as he could in the direction of Joseph's house.

* * *

Mary was surprised to see Zacharias standing in her doorway.

"Is Jesus in trouble?" she immediately asked.

"No, not from anything he's done," answered Zacharias. "Is Joseph here? I need to talk to the both of you—alone."

Mary called for her children.

"Jamie, go fetch your father and Jesus. They're out back. Rachel, you and Rebecca finish preparing the meal, would you please?"

Zacharias noticed that Mary was growing larger with her pregnancy.

"How are you feeling, Mary?"

"Well enough," she answered. "Some sickness in the morning, that's all."

"Are you sure you're up to the journey to Jerusalem for the Feast?"

"Of course, Zacharias. You know I cannot miss this Feast." She sounded adamant. "Besides, I went through much more going to Bethlehem."

Joseph and Jesus stepped through the doorway.

"Zacharias, welcome," said Joseph. Jesus was surprised to see the Rabbi and wondered if he had done something to bring the Rabbi to their home so soon after his lesson.

"Thank you, Joseph," said Zacharias. He gave Joseph a knowing look that told the subject of his visit.

"Jesus," said Joseph, "would you go see to straightening out the wood pile in back?"

"And Jamie, you keep an eye on Jude while we speak with the Rabbi," added Mary.

The three of them walked outside over to an olive tree where they could not be overheard. After sitting down, Zacharias gave them both a concerned look.

"Perhaps now is not the time to take Jesus to the Temple in Jerusalem," he told them.

Mary looked at him in disbelief.

"What do you mean, Rabbi? We've prepared everything for so long. Do you think he's not ready for some reason?"

"No. He's ready. But circumstances have changed."

"What has changed, Zacharias?" asked Joseph. He thought immediately of Pilate and feared he knew at least part of the answer.

"The situation is very different now," Zacharias answered. "We are taking Jesus to Jerusalem to reveal him to the religious leaders of the Jewish people for the first time. But now I'm not sure he should be shown to them."

"And why not?" demanded Mary.

"Because now they are all searching for him."

Mary gave him a puzzled look. "What are you saying?"

"I think it all started with the magician who was just in Nazareth," said Zacharias. Mary and Joseph now were completely confused.

"The magician was the Magi Balthazar."

"Balthazar?" said Mary and Joseph together. It seemed ages ago that they had heard his name when he gave them gifts of gold, frankincense and myrrh for the newborn baby Jesus.

"He is here looking for Jesus once again. He's been looking for Jesus ever since you left Bethlehem for Egypt, and finally tracked him down to Nazareth."

"Why is that a problem?" asked Joseph.

"Balthazar is not the only one looking for Jesus here in Nazareth," answered Zacharias. "The Sadducees and the Pharisees are looking for him."

"How do you know this? Why are they looking for him?" asked Mary.

"Because they have visited me to ask about him and his whereabouts."

"So they know who he is?" Joseph asked quickly.

"No, I don't think so. At least I did not tell them.

"Caiaphas, a priest from the Temple in Jerusalem told me the Sadducees believe the baby born in Bethlehem, whom Herod sought to kill, is the Chosen One. So they are seeking the boy they believe to be the Promised Messiah.

"But then Nicodemus visited me because the Pharisees are also looking for the boy. It was he who told me that the Sadducees are seeking the boy for the Romans who want to make him their King of the Jews to replace Herod."

Joseph could not believe what he was hearing.

"The Romans want Jesus instead of Herod to rule as king of all Palestine?"

"Yes, but the Pharisees are aligned with Herod, so I am sure they want to find the boy so that Herod can prevent him from taking Herod's place as leader of the Jewish people."

Joseph placed his forehead in the palms of his hands to think. "This is serious."

"That's why I'm here," said Zacharias, "and why I question whether we should reveal the boy in Jerusalem at this Feast."

The three of them sat silently for several moments. Finally Mary spoke in a quiet but firm voice,

> *The scepter will not depart from Judah,*
> *nor the ruler's staff from between his feet,*
> *until he to whom it belongs shall come*
> *and the obedience of the nations be his.*

The Rabbi knew the verse from the Torah.

"But Mary," warned Zacharias, "we dare not risk—"

"We have a covenant with God, Rabbi," Mary declared. "Each of us was visited by the angel. Each of us took on responsibilities for carrying out God's plan."

She looked directly at Joseph and Zacharias.

"And each of us took an oath to God Himself that we would make any sacrifice, take any risk and do whatever is necessary to see that this boy becomes the Promised Messiah."

"But Mary, this is not our risk or sacrifice. It could be the boy's," Zacharias replied.

"Rabbi, this celebration of the Feast is the first carefully timed move for which we've prepared for years. He is of age. You say he is ready. And the stage is perfectly set at the celebration of the Feast where the priests of the Temple and every rabbi in Palestine will be present along with Jewish boys who could become the core of his future followers. We will never have such an opportunity again to begin his revelation as the Chosen One."

"Mary, Zacharias may be right." Joseph was surprised Mary was so adamant about the prophesied vision in the face of the possible threat to Jesus. He tried to reason with her.

"That was our plan, and it was a good one. But the situation is different now. The Sadducees seek him for the Romans and their own gain, and the Pharisees seek him for Herod. I also know that Pilate's guards are seeking the boys involved in the incident with Pilate's helmet. If they become aware of him now through the Feast at the Temple, the plan could do the opposite of what we intend. The Prophecy could be defeated."

"But Joseph," she responded, "we can't hide him every time we think someone will seek to prevent him from becoming what God meant him to be. If we did that, he will end up being a carpenter in Nazareth.

"If there are risks, we will protect him. God will protect him. He told us in the Torah:

I will bless those who bless you,
  and whoever curses you I will curse;
  and all peoples on earth
    will be blessed through you.

"But your son is the Prophecy, Mary," Zacharias implored. "You could lose his destiny."

Mary's eyes were fixed on the ground. After a moment, she confirmed her conclusion out loud without looking up.

"If I do not take the clear opportunity to see that he becomes what

God meant him to be and to fulfill my covenant with God, then I will have lost his destiny," she answered. "Now is the time and the Temple in Jerusalem is the place."

She saw Zacharias shaking his head.

"Rabbi, you gave us God's decree for this plan at the Temple from the book of the prophet Daniel:

> *Seventy 'sevens' are decreed for your people and your holy city to finish transgression, to put an end to sin, to atone for wickedness, to bring in everlasting righteousness, to seal up vision and prophecy and to anoint the Most Holy Place.*

"Seventy 'sevens.' Do you know how many that is, Rabbi?" she asked Zacharias. "Four hundred and ninety," she answered her question.

"Do you know how many times I've recited to Jesus his lineage back to his ultimate Father? How many times I've sung it to him as a baby, taught it to him as a child, and scolded him with it as a boy?

"I can tell you exactly. Through all the years I have kept count. It's four hundred and ninety. That's seventy 'seven's.' I could say it another four hundred and ninety times and this fact would not change: Jesus was born in the lineage of Adam, and Abraham, and Moses, and David to be the Promised Messiah."

The men said nothing. A concerned look remained on their faces.

"Don't you see?" Mary urged them. "The people want the Promised Messiah now! They need the Promised Messiah now!

"The Tribes of Israel need someone to lead them out of the slavery of Rome. They need someone to give them the chance to live well from the fruits of their labors and to free the slaves in chains. They are looking for someone to prepare the way for the final coming of God.

"I've raised this boy for twelve years. You both have trained him well for twelve years. We haven't been devoted all these years to the Prophecy just to ponder these things in our hearts. It's time for action. It's time to start executing the plan. He will need the support of the priests of the Temple and the synagogues throughout Palestine. He needs to become known to the people, and that won't happen in Nazareth.

"Joseph, Zacharias," she concluded with no doubt in her voice, "The Prophecy has to start and end in Jerusalem. We are all going to the Temple in Jerusalem to 'seal up vision and prophecy and to anoint the Most Holy Place.' It is time for us to complete this first important step to make this boy King of the Jews."

They sat in silent tension for some time. Their thoughts were torn among their vows, their hopes and their fears. Finally Zacharias spoke.

"There is another reason why Jesus should not appear at the Temple in Jerusalem."

Mary and Joseph looked over at him.

"The rebel zealots are also searching for the boy who would be King of the Jews, and I told them he would be in Jerusalem."

"You told them that?" Joseph asked.

"I was just visited by the Sicarii who are looking for that boy," Zacharias informed them. "I was afraid of what might happen if they continued to look for him here in Nazareth, so without thinking I tried to throw them off the scent here by telling them such a boy would be in Jerusalem.

"I made a mistake," admitted Zacharias. "If we carry out our plan in Jerusalem now, I fear they will try to kill Jesus. That's what the Sicarii do."

This news brought fear to Mary's face.

With a look of disbelief, Joseph asked, "You actually spoke to the Sicarii, Zacharias?"

A sad look came over Zacharias's tired face.

"I spoke to my son," he confessed.

Chapter 14

TEMPTATION

He was always called "the Wine Seller Shikkor." Never just "the Wine Seller" or "Shikkor." In fact, "Shikkor" was not even his real name.

The Wine Seller Shikkor was a big man. His huge hands attached to strong thick arms could hold several wineskins and jugs of wine with ease in front of his broad chest. The mop of curly black hair and heavy beard atop his wide shoulders made him seem even larger than he was. Fortunately when he looked down at everyone in the world that moved about him, people usually were looking up into his twinkling eyes and broad smile. But if that smile went away and unhappiness appeared in those eyes, anyone looking at the Wine Seller Shikkor felt as if he were standing below a large boulder that was about to roll forward and crush everything in its path.

Shikkor is the Hebrew word for drunkard. Yet most people who knew the Wine Seller Shikkor had never seen him take a drink of anything strong, let alone seen him drunk. When the people of Nazareth heard the name "the Wine Seller Shikkor," they did not think of a drunkard. Instead the words brought to mind the image of his broad smile and twinkling eyes, and of the pleasure that would come with a cup of his excellent wine.

The name had come from another time in his life, a desperately unhappy time. After his father died and left him some money, he opened the wine shop as a young man with his new and pretty young wife. The business prospered, and the happy couple were thrilled to learn that they were going to have a child. It was a difficult birth, but a beautiful baby girl was born. Then the midwife could not stop the bleeding. He sat alone next to his wife after she died later that night and watched his tears drop to the floor into a pool of her dark red blood that looked like wine from a broken urn.

For the next two years, he was a different man. During the day, he worked in his wine shop which continued to do well by offering the best wines in Galilee. Every evening, he would watch his servant feed supper to his daughter and afterwards he would kiss the little girl goodnight. But then he would return to the back of the wine shop where he would sit staring at the floor while slowly and steadily drinking from jugs of wine until the sun rose. Over time, this routine took its toll on the man. He looked pale and sickly. He spoke only when he had to and then with slurred words. He did nothing in life but buy and sell wine with the smell of it on his breath, watch with dulled eyes as his daughter ate and went to bed, and return to the wine shop for another sleepless night. It was during that time when he became known as the Wine Seller Shikkor.

Those times ended one morning at dawn. A ray of early morning light coming through a wine shop window painted the wall behind him a soft pink. He did not notice the morning light. There was no light in his life even after the sunrise. His thoughts were as dark as they had ever been. This day, he concluded, would be his last.

A noise at the door brought him out of his stupor. He looked up to see his daughter Susanna standing there barefoot in her night dress, sucking her thumb and holding her blanket to the side of her face. While he was trying to blink the focus back into his eyes, she walked across the room, crawled up onto his knee, and fell fast asleep in his lap that was big enough to be her bed. He set the wine jug in his hand on the floor. Once again he watched tears fall from his eyes, but this time he saw them land on the soft, rosy skin of his daughter's face.

That day did turn out to be his last, but only as a drunkard. The day was also the start of his new life as a real father to his daughter. In a single moment in the dawn of that day, he realized when she crawled into his lap that she was everything in the old life he had lost and everything in the new life he had found.

His new life was filled with happiness. Susanna grew to be not only a pretty and loving daughter, but a capable assistant in the wine shop as well. Then she grew some more, and more after that. Physically, she was clearly her father's daughter. But she was also her father's daughter as a loyal and caring companion to all in her life. The wine shop, which had done well despite his neglect, now thrived with the new energy their smiles and friendly eyes gave the customers who entered their shop.

The name "the Wine Seller Shikkor" stayed with him however, and eventually lost its old meaning.

* * *

The Wine Seller Shikkor was ready to finish business for the day. It had been a good day he concluded as he slid a large handful of coins into his pouch that he set down on the counter to take home for safekeeping. And tonight he and his daughter had an invitation to dinner.

"Come, Susanna," he called to his daughter. "It's time to get ready for the evening. Nicodemus is a prompt host and dinner will be served on time."

The Wine Seller Shikkor and Susanna gave one last hurried look about the shop to see that all was in order before he closed the heavy door and locked it with a large key.

Across the market place, Peter along with several other Apostles stood at their messenger post and watched the two of them leave the wine shop. The Apostles knew exactly where the two were headed since they had delivered the dinner invitation message from Nicodemus.

"It will be dark enough soon," said Peter. "Does everyone know what he's supposed to do?"

They all nodded and waited for the dusk's light to disappear.

"I don't know if this is a good idea," Andrew said to his brother.

"It will be fun," Peter answered. "The Wine Seller Shikkor will never miss a few jugs of wine. It's time the Apostles drank some wine like real men."

"Are you sure we can pull this off?" Simon asked him.

"If everything inside the wine shop is just like I saw it, we should have no problem," replied Peter.

The day's commerce in Nazareth was done as darkness descended on the market place. When the last vendor left his stall and all was quiet, the Apostles slid like shadows around the corner of the wine shop into the passage by the side of the building where Peter, Andrew, Bartholomew and Simon stopped under a high window. Matthew, James and John went to strategic positions at the entrances to the passageway to look out for anyone who might be passing by.

Bartholomew, Simon and Andrew untied their brown rope belts that told the world they delivered messages from the market and handed them to Peter. Peter quickly tied them together with his and then carefully tied a short fishing line with his biggest fish hook to the end of the length of their combined rope belts.

"Positions!" ordered Peter.

Bartholomew stood below the window, spread his legs and leaned forward with his arms braced against the wall. Simon, standing next to Bartholomew, locked his fingers together to create a step into which Andrew placed his foot and boosted himself up to climb onto Bartholomew's shoulders. Once Andrew managed to sit on his shoulders, Bartholomew staggered slightly under Andrew's weight until the two of them leaned forward against the wall to regain their balance.

Peter slid the coiled rope over his shoulder and placed his foot on Simon's clasped hands. On the count of three, he stepped up with a firm push and placed his other foot on Andrew's leg. Then with a move that the two brothers had done for years to climb the mast of their father's fishing boat, Peter stood up onto Andrew's thigh, grabbed his brother's hand and climbed up to where he was able to place his knees on Andrew's shoulders. Once the three of them had steadied themselves against the wall, Peter carefully replaced his knees on Andrew's shoulders with his feet and slowly stood up while balancing himself with his hands on the wall.

"You all right, Bartholomew?" Peter asked below him as they all prepared themselves for the next move.

Bartholomew grunted through clenched teeth as beads of sweat broke out on his forehead.

Directly in front of Peter was the shuttered window that he had observed when he was in the wine shop earlier with Jesus. He had noticed that the shutter swung to the inside and that the wooden plank used for barring the shutter from the inside was sitting on the floor below with dust and cobwebs that indicated the window was rarely secured. He had also noticed that below the window on the floor were several jugs of wine with loop handles on the sides that he could easily hook with his large fishhook on a line. With a firm push from Peter, the shutter swung open.

"Yes!" whispered Simon watching from below.

Peter reached in with both arms and pulled himself part way through the window where his belly laid on the window ledge and his head and shoulders hovered over the floor of the wine shop. Bartholomew and Andrew breathed a little easier when his weight came off their shoulders. There was just enough light that Peter could make out four jugs below him. He pulled the coil of rope from his shoulder and lowered it to the jugs below.

With all his skill from years catching fish in the Sea of Galilee, Peter guided the fishhook to the first wine jug until the hook was firmly lodged under its handle. He carefully pulled the rope up hand over hand until the jug was within reach. Then he grabbed it, slid it by him through the window, and lowered it to Andrew's waiting hands.

"One!" said Andrew in a loud whisper to Simon below. Simon's arm was already in the air, and on Andrew's signal threw a pebble against the wall at the end of the passageway where Matthew was standing watch. Matthew immediately ran over to Simon just as the wine jug was handed down to him. Matthew took the wine jug from Simon and walked quickly to the end of the passage where he disappeared around the corner.

Above them, Peter had already fixed his hook on the handle of a second wine jug. The jug rose steadily until Peter was able once again to move it next to his body through the window and lower it into Andrew's grasp.

"Two!" whispered Andrew. Simon fired another pebble at the wall above John's head at the other end of the passage. John jogged over and took the second jug from Simon before he headed after Matthew.

"Come on!" urged Bartholomew in a low voice as his legs and shoulders began to ache with fatigue. Peter was having more difficulty in hooking the third wine jug.

"Whoa!" he blurted out as he almost lost his balance. It took several more passes at the wine jug before he felt the hook securely under its handle. When the third wine jug was safely in Peter's hands and passed down to Andrew, Andrew sounded his third signal.

"Three!"

Simon's pebble hit the wall above James's head which sent him running for the third jug of wine from Simon. Once James had proceeded with the wine jug on the route taken by Matthew and John, Simon looked up at Peter.

"Well done. Let's get moving!" Simon called up to Peter's figure still balanced in the window.

"Wait." Simon heard Peter's muffled voice from inside the shop window. "I think I can reach one more jug."

Simon saw Peter's legs kicking in the air as he was leaning farther into the shop.

"Come on. Let's go!" appealed Bartholomew who was now unsure of how long he could continue to hold up Andrew.

Peter leaned as far forward out over the wine shop as he could. Repeatedly swinging the hook on the end of the rope at the fourth wine jug farther off to the side, he was still just short of catching its handle. With his next lunging swing of the rope, the hook caught the jug. But when he tried to pull it up, he lost his balance and started to slide forward through the window. Instinctively, Peter grabbed for the shutter with one hand and slapped his other hand against the inside wall as best he could to keep from sliding down. The weight of the wine jug pulled the rope from his hand. As the jug smashed on the floor below, arcs of wine and pieces of hard clay flew across the wine shop.

After wriggling back out of the window, Peter took a long cat-like leap to the ground as soon as his foot touched Andrew's shoulder. Bartholomew quickly bent over so Andrew could climb off his sore shoulders. Simon's eyes searched up and down the passage for anyone who might have heard the commotion.

"Let's go," said Peter breathlessly. "The others should be at the barn by now."

* * *

The morning after Zacharias had visited their home, Joseph unexpectedly told Jesus that he would be leaving that day with Joseph on an overnight trip to Tiberius for meetings with Herod's chief servant Chuza to work on plans for Herod's new palace in Sepphoris. They packed and left immediately. Jesus did not understand why Joseph had suddenly announced that he would be accompanying his father. He was not ordinarily involved in meetings on plans. But he was excited to see the new town that Herod was building in the style of a Roman city.

Before they left, Jesus saw his parents arguing outside under the trees.

"He should not be in Nazareth. He's safer for the moment in the belly of the beast than at home, I tell you," he heard Joseph say.

They traveled hard to reach Tiberius where Joseph and Jesus spent a short night at the home of Chuza. The next day Joseph had a long meeting with Chuza to work on plans for the palace before starting back for Nazareth. Herod's servants in their distinctive white tunics brought food and drink as the meeting went on throughout the day without interruption.

While Joseph was in his meeting, Jesus had a talk with Chuza's wife, Joanna. Jesus found her easy to talk to and told her all about his preparation for the celebration of the Feast of the Passover at the Temple in Jerusalem. She listened intently to his words until Joseph and Chuza returned from their meeting.

"Come, Jesus," Joseph called to him. "We must hurry back to Nazareth."

Joseph thanked Chuza once again before they shook hands and parted. The return trip to Nazareth was an even harder grind. They were pushing to get back the same day which was the day before they were to leave on their journey to Jerusalem for the Feast. Barely stopping for food or rest, they made the journey through the fading sunset until they arrived home as most households had already settled in for the night. Mary started preparing a supper for them when she realized they were running short on water. Because it was dark, she asked Jesus to fetch some water from the well.

Jesus' stomach growled from hunger as he turned the corner where he could barely see the trees around the well and pools under the night stars. Although empty, the water jug felt heavy simply because he was so tired. As Jesus reached the well, he thought he saw Peter and some other figures leave the darkened market in the direction of the barn when a small figure passed by him.

"Judas!" Jesus called out when he recognized him. Judas stopped with surprise. He did not expect to hear a voice at the well in the dark of early evening.

"Oh, Jesus, it's you," answered Judas. He gave a quick look after the others who had just left the market.

"Are you ready to leave for Jerusalem tomorrow?" Jesus asked him. Jesus was starting to feel excited about the journey and was sure Judas must be feeling the same.

"Yeah, sure." Judas seemed more distracted than excited and started walking away quickly. "Listen, I have to get going. See you tomorrow."

"Is something going on?" Jesus asked him.

"Ah—not really," responded Judas over his shoulder as he headed off in the direction of the barn.

Once again Jesus was puzzled by his friend. They were about to begin the great adventure for which they had been preparing together for months. He had not seen his friend in several days. And yet Judas did not even have a moment to talk.

He pulled up the rope attached to the water bucket in the well and finished filling his water jug when a dark figure standing behind him gave him a fright.

"Hello, Jesus."

He did not recognize the strange sounding voice even though the person recognized him in the dark. The figure stepped closer where Jesus could see that he was wearing a black turban. His beard hung over the front of a long black cloak closed around him.

"You may not recognize me," he said to Jesus, "but I think you may know who I am."

"I don't think so," replied Jesus warily.

"There's no need to be afraid of me. I cannot hurt you, although there are others who can."

His voice was very unusual, but had a calming sound in it.

"I am known as someone who makes things happen and gives people what they want."

"I don't want anything," said Jesus. He dropped the water bucket and rope back into the well and turned to pick up the filled water jug. Something inside told him he wanted nothing to do with this man.

"That's not true, is it Jesus?" said the man. "At this very moment you are thirsty and would like a drink from that jug. And your belly wants some warm bread from your mother's oven right now, doesn't it?"

Jesus said nothing but could not deny the truth of the man's statement.

"You know, Jesus, that you don't need your mother for bread. You can make your own bread and in ways she cannot, can't you? And you are strong enough to draw your own water, even after a tiring journey."

Jesus looked at him cautiously and wondered how this man knew to say these things.

"You really don't need your parents to get by, do you? You're a strong and talented young man now. I think you are ready to be more than just the son of Mary and Joseph."

When Jesus did not reply, the man carried on speaking.

"The Torah says that you are to honor your father and your mother, so that you may live long in the land. But that does not mean that you can't be your own man, and do as you want on your own.

"I lead a band of men and women who have chosen to rely on themselves and me to do as they please and what they think is right for themselves. You are a man now who can rely on himself. You could be like them. You could be one of us, Jesus."

Jesus felt a strong appeal from the man's words. He liked the idea of having his independence, but thought for a moment before he answered.

"But the Book of Proverbs also tells us to listen to your father's instruction and not forsake your mother's teaching. I don't need you or your band of people to do as I please or what I think is right."

Jesus watched the man's hand reach up in a quick move to his turban, but then slowly lower and slide back inside his cloak.

"Aren't you a little worried about how you will do before the High Priest at the celebration of the Feast in the Temple?" the man asked.

"I will be fine," Jesus answered although deep down he was worried. He wondered again how this man knew so much about him.

"I will be there also," said the man. "I can help you at the Temple."

Jesus picked up his water jug.

"I won't need your help," said Jesus as he walked past the man towards home.

"You might want to go see your friends at the barn," the man called after him. "I think they could use your help tonight."

As he hurried back home, Jesus was unnerved by his encounter with this strange man. Who was he, and how did he know so much about Jesus? He seemed right in what he said, and yet it seemed wrong. And what did he know about the Apostles? Despite the questions racing through his mind, Jesus all of a sudden just wanted some food and rest, and a chance to think about everything he had just heard.

The whole family went to bed as soon as their supper was eaten. Although the caravan of pilgrims from Nazareth would be leaving for Jerusalem in the morning, Jesus thought it was odd that neither of his parents had said anything about final preparations for the journey. Joseph simply told them it was better for them all to sleep now and get up early the next morning to plan their day.

Though he was exhausted, Jesus lay on his bed too filled with his thoughts to sleep. He tried to focus on the journey to Jerusalem and his role in the celebration of the Feast at the Temple, but his mind kept returning to the strange meeting with the bearded man in the black turban. It was a complete mystery to him how the man could know about the bread at the Place of the Seven Springs, about his parents, and about his worries over reading his verse and giving his testimony at the Temple. Finally, how could the man know about his hidden feelings concerning his independence and having his parents arrange his marriage and his whole life for him?

Suddenly Jesus sat bolt upright. If the strange man knew all these things, what did he know about the Apostles in the barn that made him tell Jesus they might need his help that very night? He crawled out of bed without waking his brothers, pulled his tunic over his head, and carried his sandals across the main room of the house to the door where he silently slipped outside.

* * *

By that time, Nicodemus had drunk too much wine at his dinner. That's why he was interested in more, and in particular the new shipment of the excellent wine from the Plains of Sharon that the Wine Seller had described to him after dinner. He and the Wine Seller Shikkor were headed for the wine shop after they had dropped off Susanna at home. Nicodemus wanted to taste the delivery of new wine, but the Wine Seller Shikkor was anxious to return to the shop because he remembered that he had left his pouch full of coins on the counter.

The Wine Seller Shikkor saw the puddle of wine and pieces of broken jug at his feet as soon as he opened the door of the wine shop. He went over to the counter and lit an oil lamp. To his surprise, he saw the bag of coins still sitting on the counter. After surveying the mess from the broken wine jug, he noticed the open shutter on the window above him. He looked down at the broken pieces of clay soaking in the pool of wine below the window and leaned over to pick up something off the floor.

He held up a length of rope with wine dripping off a hook. The Wine

Seller Shikkor immediately recognized the distinctive brown ropes.

"The messengers from the market!" he growled.

The heavy shop door slammed behind him as he marched towards the barn with Nicodemus close behind. The Apostles' hideout was not as secret as the boys thought.

* * *

When Jesus arrived at the barn, he heard the Apostles before he even reached the barn door. The first thing he saw when he pushed it open was Bartholomew passed out against the wall of Jewel's stall, his head back and mouth wide open. As soon as he stepped through the door, James and John yelled "Jesus!" and ran up to him, each of them holding a handle on either side of a wine jug.

"Have some wine," they shouted together before turning the jug upside down over Jesus' head. Jesus ducked, and the twins broke out in loud laughter when nothing came out of the empty vessel.

On the floor, Matthew, Thomas and Judas were rolling dice next to the second wine jug and arguing about whether Judas had cheated. Over in the corner, the rest of the Apostles were passing around the third wine jug and drinking as they sang loudly. When they started clapping with the rhythm of their song, out of another stall came Maggie dancing and twirling so fast the bottom of her robe flared out so that her bare knees and calves were revealed. Her loose, unbraided hair was uncovered and flying about her face. She kept spinning around until she finally stumbled and staggered against the wall. The Apostles and Maggie laughed as she dizzily struggled to stand up without falling over. Maggie looked over to see Jesus standing there.

"Hello, Jesus," she smiled at him as she walked over unsteadily and draped her arms around him to keep from falling down. "I am so glad you're here," she whispered into his ear and gave him a hug. He could smell the wine in her hair and feel her body underneath her robes. It was the first time he had ever felt a woman's body against his. He sensed his body starting to react.

Maggie let go of Jesus and began dancing again as the Apostles started singing and clapping even louder. James and John started arguing and pulling on the empty wine jug. The gamblers on the floor shouted as one of them won big on a roll of the dice. Jewels started braying loudly to join in with the general commotion. Jesus looked around the barn uncertainly, not knowing what to do in all the chaos. Then his heart fell as he saw Maggie and Peter locked in an embrace and kissing passionately.

With a loud bang, the barn door suddenly slammed open and silenced everyone. In stepped the Wine Seller Shikkor followed by Nicodemus. His large figure seemed to cast a shadow over the entire barn. The anger on his face was matched by Nicodemus's angry look at Peter who still held Maggie in his arms. The frightened silence was finally interrupted by a loud snore from Bartholomew.

"You filthy thieves!" the Wine Seller Shikkor accused in a menacing voice. "I should thrash each and every one of you for stealing my wine." Everyone except the oblivious Bartholomew cowered as he stepped forward and raised his fist.

"I don't believe you will find any stolen wine in this barn," said a voice off to the side behind the Wine Seller Shikkor. He spun around and saw Jesus standing there calmly.

"Jesus, I am sorry to see you here among these common criminals. Your father would be disappointed."

"I have done nothing to disappoint my father," said Jesus. "You will find no stolen wine in this barn," he stated once again.

"These are my wine jugs," declared the Wine Seller Shikkor. "You are lying just to protect the rest of your no-good friends."

Jesus walked to each of the wine jugs and placed them on the floor before him with a lingering touch to each jug.

"If these are your wine jugs, then show us your stolen wine," Jesus dared him.

The Wine Seller Shikkor stepped over and angrily grabbed a wine jug in each hand. He held them above the snoring Bartholomew and tipped them over.

Bartholomew snorted awake shaking his head as two streams of clear, cool water splashed on his face. Nicodemus and the Wine Seller Shikkor gave each other an astonished look. So did all the Apostles.

The Wine Seller Shikkor snarled and snatched up the third empty jug. He turned it over and once again colorless water splashed on the floor. Peering into the jug, he wiped his finger around the lip and tasted it. No wine, only water.

He looked around at everyone in the barn without speaking. They, like the Wine Seller Shikkor, did not know what to say, and so said nothing.

"I'm going home," said Jesus finally in a tired voice. All eyes followed him out the door. Then they turned to the Wine Seller Shikkor.

The Wine Seller Shikkor looked confused and embarrassed. Without saying another word, he stomped past the manger and out of the barn.

Chapter 15

THE PILGRIMAGE

The excitement of a great journey arises when the desire for the destination is joined with the unknowns of the road ahead.

That excitement was felt by everyone at the market in Nazareth forming the caravan for the pilgrimage to the Feast of the Passover in Jerusalem. The few hundred people included men and women who made the three-day journey every year as well as those, young and old, who were to see Jerusalem and the Temple for the first time. They were experiencing the thrill from the urge to go to someplace new combined with the fear of leaving the safety of home.

A purposeful pandemonium filled the market. People were hurrying about to finish final preparations for the trip and find their traveling companions. The pilgrimage to the Temple for the Feast was not comfortable or easy. The three-day journey between Nazareth and Jerusalem required food and cooking utensils, bedding and tents, clothes and all else that might be needed, for there would be few places to obtain such essentials on the road. Vendors in the marketplace were scurrying to sell food and supplies to last-minute customers before they went on their way.

The pilgrims waiting to leave talked excitedly with one another and exchanged blessings with those staying behind. Horses and donkeys pawed the ground in anticipation as they were finally loaded, saddled or harnessed to carts and carriages. Only the camels seemed bored and unconcerned.

The Wine Seller Shikkor looked hurried and distracted as he pulled up in his donkey cart filled with wine for the journey. Every year he traveled in the caravan with a supply of wine jugs thinking he would make a good profit by selling wine along the way. But inevitably he would give away as much as he sold in the spirit of the group's friendly camaraderie and also to make room on his cart for travelers who were overly tired or unwell. He knew there would be enough money from the brisk sales to virtually all of the pilgrims at his shop where Susanna was busy helping the last who were purchasing wine for the journey.

He saw the Iscariot family looking proudly at their son Judas who would be participating in the Feast at the Temple. The sight of Judas reminded him of his embarrassment the night before. He glanced about for any of the Apostles who might be delivering messages in the market and was relieved when none of them were in sight. Nor did he see Jesus which was also a relief to him. There were many other familiar faces though—his many customers, other merchants, fellow worshippers from the synagogue and Lazarus who was meeting his sisters from Bethany. But he did not see the Rabbi Zacharias anywhere.

"That's odd," he thought. The rabbi often traveled on the pilgrimage with Joseph the carpenter and his wife, but they too were nowhere to be seen. The Wine Seller Shikkor concluded that they must be among some of the other many groups in the caravan. With all those people and the commotion, it was easy enough to lose someone for a while.

The route they were traveling was neither the safest nor the most direct. Jerusalem lay straight south of Nazareth at the end of a good road maintained by the Romans for troops and supplies to move back and forth. It was by far the shortest and best route. But that road took the pilgrims through Samaria, and no pilgrim going to the Temple would set foot in Samaria if there were any way to avoid it.

"May I never set eyes on a Samaritan" was a saying often heard in Judea and Galilee. Samaritans were called "the foolish people" and treated with every mark of contempt. Being called a "Samaritan" meant that someone was considered a "stranger" as much as it meant someone was from that region. To partake of Samaritan bread was like eating swine's flesh. The priests of the Temple in Jerusalem would not drink wine from Galilee simply from the attitude that it was defiled by being shipped through Samaria.

The hatred between Samaritans and Jews ironically did not come from the fact that they were very different. As often happens, their intense contempt and intolerance for one another arose from the fact that they were only slightly different. Centuries earlier, Samaria was settled by foreign colonists who worshipped false idols. Their religion eventually evolved into a mixture of superstitions with Jewish doctrines and rites. Then a disagreement between a High Priest of the Temple and his brother resulted in the brother establishing a rival temple on Mount Gerizim in the middle of Samaria. That temple was destroyed and never rebuilt, but the religious separation became permanent. Samaritans took every opportunity to insult Jews. Jews treated Samaritans with complete disdain since their mixed blood and religion made them neither Jews nor Gentiles.

So instead of taking the good road south through Samaria that led directly to Jerusalem, pilgrims from the north traveled east across the River Jordan to Perea and then south through its wilderness until they crossed back over the Jordan to Jericho and on to Jerusalem. It was rough and dangerous country filled with bandits who preyed on the pilgrims. The bandits lived well from the pilgrims' supplies and money for the many tolls required to use roads and to enter the gates of towns on the way.

Despite the hardship and danger ahead, the pilgrims were in a festive mood. They were generally grouped together with their friends and family, but also enjoyed the company of others they had not seen in a while. Along the way, they had the chance to meet new friends who fell in with the caravan on the same pilgrimage.

The pilgrims knew that it was almost time to depart when the Pharisees arrived and gathered at the front of the caravan to lead the group. The Pharisees looked almost like a caravan by themselves with their fine carriages, many servants and carts carrying their baggage. Nicodemus in his carriage fell in line along with his fellow Pharisees behind their leader Samaias.

When Nicodemus got out of his carriage, the other Pharisees immediately gathered around him in admiration. On his arm, he was wearing a new tephelin, a shiny black leather capsule that contained a concealed parchment on which four special passages of scripture were written. It was positioned on the bicep of his left arm so that it sat next to his heart and fastened with long black leather straps wound carefully around the arm seven times and three times around the fingers of his hand. The other Pharisees jealously admired the extraordinary tephelin on Nicodemus's arm because it had two Hebrew letters molded in gold into the top and side of the capsule and the black strap tied to the hand with a knot in the shape of a third Hebrew letter. The three letters spelled *Sha-dda*, one of the Hebrew words for God. He had the tephelin made at great expense especially for this pilgrimage.

A tephelin was considered a valued and important symbol of past deliverances of the Jewish people. Some rabbis said that a tephelin was more valuable than the gold headband on the forehead of the High Priest since the inscription of the sacred name Jehovah appeared only once there, but twenty-three times in the verses on the parchment concealed inside the tepheilin. There was even a special blessing said when the tephelin was tied to the arm. But the unspoken belief was that the tephelin was an amulet that could be used to rid evil spirits or even conjure up demons. There was the legend of a rabbi who turned his back on the king and would have been killed save for the power of the tephelin he was wearing. Some scribes of the Temple held that it was a punishable offense to question the powers of a tephelin.

A respectful quiet fell upon the large crowd of pilgrims as the Pharisees moved into a circle. When everyone's attention was focused on them, the Pharisees started praying loudly for a very long time. These prayers were the first of at least a hundred each day for they believed that much prayer was more sure to be heard. They prayed with a great demonstration of piety before entering or leaving any city, and the longer the better. As the Wine Seller Shikkor watched, he thought it was more like a show than a prayer. It was clear to him that the Pharisees were praying in order to get the pilgrim's attention rather than God's.

Anxious to start their journey, the pilgrims were beginning to think the Pharisees' prayer would never end when finally several loud blessings were given, and the Pharisees began moving to their carriages. Nicodemus moved over next to Samaias and spoke cautiously so no one would hear.

"Have you learned anything more about the Romans' boy king?"

No," answered Samaias. "But Herod has put many secret police here among the pilgrims and in villages throughout Palestine looking for any boy who might be suspected. His agents in Jerusalem are also watching the actions of the Romans and Sadducees.

"Have you any news about the boy?" Samaias asked Nicodemus.

"No," he answered.

Samaias gave him a critical look.

"Be glad we are not here for Herod's wrath when he arrives," he said as a servant helped him into his carriage.

Like a large caterpillar that slowly manages to move its many parts in a single direction, the long line of pilgrims behind the Pharisees headed out of the town. The Wine Seller Shikkor urged on his donkey with a flick of his reins as he looked about unsuccessfully one more time for the Rabbi and Joseph the carpenter. As the end of the caravan finally left Nazareth, the two vinedressers slid unnoticed in among the pilgrims.

* * *

Jesus was sitting at home and did not know why. All he knew was that the caravan of pilgrims was leaving for Jerusalem that morning, and he, his parents and the rabbi were not in that caravan.

He was confused and disappointed about everything. The night before at the barn had been a great disappointment for him. The Apostles had behaved badly and caused him to do something he was not sure he should have done. In the process, he had surely angered the Wine Seller Shikkor which would not please his mother. He knew there would be another lecture with the list of his ancestors. And he could not rid his mind of the image of Peter kissing Maggie. His affection for her clearly meant nothing. Then there was the uncomfortable and puzzling encounter with the mysterious stranger at the well. Now after many weeks and long hours of preparation for his part in the celebration of the Feast at the Temple, it looked like Judas would be there, but not him. And he had no idea why.

While Jude rocked back and forth quietly next to him, Jesus talked to Rebecca with his hands as he halfheartedly watched Jamie and Joses playing a game with their dreidel. Rachel brought them all sweetbread that she had baked. Jesus smiled his thanks to her, but rose without eating to look out the open door yet again.

He could see Mary, Joseph and Zacharias still sitting outside under the trees. After the family had awakened and eaten, Jesus expected that Joseph would finally give the instructions for preparation for the journey and then send his brothers and sisters off to stay with the rabbi's wife Elizabeth. Instead, the rabbi showed up at their door. The three of them had been talking for a long while and at times even seemed to be arguing.

In the shade of the trees, Mary tried to sound certain of her words despite the doubts in her mind. "We must take him to Jerusalem. How else can we show the world who he is? The Temple is where God is worshipped. The Priests lead the people in their worship of God. The rabbis and elders from every synagogue among the Tribes of Israel will be there. And all the people gathered there are looking for the Promised Messiah."

Joseph was not convinced. He could not overcome his worry. He had no doubts about the power of the Romans, the influence of the Sadducees and Pharisees, the ruthlessness of Herod's secret police and the deadliness of the Sicarii. An old rabbi and a pregnant woman would not be able to protect his son from these dangers. It would be up to him. And Joseph knew he was no match for men who were trained to kill.

Zacharias too was torn. He loved the boy and did not want to do anything that would cause him harm. But there was so much at stake for the old man who could see the end of his days. Taking this important step to see that the Prophecy was realized could mean everything for his own dreams, his lifetime's work and years of dedication, and, finally, his response to the priests of the Temple for their rejection of him.

But in the back of Zacharias's mind, another question weighed heavily on his thoughts. What would the risk of taking Jesus to Jerusalem mean for his own son? The angel in the Temple had also told Zacharias of a prophecy and a path for his son. Yet his son was on a path heading away from that prophecy. If something happened to Jesus, would it risk the destiny of his own son as well?

The three of them sat in silence struggling with their uncertainty until Mary finally spoke the words that all of them knew was the truth they must face.

"When I give birth to my children, I give them life at the beginning. But when they are ready for their own life, though I wish it were otherwise, I cannot know or tell them what that life is to be.

"This could be the start of the Prophecy, and we worry that this might also be its end. But it is not for us to determine how the Prophecy will end. That is for God alone.

"We are here only to see that it begins and goes forward. We cannot give him a Temple. We cannot give him a kingdom, an army or followers. We can only give him the chance to be who he is and do what he must to fulfill the Prophecy."

The two men could not disagree.

Zacharias finally nodded. "You are right. The Prophecy will be fulfilled only by Jehovah and Jesus."

Joseph looked at them. "But we must still try to protect him. And hopefully God will protect him so that one day he will protect all of us."

Such was their decision to go. In their uncertainty, they felt the need to pray. Zacharias simply asked of God "that our hearts may not be faint, and our vision may not be darkened."

The old man climbed to his feet.

"One should pray on the road, but only short prayers," he said with a smile. "Let us be going."

**

It was a meeting Caiaphas had been dreading for some time. He had received the Roman soldier who delivered the message from Pontius Pilate. The commander had arrived in Jerusalem and had ordered an immediate audience with the priest. Pilate once again would want to know the identity and location of the boy born in Bethlehem whom Herod the Great had tried to murder. Once again Caiaphas still would be unable to give him that information. This time, however, Caiaphas feared that Pilate would not ask. He would demand to know details of the boy, and there would be consequences if Caiaphas had no answer.

Caiaphas checked again urgently with all his sources, priests, rabbis, scribes, Levites, tax collectors and even servants who had been on alert for any signs of a boy born in Bethlehem and later of Nazareth who might be the one who could be turned over to the Romans. They all had nothing. A few made suggestions. But in the end, Caiaphas had no more news of who and where the boy was than on the day the priest promised Pilate he would be found.

He brought several other priests and scribes with him to Pilate's headquarters in the Tower of Antonia occupied by the Romans and overlooking the Temple. He hoped that their number would give a better appearance of substantial effort and maybe deflect some of the displeasure that Caiaphas knew Pilate would express in no uncertain terms when he failed to give the commander any information about the boy. But when they reached the commander's headquarters, only Caiaphas was escorted in to meet with Pilate.

Pilate dispensed with any greetings. "What news do you have of the boy? Do you have him?" he asked immediately.

"Well," replied Caiaphas, "As we informed you, we believe he was living in Nazareth, and we expect with the large number of pilgrims attending this ceremony of the Feast that we may be successful in learning more—"

"Is that all you have to tell me?" Pilate interrupted, his face growing red with anger. "You told me that when I first gave you the order to find the boy.

"Here me and hear me well, Priest. The security of Palestine and Rome itself is at stake. I have very little time before Herod—before I must take action.

"Find me that boy from Nazareth, because if you don't, what you will find is that you priests will have lost your positions and your income from taxes. I have the full force of Caesar's authority in Rome and a Legion of soldiers outside who will help me see to it. Is the situation clear enough for you?"

Caiaphas went pale, but quickly gathered his wits.

"We will take further action, Commander. The Temple guards will watch all who enter and leave the Temple during the celebration of the Feast. Anyone who knows of the boy is sure to be at the Temple during Passover. We will be able to examine anyone who might have knowledge of the boy.

"And after the Feast, almost every priest, rabbi and scribe in Palestine will be gathered at the Temple for the Holy Conclave. We will impress on them the importance of this search. Someone in that gathering is sure to have knowledge of a boy with his history and destiny. We will find him most certainly," Caiaphas concluded with as much confidence as he could summon.

"It had better be done, for your sake and his," growled Pilate as he waved Caiaphas out of the room. "And for my sake especially," he thought after the priest had gone.

Then he called in his chief officers and gave them his own instructions for finding the boy who would be the king through whom Pilate intended to rule.

* * *

A great journey puts its purpose before you and all other things at your back.

Jesus was thinking about the Feast at the Temple. He was on his way to Jerusalem. All of his other concerns were now behind him.

He and his parents and the rabbi were following the other pilgrims from Nazareth, but by the time they had left the town after getting packed and leaving the children with Elizabeth, they were over a half day behind the caravan. They tried to maintain a pace that would catch up with the caravan. But the old rabbi could no longer walk swiftly, and both Mary and the old donkey Jewels on which she rode needed to stop often. As the sun grew lower on the horizon, Joseph knew they had only fallen farther behind the other pilgrims.

Joseph stopped early to camp at a good spot protected by some large rocks near a brook. Mary and the Rabbi needed to rest. He too was tired, but more from the burdens of doubt than the road traveled. After a light supper, Joseph and Jesus sat by the fire as the others slept. Joseph tried to stay awake to stand watch, but Jesus saw his father's eyes struggle to stay open.

"Father, I'm wide awake. Why don't you sleep now and I'll watch by the fire."

"Are you sure you are awake, son?" Joseph asked.

"I'm fine. You sleep. I'll wake you if I need to."

Jesus laid back watching the stars and thinking about the Temple. It occurred to him that for all the preparation he had done for the celebration of the Feast, he did not really know anything about what would happen except the words he was to read and his thoughts for his testimony. His concerns were interrupted by a rustling sound near the rocks where the donkey was tethered. Jesus rose and silently walked towards the rocks. There he saw a boy about his age rummaging through their packs.

"Are you hungry?" Jesus quietly asked him.

The startled boy leaped up and raised a wooden staff to deliver a blow.

"Are you hungry?" Jesus repeated. "Or are you stealing to destroy our pilgrimage to Jerusalem?"

The boy stood there not knowing what to do.

"'People do not despise a thief if he steals to satisfy his hunger when he is starving.' That's written in the Proverbs," said Jesus.

"What are the Proverbs?" asked the boy whose staff was still ready to strike.

"It's a book of wise sayings written long ago by King Solomon."

"I have heard of King Solomon," said the young thief as he slowly lowered his staff.

Jesus watched him closely and went on.

"King Solomon also said in the Proverbs that if men band together to lie in wait to shed the blood of others and steal their precious possessions, the greed of those men actually makes them lie in wait for their own blood and lurk secretly to take away their own lives.

"But I'm sure you are just hungry, aren't you?" Jesus told him.

Before the boy could answer, several rough-looking bandits came out of the dark. They saw Jesus facing the boy and raised their staffs to attack Jesus.

"Wait!" said the boy. "Don't waste your time."

The bandits hesitated.

"They have nothing," he told them. "I looked though their packs. They will starve before they get to Jerusalem."

The largest of the thieves lowered his staff. "How can these pilgrims travel with nothing to eat but their foolish faith?" he asked with a disgusted look. "Let's go."

The boy paused as the other bandits disappeared behind a boulder.

"Maybe I will see you again," he said to Jesus. Then he turned to follow the other thieves.

"I hope so," answered Jesus. Jesus did not know how or where he could possibly meet the young thief again, but for some reason he had a feeling that he would.

Joseph suddenly rushed in with his walking stick clenched in his hand. Zacharias followed close behind.

"I heard voices," said Joseph. "Are you all right?"

"Yes, Father. There were bandits, but they left. They took nothing."

Jesus told them about the encounter with the boy and how the young thief had protected him from the band of thieves.

Zacharias shook his head sadly. "Whoever does not teach a son a trade is as if he brought him up to be a robber."

"Rabbi, that boy was taught a trade. He was taught to be a robber," said Joseph as he turned to go back to their fire. "You try to sleep, Jesus. I will watch for the rest of the night."

The next morning the three men were extremely tired for they all stayed awake during the night standing watch on their own without any rest. Mary too was exhausted from the discomfort of sleeping on the ground.

They discussed the difficulty of their situation. On the second day of their journey, they were already more than a half day behind the caravan from Nazareth. Mary was struggling, the aged Zacharias was not doing well walking on the rough wilderness ground, and one man, a boy, a pregnant woman and an old man were easy prey for bandits. They would not be that lucky again with another band of robbers.

There was only one option. That was to return to the main road south from Nazareth to Jerusalem through Samaria. Mary and Zacharias were not particularly happy about taking that route. But they could not argue with Joseph's conclusion that there was no other choice if they hoped to arrive in Jerusalem in time for the start of the celebration of the Feast of the Passover.

By the time the sun was at full height, they were back on the main road through Samaria and moving steadily south at a good pace. They were able to keep moving and keep up their strength with many short breaks for rest, food and water whenever they stopped to pay tolls to use the road. Jewels kept moving steadily under the familiar weight of Mary and her unborn baby. The sight of Mt. Gerizim told Joseph that they were nearing the middle of Samaria and the halfway point of their journey. Before long he would start looking for a safe and comfortable place for them to spend the night.

Eventually Joseph saw a village in the distance. As they came to the edge of the village, they spotted some people standing near a figure lying on the ground. Two of the people left the group and walked away quickly in their direction. One wore the robes of a rabbi and the other the clothes of a Levite who by tradition held religious and political duties. They stopped to speak with Zacharias as Jesus walked past them to get a closer look at the person on the ground.

"Blessings unto you, brothers," greeted Zacharias. "What is happening up there?"

"A man has been badly beaten."

"By robbers?" Zacharias asked.

"No, by Herod's men," answered the rabbi. "They are going to every village asking about people's sons. For some reason they beat him when they questioned him and found that he had a son. No one knows why. But they did not like his answers."

The two of them continued to head away with some haste.

"You had best stay away," the rabbi warned Zacharias. "There is no telling what Herod's men might do or why. They're vicious."

Zacharias and Joseph quickly looked at each other and then down the road at Jesus who was approaching the injured man. They hurried to catch up to him.

Jesus was horrified when he looked between the people standing there to see the man lying on the ground. The clothes were mostly torn off the half dead man whose bloodied body lay in the dirt next to the road. He could not believe that the rabbi and Levite had just walked away from the man without helping, and the others standing there seemed too afraid to do anything but look down at the man.

From the other direction, another traveler arrived, a Samaritan. He kneeled down next to the injured man and looked at his wounds to see if he was still alive. He immediately poured some water on the man's lips and then opened his pack to pull out a cloth which he soaked in some oils and wine from his wineskin. With gentle dabs, he began to wipe the blood and dirt from the man's wounds.

Joseph and Zacharias quickly walked up to Jesus and looked at the injured man and the Samaritan.

"Come, Jesus," said Joseph.

"But, Father—," Jesus turned and gestured at the injured man.

"Is there somewhere I can take this man to be cared for?" the Samaritan asked the people standing around him.

"There's an inn in the village," one of them finally said, hesitant to appear too helpful.

The Samaritan placed the injured man's arm around his shoulder and lifted the man up onto his donkey. He spoke to the injured man whose pain from being placed on the donkey had made him more conscious.

"Hold on, my friend. We are going to an inn where you will be comfortable." When the injured man grimaced, the Samaritan tried to reassure him. "I will see that the innkeeper has money to look after you, and when I return in a few days, I'll check on you and make sure he is paid more if necessary."

Jesus was not sure the hurt man even heard the Samaritan. Joseph pulled Jesus away by the arm.

"We must go quickly, Jesus."

"Who did this to that man, Father?"

"Robbers, I expect," said Joseph as he and Zacharias looked around nervously while hurrying the donkeys along. Jesus watched the Samaritan leading his donkey with the injured man toward the village, and then looked back one last time at the rabbi and the Levite off in the distance.

***

A short distance behind the caravan of pilgrims from Nazareth, the two vinedressers sat next to each other by their small fire and took large swigs of wine from a wineskin.

"I don't know why we are so worried about finding a boy," the one vinedresser said to the other. "It's a woman I'd rather be looking for."

Their laughter stopped short when each of them felt the sharp edge of a dagger against his throat. The strange voice they knew well spoke from behind them.

"You will look for the person I order you to look for!"

The Black Turban drew away from their throats the daggers he held in each hand and stood up. The vinedressers stumbled to their feet as quickly as they could to face him.

"And when you are ordered to look for that person," the Black Turban reached out with both hands and pointed the tips of his daggers at their throats, "you will find him. Do you understand?"

With fear in their eyes, they looked at the ground and nodded several times.

"Tell me what you know from the caravan," the Black Turban ordered.

"We know that Herod's secret police are watching closely a boy from Nazareth. His name is Iscariot, Judas Iscariot."

The Black Turban frowned.

"Look for another," he told them. "The boy who made you look like fools after the magician's show at the market in Nazareth."

The two vinedressers smiled at the news of their new prey.

"Yes, my Lord," they said as each of them touched the handle of his dagger. The Black Turban watched their hands.

"Don't hurt him once you find him," he ordered in a firm voice. "Just bring him to me. I want him as one of my own."

The vinedressers looked disappointed.

"I said don't hurt him. I didn't say you had to make him comfortable." The Black Turban gave them a malicious grin.

"Yes, my Lord." They returned his smile.

* * *

Joseph woke the others before dawn. With an early start, they might be able to reach Jerusalem that night and possibly arrive at about the same time as the main caravan of pilgrims from Nazareth. The third day on the road passed quickly for Jesus who was fascinated by Zacharias's tales that turned their journey into a path through the echoes from the past of their people.

They first passed by Shiloh where Moses had built under direction from God a tent tabernacle to serve as a sacred sanctuary for the Ark of the Covenant. The Ark was a large ornate chest built to house the two tablets with the commandments given by God to Moses on Mount Sinai as the tribes of Israel fled their slavery in Egypt. For the next three hundred sixty-nine years, the whole congregation of Israel assembled at Shiloh until the sad day when the Ark was taken into battle and captured by the Philistines. At some point, the great tent was replaced by a building that became the first temple for the feasts and sacrifices of the people. It was here that lots were cast to determine the lands of each of the tribes of Israel.

Next they passed to the east of Bethel where Jacob in his sleep dreamt of the angels coming up and down a ladder. In this place, Zacharias told them, even the angel of death was shorn of his power.

Soon after, they stood on the plateau of Ramah and looked at the nearby heights of Gibeon, where God made the sun stand still during the Israelites' war with the Amorites, and at Gibeah, where Saul, as handsome a young man as could be found anywhere in Israel and a head taller than anyone else, reigned for thirty-eight years as Israel's first king.

Near Ramah, Rachel died after the remarkable tragedy of her life and love told by Moses in the Torah. She met her husband Jacob who had come from faraway Canaan to live with her father Laban in order to be safe from the anger of Jacob's jealous brother Esau. Jacob fell in love the first moment he saw Rachel as she was watering her lambs. He worked seven years for Laban in return for permission to marry Rachel. On the night of their marriage, the bride's face was hidden by her veil, and it turned out that Jacob had been married to Rachel's sister Leah who had not the figure and beauty of Rachel. When Jacob confronted Laban with this deception, Laban explained that the older sister had to marry first by custom, but assured Jacob that after his wedding week was finished, he could take Rachel as a second wife so long as he worked another seven years as payment for her.

Leah gave birth to four sons, but Rachel was unable to conceive a child. She became jealous and insecure, and told Jacob to "give me a child or I shall die." She gave him her maidservant to be a surrogate mother for her. Her maidservant gave birth to two sons that Rachel named and raised. Leah then also offered Jacob her handmaid who bore two sons that Leah named and raised. After Leah conceived again, Rachel was finally blessed with a son named Joseph who would become Jacob's favorite child.

Jacob decided to return with his two wives and twelve children to his family in Canaan. He wanted his own place in his own country and doubted whether Laban would let him keep the wealth that he had acquired from his distinctive flocks of spotted and speckled livestock. Because he was afraid that Laban would stop him, he left with his family without telling his father-in-law. Laban chased him down in seven days and accused him of stealing religious idols from his house. Jacob denied it and went so far as to put a death curse on anyone who would have stolen Laban's idols. He had Laban do a search and then scolded Laban for his accusation after nothing was found. They made peace, had a feast and built a pillar of rocks to honor their friendship.

But Jacob did not know that it was Rachel who in fact had stolen the idols and hidden them on the camel on which she was sitting while Laban was doing his search. Without realizing, Jacob had put the curse of death on his own wife, the mother of his favorite child and the love of his life for whom he had given fourteen years of labor. After he had returned to his home, made peace with his brother, and was visited by God who told him he would start the nation of Israel, his beloved Rachel died painfully in childbirth.

As soon as Zacharias finished telling Jesus the story of Jacob and Rachel, he stopped and pointed to the west.

"See where the mountains fall sharply towards the sea? That open land called Shephelah is where our people have seen great triumphs. There Joshua chased down and defeated the kings of the south, and the strong Samson, during the forty long years of war with Israel's arch enemy Philisitia, killed one thousand Philistines with only a donkey's jaw bone."

Then Zacharias pointed in the opposite direction.

"To the East, one finds the extremes of God's judgment and blessings. In a mysterious hollow lies the Dead Sea, and beyond is the desolation of the wilderness where Herod's fort and the fort at Masada are built for protection. But not far from there lies the earthly paradise of Jericho."

Zacharias told Jesus of how the tropical fruits and balsam wood that grew in Jericho made its air smell like perfume. It was no wonder that Herod the Great had built a theatre and amphitheatre behind its walls, and Archelaus had built a palace surrounded by splendid gardens.

"And once the pilgrims reach Jericho," said Zacharias, "they can almost hear the sacred sound of the trumpets from the Temple Mount in Jerusalem."

"We hopefully should hear the sounds of Jerusalem before long," Joseph told them. He wanted to cheer up Mary who looked very tired.

"Rabbi, what lies to the south of Jerusalem?" asked Jesus.

"The wilderness of Judea, solitary shepherds, hiding outlaws, fanatic holy men, and caves with the most precious dust in Palestine," answered

Zacharias. "Those limestone caves were the hiding place of David and his followers and are now the home of the Essenes, the holiest of men who seek a pure life separate from the world."

Joseph tried to press them on to reach Jerusalem ahead of the setting sun. But as the sun lowered in the sky, they were slowed by several hills that were each higher than the one before. Finally Mary and Zacharias could go no farther.

"When we reach the top of this hill, we'll stop for the night and enter the city in the morning," Joseph announced. "We'll still arrive in time for the start of the celebration of the Feast."

Once they had labored to the top of the last hill of the day, they were greeted by a large flock of sheep. The shepherds were already cooking over a fire and welcomed the four hungry and grateful pilgrims with an invitation to join their meal. When the shepherds asked the rabbi to bless their food, Mary reminded Zacharias that on the road, prayers were short.

The shepherds told their guests that they had brought their sheep here, as they did every year, to sell to the pilgrims for the many sacrifices the worshippers would be making for the Feast of the Passover. When they mentioned they lived near the watchtower outside of Bethlehem, Joseph told them that he too was originally from Bethlehem and that his son Jesus had been born there.

In the glow of the firelight, an old shepherd who was almost blind looked up quickly and cocked his cloudy eyes in Joseph's direction.

"How old is your son?" he asked Joseph.

"He is twelve and has come to Jerusalem for his first Passover Feast. He is sitting right here, my friend. Give a greeting to this good shepherd, Jesus."

"The peace of the Lord to you and my thanks to you for your kindness to us," Jesus said to the old man.

The shepherd abruptly set down his food and asked Joseph, "How is it your son was not killed by Herod's murderers like the rest of our sons?"

An uneasy silence fell over them before Joseph answered.

"We luckily were given a warning and left before the killing started."

The old shepherd said no more during the rest of the supper. His squinted eyes often turned to Jesus.

After their supper was finished, the tired travelers started settling in for much needed rest. Jesus was spreading out his bedroll when he noticed someone standing behind him. He looked up and saw the old shepherd.

"Walk with me, young man. Take my arm and lead me up that hill," the old man pointed his shepherd's crook toward Jerusalem. Jesus took his arm, and the two started climbing a path through groves of olive trees lit by the light of the full moon above.

"What is this place?" Jesus asked him.

"It is the Mount of Olives," he answered. "It is sacred ground. People have been buried here for a thousand years."

As they neared the top of the hill, the shepherd said to him, "We have met before, Jesus."

"I don't think that could be," responded Jesus. "This is my first time in Judea."

"No, you were born in Bethlehem. I met you there not long after you were born," the shepherd replied.

Jesus was wondering how this could have been possible, when they reached the end of a ridge at the crest of the hill. Looking into the distance, Jesus' breath stopped. There below them on the next hill were the lights of Jerusalem.

Torches burned brightly at the gates and palaces and monuments. Even from this distance, he could see throngs of pilgrims moving about. But standing above them all, stood the Temple on the Mount. Hundreds of torches lit up its snow white marble. The land within the Temple's walls alone looked to be as big as all Nazareth.

Reaching high up above the Temple walls was the Holy Place, an edifice so tall and large it was as if its flat roof was a seat for God to sit upon the earth. Even in the distance, Jesus saw the gold on its huge doors glittering in the torch light.

They sat down and for a long while took in the beauty of the city before them. Jesus had wondered often what Jerusalem would be like, but it was far beyond anything he imagined.

"The lights are so beautiful," Jesus finally remarked with awe. "Can you see them?" he asked the shepherd.

"Oh yes. I can see the light in the dark," he replied. "When you become so old that your eyes start to fail, sometimes only then can you see some things very clearly for the first time."

His statement made Jesus curious.

"What can you see better with old eyes that have grown weaker?" he asked.

"My purpose," the shepherd answered. "Looking at my life, I can now see clearly that a shepherd has one purpose—to nourish and protect his flock. A good shepherd will lay down his life for his sheep.

"Everyone has a purpose," he went on. "The question is, when they finally see it, are they willing to lay down their life for their purpose."

They sat in silence for a few moments looking into the distance at the torch lights of the city on the hill. A warm breeze touched their faces.

"What is your purpose, Jesus?" the shepherd asked.

Jesus saw the shepherd's eyes close, waiting for an answer. Jesus wondered what purpose he could ever have for which he would be willing to die.

"My eyes are not yet old enough to see that well."

The old shepherd smiled.

"Well, tomorrow you will enter the gates of Jerusalem for the first time. Perhaps there you will learn your purpose."

Jesus felt a shiver of excitement. Tomorrow he would be in Jerusalem. As Jesus looked off at the torches burning brightly at those gates, he could see long lines of pilgrims backed up a great distance before the gates they were trying to enter. He could not wait to walk through the gates of Jerusalem.

At the end of a great journey, one is even more excited than at its beginning.

**

When thousands of weary pilgrims finally reached the gates of Jerusalem that night, they were stopped by several Roman soldiers standing alongside the city guards. None could pass through the gates until they each answered two questions asked by the soldiers on the order of Pontius Pilate.

"Are you from Bethlehem or Nazareth? Do you have a son?"

Chapter 16

THE TETRARCH

It was a grand entrance attended by almost everyone in the city. Those people standing next to the road threw palm branches of welcome on the path and the rest of the crowd clapped out of curiosity, respect and fear.

But then, they had been paid to lay down the palm branches given to them by Herod Antipas's secret police who had also ordered the people to clap when Herod Antipas arrived in Nazareth. The large sleek black stallion on which Herod was mounted did not like walking on the palm branches below its hooves any more than the people liked placing them on Herod's path.

Herod Antipas gave the crowd a royal wave as if he were their king. But he was not. He was the Tetrarch of Galilee and Perea, the office of administrator given him by Caesar Augustus as suggested by his father's seventh will and testament. It irritated Herod Antipas to no end that after seven bumbling decisions by his father, he had ended up the administrator of some out-of-the-way farmlands and deserts rather than the sovereign of all Palestine appointed by God with Caesar's nod.

He had tried mightily and still intended to become the king of all the Jews. But first his father, and then his brothers Archelaus and Philip, and finally Caesar Augustus had thwarted his ambitions. Now his father was dead, Archelaus had been exiled to distant Gaul, Philip had managed to lose his wife and was off living happily in the north, and Caesar seemed willing to install any leader who could bring Palestine and the

Jewish rebels under control. Herod Antipas was ready with his army and secret police, and was willing to shed blood to show Caesar he was that leader.

Then his informants revealed that Pontius Pilate, Rome's "destroyer of rebellions," was secretly planning to keep the crown from going to Herod by removing him and making a boy from Nazareth the King. There were very few secrets in Palestine. The one secret he still needed to solve was the identity of that boy. Pilate's plan clearly was being executed carefully because neither Herod's informants nor his secret police had been able to locate the boy.

So Herod decided to take matters into his own hands during a visit to Nazareth while Pilate was away in Jerusalem for the Feast of the Passover. He had the perfect cover of a tour to review the construction of his new city Tiberius followed by a visit to Nazareth for an inspection of the recent fortification of the garrison. He did not like being exposed to threats from the dangerous and active rebels in Galilee, but he was relieved to avoid the dreadfully dull celebration of the Feast in Jerusalem. Above all else, he was in Nazareth to find the boy who would be King, and secretly do what was necessary to stop him.

Herod and his large entourage of guards and servants moved through Nazareth towards the garrison where they would be billeted. They passed the marketplace and then the lovely trees and pools around the well which Herod noted with interest. Carrying on through the town to its outskirts, they eventually reached the garrison. But there were no trumpets or lines of soldiers assembled to welcome him.

A Roman officer and a small complement of guards at the gate came to attention as Herod stopped to enter.

"Welcome, Herod Antipas, Son of Herod the Great and Tetrarch of all Galilee and Perea," the officer said with a salute. "I am Decimus, second in command after my commander Pontius Pilate. The Roman garrison at Nazareth is here for your protection."

When Herod rode through the gate into the parade ground, a dozen Roman soldiers divided into two short lines rendered a salute. He stopped and with a chagrined glance around the quiet and empty garrison looked down from his large black steed at the officer.

"Thank you for your welcome and your—protection," he said with a dismissive gesture at the soldiers. "I see that it is not Rome's strategy to defeat the rebels in Galilee by outnumbering them."

Herod's soldiers behind him laughed. Decimus turned red faced.

"My commander sends his regrets for not being here to meet you. He has taken the Legion to Jerusalem to give protection to over a million of your Lordship's people gathered for the religious celebration there. This garrison is strong and can defend you with very few men, Your Grace," he answered.

"Besides, it is the bravery, not the number of soldiers that ultimately protects your Lordship," Decimus added. His scornful look quickly removed the smiles of Herod's soldiers.

"If you will come this way, your Lordship," the officer pointed across the parade ground, "I will show you and your servants to your quarters." Cold looks again came from Herod's officers who did not like being referred to as servants.

Herod decided to let the insult of this unceremonious welcome pass since there was nothing to be done about it there and now. He dismounted from his tall horse with the help of several servants in their bright white tunics who scurried up to the black horse's side. Decimus was surprised to find that Herod only came up to the soldier's shoulders and was a bit plump under his robes. The Roman officer could see the curls of hair on Herod's head carefully arranged to cover areas where the hair was already thinning. Up close, the soldier could detect a flesh-colored salve on Herod's face to cover blemishes on his skin.

He handed his horse's reins to a servant.

"Take my horse back to the pools at the well. Give him a proper bath." Herod ordered. He walked to the horse's head and reached up to pet its nose.

"You've earned it, my handsome boy. Now give your Papa a kiss," Herod said to the strikingly beautiful animal. He took an apple from a servant who was standing ready to hand it to him, bit into it and held his face up so the horse could take the apple from his mouth. Herod clearly enjoyed the horse's lips and tongue exploring his face for the apple.

"Let me take you to your rooms, Your Grace," said Decimus with a look of distaste shared by the other Roman soldiers. Several more servants gathered around to escort Herod as he turned to follow the officer.

Chuza, the head of Herod's household, made his introduction to Decimus as they proceeded down the corridor lit by torches to the Tetrarch's chambers. Once he had seen all the rooms set aside for Herod's entourage, Chuza knew they would be a bit crowded for he was accompanied not only by the usual large number of personal servants, but also extra secret police and soldiers. Herod had a small frown as he inspected the plain rooms where he would be staying until they walked through the next door. His face took on a look of sheer admiration. Chuza and his servants stood speechless.

There before them, hidden away in this plain and efficient fort, were baths that were luxurious enough for a king's palace. One in particular caught Herod's fancy. Its tiles were like a work of art, and it was big and deep enough that a bather would have to swim. Chuza kneeled down and dipped his hand in the water.

"It's warm, my Lord," he informed the much impressed Tetrarch.

* * *

Peter and Maggie walked up to the pools around the well and sat down under the trees. His tunic was slightly askew, and there was grass from the hills outside of Nazareth on the back of Maggie's headscarf. No sooner had he sat down then he was back up kneeling forward on one knee.

His eyes caught sight of a spectacular black stallion tied to a tree by one of the pools. By far the largest horse he had ever seen, it looked like an oversized statue carved out of shiny black marble except for the swishing of its long tail and the occasional quiver of a heavy muscle under its thick mane. Peter was smitten by its astonishing beauty and strength.

Around the horse's flanks came a servant who moved to the other side of the horse to brush its coat. His white tunic created a bright contrast against the horse's ebony coat as he reached up to slap the brush against its haunches and vigorously stroked it downwards. After each brush stroke on the horse, the afternoon sun reflected off its sleek coat like small flashes of lightening. The horse slowly picked up its front right hoof and then suddenly stomped the ground. Even with the distance between them, Peter could feel the horse's power through the earth where he was kneeling.

"Have you ever seen anything so beautiful?" he said to Maggie. Although slightly jealous at the question, Maggie had to admit that she had not.

Another servant wearing a white tunic arrived from the direction of the Wine Seller Shikkor's shop. He held up a newly purchased wineskin to the other servant who tossed his brush to the ground, grabbed the wineskin and threw his head back to drink deeply. When the wineskin eventually came down, the second servant took back the wineskin for his turn at a long swig. They happily climbed over a low wall nearby the pools and sat behind it to continue drinking in its shade.

"Come on!" said Peter as he grabbed Maggie's hand and pulled her to her feet.

They walked over to the horse and circled it with admiring looks. Peter glanced over at the wall. The two servants were busy drinking and could not see Peter from where they sat facing the opposite direction with their backs against the wall. He stepped over to the horse and reached up to pat its neck.

"Come over and give him a pet," he whispered and waved at Maggie.

Maggie stepped up and rubbed her hand over the horse's soft nose. Its lips played with her fingers without biting. Suddenly the horse lifted its head and its ears went back. Maggie raised her eyes and saw Peter sitting on the horse's back holding its halter rope that he had untied from the tree.

"What are you doing, Peter?" she said in a frightened whisper as she looked over her shoulder at the wall that hid the servants. They carried on drinking without noticing a thing.

"I'm just sitting on its back," Peter replied. "He's huge! You can see everything from up here. Come up and have a look."

Maggie shook her head. "Peter, come down!" she urged, glancing once again at the wall.

"He's so beautiful! What an animal! Come up here—just for a moment," he repeated.

She hesitated, slightly fearful but excited. Then the horse shook its head up and down as if to say it was all right. So she grabbed Peter's hand and pulled herself up. It took some doing to scramble up the tall horse, but she finally made it and was mounted behind Peter. He was right. They were sitting high above the height of a man's head, and the ground seemed very far below them. Her legs could feel the warmth and immense strength of the animal. Peter gave the horse a little kick with his heels.

"What are you doing?" she whispered to Peter.

"Let's just walk him around the pool and back. The servants won't even know he's been gone."

Peter gave the horse another little kick, but it still did not move. He broke a small switch off a branch of the tree above him.

"Peter—don't!" she warned, but it was too late. He gave the horse a little slap on the shoulder.

With a loud whinny, the horse reared up, standing high on its back legs and pawing at the air with its front hooves. The servants scrambled from behind the wall to see the horse's hooves hit the ground and immediately rear up again. Then they saw two figures fly off the horse's back through the air to the ground with a hard thump. They leaped over the wall and reached the horse at the same time two Roman soldiers who were passing by the well ran up to the two figures lying on the ground behind the horse.

Both Peter and Maggie had the wind knocked out of them from the fall. Struggling to breathe, neither of them heard the words hurriedly exchanged between the servants and the soldiers. But after their first breaths, they looked up to see two swords pointing at them and felt themselves being pulled roughly to their feet before being thrown back down to another hard landing on the ground.

* * *

Although he was eager to swim in the beautiful baths, Herod decided to tend first to his business as Tetrarch and hopefully dispense with the troublesome concerns that brought him to Nazareth. He sent out orders for the Pharisees on the local Sanhedrin to appear before him and had his servants prepare his robes for official business.

Several servants in their white tunics hovered around him. One servant stood by handing Herod pieces of fruit or sweets whenever the Tetrarch's open hand reached out. Another worked carefully to arrange the curls on his head while two more bathed his face and feet. Once his white robes with golden embroidery were placed over his shoulders, another servant swept in to apply more flesh colored salve to his face in careful strokes from a delicate brush made of the soft hair from a camel's belly. Finally, Chuza removed from a small chest a simple but elegant crown with brightly colored jewels around its base. It was Herod's business crown. He kept a much larger and ornate crown at his main palace for formal occasions and religious feasts.

Herod's messenger entered the room just as the Tetrarch finished examining himself in framed polished metal held by a servant girl.

"Ah, very good. You've returned just in time. I am ready to receive the Sanhedrin," Herod announced.

"The Sanhedrin are not here, my Lord," said the messenger. "They have all gone to Jerusalem to attend the Feast of the Passover."

A displeased look came over Herod.

"All of them? But they knew I was arriving today. Not one remained behind?"

"No, my Lord." The messenger answered. "But I do have a message that just arrived from your wife."

He pulled out an unusually large piece of sealed parchment. Herod sighed and rolled his eyes at the sight of another long missive from Herodias. One always arrived from her whenever he reached the next city in his travels.

"Take the message and read it to me, Chuza," he directed without enthusiasm.

Chuza broke the seal on the parchment, unfolded the letter and began to skim through its long paragraphs. Instead of reading the message, he summarized its points in the manner Herod preferred.

"She inquires about your health, your Grace, and says the children are well. The weather is—"

"Yes, yes, I know. Just tell me what she wants this time."

As Chuza detailed Herodias's demands for additional servants, Herod thought back to how he should have seen the warning signs from the beginning. Perhaps he had lowered his standards after being married to a Nabatean princess whose foreign ways and language had always got in the way of a complete and fulfilling relationship. But when he met Herodias, even though she was his niece and the wife of his step brother Philip, she seemed to be perfect for the wife he wanted who would share his needs and support his ambitions.

She was attractive, alluring and appreciative of nice things. What appealed to him most, however, was that she, like him, was desirous of power and was willing to use it. Her first husband, Philip, was a quiet man of simple pleasures and content simply to govern his lands to the north where nothing of any consequence happened. But Herodias was bored and going nowhere. She wanted more. She saw that Herod Antipas did too. It did not take long for her formidable powers of persuasion to convince Herod that he could divorce his foreign princess, safely risk his docile brother's wrath, marry her, and then all of Palestine could be theirs.

Herod now knew that there were signs he should have observed. When he told Philip that he and Herodias were going to divorce and marry, his brother showed no anger and did not even threaten revenge. Philip made a bit of a protest, but then immediately returned to his palace in Perea where he held a month-long feast with circuses and banquets. Not exactly mourning his loss was Philip.

At first, Herodias gave her new Tetrarch everything he wanted, but after a short while, Herod got everything he wanted only after Herodias got everything she wanted. After a while longer, he got less and less of what he wanted despite having to meet Herodias's increasing demands. He eventually found himself trapped for he could not divorce her so soon. He would have been completely unhappy in their marriage except for two important things. She would still excite him by sharing and encouraging his plots to become King of the Jews and ruler of all Palestine. And she never objected to his taking pleasure from the company of beautiful young girls. She sometimes even made arrangements for such pleasures. Whether at his main palace or traveling, Herod enjoyed himself through the selective efforts of Herodias and Chuza.

"She adds one more thing in her message, your Grace," Chuza read on. He waited until Herod's attention returned to his summary of the message from Herodias.

"Her Grace is fully convinced of Pilate's plot to remove you from power and make the boy born in Bethlehem King of the Jews, and firmly believes that he must be found and killed."

"She said that?" Herod asked. "She used the word 'killed'?"

"Yes, my Lord," confirmed Chuza. "She notes that the boy born in Bethlehem has been the only serious threat to claim the throne of the Herodeans since the beginning of their rule, and is surely a real threat now with his protection and advancement by Pilate. Consequently, if he now lives in Nazareth and cannot be found, she urges you, my Lord, to take the action that your father Herod the Great took when facing the same threat. She encourages you to kill all boys of his age in Nazareth."

Herod contemplated her advice for a few moments.

"And what do you think of this counsel, Chuza?"

"Her Grace is wise and seeks only to protect you and your rule, my Lord. Her loyalty is beyond reproach," he answered.

"Yes, I know, Chuza. But what do you see in her advice beyond her wisdom and loyalty?"

Chuza paused before answering.

"I am sure that if her Grace were reminded that your father's tactic apparently did not work previously, she might reassess its effectiveness. And if she weighed the effect of such action on the attitudes of those foolish people in Galilee who support the rebels and currently fail to appreciate the beneficent rule of your Grace, she might conclude that her preliminary recommendation might have the undesirable result of turning the affections of your subjects away from your Grace at this sensitive time."

"I see," responded Herod. "Would you please write her a message from me indicating that those are my grateful concerns about her selfless and loyal recommendation?"

"Yes, my Lord."

"And tell her the weather has been quite temperate," added Herod.

"Yes, my Lord. Would you like me to call in Nazeera?" asked Chuza. "He is waiting to brief you on the situation in Nazareth."

Herod told Chuza to call in the chief of his secret police. An air of unease fell on everyone in the room when the man came through the door. Below his receding line of long thin greasy hair were two slits with eyes that never stopped darting about. A long bony nose curved over his thin unsmiling lips. His lean angular body moved like a skeleton wearing a dingy white robe. Even Herod suppressed a shudder of revulsion as the man bowed low before the Tetrarch.

"Your trusted servant, my Lord. I am summoned," Nazeera announced in a breathless wheeze without a hint of trustworthiness.

At the beginning of these briefings, Herod always felt extremely relieved that the man worked for him and not any of his enemies.

"What is your report on the boy from Nazareth who is a threat to my crown?"

"My Lord, the Pharisees' reports of the plot to make a boy from Nazareth king have been confirmed once again. Pontius Pilate has been communicating with the Sadducees who have had repeated discussions about the boy. However, the Pharisees in Galilee have not provided any further information about the boy's identity or location. Nor have the Romans or Sadducees taken any actions which have revealed that information."

Herod's face took on a look of serious concern.

"Do you have any information on when this plot might be carried out?"

"No, my Lord. Consequently, we are taking extensive actions that should reveal the boy to us soon. We are starting tonight to undertake— shall I say— more 'serious' interrogations and searches now that I am here in Nazareth.

"In addition, we have been conducting extensive searches and interrogations of pilgrims in villages on the routes to Jerusalem through Perea, Samaria and Judea. Our agents are also actively infiltrating pilgrim gatherings and celebrations throughout the Feast in Jerusalem."

"But Samaria and Judea are not within my jurisdiction," replied Herod.

Nazeera's eyes darted back and forth several times before looking at Herod.

"Let us simply say, my Lord, that I failed to note that fact and recall my agents in a timely manner," he answered. His breath rattled in his chest before he went on.

"With your indulgence, my Lord, I'd like your permission to execute a few 'uncooperatives' to make the Nazarenes take notice of the importance of our inquiries."

"Do you really think that's necessary?" Herod asked.

"In light of how little information we've been able to obtain, I do, my Lord."

Herod furrowed his brow for a few moments.

"Were you thinking of a couple crucifixions?"

"Your Grace, I was thinking a few beheadings might be more effective."

The image of a beheading made Herod uncomfortable.

"Must you behead them? Beheadings are so unpleasant."

"But they are quick, my Lord. And they get the people's attention very effectively. I would prefer not to take several days necessary for death by crucifixion to make our point while we are in Nazareth."

Herod understood that the shedding of blood was an essential part of exercising power. But he did not like the sight of it and would never consider literally having blood on his hands. He did not even particularly like the idea that there was "blood on his hands" from taking the responsibility for bloodshed. But he played the game of power, and bloodshed was a fundamental part of that game. Anyone who played the game of power in Palestine knew that he risked the sight of blood, even his own. That was his greatest fear, the sight of his own blood, for he knew that the rebel zealots wanted it.

"All right, have them beheaded if you must," Herod consented. "But announce that it was done by authority of the local Sanhedrin," he added.

"But, my Lord," responded Nazeera, "the local Sanhedrin does not have the authority to order a beheading."

Herod looked irritated.

"Let us simply say the Sandedrin failed to note that fact and recall my soldiers in a timely manner," he answered.

Nezeera nodded with an approving look.

"And what of the rebels?" Herod next asked Nazeera.

"The rebels in Galilee are continuing to increase the number and violence of their attacks. Fortunately for us, they seem to be targeting Roman forces principally and not your troops or palaces. However, there continue to be reports from informants, as I warned you before coming here, that extreme violent elements of the rebels are targeting ruling officials for attacks and possible assassination."

"The Sicarii?" asked Herod.

"Yes, my Lord. They see no difference between your rule and the Romans."

A shudder ran up Herod's spine. He was certain the image of a figure appearing silently out of nowhere with a deadly sharp dagger would haunt him once again that night as he tried to fall asleep. He secretly wished he had the courage of the Roman soldiers in the fort around him, but knew that he did not.

"But we are secure here in the garrison, aren't we? That was the plan in staying here."

"Most assuredly," answered Nazeera although he was thinking that no man in Palestine was safe from the murderous methods of the Sicarii. "The fortification of the garrison can protect you even with the undermanned Roman contingent, and your guards are always ready, my Lord.

"Will there be anything more, my Lord?" Nazeera asked.

Herod seemed distracted for a few moments, but then stopped chewing his thumbnail to respond.

"One final thing. When you find the boy from Nazareth, you know what to do with him, do you not?"

The man bowed low and with a final rasping breath answered, "I do indeed, my Lord. It shall be done."

Before Nazeera withdrew, one of Herod's officers hastily entered the room.

"My Lord, with your leave," he kneeled before Herod.

"What is it?" Herod asked.

"My Lord, two people were arrested for trying to ride your horse while it was being groomed at the pools."

"What? Was he hurt? Kill the horse thieves!" Herod sounded furious.

"Your horse is unharmed, my Lord," said the officer. "And I am told the boy and girl did not appear to be trying to steal the horse."

"Did you say a boy?" asked Nazeera.

"And a girl?" asked Herod.

"Yes, my Lord," answered the soldier.

"Is the boy from Nazareth?" Nazeera asked him.

"I believe so, sir."

"And what does the girl look like?" Herod asked him.

"She is very comely, my Lord."

"Bring them here immediately!" both men ordered simultaneously. As the officer hurried from the room, Nazeera immediately apologized for his affront in speaking over the Tetrarch's command. Herod ordered a servant to check on his horse and have the grooms who were in charge of the horse brought before him.

The officer returned with two soldiers who pulled their prisoners into the room. Peter and Maggie stood before Herod with their hands tied and looking frightened. The officer stepped over to them, grabbed each of them by the hair and pushed them to their knees.

"Kneel before your ruler, you Nazarene scum!" he ordered.

Herod rose from his chair and came over to where they were kneeling with their heads down. He stopped in front of Maggie and lifted her chin to look up at him. A loosened shock of her black hair fell across her closed eyes.

"You are a lovely, young thing. How could someone like you have—"

Herod stopped mid-sentence when Maggie opened her eyes and looked up at him through the strands of her hair. A surprised and pleased expression came over his face. He circled idly behind her and gently lifted her heavy braid to look at the back of her neck. He set her braid back down and lightly stroked her head.

"This poor girl has gotten dirty." He turned to a couple of his servant girls. "Take her to the baths and see that she is cleaned and refreshed."

Herod looked down into her face again.

"Go," he ordered gently with a smile. "They will take care of you."

The servant girls hurried over to help Maggie stand up and took her out of the room. Herod looked over at Peter and continued walking around him almost lazily, examining him up and down, until the Tetrarch was looking into his face. After a brief inspection, he smiled at Peter.

"Is that a beard or do you like imitating a camel with mange? You do the imitation very well."

The servants and soldiers starting laughing at Herod's mockery of the boy, when suddenly Herod lashed out with the back of his fist and struck Peter's face hard. Blood instantly starting streaming out of Peter's broken nose.

"That is for touching my horse with your filthy hands, you mangy animal!"

Nazeera could see that Herod's rage was not finished. He stepped up next to Herod.

"May I continue with him, your Grace?" he interrupted. When Herod stood there not answering, his lips pulled back and his jaw clenched in fury, Nazeera stepped between them and faced Peter.

"Do you live in Nazareth?" he asked Peter.

Wiping the blood from his nose with his tied hands, Peter nodded. Nazeera looked over at the officer who pulled his long sword out of its scabbard and pressed it against Peter's throat.

"Speak when you're spoken to!" the soldier ordered, his face in Peter's.

"Y—yes," Peter stammered.

"How old are you?" Nazeera continued.

"Thirteen," answered Peter. His voice broke with fear.

"Where were you born?"

"Capernaum."

Nazeera frowned.

"Do you know a boy in Nazareth, a special boy, who is known to the Romans and works with them?"

Peter's eyes involuntarily revealed a glimmer of acknowledgment and then quickly lowered.

"No," he mumbled.

"No, *sir*!" the soldier shouted in his face and pressed the sword against his neck more firmly.

"No, sir," repeated Peter in a choked voice.

Herod turned away and walked back to his chair after he saw some of Peter's blood run down onto the blade of the soldier's sword. But Nazeera had seen the hesitation in Peter's eyes and continued staring intently at him for another moment. Nazeera finally turned and went over to Herod.

"He knows something about the boy from Nazareth, my Lord," Nazeera whispered. "I saw it in his eyes. Let me take him away to interrogate him further."

Herod did not bother with a whisper.

"Get it out of him!" he ordered loudly. "Make him tell you what he knows!"

With a wave from Nazeera, the soldier quickly dragged Peter out of the room.

"My Lord," said Nazeera parting with a hasty bow as he followed them out.

"And when you're done, make sure he'll never forget your interrogation!" shouted Herod after them.

No one moved as Herod sat in his chair, staring ahead of him and breathing hard. A servant entered the room.

"The horse's grooms are here, my Lord."

"Take them to Nazeera," Herod snapped at the servant. "He'll know what to do with them."

After a while, his breathing calmed and his face softened. He rose from his chair.

"I do believe it's now time for a bath," he announced with a wink at Chuza.

Chapter 17

THE TEMPLE

The full moon lay low on the horizon, desperately holding on to the dark sky for those last moments before the rising sun would steal it back to start a new day. Jesus opened his eyes just as the moon surrendered the sky to the sun. The first calls from the hungry lambs for their mothers had awakened him. He rubbed the sleep from his eyes and rolled over to see the three silhouettes of Mary, Joseph, and Zacharias looking off towards Jerusalem.

Jerusalem. The thought sent a shiver of excitement through his body. Today on the eve of the Feast of Passover, he would leave the outer court of Rome's Palestine and walk through the gates of the inner sanctuary of the people of Israel.

He felt the edge of cool morning air against his skin as he threw back his bed roll and rose to his feet. Walking over to where the rabbi and his mother and father were standing, he heard them finishing a prayer as he arrived at their side. There was a tension behind their good-morning smiles and greeting.

The shepherds called everyone to the fire for breakfast. There was eagerness in the company's conversation as they talked of the day to come. For the shepherds, it would be the most profitable time of the year as they sold their lambs to the pilgrims for sacrifices at the Temple. The lambs were carefully selected for the sacrifices, neither less than eight days nor more than one year old, and free from all seventy-three blemishes forbidden in sacrificial lambs. The pilgrims were ready and eager customers willing to pay well for the select flock.

Zacharias seemed a little nervous even though he was returning to the familiar courts and chambers of the Temple where he had spent many years. Joseph looked forward to connecting with his friends among the pilgrims from Nazareth. Mary's excitement for her son's first Feast was distracted only by the kicking in her belly that reminded her of her next child's arrival. Jesus said very little, but his excitement grew as it fed off the energy in everyone's words.

Just as they started to rise to pack up their belongings before heading to the city, a young shepherd boy led the old blind shepherd up to the group. The old man held a young lamb resting comfortably in the warmth of his arms. He stood there silently for a moment as the group waited for him to speak.

"Jesus, come to me, my boy," he said. "This lamb is of the age for sacrifice, just weaned from its mother. It is without blemish. I give it to you for sacrifice at your first Feast of the Passover. Go with our blessing."

He handed the lamb to Jesus. After a small struggle from the uncertainty of being passed to another set of arms, the lamb soon settled into the protection of his new shepherd. Jesus thanked the old man and felt an immediate bond with the helpless little animal who had given itself completely to his care.

Once the three pilgrims from Galilee had packed up their things and the shepherds had gathered their flock, they all headed over the crest of the Mount of Olives towards the gates in the walls of Jerusalem. The thrill of seeing Jerusalem was as great for Jesus in the daylight as the night before. The sunshine revealed the bright flowers of early spring, the dark green leaves of the olive trees and the white tents dotting the grass around the city walls. Lines of pilgrims, singing psalms and eager to worship, wound their way towards the city gates that led to the Temple where rising up majestically from its walls and courts was the Holy Place, God's own sanctuary with its dazzling snow white marble and gold that reflected the slanting rays of the sun.

The shepherds were working hard to keep their flock together among the travelers and camps along the road to the city gate. Joseph left Zacharias with Mary and the donkeys and went to help the shepherds. Jesus walked along carrying his lamb and helping keep the sheep from straying. The flock moved slowly but steadily past the long lines of frustrated pilgrims who were waiting hours to enter through the city gates.

When the shepherds finally reached the gate to the city, they saw the reason for the long delay. A large number of Roman soldiers were stopping every pilgrim entering the city with the questions about the pilgrims' home and whether they had sons or male relatives around the age of twelve years. Those pilgrims who gave any reason for suspicion were taken away for further questioning. As a result, the thousands upon thousands of pilgrims entering the city walked through the gates one at a time, instead of in a smooth flowing line.

The Roman officer in charge of the guard at the gate frowned at the shepherd who asked about entry of the flock of sheep. He was as frustrated by the crush of pilgrims as the irritated travelers who stood for hours before answering the guards' questions. Now he had a flock of noisy, nervous sheep to deal with on top of the impatient crowds.

"They are for tomorrow's sacrifices," the shepherd informed the officers. "We have to get them to the Temple so that the pilgrims can pick out their sacrifice today while they can before the first Holy Day of the Feast."

The Roman officer was smart enough to know that there would be more trouble if he were held responsible for limiting the sacrifices in the Temple than for delaying the entry of the pilgrims. He ordered his guards to clear the pilgrims out of the gate so the shepherds could move the flock through.

"Get 'em through fast!" the officer barked at the shepherds.

The shepherds scrambled to hurry the sheep through the gate without losing any strays. Among the shepherds, Joseph used his walking stick to help keep the animals together, and Jesus looked just like one of the shepherd boys as he carried his lamb among the sheep. Once through the gate, Joseph looked back at Zacharias and Mary on their donkeys behind the flock. The blind old shepherd and a shepherd boy were at their side.

A guard raised his hand to stop them as they followed the sheep into the gate. The old shepherd looked up and squinted at the Roman soldier.

"They're with us," the old man growled at the guard as he gave the donkey a slap on the rump to get it moving.

Before the soldier could protest, the irritated pilgrims in the line behind crowded back up to the gate. The harried soldier decided to let it go.

"Watch your step, Rabbi" the guard said to Zacharias, pointing at the sheep droppings with the end of his spear.

"I will indeed, young man," answered Zacharias. "So I will."

The rabbi and Mary caught up with Joseph and Jesus as they were giving the shepherds a final thank-you for their hospitality and gift. Mary and Joseph took the old blind shepherd aside and spoke with him quietly for a few moments before exchanging an emotional embrace and blessings. Jesus came up, petting the lamb in his arms, and thanked the old man once more for the gift of the lamb.

"The first of my flock," said Jesus proudly to show the old shepherd his gratitude. The old man seemed choked up, and could only give him a small wave.

As the shepherds moved off, Jesus stood next to Zacharias with eyes wide at the sight of the city filling with crowds of passing pilgrims. There were people everywhere. Once through the gate, most were singing and talking excitedly, although many were silent in awe or reverence from their first time in the "city of our God." Jesus had never seen so many in one place. There were more people on the crowded street ahead of him than in the market on a busy day in Nazareth.

"How many people could there be here?" Jesus wondered.

"Well, about six hundred thousand people live in the city, and over two million pilgrims come for the Feast," replied Zacharias.

Jesus could not imagine those numbers of people, let alone in one place. He tightened his hold on the lamb in his arms.

"How do you know that, Rabbi? Does someone count them all?"

"No, Jesus," replied Zacharias with a smile. "But the priests of the Temple do count the lambs that are sacrificed. In my last year in the Temple, there were over 256,000 lambs sacrificed, and there is one lamb sacrificed for each company of at least ten to twenty people. We also know the Temple can hold about 210,000 people. Then there are the taxes collected by the priests for entering the Temple. So the priests can calculate the numbers of worshippers from all these figures."

"The priests collect taxes from the worshippers in the Temple?" Jesus asked.

"Yes, the High Priest has that power from the Romans."

Jesus frowned as he contemplated this information, when Joseph and Mary joined them.

"We are going right to the home at which we will be staying," announced Joseph. "I want Mary to rest before supper.

"Will you be all right going to your lodging, Rabbi?" he asked Zacharias.

"Oh yes," replied Zacharias. "My friends have a lovely home not far away."

Once they agreed on when and where they would meet for the sacrifices the next day, Zacharias and Joseph's family moved off in opposite directions.

"Where are we staying, Father?" Jesus asked. In all the excitement, it had not occurred to him to ask.

"We're staying at the home of Abbas and his wife Imma. Your mother and I have stayed there for some years when we come to the Feast. They are a very nice family with a son about your age."

"Where do all these other pilgrims stay?" wondered Jesus.

Joseph explained that many of the pilgrims camped outside the city walls, but within the walls of Jerusalem, pilgrims found accommodations in a remarkable manner. The city did not belong to a particular tribe of Israel, but was considered equally the home of all Jews. Out of that view arose the tradition that homes and rooms were offered without charge to pilgrims as brothers and sisters. He pointed to a curtain hanging at the entrance to a house which indicated that there was room for guests, and a table spread in front told visitors that food was available. In exchange for the hospitality, pilgrims would offer the skins of the sacrificed lambs or vessels they had used in the sacred services in the Temple.

"I usually do some work and repairs on Abbas and Imma's home to help out," Joseph added. "Here we are," he pointed to a house that looked like it needed some work. Mary looked relieved when they finally arrived.

"Look at you!" Coming out the door, Imma welcomed Mary by pointing at her pregnant belly. A pleasant, plump woman holding a baby over her shoulder, she apparently had been in the same condition not long before. Several other small children scurried to her side when they heard their mother's greeting.

"Welcome, good Joseph," she beamed at him. "Did you bring your tools?"

"Of course I did, Imma," he smiled at her.

"And this must be Jesus."

She walked right up to him, and despite the baby in her arms and the lamb in his, gave him a big hug. The lamb started kicking and the baby started crying which she did not seem to mind or even notice. The little children hanging onto her skirts stared with curiosity at Jesus and his lamb.

"Why, you're just as tall as my oldest. Where is that boy?"

Imma turned and called over her shoulder into the house.

"Barabbas! Come out here and meet our new guest."

A stocky, strong-looking boy stepped out into the sunshine.

"Jesus, this is my son Barabbas."

The two boys gave each other a nod as they sized up one another. Barabbas looked at the lamb in Jesus' arms.

"Are you a shepherd or something?" Barabbas asked him.

"No," answered Jesus. He did not like the way the question sounded from Barabbas. "He was a gift from a shepherd for sacrifice at the Temple."

Before Barabbas could say anything more, a man came up behind them from the street.

"Well it looks like Nazareth is missing its finest carpenter," the man exclaimed loudly.

"Abbas!" Joseph greeted him with a hearty handshake.

"Joseph, my good friend," he replied. "And I see you've been working with more than wood and stone," the gregarious man said as he took Mary's hands and smiled at her pregnant belly. Mary blushed. Abbas was the only man who ever dared to tease her, and the only man from whom Mary would tolerate it.

"Who is this fine looking young man?" Abbas turned to Jesus. "Another carpenter from Nazareth? I certainly hope so. Joseph should have some competition. Jesus, my name is Abbas." He shook Jesus' hand as best he could with the lamb in Jesus' arms.

"A sacrifice for the Feast, Jesus?" Abbas nodded at the lamb.

"Yes, sir."

"Very good. Barabbas, take Jesus out back and show him where he can keep his lamb until tomorrow. Now, Joseph, did you bring your tools?"

Barabbas led Jesus out back to a small space where the lamb could be tied up. Once the lamb was safe and drank some water, Barabbas turned to Jesus.

"Come on," Barabbas said to Jesus as he headed for the alley behind the house. "Let me show you some of Jerusalem. I'll take you to where we can drop pebbles on the helmets of the Roman soldiers."

Jesus followed him, excited to see the city but unsure about doing anything involving Roman soldiers.

"Do you have Roman soldiers in Nazareth?" Barabbas asked Jesus.

"Yeah. They're building a new garrison."

"Don't you hate the Romans?"

Jesus decided not to mention that he and Joseph were doing work on the building of the garrison. "Well, I wish they would go home to their own country."

Barabbas led Jesus though the crowds of people in the narrow streets as easily as if he were dodging trees in a forest. As they climbed in a sort of circle, Jesus saw deep ravines on three sides of the city which made it look like a fortress. Another valley ran right through the center of the city. Around this valley were hills that looked almost like islands. On the slopes of these hills, Jesus could see rising terraces with people bustling down streets to houses, market shops and bazaars. As his gaze moved up the hills, he saw many palaces until his eyes reached the white marble of the Temple behind its tall walls on the Temple Mount above the city.

Jesus hoped that they would go closer to the Temple, but Barabbas headed the other direction. The boys stopped when they reached a low stone wall that looked down quite a distance to the ravine below. Barabbas picked up a handful of pebbles and peeked over the wall.

"The Roman soldiers usually travel back to their quarters on this road. They can't see us up here when we drop pebbles on their helmets."

He looked over the wall in both directions on the road below for targets. Then he noticed that Jesus had not picked up any pebbles.

"Are you scared?"

"No."

Barabbas snorted. "I think you're afraid of the Romans."

"I am not! In fact, my friends and I snatched the helmet from the head of the new commander of the garrison in Nazareth."

"Really?" responded Barabbas. "Did they chase you?"

"Of course," replied Jesus. "When they didn't catch us, I walked right up to the commander, gave him back his helmet, and ran off again without getting caught."

Barabbas was doubtful. "What did the helmet look like?"

Once Jesus described the helmet in detail, Barabbas was much impressed. He had tried to drop pebbles on such helmets worn by Roman officers in Jerusalem many times. They waited a while, but no Roman soldiers passed below.

"I wonder where all the soldiers are?" the disappointed Barabbas asked. "We'd better head home for dinner or we'll be in trouble with my mother," he said finally.

When the boys returned home, everyone was busy preparing for the evening meal and the holiday ahead. Mary, with a worried look, asked Jesus where he had been and seemed relieved when he told her what Barabbas had shown him of the city. He went out back to check on his lamb and was pleased when the lamb's stubby tail wagged fast with happiness from seeing him.

Abbas summoned everyone to the supper table. After eating, when they were settled, he announced that it was the duty of Abbas and Joseph, as the head of their households, to retell the history and rituals of the Feast of Passover.

Joseph then told them that the Feast of the Passover was the most important of three festivals for which all males in Israel were commanded in the second book of Moses to appear before the Lord in the place He would choose. The feast they would celebrate, Joseph explained, was actually two religious feasts combined, the Feast of the Passover and the Feast of the Unleavened Bread.

The Feast of the Passover, as they had all been taught, was to celebrate God's sparing the first-born children from the plague that fell on Egypt for enslaving Israel. The plague passed over the homes where there was the blood of a spring lamb on the doorpost. The Feast of Unleavened Bread came from the command from God to Moses that only bread made with bitter herbs and without yeast—unleavened bread—would be eaten for seven days. "*'On the first day remove the yeast from your houses, for whoever eats anything with yeast in it from the first day through the seventh must be cut off from Israel,'*" said Joseph quoting Moses.

"So there are three symbols in the Passover," he concluded. "The Passover lamb, the unleavened bread, and the bitter herbs. The Passover lamb means that God passed over the blood-sprinkled on the houses of our fathers in Egypt; the unleavened bread means that our fathers were delivered out of Egypt in haste; and the bitter herbs mean that the Egyptians made bitter the lives of our fathers in Egypt."

Abbas next explained that on the first and then on the seventh and last day of the Feast, there would be special services for worship at the Temple according to the law set down in the Torah. No work was to be done on those days except the preparation of food.

"The first day of the Feast is devoted mainly to special sacrifices which start midday and last much of the afternoon. The last day of the Feast is also a special day for us."

Abbas gestured to Jesus.

"Our Yeshua will be in the service and will read and give a testimony before the High Priest of the Temple."

Jesus blushed at the respectful attention of everyone in the room, and felt a little nervous when reminded of his responsibility.

"Tomorrow morning on the first day of the Feast," Abbas continued, "the priests of the Temple will lay two cakes with leaven on a porch of the Temple as an offering of thanks. While the two cakes lay there, we are still permitted to eat leavened bread. But when one of the cakes is removed just before the mid-day meal, no one is then permitted to eat leavened bread. And when the second cake is taken away, everyone is required to burn their leaven.

"So tonight it is very important," Abbas held up a candle and all the children grew excited, "that we search for and find all the yeast and leaven in the house so that tomorrow we do not eat leavened bread, not even a single crumb, and can burn the leaven when the priest takes away the second cake. All right, come up and let's start our search!"

The children eagerly crowded around him. He let one of his children light the candle, told his youngest that she would help him hold the candle, and then whispered his next instructions.

"We must look everywhere where yeast or any leavened bread might be kept or where even the crumbs of leavened bread might have fallen. To be sure that not even a single crumb is missed, we must search in strict silence to be careful. When you find any leavened bread, you must bring it to me and place it in this basket that I will put in a safe place where none of it can be used or taken by accident. Is everyone ready?"

The children nodded. Their serious looks indicated the importance with which they viewed their task.

"Let's go," whispered Abbas who turned and started their search. The silence in the candlelight created as much excitement as if they were hunting wild game in the wilderness. When a child found a small piece of bread, many of which were conveniently left out by Imma, it was held up in jubilant silence like a trophy from a great contest and then placed carefully in the basket held by Abbas so that not a crumb was lost. After a while, it looked like the search might be over, when suddenly Abbas stood up and hurried over to a far corner near the cooking fire where he reached down in the corner and held up a crumb for all to see before placing it carefully in the basket. He gave the children a look of relief, as if he had narrowly avoided a catastrophe, so that they renewed their search in earnest for even the tiniest crumb.

Every speck of dust became a target. After a few more crumbs, no further contributions were found for the basket held by Abbas. He broke the silence by asking each of the children one by one whether they had found all the leavened bread that could be found. Once they had each answered, Abbas held up the basket and announced, "All the leaven that is in my possession, that which I have seen and that which I have not seen, be it null, be it accounted as the dust of the earth."

With the end of the children's hunt, the three pilgrims from Nazareth all realized how tired they were from their long journey. Mary excused herself to prepare for bed, while Joseph went to check on the donkeys and Jesus went out back to see that his lamb was all right. Sound asleep, the little animal barely stirred as Jesus sat down next to it and laid its head on his lap. He petted the lamb gently as he watched the large round moon in the sky. Despite the many thoughts and scenes from the last few days racing through his mind, his hand soon grew still on the tiny warm body as both of them breathed deeply in restful sleep.

* * *

It was the fourteenth day of the month of Nisan, the day of the full moon and the first day of the Feast of Passover. Mary, Joseph, and Jesus with his lamb held tightly in his arms went with Abbas and Imma to meet up with Zacharias to go to the Temple for the sacrifices that would begin midday. Among the huge throng of people moving towards the Temple Mount on the eastern edge of the holy city, it was not easy to spot the rabbi. But eventually they saw him standing with Judas and Judas's father, Simon Iscariot.

Moving slowly behind Zacharias in the great crowd of pilgrims, they finally reached the Royal Bridge which led to the Temple walls. The bridge with its arches was itself colossal as it spanned the Tyropoeon

Valley far below to connect the ancient city with the Temple Mount. Joseph, with the detailed attention of a carpenter, told them as they crossed that the Royal Bridge was over one hundred fourteen full paces long and almost twenty paces broad, and its arches each spanned almost fifteen full paces. Underneath them, the stones he pointed to were each eight full paces long.

The Royal Bridge brought them to the western wall of the Temple where the pilgrims were turned to head for the Temple's southern wall. There they entered the Temple through the Hulda Gates. Once through the gates, they climbed the stairs to cloisters underneath double rows of marble pillars that ran along the temple walls as far as they could see.

"Taller than six men and each cut out of a single block of marble," Joseph announced. But then they reached a set of even taller pillars.

"A treble colonnade of one hundred sixty-two pillars arranged in four rows of forty pillars each. Taller than eight men," observed Joseph. "Plus those two at the end which are the entrance to—"

"The Royal Portico—the site of the ancient palace of Solomon," Zacharias excitedly finished Joseph's sentence.

They came into an aisle about ten paces wide lined by pillars twice as tall as the pillars they had just passed. Passing through the aisle, they entered a central nave and stopped, looking up along with all the other pilgrims in complete awe at the ceiling that was held up by gigantic pillars three times as tall as the pillars they had first passed.

"It would take twenty men standing on each other's shoulders to touch that ceiling," Joseph told them.

Jesus stood there with the others, staring up at the tops of the massive pillars. He had worked on many projects with his father, but had never realized that emotions like he was experiencing could come from a building. Feeling a hand on his shoulder, he looked at Zacharias.

"We must move on," said the Rabbi, "or we'll be late for the sacrifices."

From the hushed reverence of the Royal Portico, they passed back into the sunlight shining over a mass of people and activity in a great square courtyard which Zacharias told them was the Court of the Gentiles. Jesus had expected that the celebration of the Passover in Temple would be a solemn occasion, but here the noise was overwhelming. Though their feet stood on multicolored marble stones, the Temple court felt more like a marketplace. The square was completely filled with pilgrims buying sacrificial sheep, oxen and doves, Levites who worked in the Temple coming and going from their apartments that lined the walls around the courtyard, and priests hurrying from all directions to position themselves for the coming ceremonies.

Then Jesus felt himself being moved with the others to the right where they stood in lines before men sitting behind long tables. Levites walked along the lines reminding the men that Temple rules require that no money shall be tied to them in a purse and the tribute must be in their hand to enter.

"Why are we standing in line here, Father?" Jesus asked Joseph.

"All males entering the Temple must have in their hand a half shekel tribute to pay for the cost of the Temple's activities, and we must exchange our money here with the money changers for the Temple shekels. They are the only coins that can be spent within the Temple walls," he explained.

"The Temple shekels now cost twice what our regular shekels are worth, so the half shekel tribute now costs two denarii," complained Abbas. "And the money changers are charging us a silver meah on every half a denar they exchange."

"That's a one-fourth of a denar!" exclaimed Joseph. "Two denarii for the tribute for me and also for Jesus and a quarter of a denar for the money changers—that's a week's wages for me."

Jesus could not believe what he had just heard.

"Rabbi," he turned to Zacharias. "Does the Torah require us to pay to worship God in the Temple?"

"No. But the priests of the Temple do," he admitted.

They moved forward through the press of people in the Court of the Gentiles until they passed through a beautifully ornamented marble screen about as high as their chests. Inscribed on the marble in Greek and Latin was a warning to Gentiles not to proceed past the screen upon penalty of death. Just beyond this warning, they reached a flight of fourteen steps that led up to a terrace.

"This is the *Chel*," Zacharias told them. "It forms a boundary around the inner wall of the Temple. There are nine gates into the three courts in the Sanctuary. Each court is higher and smaller than the one before and leads to the Holy Place and the Most Holy Place. Only the priests of the Temple are allowed in the Holy Place, and only the High Priest is allowed once a year to enter by himself the Most Holy Place."

They came to a gate with massive ornamented brass doors at the top of twelve steps.

"The Beautiful Gate," Zacharias announced. "It takes the strength of twenty men to open and close it."

"And this is the Court of the Women," he told them. Through the gate they saw a court surrounded by a colonnade of tall columns. Along three sides of the court was a raised gallery. "Except for sacrifices, women are not allowed to proceed further into the Sanctuary. They take their place in the gallery around this court where all can worship in common."

His words were interrupted by a blast of trumpets. They looked up to see priests with silver trumpets next to the altar standing above in one of the Sanctuary courts ahead of them below the towering Holy Place.

"We are here just in time," said Zacharias. "Watch the Gate of Nicanor." He pointed to a large copper gate sitting at the top of fifteen semi-circular stairs.

The trumpets sounded a herald signal seven times, each signal a short blast followed by a longer tone and then another short blast. When the silver trumpets were lowered, the copper gate slowly opened. In the sky behind, a column of black smoke rose as more wood was thrown into the eternal flame of the altar for the coming sacrifices. A line of several hundred barefooted priests in white robes filed out followed by the High Priest in his resplendent robes.

The High Priest raised his arms to pray. All the worshippers stood and turned towards the Holy Place, drawing their feet together and crossing their arms over their breasts to stand with fear and reverence as a servant before his master. At the end of each of his prayers, they responded by saying "Blessed be the name of the glory of His Kingdom forever." When he finished, the priests began moving into the crowd of worshippers to lead them up the stairs into the next court for the sacrifices.

Jesus once again expected a somber ritual, but with the thousands of pilgrims there to offer their sacrifices, the noise of the bleating sheep and the priests giving instructions to the worshippers, he could barely hear Zacharias.

"Through the Gate of Nicanor, we will enter a single court that is divided in two by a low wall. We will be in the Court of Israel to offer our sacrifice. The priests will take our sacrifice up the two steps to the Court of the Priests where we will watch the sacrifice on the altar before the Holy Place."

After they entered the Court of the Women under the close inspection of the Temple guards looking for the unclean who were forbidden to enter, a young priest came up to them and after a blessing instructed the group to follow him to the Court of Israel. When they entered the Court of Israel, Jesus saw a flurry of organized movements urged on each group of ten to twenty pilgrims. He looked up at Zacharias who, despite all the noise of blessings, prayers and instructions to the worshippers, was calm and composed. He tried to look at the Holy Place and the immense altar of white unhewn stones rising high above, but was interrupted when the young priest moved them to the right where they were stopped at the steps to the Court of Priests and given to another priest.

Even with all the commotion, the lamb in Jesus' arms rested quietly in their warmth and protection. The priest reached over and took the lamb away from Jesus. When the lamb struggled, Jesus instinctively wanted to take his lamb back into his grasp. But the priest firmly held the squirming lamb and instructed each of the men to look to the west, lay a hand on the animal and repeat a prayer after him.

"I entreat, O Jehovah; I have sinned, I have done perversely, I have rebelled, I have committed trespasses; but I return in repentance, and let this be for my atonement."

With their hands still on the lamb, the priest moved it upwards and downwards, then right to left. Then in a quick motion the priest handed the lamb to another priest. Jesus tried not to hear the lamb's frightened cries as he watched the priest pick up a gold vessel with a pointed bottom that prevented it from being set down when filled.

Suddenly the lamb went silent. Jesus looked over just as the hand of the other priest finished moving a knife across the lamb's throat and thrusting it upwards. The first priest adroitly moved the gold vessel to catch the blood as it flowed out of the small limp body.

Jesus stood there numbly watching the priests move efficiently through their practiced ritual. The first priest with the pointed cup walked up the long ramp to the altar at one corner and then the other where he twice dipped the forefinger of his right hand into the blood and sprinkled it with a motion of his thumb so that each time two sides of the altar were covered. As he poured the remaining blood from the cup at the base of the altar, the second priest skillfully finished skinning and cutting up the lamb leaving its innards in a pile. Some priests washed the meat and entrails and tossed sacrificial salt on the flayed sacrifice while the skin and fleece were carried away. Other priests came to take the meat to a nearby chamber for storage and the innards up to the altar where they were tossed on the fire and arranged for burning.

Another priest came up to lead them away walking backwards to the Gate of Nicanor where he told them to bow their heads as they left. But Jesus could not stop himself staring at the dozens of priests steadily shedding the blood of unblemished innocents for the sins of the pilgrims as the smell of burning flesh surrounded them and the smoke of the burnt innards billowed into the sky above.

Jesus did not hear the flutes or harps with the chorus of Levite boys singing their *Hallels* from the Psalms as he walked away. He could only hear the moment when his lamb went silent.

* * *

After the service ended at the Temple, the group along with Zacharias returned to the home of Abbas and Imma for the Paschal

Supper, named from the Hebrew word *pesach* for Passover. The Paschal Supper was the dinner to celebrate the Passover. It was a joyous occasion for which people dressed in their festive clothes to enjoy the meal with all its traditions. But while the food was being prepared, Zacharias noticed that Jesus was very quiet.

"Is something wrong, my son?" Zacharias asked when the two of them were alone.

"I was thinking about the sacrifice today, Rabbi. Was it really necessary to shed the blood of the lamb? What good did it do?" Jesus asked.

"The idea of sacrifice taught to us by Moses is punishment and forgiveness through substitution. In that way we receive atonement and redemption," answered Zacharias.

"But why take the life of an innocent and perfect lamb? Couldn't we offer money or the first fruits of harvest instead?"

"Real punishment is the giving of the life of the sacrifice which is in its blood. Without the shedding of blood, there is no remission of sin. It is the sprinkling of blood, made pure by the salt, and accepted by the priests at the altar which purifies and redeems us."

"I understand, Rabbi. But how can the priest taking the blood of lambs and oxen and doves day after day, again and again, take away sins? How are we redeemed by the blood of animals?"

Jesus had tears in his eyes from thinking of the lifeless body of the lamb, for which he as the shepherd was to lay down his life.

"Can't we do one sacrifice to God made pure by Him, without priests or temples, for all time?"

Before Zacharias could answer, the call came for everyone to come to the supper. Since the supper was a celebration of their people's deliverance from bondage, the first tradition was that everyone would sit or recline as they ate as free men do, and not eat while standing in the manner of slaves. Each person was given a space at the table with room to place their left elbow to rest their head and gesture with their right hand. The other tradition of the Paschal celebration was the wine. By custom, even the poorest in the land was to have at least four traditional cups during the meal.

Abbas, as the head of the household, began the supper by taking the first cup of wine, and giving thanks over it with the traditional prayer in which Jehovah their God was blessed for choosing and sanctifying them among all nations, and preserving and sustaining them to this season. The men then drank their first cup and washed their hands. The low table with the supper was brought before them. Next, Abbas took up some herbs from the table, dipped them in salt water, ate them and gave some to the others.

After this, the dishes and food curiously were removed from the table and the second cup of wine was poured before the next ceremonial event in which the head of the household fulfilled his obligation to explain the importance of Passover. This task was done by having his son recite certain questions which the father then answered.

Barabbas asked his father, "Why is this night different from all other nights? On all other nights we eat leavened or unleavened bread, but this night only unleavened bread. On all other nights we eat all kinds of herbs, but this night only bitter herbs. Why do we dip the herbs twice? On all other nights we eat meat roasted, stewed, or boiled, but on this night why only roasted meat?"

Abbas answered by telling the history of Israel from Abraham to Moses and the giving of the Law. When he had finished, the dishes of food were returned to the table. Abbas took each dish with the Passover lamb, the bitter herbs and the unleavened bread and explained why these dishes were chosen for the Paschal supper. Then the second cup of wine was drunk, their hands were washed again, and the prayer said earlier was repeated.

Next Abbas took one of two unleavened cakes and after breaking it into pieces, gave thanks. The thanksgiving was to follow the breaking of bread because it was the bread of the poor who have only broken pieces and not the whole cake. The pieces of bread and herbs were dipped by Abbas into a mixture of dates, raisins and vinegar and handed to each of them. The meal of unleavened bread, herbs and lamb was then eaten.

When they finished eating the lamb, their hands were washed once again and the third cup was poured. Then the last of the unleavened bread was blessed, broken, and eaten. A special prayer for the creation of the fruit of the vine was said over the third cup before it was drunk. The men were then permitted to drink wine that was not part of the rituals while they talked of the day's sacrifices and the coming week. Finally the formalities of the supper were concluded with the last cup over which a *Hallel* was sung from the Psalms.

Jesus watched quietly as the men finished drinking the fourth cup. They clearly were feeling its effects. As the dishes were being cleared, Abbas leaned over to fill their cups with the last of the wine.

"Drink up, Joseph, Rabbi. We cannot let the wine go to waste."

Joseph signaled for Abbas to stop.

"I can bear no more, Abbas. Please take this cup from me."

When he heard his father's words, Jesus wished he could use them to take from his memory the image of the priest's cup holding his lamb's blood.

* * *

The days that followed before the final service in the Temple were enjoyable for Jesus. With Barabbas, he and Judas explored the markets, palaces and gardens of the city. Zacharias took Jesus and Judas around the Temple to show them the innermost places where the priests and scribes did their work. They saw the Chambers in the Court of the Women where the tribute was stored in chests, the Chamber where the Great Sanhedrin met, and the largest stones over thirty-five paces long. They were not able to go up in the Tower of Antonia looking down upon the Temple because that was where the Roman army was headquartered in Jerusalem to keep a strategic eye on the heart of the nation of Israel. Jesus was not surprised that it took forty-six years for Herod the Great to build the vast Temple.

The week did not go as well for others. Pontius Pilate received no promising reports from the questioning by his soldiers at the gates to the city, and his pressuring of the High Priest and the Sadducees still produced no results. Herod's secret police had nothing to reply to Nazeera's repeated messages demanding news of the plot to make the boy from

Nazareth king. The vinedressers' nonstop searches for J.B.'s cousin were virtually hopeless among the hundreds of thousands of people coming and going from the Temple. The Pharisees similarly had no news, but Nicodemus kept returning to the one source he was convinced might have an idea about the boy—the Rabbi Zacharias.

"Rabbi," inquired Nicodemus yet again when he sought out the old man, "you must have some idea of the identity of the boy that the Romans are looking for?"

Frustrated by the repeated questions, Zacharias looked Nicodemus straight in the eye.

"What if the Promised Messiah were someone from Galilee? Someone from our own country to free us from the Romans according to the law set down in the Torah, to let us keep the fruits of our labor so that everyone can live a comfortable life, to give us God's wisdom and prepare us for His coming. Would that be such a bad thing, Nicodemus? No Herod has ever done that. Why would you want to reveal his identity to anyone in power now?"

He turned and walked away, leaving the young Pharisee standing there with that new thought instead of new information. Zacharias went directly to the garden where he was to meet Mary and Joseph.

"We seem to be safe for the moment," Zacharias concluded the discussion with their agreement. No attention from any authorities had come to Jesus after their arrival in Jerusalem, and from Zacharias's encounters with the priests and Nicodemus, no one seemed to have any suspicions about Jesus that gave them concerns for his safety and their purpose at the Feast of Passover.

"Do we dare change his verse to read before the High Priest?" asked Joseph.

Zacharias considered the question for a moment.

"If all remains well, as it is now, I think we can. But let's wait until we know it's the right thing to do."

Mary and Joseph nodded with anxious agreement.

* * *

It was this last part of the last day of the Feast of the Passover that the High Priest Annas truly hated. Following weeks of preparation, endless details to decide, innumerable people to meet, unpredictable problems to solve, service after service, sacrifice after sacrifice, here on the last day at the end of the last service of the Feast when he was most tired, he had to sit in the Court of the Women wearing his breast plate over eight sacred vestments of woven gold, blue and scarlet, his headpiece and golden bells, and then listen to twenty boys from ten synagogues throughout Palestine read from the scrolls, usually badly, and testify about the meaning of their verses to their lives, always boring. Then he had to pretend to be interested and nod his approval, while the other priests could bow in respect and nod off to sleep under the shawls covering their heads.

The High Priest was even more tired than usual this year with the distraction and the pressure from the Romans over looking for a boy. A boy from Bethlehem, or Nazareth, whose name was unknown, and who, for all they knew, might not even be alive. What did Pontius Pilate really hope to accomplish with an unknown boy? The High Priest considered the whole thing ridiculous and unnecessarily dangerous.

"Here are twenty boys, Pilate. Take your pick," thought Annas as he nodded with approval at a boy who had just finished rambling on about his brothers and sisters. "And leave us out of your foolish political ploys."

When the boy was done, a young scribe of the Temple named Joseph escorted the next boy up to the priest holding the scrolls with the books of Moses and the Prophets. He would tell the priest the verses the boy was to read, and then announce the boy's name and synagogue. The priest would turn to the passage and ceremoniously step aside for the boy to stand before the scrolls and begin reading. More than reading the passage and giving his testimony, it was those long nervous moments standing before the High Priest and thousands of worshippers while watching the scrolls turn slowly that turned a boy into a man.

The young scribe returned to the line of waiting boys. Since coming into service at the Temple from his home in Arimethea, the scribe Joseph had impressed the other scribes and priests with his knowledge of the law and his ability to argue its finer points. His part in this final service of the Feast, where he physically and symbolically brought these boys to the laws of Moses and the word of the Prophets, was an indication that the young scribe was favored and his career was on the rise.

There were only three boys left. As Joseph was learning the name and verse of the next boy to read for his introduction, he noticed an old rabbi hurrying over to the last two boys in line. The rabbi nodded courteously to Joseph and started whispering to the two boys.

"Judas," said Zacharias quietly. "Do you feel ready?"

Judas nodded nervously.

"You will do well, I know," the rabbi said with a comforting smile. He quickly turned to Jesus.

"Now Jesus, listen carefully. I am giving you a new passage to read."

Jesus could not believe what Zacharias was telling him. He looked up at the High Priest and out at all the worshippers, turned white and started to feel sick to his stomach.

"Don't worry, Jesus. It's a verse you already know well," Zacharias whispered to him calmly. He handed Jesus a piece of parchment with the passage written on it.

"Why are you doing this, Rabbi?" asked Jesus as he looked at the paper. "I haven't prepared a testimony on this verse."

He gave Zacharias a look of uncertainty that was quickly turning to fear. The scribe Joseph gave them a questioning look as he started to lead another boy up to the High Priest and the scrolls. Jesus would read next.

"I can't tell you why right now, Jesus," replied Zacharias. "Someday you will understand. But you must read this verse now."

Zacharias rose to leave.

"But my testimony, Rabbi?"

Zacharias put a reassuring hand on Jesus' shoulder.

"You will know what to say, my son. God has already told you, and I have already prepared you."

As Zacharias walked away, Jesus stared numbly at the piece of parchment, his eyes unable to focus. He looked up when he felt another hand on his shoulder.

"Are you all right?" The young scribe gave him a concerned look. Jesus could only nod.

"Tell me your name," the scribe said to him.

"Yeshua," he answered in Hebrew.

"Where are you from, Yeshua?"

"Nazareth."

"And what is your father's name?"

"Joseph."

"That's a good name."

The comment made Jesus look back at him. "It's my name too," the young man smiled at Jesus. "I am Joseph of Arimathea, but my friends call me Ari." He glanced over at the boy reading from the Torah to see how much time he had.

"Is everything all right? Who was that man talking to you just now?"

"He's my rabbi. I'm all right, I guess. But he just gave me a new verse to read at the last minute."

Ari asked Jesus what the passage was. When he heard the answer, he frowned. It seemed a harsh thing for the rabbi to do to a nervous boy in this demanding situation, and the scribe did not want an embarrassing moment for the boy or the High Priest at the end of the service. Jesus saw the concern on his face.

"It's all right," said Jesus. "I have read the verse before."

Ari was struck by the fact that now the boy was trying to comfort the scribe instead of being nervous for himself. He looked back at the boy standing before the scrolls.

"Are you ready?"

Jesus smiled hesitantly and nodded.

"Good. We'll go up in just a moment. You will do well, Yeshua. I can feel it."

Jesus gave him another faint smile and then stared at the marble floor beneath his feet. All of a sudden, Judas grabbed Jesus' hand nervously. They exchanged a squeeze of luck between friends facing the same fear and challenge. Then Jesus heard Ari's voice.

"It is time, Yeshua. Come with me."

Judas watched Jesus walk away. He remained there where he had been placed, alone and unsure of himself, waiting to be told what to do.

Jesus stood before the scrolls. He looked up at the High Priest sitting above him like a king on his throne. Then he looked out at the worshippers in the Temple hoping to see the familiar faces of his father and rabbi. When all he saw was a huge crowd of unidentifiable faces, his mind went blank. He did not even hear the scribe tell the priest the verse that Jesus was going to read.

"Yeshua, son of Joseph of Nazareth," Ari announced in a loud voice.

Jesus watched the priest with the scroll slowly turn the handles until he carefully stopped at the book of the Prophet Isaiah and the place with the passage to be read. The High Priest was thinking thankfully that there were only two more boys to go. There was a growing hum of noise from the movement and low conversation from the impatient multitude of worshippers who had been standing for hours barely able to hear what most of the boys were saying.

Caiaphas's attention perked up, however, when his ears caught the word "Nazareth."

No words came from Jesus' mouth. He stood still, just looking out at the back of the Temple. Ari lowered his head, trying to think of something he could do to save the boy great embarrassment. Caiaphas leaned forward in anticipation. After a moment, the High Priest realized that no one was reading and looked down at the boy. The entire Temple became aware of the silence, and all eyes turned to the boy who stood unmoving before the scroll.

Jesus' eyes did not look to the scroll, yet he began the passage in a voice that all could hear.

The Spirit of the Lord God is upon Me
Because the Lord has anointed Me
To preach good tidings to the poor.

Caiaphas and the High Priest quickly exchanged looks. Jesus carried on speaking without looking at the scroll.

He has sent me to bind up the brokenhearted,

To proclaim freedom for the captives
And release from darkness for the prisoners,
To proclaim the year of the Lord's favor
And the day of vengeance of our God . . .

Then Jesus' voice softened, yet the thousands standing before him could still hear the rising conviction in his words,

To comfort all who mourn
And provide for those who grieve in Zion,
To bestow on them a crown of beauty
  instead of ashes,
The oil of joy
  instead of mourning,
And a garment of praise
  instead of a spirit of despair.

"My friends, and God's people of Israel," the boy now addressed them in his own words. "This is my testimony of the meaning in my own life of these words from the Prophet Isaiah as taught to me from the lessons of my rabbi, Zacharias.

"God has sent us someone to bring good news to all. Not just the rich, but especially the poor and those who truly need His love. Someone who can heal not just the sick and infirm, but also bind up the wounds of those with hearts broken from the burdens of caring.

"And God has sent us someone to proclaim freedom today for those who feel trapped and release for those whose whole lives are imprisoned in darkness."

The heart of every man standing in the Temple began to beat faster when he heard the word "freedom" echo off the walls. Every woman felt something deep inside move at the thought of release from a life imprisoned in darkness. With unsuppressed pride in her son, Mary, standing among the women, clenched her fist with one hand and covered her heart with the other.

"Someone who proclaims God's love so that everyone can understand the Lord's favor in every passing year of their lives and recognize the protection of our God against our enemies and His."

Hearing these words, the priests and rabbis assembled in the Temple sensed a strengthened resolve for their faith and service.

"And for those who grieve and mourn, God has sent us someone to give comfort.

"And for *everyone*, as they go through life with its troubles and pain, God has sent us one who will give us all, '*a crown of beauty instead of ashes . . .*'"

His voice began to rise. "'*The oil of joy instead of mourning,*'"

Jesus' final words rang out through the Temple, "'*And a garment of praise—instead of a spirit of despair.*'"

"God has sent us this person," Jesus finished. "Thanks be to God!"

Every worshipper listening to those words spoken by the boy felt something within that they had not known for years.

Hope.

Not since the day he stood alone offering incense on the Golden Altar in the Holy Place had Zacharias heard such a silence throughout the Temple. He could not help but look around for the stranger who had spoken to him from beside the altar for there was once again a feeling of great power present within its walls. Nothing moved except the churning sea of emotions inside the souls who had heard the words of the Prophet Isaiah spoken by this boy from Nazareth.

Finally the High Priest nodded at Jesus with approval and hastily turned to signal Caiaphas.

Ari, like everyone in the Court of the Women, stood there watching Jesus walk away from the scroll when all of a sudden he was startled by someone standing next to him. He looked down to see Judas whom he had forgotten.

"What is your name and your father's name and your verse?" he asked Judas quickly. With the answers, Ari hurried Judas up to the priest holding the scroll who was still watching Jesus depart from the Court. He interrupted the priest with the boy's verse before turning to the High Priest and worshippers and announcing, "Judas

Iscariot of Nazareth, son of Simon of Kerioth."

No one heard him. The High Priest was beckoning for Caiaphas while the thousands of worshippers were talking among themselves about the message they had just heard and the remarkable boy who had just delivered it.

"Judas Iscariot of Nazareth," the scribe announced again more loudly without it doing any good. "Go ahead, son, and read your verse," he finally told Judas. Judas looked about helplessly. The only person he saw looking at him was his father. He looked down at the scroll before him, but the tears forming in his eyes made it difficult to read. Swallowing hard, he began. Only he could hear the words he read.

> *The Lord Almighty has a day in store*
> *for all the proud and lofty,*
> *for all that is exalted*
> *and they will be humbled.*

He paused and saw his father struggling to watch him through the throngs of worshippers leaving the Court. He looked up to see the High Priest walking away with Caiaphas as another priest was quickly giving the closing benediction to end the service and the Feast.

Judas's tears stopped. A hard look entered his eyes. He looked back down and finished his verse in a low voice filled with bitterness.

> *The arrogance of man will be brought low*
> *and human pride humbled;*
> *the Lord alone will be exalted in that day,*
> *and the idols will totally disappear.*

With no thought of giving his testimony, Judas turned and walked out of the Temple.

Only a single pair of eyes far back in the Court of the Women watched him until he was out of sight. Once Judas was gone, the Black Turban moved out of the shadows and gave a confident, sinister smile at the altar.

Chapter 18

MISSING

Zacharias, for the first time in his life, was looking forward to leaving Jerusalem. While he knew the journey back to Nazareth would be punishingly hard on his old body, he wanted very much to rejoin Elizabeth, return to his humble synagogue and relish the triumphant moments of his return to the Temple.

Following Jesus' reading at the Temple the day before, Zacharias was sought out by many Temple priests who had been his former colleagues to congratulate him on the performance of his student. Even those priests who had supported his removal from the Temple gave him a respectful bow as the old priest walked by. As he was leaving the Temple, he noticed Caiaphas giving him a long look from a distance. Zacharias gave Caiaphas a smile and nod of his head.

Numerous priests introduced themselves to the now admired teacher of whom they had only heard the stories of being struck mute. They were disappointed to hear that Zacharias was not planning to attend the Holy Convocation of rabbis for the next three days because they had hoped to learn from him how his teaching produced such excellent students. But he had finished what he came to do. He was now done with Caiaphas and the priests in his past. It was time to go home for good.

The next morning, just as the old rabbi finished putting together his things for the journey home and began thinking about how he might ask the Wine Seller Shikkor for a ride on his cart, he was interrupted with the message that there was a guard from the Temple to see him.

The guard informed him that the High Priest Annas had requested an immediate audience with Zacharias at the Palace of the High Priest and asked that he bring along the two boys from his synagogue.

Zacharias was disturbed by the guard's message. After the demands of the long Feast, the High Priest ordinarily would be resting and preparing for the Convocation of the rabbis. He suspected Caiaphas might be the cause of the meeting. Everything in their plans for Jesus at the Feast had gone well up to this point. There was little good that could come out of such a meeting, he thought.

The rabbi hurried to the home of Abbas and Imma looking for Mary and Joseph. He found Jesus and Barabbas minding the children while their parents were out buying supplies for the journey back to Nazareth.

"Jesus, you must come along with me and Judas to the Temple. We have been asked to meet with the High Priest."

Jesus could hardly believe this exciting news.

"But Rabbi, we're supposed to leave for the trip home with the caravan to Nazareth as soon as my parents return."

Zacharias frowned. He too was to depart with the Nazarene pilgrims and wanted very much to talk to Mary and Joseph before going to meet the High Priest.

"Are you packed and ready for the trip?" asked Zacharias.

"Yes."

"Then get your things and come with me."

Zacharias turned to Barabbas.

"Can you tell Jesus' parents when they return that Jesus left with the Rabbi Zacharias, and we will meet them with the caravan going to Nazareth?"

"Yes, Rabbi," answered Barabbas.

After Jesus said goodbye to Barabbas and the children, he and Zacharias hurried to the home where Judas was staying. "I don't know yet," was the only thing Zacharias said in a distracted response to Jesus' question about why they were meeting with the High Priest.

Simon Iscariot was more than pleased to hear that the High Priest had requested his son go with the rabbi to meet at the High Priest's palace.

"We are staying in Jerusalem another three days before returning to Nazareth," he informed Zacharias. Because Zacharias and Jesus would be hurrying to meet the other pilgrims heading for Nazareth, Simon told Zacharias it was all right for Judas to return alone from the High Priest's palace since it was nearby.

Zacharias and the boys spoke little though all three were filled with questions as they hurried the short distance to the palace of the High Priest. Jesus wondered not only about why they were going to see the High Priest, but also about why the Rabbi appeared to be disturbed and why Judas would not even look at him.

The Temple guard who had delivered the message to Zacharias was waiting for them at the entrance to the palace on the slope of the hill connected to the Temple through a long colonnaded walkway. He escorted them immediately through the courtyard and halls of beautiful marble and cedar up a flight of polished stone stairs to a room where the High Priest awaited them. Zacharias was not surprised to see Caiaphas waiting outside the room.

"Blessings be upon you, good Zacharias," Caiaphas greeted him.

"And you, Rabbi," answered Zacharias.

"And here are the boys from your synagogue," Caiaphas turned to Jesus and Judas. "Boys, the priests of the Temple were all very impressed yesterday. You did very well. Now would you wait here a few moments while the High Priest speaks with the rabbi?"

Caiaphas nodded at a Temple guard who stepped next to the boys while Caiaphas motioned to Zacharias to enter the room with him. As the ornately carved cedar door closed behind them, Jesus started to wonder once again why the three of them had been summoned by the High Priest, when he heard a familiar voice.

"Yeshua, it's good to see you again."

Jesus looked up to see the young scribe who had befriended him before his reading in the Temple the day before.

"It's me, Ari, Joseph of Arimathea, The same name as your father, remember?"

"And here's your friend from Nazareth," the young man turned to

Judas. "I'm sorry. I don't remember your name."

"Judas," he muttered.

"Isn't it good news, Judas and Yeshua?"

"What do you mean?" asked Jesus.

"Haven't you heard yet? The High Priest is inviting you to stay for the Convocation of priests and rabbis. Your reading and testimony at the Temple were so impressive, that he would like you to observe as students the discussions of the rabbis and scribes.

"That means you can stay in Jerusalem for three more days before the Temple guards will take you back to Nazareth, and you get to stay at my home. It is a great opportunity for you both, and my wife is looking forward to meeting you. Come, let me show you where you will be staying and then we can go to the first meeting of the priests and scribes."

Jesus was thrilled at the opportunity, but was concerned about whether he should return with his family to Nazareth. He and Joseph had much work to do. Judas felt better about his reading at the Temple. Someone must have been listening and noticed him after all. But he was hesitant about the prospect of having to sit through boring sessions with priests and scribes talking about the Torah. He did not want to be stuck in the Temple and the house of some stuffy scribe.

"My family is staying in Jerusalem for three more days," Judas told him. "I can stay with them."

Jesus was torn. "I should speak to my mother and father first."

"But everything has been arranged," the young man stated. "The High Priest is talking with your rabbi who will sort everything out with your parents. We should go now. The opening and first meeting of the Convocation will start soon and you don't want to miss it."

Judas had had enough of the priests and temples and scrolls. He wanted to go to the bazaar. "I can't go now. My parents are expecting me to return right away. I can meet you later."

Jesus was convinced that when Zacharias talked to his parents, Mary and Joseph would approve of his staying. Feeling excited, he picked up his bedroll to follow the young scribe and turned to Judas.

"Judas, will you please tell the Rabbi where I've gone and ask him to be sure to talk to my parents?" he asked as he started to follow Joseph down the hall.

* * *

Behind the cedar door, Zacharias listened respectfully to the High Priest as Caiaphas stood by.

"The boys clearly are students of great promise, Zacharias. Their readings at the Temple were quite out of the ordinary. Therefore, I believe it would be a worthwhile experience for them to see and hear the discussions of the priests and scribes at the Convocation. We, of course, will take care of their accommodations and see them safely home with the Temple guards in three days after the Convocation. Caiaphas has already made the arrangements. We simply need you to inform their parents and assure them of the wonderful opportunity we are making available to their sons."

"Thank you, Annas," responded Zacharias. "And to you also Caiaphas," he nodded in the direction of the younger priest. "I will certainly speak to the boys' parents, but I cannot commit that they will approve. They are simple working people from faraway Galilee and may not know what to think of their sons staying behind on their own for such a grand occasion."

"I should think they would be grateful for such an opportunity for their sons," the High Priest replied. "And I'm sure it will not be a problem once you speak to them.

"Now I must be off to the opening of the Convocation." The High Priest rose from his chair. "Too bad you could not stay to join us, Zacharias. But it was good to see you again. I do hope you have a safe journey back to Galilee."

Once Zacharias had left the room, Caiaphas's face took on a serious look.

"Do you think we should tell Pilate about the boy?" he asked the High Priest.

"Not yet," replied Annas. "We dare not risk Pilate's wrath and response if we fail to give him the right boy. These boys are sons of simple working men, after all. Not exactly the stuff kings are made of. No, I want further proof and confirmation about the boy before we reveal him to the Romans."

"Well, I've sent the scribe Joseph to take the boy to the Convocation so we can ask him more questions and find out more about him," said Caiaphas.

"Does the scribe know who the boy might be?" Annas asked.

"No," responded Caiaphas. "But Joseph likes the boy and was impressed with his reading in the Temple. He thinks we are just interested in the boy's further education."

***

Zacharias hurried out of the room. He was very troubled by the attention being focused on Jesus. The motives of the Sadducees could not be trusted at this point, he thought. There was no way he could leave Jesus in their hands unprotected for three days. He had to get Jesus to Mary and Joseph and out of Jerusalem.

As he closed the door, he felt panic when he saw Judas sitting there alone.

"Where's Jesus?"

Judas was taken aback at how sternly the question came from Zacharias.

"Joseph came and took him away."

"Thank God," the old rabbi said with a rush of relief. His attention immediately turned to getting to the caravan of pilgrims quickly before they left.

"Go straight to your parents," he called over his shoulder as he strode swiftly down the hall. "I will see you in Nazareth in a few days."

"But Rabbi," Judas called after him, "it was Joseph of —"

Zacharias hurriedly turned the corner without hearing Judas.

"Arimathea," he finished after Zacharias disappeared.

Judas did not know what to do next. He looked up at the Temple guard who had been standing there silently.

"This way," said the guard pointing down the hall.

* * *

Judas walked from the palace of the High Priest down the street towards the house where he and his parents were staying. But instead of stopping, he walked past and kept walking a long ways, his thoughts wandering in his mind while his footsteps wandered through the city.

He did not want to talk to his parents. He knew what would happen. It would be the same scene all over again, as it happened every day. They would be all excited about his visit to the High Priest's palace, just like they had been excited about his studying with the Rabbi, and being selected to read at the Temple, and then participating in the Feast. And then they would start questioning how well he was doing, and finding fault with what he was doing until finally he would end up being punished, sometimes painfully, for doing the thing about which they were originally excited.

And Jesus always seemed to be his problem. Whenever his friend was involved in what Judas was doing, Jesus would do it better. People would notice what Jesus did. Everyone would talk about Jesus. His parents would point out to him what Jesus had done and ask him why he had not done something like Jesus did it. But then Jesus would pretend like nothing had happened to Judas. The scene kept being repeated. He would do everything Jesus did, but it ended up as if he had done nothing and Jesus had done everything. It embarrassed and infuriated him.

Only when his stomach growled and he realized he was hungry did he finally stop and look around to see where he was. He found himself next to a bazaar near the edge of Jerusalem in a poor part of the city he had never seen before. Looking at a stall that offered some stale-looking bread, he reached into his tunic for the pouch where he kept his coins and realized he had not brought it when he went on short notice to the palace with the rabbi. Feeling frustrated, lost, friendless and hungry without money, he angrily picked up a rock he saw lying at his feet and threw it as hard and far as he could.

"Nice throw!" he heard a voice say behind him. Turning around, he saw a bearded man wearing a black turban. The man was leaning against a wall and tearing off a piece of bread from a loaf he was holding.

"I know you," the Black Turban said, chewing on his bread. "I saw you reading a verse at the Temple yesterday." He tore off another chunk of bread and held it out towards Judas. "Hungry?" he asked. When he saw Judas hesitate, he spoke again.

"You know, I really liked the verse you read—even if no one else seemed to. You did well." The Black Turban offered Judas the bread once more. "Go on, have some bread. You look hungry. You can't eat that stone you threw."

Judas reached out and took the piece of bread. He was surprised to find that it was warm as if it had just come off the coals in a baking oven.

"Thank you," said Judas.

"Are you enjoying your time in Jerusalem?" the Black Turban asked.

"Not really," answered Judas with his mouth full.

"How could you not? After all, this is the City of God." The Black Turban tore off another piece of bread for Judas.

"I don't know," said Judas. "It just hasn't gone like I hoped. Jerusalem hasn't been that much fun or special."

"Well, I can show you some fun and someplace very special in Jerusalem. Would you like that?"

Judas felt warmed by the man's attention and better than he had in quite a while.

"All right," he smiled.

The Black Turban did not take him far when he stopped on the other side of the bazaar. A group of tough-looking men in a circle on the ground were rolling dice.

"Room for another player?" the Black Turban asked them.

"There's room for another player's money," said a rough-looking character with a long scar running up his cheek to a missing eye. The other gamblers laughed and looked Judas up and down like predators eyeing fresh prey.

"Well here's a player for you," responded the Black Turban who prodded Judas towards the game.

"But I don't have any money," Judas told him.

The Black Turban flipped a large silver coin in the air which Judas caught.

"You do now," he said. "Roll those dice!"

When the gamblers saw Judas's silver coin, they quickly invited him to join their game. The Black Turban cheered when Judas won, and urged him to try again with more coins when he did not win. After a while, when all his money had been lost, he turned to the Black Turban and apologized.

"It doesn't matter," said the Black Turban. "That's what the money was for."

He gave the boy a friendly slap on the shoulder.

"Come on. Let me show you someplace really special."

Judas followed him and was surprised when he eventually led Judas through a gate of the Temple. They headed to the Royal Portico, but instead of entering the Court of the Gentiles, the Black Turban made a quick turn and opened a low door that led into a very narrow staircase. The stairs climbed for quite a distance until a sharp turn at the top opened up to a small perch on the roof of the Portico. Judas could tell that few people went there as the pigeons and doves flew off in surprise from their nests. The view was like none other in Jerusalem. There on the roof next to the Royal Bridge, they were twice as high above the valley below. Looking down made him feel slightly dizzy.

The two of them admired the view without speaking for a few moments. Judas thought about how he was actually enjoying himself for the first time in a long time. He looked over to see the Black Turban staring at him intently.

"You know, Judas, it was really unfair at the Temple yesterday how your friend got all the attention so that no one heard what you had to say."

Judas looked back at the Temple court below. He felt the anger returning from the previous day. The Black Turban continued.

"I don't understand it. You're just as talented and still he gets all the attention. Your rabbi gives him more attention than you and seems to like him better."

Inside, Judas became even more irate since what the man said was true.

"But you know what was really unfair?" the Black Turban asked him. "I was there at the well and saw you try to save the girl from the vinedressers. That was really brave. But then you get tossed into the pools and your friend got all the appreciation for looking brave while you, who stood up to the vinedresser in the first place, looked like a fool. That wasn't right."

The Black Turban saw the muscles in Judas's jaw clench tightly.

"I know he's your friend. But what kind of friend is that?" The Black Turban sadly shook his head.

"That's why the words of the verse you read at the Temple seemed so fitting:

The Lord Almighty has a day in store
for all the proud and lofty,
for all that is exalted
and they will be humbled.

"You know, Judas, your friend gets all the attention, so I think you should get something he doesn't have."

The Black Turban reached into his robes, pulled out a beautiful black tephelin with gold lettering on it, and handed it to Judas.

"Here, this is for you."

Judas's eyes grew wide. His fingers stroked the smooth black leather and touched the gold of the letters.

"Let me show you how to put it on," the Black Turban offered. He placed it on Judas's left arm and carefully wound its straps down to the left hand where he showed Judas how to tie the special knot that looked like the Hebrew letter.

They admired the tephelin on Judas's arm for a few moments and then enjoyed the view once more. Eventually, the Black Turban turned and looked Judas in the eye.

"Judas, you are a very smart and talented boy. You are capable of being a very important and well-known person someday. Don't you think so?

Wouldn't you like that?"

Judas looked at the beautiful tephelin on his arm.

"Well I think you should be someone important," the Black Turban concluded. "So it's a good idea for you to know other important people. Would you like to meet someone right now who is very important?"

"Well—" Judas hesitated.

The Black Turban gave him a serious look. "Judas, can you keep a secret?"

Judas gave him a determined nod.

"Come with me," the Black Turban said turning to leave. "It will be a great experience and an adventure." He stopped and looked back at Judas. "We can only get to him through an underground tunnel that needs a key."

The Black Turban pulled out a large key from inside his robes and tossed it to Judas.

"Come! We must go now to see him."

Judas stood there a moment looking at the key and watching the Black Turban start to walk away. The weight of the key in his hand seemed to command that he go with the Black Turban. His excited curiosity wondered who the important person could be. He hurried to catch up with the Black Turban.

* * *

At the main gate at the walls of Jerusalem, there was complete chaos. A massive crowd with tens of thousands of pilgrims was backing up, trying to get past the Roman guards who were doing their best to inspect and question everyone passing out of the city. But even those who were trying to answer the guards' questions respectfully were being pushed along involuntarily by the press of thousands behind them.

Back in the throng of people, Joseph along with Mary sitting atop Jewels were looking about anxiously, straining to see as far as they could to locate Jesus and Zacharias. Barabbas had told them that their son was with the rabbi, but they had not seen the two when the pilgrims from Nazareth gathered to leave. Then the large caravan of Nazarenes was broken up when it was swallowed into the mass of pilgrims at the city gates where they were held up by the Roman guards. The rabbi and their son were nowhere to be seen.

The pushing and shoving in the huge crowd of pilgrims grew worse as their number increased and their patience became strained. Jewels' ears were laid back and he looked ready to kick. Joseph was almost knocked to the ground. His attention turned away from his son when he began to fear that the situation could become seriously out of control and dangerous for Mary.

Up at the gate, the Roman officer watched in frustration as both his guards and the people they were questioning were being pushed through the gate so that their questioning could not be completed. Hearing the shouts of anger and fear from the crowd, he realized that there was nothing they could do to stop the surging mass of people without his guards or the pilgrims getting trampled.

"Let them pass through!" he finally ordered. But at that point, the order was unnecessary. The pilgrims pushed from behind were already stumbling past the struggling guards.

A few moments later, Mary and Joseph moved through the gate as if they were being carried down a flowing stream.

"Where's Jesus? We must find Jesus!" cried Mary as she strained to look around for her son.

Doing his best just to stay on his feet among the shoving crowd, Joseph tried to comfort her.

"He'll be all right, Mary. He's with Zacharias. We'll meet up with them later."

*　*　*

Ari and Jesus walked from the High Priest's palace along the colonnade that connected it with the Temple. After they dropped off Jesus' things at Ari's home, they arrived at the Great Sanhedrin's Chamber of the Unhewn Stones where the Convocation was taking place. The Convocation had already begun. A priest and a scribe stood addressing one another while the learned men filling the large chamber listened intently.

"They are discussing the interpretation and meaning of dreams," Ari explained in a whisper after he and Jesus slid into the only two remaining empty seats at the front of the room.

The scribe was concluding his point. "So it is that our history makes quite clear that God uses dreams to serve His purpose.

"Did not Jacob dream of a ladder from earth to heaven where God first told him of how his descendants would be as the dust of the earth and would then become our nation? And then did not God in a dream tell Laban how not to speak in judgment to Jacob, husband of his daughter Rachel, after Jacob had fled? And did not Jacob's son Joseph interpret dreams of the Pharoah's servants and the dreams of the Pharoah himself so that he came to great power?

"Then Daniel read the dreams of King Nebuchadnezzar such that the King prostrated himself before Daniel who said, 'No wise man, enchanter, magician or diviner can explain to the king the mystery he has asked about, but there is a God in heaven who reveals mysteries.'

"Finally, as Moses' book revealed, God himself came down in a pillar of cloud and in the door of the tabernacle said:

Listen to my words: When there is a prophet among you, I, the Lord, reveal myself to them in visions, I speak to them in dreams."

The scribe gave a self-satisfied look to those listening and nodded to the priest as if the matter were closed and there was nothing more to say on the subject. But the priest stepped forward and dramatically raised his hand as if he were signaling the rabbis and scribes to stop their conclusions.

"Beware! Beware of what my learned friend has told you.

"We have been warned by the prophet Jeremiah who gave us these words from the Lord of Hosts:

I have heard what the prophets say who prophesy lies in my name. They say, 'I had a dream! I had a dream!

"King Solomon wisely concluded in his writings that, 'Much dreaming and many words are meaningless."

The priest shook his finger at the audience.

"And the prophet Jeremiah has warned us. He has warned us:
> *Do not let the prophets and diviners among you deceive you.*
> *Do not listen to the dreams you encourage them to have.*"

The priest began pacing about looking directly at his listeners to emphasize his points.

"My learned friend would have you accept the dreams of prophets when those very visions may be leading to the worship of a false god! Yet the prophet Jeremiah has warned us, those prophets '*speak a vision of their own heart, not from the mouth of the Lord.*'

"Moses himself has instructed us not to listen to the dreams of prophets that may be blasphemous:
> *If a prophet, or one who foretells by dreams, appears among you and announces to you a sign or wonder, and if the sign or wonder spoken of takes place, and the prophet says, 'Let us follow other gods' (gods you have not known) 'and let us worship them' you must not listen to the words of that prophet or dreamer. The Lord your God is testing you to find out whether you love him with all your heart and with all your soul.*

"In these dangerous days, my friends, God is indeed testing us. Each day brings new messiahs claiming to speak for God, and even claiming that they are God himself. And they have no more basis for these claims than someone's dreams.

"We must not accept my learned friend's claim that dreams are God conveying his vision when they in fact are likely to be 'meaningless' or, even worse, mere visions from a prophet's own heart that are nothing more than false beliefs in a false god."

The priest stopped walking and looked down where Jesus was sitting. Seeing the boy inspired his conclusion.

"My boy, do you have dreams?" The priest smiled at Jesus and returned to his oratory. "Why even a boy can have a dream, a boy's dream of sweets or games or girls.

"Yet how do we know that a boy who dreams is not a prophet? Are we to believe such a person's dream might be a vision of God? Of course not. My learned friend's position on dreams leads us to a dangerous threat to our religion."

The audience turned their eyes to the scribe to hear his rebuttal when a voice behind the priest spoke up first.

"A dream unread is like a letter unopened."

The room's attention quickly swung back see who had spoken. To everyone's surprise, it was the boy the priest had just addressed.

Jesus was surprised at himself for speaking out. He felt uncomfortable with all eyes now gazing at him, but carried on speaking.

"God can talk to people as they sleep just as He can talk to them when they are awake. Job wrote:

For God does speak—now one way, now another—
though no one perceives it.
In a dream, in a vision of the night,
when deep sleep falls on people
as they slumber in their beds,
He may speak in their ears
and terrify them with warnings."

Seeing some of the priests and scribes nodding their agreement, Jesus continued.

"Dreams are messages from God, but they are not the Word of God.

"It's like when Isaiah said, dreams are like 'when a hungry person dreams of eating, but awakens hungry still; as when a thirsty person dreams of drinking, but awakens faint and thirsty still.'

"King Solomon had his dream in which God told him to ask for whatever he wanted. God was pleased with his answer and offered Solomon what he asked for as well as both wealth and honor so that in his lifetime he would have no equal among kings. But Solomon awoke and realized it had been a dream. It was a message, but not the Word of God.

"Rabbi," Jesus added, "I think Jeremiah also wrote:

Let the prophet who has a dream recount the dream, but let the

> *one who has my word speak it faithfully. For what has straw to do with grain?' declares the Lord.*

So there is a difference, I think, between the Word of God and the dream of a prophet."

An audible murmur ran through the Convocation. Some were commenting among themselves on what Jesus had just said. Others were asking about who that boy was. The priest replied to Jesus in a stern voice.

"My boy, you recite well from the books of Moses and the prophets. So you must know also Moses' serious concern and command to us about those prophets whose dreams lead us to a false god:
> *That prophet or dreamer must be put to death for inciting rebellion against the Lord your God, who brought you out of Egypt and redeemed you from the land of slavery. That prophet or dreamer tried to turn you from the way the Lord your God commanded you to follow. You must purge the evil from among you.*

Jesus lowered his head and was now embarrassed he had spoken out. He could hear in the background the scribes and priests whispering "the boy who read at the Feast."

"Yes, Rabbi. I'm sure it is as you say. I only know Moses commanded:
> *It is the Lord your God you must follow, and Him you must revere. Keep His commands and obey Him; serve Him and hold fast to Him.*"

Sitting next to Jesus, Ari looked at him proudly and laid a reassuring hand on his shoulder.

* * *

Keeping to the shadows of side passages under the colonnades along the Court of Gentiles, the Black Turban led Judas to a part of the Temple where there were no priests, guards, workers or worshippers. Judas almost bumped into him when he turned a corner and stopped suddenly in front of a low, heavy wooden door.

"Give me the key," the Black Turban ordered. Judas was surprised at how cold the Black Turban's hand felt when his long-nailed fingers took the key from Judas's hand.

A ponderous click and creaking noise echoed down the passage as the Black Turban turned the key and pushed open the low door. Although it was pitch black behind the door, the Black Turban did not hesitate. Judas felt the chilling hand of the Black Turban take his and pull him into the darkness where they descended a short flight of stairs. At the bottom, Judas could not see a thing, but the Black Turban led him along and turned corners as if the man could see perfectly. Eventually they reached a narrow stairway against the wall and started climbing a long ways up. The Black Turban kept jerking Judas's hand as they climbed the stairs quickly. Judas tried to steady himself by feeling for the wall and became increasingly frightened as they climbed higher and higher. There was nothing on the other side of the stairs but darkness. One misstep would send him falling into the black below.

Suddenly the Black Turban stopped. Judas saw a small crease of light at the bottom of a door before the Black Turban. One of his cold hands reached into the air and carefully closed into a fist. Judas jumped as the fist struck the door with a hard, echoing knock. Five more methodical knocks followed with a long pause between each. The Black Turban's fist stayed suspended in the air. After a longer pause, he repeated the six slow measured blows to the door. The fist still did not come down. For a third time, it struck the door with the rhythm of six more firm knocks. His fist lowered to his side and he stood motionless.

"If anyone picks a boy to be King of the Jews, it will be me, not the Sadducees or the Romans," thought the Black Turban.

Blinding light hit Judas's eyes when the door swung open without warning. He stumbled as the Black Turban pulled him forward through the door. After a couple more steps they walked through a second door opened to them into a room where Judas's eyes started to grow accustomed to the light.

As the door closed behind them, he saw the man who was staring at him from a chair on the other side of the room. Fear in his face,

Judas frantically looked about for a place to run for escape. When he tried to move, the Black Turban's hand grasped his tunic and held him there.

Pontius Pilate turned his hard stare at the boy to the Black Turban.

"Do you have news? Have the Pharisees or Herod's secret police found the boy from Nazareth?" Pilate asked.

"I have more than news for you," the Black Turban answered. Without letting go of Judas's tunic, he shoved the boy out in front of him. "I am giving you that boy."

Pilate once again studied him closely. "What is your name?"

Judas was frozen from fright.

"Tell him your name!" the Black Turban commanded Judas with a rough jerk to his tunic.

"Judas Iscariot." When the choked words came out of his mouth, Judas was certain he was a condemned man.

"Are you from Nazareth?" Pilate asked.

Judas nodded.

"He was chosen from the synagogue in Nazareth to read a verse for the Feast of the Passover in the Temple," the Black Turban told Pilate. "I noticed him when no one else did."

Pilate watched the boy struggling not to sob. "Where were you born?"

"Kerioth."

"In Judea?" Pilate asked.

Judas nodded. "My father's name comes from 'Ish Kerioth.' That means 'a man of Kerioth.'"

Pilate gave the Black Turban an angry look.

"I have relied on you and your information ever since you revealed to me that the Pharisees and Herod are also actively looking for the boy from Nazareth. I have rewarded you and even held off exterminating those vermin you call Warriors of the Wilderness though you can't control them enough to stop them from killing my soldiers.

"And now you bring me this insignificant creature? He isn't the boy. He wasn't even born in Bethlehem."

Pilate rose from his chair and walked over face to face with the Black Turban.

"I'm looking for the boy born in Bethlehem who struck fear into the heart of Herod the Great. I am looking for the next King of the Jews for whom Herod killed hundreds of babies. Bring me that boy from Nazareth born in Bethlehem, not this sniveling child from Kerioth."

With a look of disgust, he pointed at the door.

"Go! And don't waste my time further."

Judas felt the flesh of the hand on his tunic turn searing hot as the Black Turban dragged him through the door where the dark surrounded him once again.

Pilate stepped to the window and gazed out of the Tower of Antonia at the Temple below, frustrated yet again with another failure in his search for the boy from Nazareth.

"Maybe Herod did manage to kill the baby," mused Pilate. "Yet others have been looking for him before I began my search and are still looking for him," he thought. His instincts still felt strong. The boy was out there and could be his King of the Jews.

His instincts were also strong about something else. There was something familiar about the boy he had just seen. He called for his aide who entered immediately.

"Marcus, a boy just left through the tunnel to the Temple with one of our spies. I want you to go fetch the boy back—alone."

Pilate thought of the fear in the boy's face and reached into the pouch tied to his belt.

"And here, give him these," Pilate handed the aide some silver coins, "to make him feel better about coming back with you."

Marcus took the coins and headed for the door.

"Take a torch," added Pilate. "You could easily kill yourself on those stairs."

* * *

The long wide procession of pilgrims slowly departing Jerusalem started splintering apart as groups broke off in the direction of their homes. The many pilgrims from the north headed east through Jericho and across the River Jordan into Perea to avoid Samaria. Once they had crossed the river, they turned north and after a few hours began to stop at different points for the night's food and rest.

The caravan of pilgrims heading home to Nazareth had not managed to reassemble after they were separated at the chaotic departure through Jerusalem's gates. Mary and Joseph happened to locate a few of their group. But despite constant searching, they saw no sight of Jesus. Once Joseph had collected wood for a small cooking fire, Mary insisted that he go looking for Jesus and Zacharias among the groups of pilgrims while she prepared a supper and their bed for the night.

Joseph returned after an unsuccessful search when the sun had gone down. He had found a number of the Nazarene pilgrims and arranged to meet in the morning for the day's journey. But no one had seen the rabbi or their son. They ate without speaking as they each struggled with worry and fatigue. Even before she finished eating, Mary could barely keep her eyes open. Joseph finally persuaded her to lie down and get some rest with the promise that they would surely find him and Zacharias the next day as the caravan to Nazareth came together.

* * *

Jesus did not sleep well that first night despite his own room with a comfortable bed in Ari's home. He did not know what had possessed him to speak out in front of all the distinguished priests and scribes at the Convocation, and was sure he had embarrassed not only himself, but also his host Ari and his rabbi Zacharias who would surely hear about what Jesus had done. But Ari did not seem at all concerned about Jesus speaking up at the Convocation. In fact, he made Jesus promise to meet him at the Temple gate with Judas before the afternoon session of the second day of the Convocation.

Judas was not excited about going to the Convocation, but Ari had made the arrangements with Simon Iscariot and instructed Jesus to fetch his friend before meeting Joseph at the Temple gate. Just as Jesus arrived at the house where Judas was staying, Judas arrived in a hurry looking over his shoulder down the street behind him.

"Let's go!" he said to Jesus out of breath. Jesus started heading down the street that led to the Temple gate.

"No, let's go a different way," ordered Judas as he ducked down an alley. Jesus was puzzled but followed his friend.

The unexpected diversion did not fool the two vinedressers who were watching the boys closely. It had taken them over a week, but the reading at the Temple at the Feast had given them a trail that eventually led to where Judas was staying and now to their intended target. They followed the boys closely down the alley and through small twisting streets that wound their way towards the Temple. As the Temple grew closer, they nodded at one another, slid their hands to the daggers in their sleeves and started to move to the boys. A step away from grabbing Jesus, they were pushed roughly to the side.

"Get out of the way!" snarled a scar-faced one-eyed man who shoved the vinedressers out of his path without a glance. A group of tough-looking men following right behind the one-eyed man pushed them aside once again. The ugly scarred brute reached out without hesitation and grabbed Judas by the tunic, lifting him up and slamming him against a wall.

"Where's our money?" he barked at Judas. He cocked his head so that his one eye was peering right into the fearful eyes of Judas.

"I said you'd get it," answered Judas.

"You said that when you left after your other visit to our little game and never came back!" The man shook Judas by his tunic.

"Let me go so I can give it to you," Judas told him.

The one-eyed man set him down after the other men moved in closely so that there would be no escape. Judas reached into his tunic and pulled out a pouch from which he poured a large handful of silver coins. The one-eyed man took the coins from Judas's palm and then grabbed the pouch from his other hand.

"That should do it," he said, "plus this for the inconvenience." He held up the pouch.

Spinning around with a laugh, he again pushed away the

vinedressers who had drawn in close behind. In the moment it took for the vinedressers to regain their balance with a curse, the boys were gone. The vinedressers hurried around the corner just in time to see Jesus and Judas walking with a young scribe through a gate into the Temple.

After Ari greeted them with excitement, the boys followed him to the Convocation without talking. When they were seated, Jesus finally asked Judas who those men were and why Judas owed them money.

"It's none of your concern," answered Judas.

"Where did you get all that money?" Jesus asked. Judas did not reply.

"Judas, there's only one place where you and I have seen that many coins. The Apostles' money from delivering messages."

"I said it's none of your concern!" Judas snapped at Jesus. He turned away at first, but then looked back at Jesus with anger in his eyes.

Before Jesus could say anything else, the Convocation began with a prayer and announcements of the subject of their discussion. His thoughts were distracted for some time until he heard the rabbis and scribes talking about the meaning of the Feast of the Passover. He did not notice that he was being watched closely.

Caiaphas sat off to the side where he could observe the boy. Accounts of Jesus' words at the first day of the Convocation had passed quickly through the priests and scribes of the Temple and eventually were reported to Caiaphas. Caiaphas advised the High Priest of the second occasion in which this boy had made a significant impression at the Temple. Annas directed Caiaphas to scrutinize the boy's behavior and judge whether he should be made known to Pilate.

A while later after the discussion of the meaning of the Feast had moved through several points, another pair of eyes interested in seeing the boy entered the Chamber and began watching him closely. Nicodemus had been instructed by Samaias to witness the boy's actions and words at the Convocation. The first words he heard were from a respected elderly priest.

"I am afraid I must agree with our young friend Yeshua. The Feast of the Passover should be viewed principally as a celebration of freedom of our people from bondage. It is not symbolic of our bondage, but of our deliverance from bondage.

"And the unleavened bread which once had been the result of our hasty escape from slavery became the bread of our new state of freedom. No yeast of Egypt was to taint it. The leaven which stood for the imprisonment and death of our people was to be banished from our homes.

"Thus, the sacrifice of this necessity in our bread became the symbol of our new life in which all, even our humble bread, was devoted to the Lord."

The elderly priest turned to Jesus.

"But my young friend, I still do not quite understand how the Feast as a symbol of our deliverance ties into what you call the 'middle way.'"

"It is a very simple idea, Rabbi, not worthy of your attention," answered Jesus. "I was just thinking that if the Feast of the Passover celebrates our deliverance, that means after our deliverance we are headed towards something new. But if we don't know where we are headed after our deliverance, we must pass through a middle way to find out where the journey takes us and ends.

"There is no middle unless there is something before it and something after it. What came before is given meaning from what follows, and that which happens then, in the middle way, is understood from what follows from it."

"But my son," responded the priest, "I know of no words in the scriptures that speak of such a 'middle way.'"

Jesus thought for a moment.

"After our deliverance from bondage, we were given the laws of Moses and then the books of the prophets. Could it be that the prophets of the scriptures are pointing us to the middle way and to where God is sending us on the journey?"

"I do not know," the priest replied. "But surely the end of our journey and the purpose of our deliverance is the second coming of God. What would be the purpose of a 'middle way' other than this ending?"

"Well—" Jesus hesitated. He did not want to say something foolish once again or offend these learned men. After all, he was just a boy from faraway Galilee who had simply read in the Temple a passage from a prophet. He thought it would be safest to recite another verse.

"The Lord said in the book of the prophet Isaiah:
I will lead the blind by ways they have not known,
along unfamiliar paths I will guide them;
I will turn the darkness into light before them
and make the rough places smooth.

"I was thinking that maybe God was referring here to the middle way after our deliverance and that he would show us how darkness can be turned into light and rough places made smooth."

The priest smiled at the boy.

"Ah, my young friend, would that we could be shown how to stop the evil that sin does, and eliminate the hate and death in our lives. Those would indeed be unfamiliar paths and ways we have not known."

Jesus sat quietly while the priests and scribes carried on their discussions. He was wondering how God could turn darkness into light and make the rough places smooth.

* * *

On the second day of their journey homewards, more and more pilgrims from Nazareth found each other and reunited as a caravan to travel together for safety and good company. With every discovery of a new group of neighbors and friends, Mary and Joseph expected to see the old rabbi and their son. But the day continued with no sign of them.

"Maybe they are ahead of us," Joseph said to ease Mary's worry. "Hopefully we will catch up with them soon. Zacharias can't move that fast anymore, and Jesus will stay with him, I'm sure."

Joseph tried to appear unconcerned even though he knew Zacharias and Jesus could be anywhere ahead or behind them on the long road. Whenever any pilgrims heading for Nazareth joined them, he would seek them out to ask about the rabbi and Jesus. But when none had seen any sign of the two at all, he too began to worry.

With the midday sun directly overhead, Joseph shielded his eyes as he turned to look behind him yet again. This time he saw a familiar figure in the distance. Sitting atop his cart above the crowd was the large contour of the Wine Seller Shikkor. And to Joseph's relief, next to him sat Zacharias.

He pulled Jewels off the side of the road to let the cart catch up to them. The three men exchanged smiles and a greeting. But before they could share the stories of their departure from Jerusalem and their journey, Mary asked abruptly, "Where's Jesus?"

Zacharias gave her a puzzled look.

"What do you mean? He's with you, isn't he?"

"Abbas and Imma's son Barabbas told us that he was with you at the Temple," said Joseph. His voice was tense. Mary's face went pale.

"And Judas told me at the Temple that you had fetched Jesus, and that he went with you while I met with the High Priest. I would have taken him with me out of Jerusalem otherwise," said Zacharias.

"He did not leave with me," Joseph confirmed.

"Oh, Dear Lord!" exclaimed Zacharias. His words sounded both his fear and an unspoken prayer. "We must go back to Jerusalem now and find him!"

Joseph had already turned Jewels around and was hurrying back against the stream of pilgrims.

* * *

It was late morning on the third and last day of the Convocation. Word had spread once again about the words of the boy from Nazareth who conversed with the most learned scholars of the Temple as if he were one of them. There was a larger crowd of priests of the Temple than normally attended the Convocation. It was the day the High Priest would attend the discussions, and many were curious and interested in the High Priest's reaction if the boy spoke again while in his presence.

Annas had been fully briefed by Caiaphas on the previous day's Convocation. There was little doubt in Caiaphas's mind that the boy, although they knew very little about him, was someone they could turn over to Pilate. Whether or not he was the boy born in Bethlehem to be King of the Jews, he might keep Pilate satisfied and the priests safe in their positions in the Temple. Annas was more cautious.

"We cannot make a mistake turning this boy over to Pilate if he is not who the Romans are seeking. If we give Pilate the wrong boy, the risk of the Romans' wrath and punishment would be even greater. I must have no significant doubts.

"While I am presiding over today's Convocation, Caiaphas, I want you to ask the boy questions that will convince me he is the one we should give to Pilate. Once I am convinced, I will signal the guards to take him at once."

There were others besides the priests and scribes of the Temple who were at the last session of the Convocation to observe the boy closely. Nicodemus and Samaias were as near as they could seat themselves with several of Herod's secret police waiting for their instructions. In the back of the Chamber of the Hewn Stones with the worshippers who had heard word of the boy, the two vinedressers tried not to look as out of place as they felt. Then just before the Convocation was to commence, a squad of Roman soldiers filed in and positioned themselves around the perimeter of the Chamber,

Ari and Jesus entered the Chamber and took their seats, saving a seat for Judas. Jesus looking about finally saw Judas at the far side of the room talking with two dark-haired men. Unable to see who they were, Jesus was slightly surprised and uncomfortable when Judas turned and carefully pointed at Jesus before leaving them to come sit next to him.

Before Jesus could ask Judas about the men, everyone rose as the High Priest entered. In his embroidered robes over his breast plate with twelve jewels representing the tribes of Israel, he raised his hands and blessed the Convocation before sitting in a large throne-like chair. The proceedings began with some scribes and priests reporting to the High Priest on the previous subjects of their discussions and debates. While the High Priest pretended to listen thoughtfully, his eyes stole glances for the sight of the boy in the audience.

Caiaphas knew exactly where the boy was sitting. He gave an irritated look at the boy next to Joseph of Arimathea. He wanted to be done with him, with Pilate, with all the pressure of the Roman plots and plans. He had not asked for the impossible task of finding an unidentified boy who might not even be alive after twelve years and wanted to be finished with it, even if that meant handing over a boy from Nazareth regardless of who he was.

"Let's get this over with once and for all," he told himself as he heard the High Priest call his name to address the Convocation.

Walking to the center of the room, he turned slowly in a complete circle while giving an intense silent glare at the entire assembly. Then in a low voice that all strained to hear, he began.

"Every day we come to this Temple, the House of our God, to offer our prayers, our sacrifices, our very lives. And as we walk to this holiest of places, what do we see?

"We see the Promised Messiah. He is next to us on the street wearing the robes of a rabbi and claiming that he will deliver us from all evil. And we see him in the market, wearing a hairshirt and demanding that we follow him into the wilderness to find God's deliverance. Then we see him on the next street corner, half naked and dirty claiming once again that he is anointed by God and commanding that we follow him."

Caiaphas paused and let his silence command the room.

"Blasphemy!" he shouted, startling everyone. "All blasphemy!

"As we sit here in this holy place, we are surrounded by all manner of men who would have us believe in their false gods and false religions. They command that we even worship they themselves as false gods!

"What does God think of these people? Moses told us:
> *They made him jealous with their foreign gods*
>   *and angered him with their detestable idols.*
> *They sacrificed to false gods, which are not God—*
>   *gods they had not known,*
>   *gods that recently appeared,*
>   *gods your ancestors did not fear.*

Caiaphas carefully timed his movement and words so that he now was standing next to Jesus.

"What are we to think of these men? What are we to do as they poison the minds of our worshippers, and our pilgrims." Caiaphas placed his hand on Jesus' shoulder, "and the minds of our children who worship in the Temple?"

He looked down at Jesus.

"My boy, have you heard the words of these messiahs as you have come to worship at the Temple?"

Jesus nodded. The priests and scribes were pleased that Caiaphas had spoken to the boy who had impressed them at the Convocation and who the newcomers had hoped to hear. Three people who had just entered were not pleased, however. Mary and Joseph with Zacharias had managed to find a place in the back of the crowded room and were straining to see their son as Caiaphas addressed him.

"But you have not listened to this blasphemy, have you?"

"I have," Jesus answered to everyone's surprise. "As wheat alone is not possible without the chaff, truth can be seen only by considering that which is untrue."

Caiaphas gave Jesus a hard look. He became irritated yet again.

"Ah, you have been considering words that are untrue—and blasphemous. Interesting. Let me ask you, the verse you gave at the Temple during the Feast, it was from the prophet Isaiah, wasn't it?"

"Yes."

"What was that verse?"

In the back, Mary and Joseph gave Zacharias a concerned look.

"The Spirit of the Sovereign Lord is on me because the Lord has anointed me—"

"That's enough," Caiaphas stopped him short. "Did you choose these words to say to the High Priest, the elders and all the worshippers at the Temple?"

"Yes. I chose them with the help of my rabbi."

"Your rabbi is Zacharias, the rabbi of the synagogue in Nazareth and a former priest here at the Temple, is he not?"

"Yes."

Caiaphas looked at Jesus accusingly.

"Did you choose those words to read in the Temple because you and your rabbi are claiming to all that God has specifically anointed you?"

Audible gasps came from the listeners.

"I was only reading from the book of the prophet Isaiah," answered Jesus.

"But I saw you at the Temple at the Feast," replied Caiaphas, "and you did not read those words. Your eyes never went to the scrolls. You spoke those words as if they were your own and applied to you.

"Were you not trying to make people believe that you are claiming to be the Chosen One?"

"What on earth is he trying to do?" thought the concerned High Priest as he tried to catch Caiaphas's eye. "We're trying to find a boy for the Romans, not someone to be stoned for blasphemy."

But all eyes were on Jesus. Mary grabbed Joseph's sleeve in fear as he and Zacharias leaned forward.

Jesus looked at Caiaphas intently for a moment before answering.

"Your question claims the words are mine. Yet they are the words of the prophet no matter how they come out of any man's mouth."

Zacharias realized that he had just heard Jesus fire the first arrow in response to Caiaphas. Jesus had attacked Caiaphas's question.

Jesus went on. "Isaiah also wrote, '*I am the Lord, that is My name—*'"

"There!" Caiaphas interrupted him. "Again you chose to speak words in this Holy Temple that are claiming you are the Promised Messiah. Do you not say them because you would have us believe you are the Chosen One?"

Jesus waited for Caiaphas to stop speaking, paused and then started again.

"Isaiah also wrote:
> *I am the Lord; that is my name!*
> *I will not yield my glory to another*
> *or my praise to idols.*
> *See, the former things have taken place,*
> *and new things I declare;*
> *before they spring into being*
> *I announce them to you.*

"Rabbi," Jesus said to Caiaphas, "when the Promised Messiah comes, God will tell us, not a boy pilgrim from Galilee."

"The second arrow," thought Zacharias. "He has appealed to a higher authority."

Caiaphas pointed at Jesus.

"Have you not spoken the Lord's words in the Temple and do not those words you have chosen speak as one anointed by God?"

"The third arrow," whispered Zacharias, anxiously anticipating an attack on the interrogator. Not one person breathed, waiting for Jesus' answer.

"You are claiming that I use God's words as my own, but it seems you are using God's words as your own against me. But did not the prophet Isaiah say:

> *For my thoughts are not your thoughts,*
> *nor are your ways my ways, says the Lord.*
> *For as the heavens are higher than the earth,*
> *so are my ways higher than your ways*
> *and my thoughts than your thoughts.*

"I spoke God's words given to us by the prophet Isaiah, Rabbi. Neither you nor I can claim God's words as our own."

The priests and scribes nodded and murmured their approval at Jesus' answer. Unseen in the back, Zacharias smiled.

"Three arrows," he thought proudly. But his concern returned as Caiaphas stepped in front of Jesus and looked directly down at him.

"Answer me this," ordered Caiaphas. Everyone hushed expectantly. Jesus inwardly braced himself.

"Where were you born?"

The simple question surprised Jesus.

"I was born in Bethlehem."

Caiaphas turned and looked up at the High Priest. Annas nodded to him and signaled to one of the Temple guards. Among the priests and scribes, Nicodemus and Samaias were waving to Herod's men. A Roman officer was directing his troops to secure the exits. In the back, the vinedressers were nowhere to be seen.

"May I go?" Jesus looked up at Ari and asked. He could see the boy was very upset from the harsh exchange of words and nodded.

Jesus stepped past Judas and tried not to look at anyone as he quickly walked away. Turning a corner to leave the Chamber, he heard a voice address him.

"Jesus of Nazareth?"

Jesus looked up, but had no chance to see who had spoken. A hood was thrown over his head. His hands and feet were bound in one swift motion, and his feet were pulled out from beneath him. Unable to resist, he felt himself being speedily carried off.

One angering thought engulfed all his emotions—the image of Judas pointing at him.

Chapter 19

REVELATIONS

Jesus' world was dark and unmoving. His hands and feet were bound, and the hood covering his head kept out all light. He had been carried away hurriedly, placed in a room on some sort of cot and left alone in silence. Unable to loosen the leather straps tied around his wrists behind him and unable to figure out who had done this to him, he laid there focusing hard on breathing and thinking of his family, his friends, Zacharias—anything to keep away the nightmarish vision of the condemned and bloodied criminal fallen under his cross. He could not bear the intruding image of the criminal whispering "Save me, save me ... ," when he was helpless to save himself.

Then he heard the sound of a door opening and closing, followed by the shuffling of feet. Two strong hands sat him up. He felt the pressure of the leather straps around his wrists and ankles ease as they were untied. When the hood was lifted off his head, he squinted while his eyes adjusted to the light in the room. They focused after a moment on a sight he never would have expected.

Jesus was looking directly into an intense gaze from the ancient wrinkled face of a tiny old woman. On either side of her stood two young men poised to protect her against any move from Jesus. They were the men to whom Judas had pointed him out earlier.

"I know who you are," she said.

"Where am I?" asked Jesus.

"You are safe here," she answered. "You did not know it, but you were in great danger until my servants brought you to me."

"Danger from what?"

"You will know soon enough."

Jesus was certain she was the oldest woman he had ever seen. Her stooped and frail figure under her robes was so small that she stood looking straight into Jesus' eyes as he sat before her. But her eyes, staring intently into his, were clear and bright. Their steady calm suggested authority and commanded immediate respect.

"I don't know who you are," said Jesus as if apologizing.

"I will tell you," she said. Jesus saw tears begin to fill her eyes. "But first, I ask your permission to let me do one thing."

Though he thought nervously of his being bound and carried away, Jesus nodded respectfully to her.

The old woman gestured to her servants who immediately left her side. One of them picked up a small rolled-up rug from the cot where Jesus was sitting and spread it before his feet. The other servant fetched a bowl of water from the side of the room and set it down on the rug. Then they each took her by the arm and carefully helped her kneel down on the rug before Jesus.

With some difficulty, her gnarled fingers removed Jesus' sandals. He felt uncomfortable, but remained still. The old woman began rocking back and forth gently and mumbling a prayer. He could not make out her prayer, which was interrupted often with gentle sobs, except for the repeated words "He who is. . . . He who is." Then, taking great care, she began to wash Jesus' feet.

Jesus had no idea what to do or how to act. Never before had anything like this been done to him. No one had ever touched him in such a supplicant manner, let alone an older woman to whom he normally would be showing great respect. He was perplexed by the strange actions of these people and still wondered about the danger to him.

In his discomfort, he instinctively stood up. He saw that her servants who had bound him and carried him away also had tears in their eyes. They too kneeled down next to the old woman. He was tempted to bolt for the door when suddenly it swung open. The four of them tensed as they quickly looked over at the entrance.

Into the room hurried Zacharias, followed closely by Joseph and Mary.

Seeing Jesus, Mary rushed over and hugged him. "Jesus, thank God you're safe!" Joseph walked over and put his hand on Jesus' shoulder. Jesus gave him a grateful but puzzled look. Zacharias walked over to the old woman and helped her to her feet.

"Thank you, Anna. We came as soon as we received the message he was here," said Zacharias. "Are you all right?" he asked her.

She smiled at him. "I have never been better or happier in my entire life, Zacharias."

Mary's relief at her son's safety turned into motherly irritation. "Jesus, where have you been? Why didn't you leave with the rabbi and the caravan to Nazareth? We have been looking for you for three days!"

"Didn't you get the message from the rabbi when you left?" Jesus asked her. "He was supposed to tell you that I was invited by the High Priest to stay in Jerusalem to attend the Convocation of priests and scribes."

Joseph answered. "No, Jesus, we did not. What have you been doing for three days?"

"I spent them in the Temple at the Convocation listening and learning so much. I even got to talk with the priests and scribes about so many interesting things. I wish you'd been there."

"It was a marvel to behold," the old woman said to Zacharias. "I could not help but notice him as did everyone at the Convocation. Not only were the priests and scribes engaged with him and moved by his words, there were the Sadducees and Pharisees as well as many I did not recognize who were watching him closely and sending out word of him to others.

"Then I received your message to look for the boy, Zacharias. We found him and realized he was in danger. So we took steps to protect his safety." The old woman lowered her eyes and turned to Jesus. "I apologize for what I had my servants do, but we could take no chances."

"What danger was I in?" Jesus asked them.

Zacharias, Joseph and Mary glanced hesitantly at Jesus and then at one another. No one answered. After a moment's silence, a frustrated look came over Jesus' face.

"What is going on?" he asked. "I am among the priests of the Temple and yet you say I'm in danger. Then I am bound, hooded and taken by strangers to an unknown place where strange things happen, and you say I am safe? None of this makes sense."

Jesus' voice raised as his irritation turned to genuine anger and his question turned into a demand. "I want to know what is going on!"

There was another moment of awkward silence. No one dared look at each other or at Jesus. Finally it was the old woman who spoke.

"He needs to know now," she said to Mary, Joseph and Zacharias. "Others already know or suspect. It is time to tell him."

The old woman turned to Jesus. She took a deep breath and looked into his eyes.

"We were told in the Psalms, '*He shall give His angels charge over you to keep you.*' Jesus, God has given his angels charge over you and through those angels has commanded us in this room to keep you from harm and to do God's plan.

"My name is Anna. I am the daughter of Phanuel of the tribe of Asher. During the many, many years that I have been a widow, I have never left the Temple. I worship day and night, fasting and praying. I am completely devoted to God and His work. Because of my devotion, God has given me a special power."

At these words, Jesus and Zacharias exchanged looks.

"Some have called me a prophetess," she answered the questions in Jesus' mind. "I only know that I sometimes can see the end of a story when it has only started.

"Twelve years ago, a young couple brought to Jerusalem a newborn baby to present him to the Lord at the Temple after his circumcision. After his parents offered the traditional sacrifice of two turtledoves, they were approached in the Temple by a man named Simeon. Simeon was a devout and just man who sought to find the Lord so that he could die in peace.

"When he saw the baby, Simeon was moved by God and knew that this baby was special. He took the baby in his arms just as I entered to offer my daily sacrifice. I heard Simeon bless God and call the baby 'the glory of Your people Israel.' He gave the baby back to his mother and told her that the child was destined to cause the fall and rise of many in Israel and destined to be a sign which will be spoken.

"I had no doubt as I witnessed Simeon that he was moved by the Holy Spirit. And I could see the end of the baby's story when it had only started."

Anna's voice choked with a small sob.

"For the last twelve years, I have given thanks for that moment and have spoken of that baby to all those who have been looking for redemption in Jerusalem. Now I only wait for the end of the story I know is coming."

The old woman swayed unsteadily. Her two servants moved quickly to her side and helped sit her down in a chair. Zacharias walked over to her and placed his hand on her shoulder until he was sure she was all right.

Joseph stepped forward uncertainly. He looked at Mary who nodded to him, and then spoke to Jesus.

"Son, what the Prophetess Anna said is true. God did give his angels charge over you. After you were born in Bethlehem, I was visited by an angel in a dream who told me that you were in great danger."

Jesus was surprised to hear this from Joseph. He was a practical man who normally spoke only of building and business. To hear him speak of being visited by an angel was unusual and unexpected.

"I was told to take you and your mother and flee to Egypt to await further word from the angel when the danger to you had passed. Three years later, an angel visited me again in a dream and told me that I should return to Palestine with you and your mother. We thought the danger had passed, but then I was warned in another dream to take you to Galilee where you would be safest from any danger."

"What kind of danger, Father?"

"There was someone who wanted to have you killed, Jesus."

"Killed? Me?" Jesus could not believe what he had just heard. "Why would someone want to kill me? I was just your little boy."

Joseph tried to answer, but the words caught in his throat. He swallowed hard twice until he could speak.

"Jesus, you were not my little boy." Tears welled up in his eyes. "I am not your real father."

Jesus was stunned. He stared at Joseph in disbelief, then looked over to Mary and back at Joseph.

"Who—then who—" Jesus could not finish.

Mary moved toward Jesus and reached out to him. Confused and hurt, Jesus stepped back to avoid her touch.

"Jesus, remember you are from a long and distinguished lineage of forefathers—" she started.

"Mother," Jesus interrupted her angrily, "don't ever tell me again about my lineage. It's all a lie!"

"It's not a lie." Mary responded. "But I didn't tell everything. I never finished the list of your forefathers."

Jesus looked away and said nothing.

"You can never know, Jesus, how much Joseph has loved and protected you better than any other man or father on this earth could have done. You are, like Joseph, from the house and lineage of David, and before him, all the others going back to Moses and Abraham and to Adam. But when I told you of your lineage, I stopped there and did not go further. I left out your first forefather and your true father."

Jesus turned back to her with a questioning look. She went on.

"Your full lineage goes directly to Adam—who, as the Torah says, was the Son of God."

Mary looked relieved as she finally spoke the secret of her heart.

"Jesus, you are—at the beginning of your lineage and again at your birth—the Son of God."

Jesus did not move.

"I was also visited by an angel," Mary went on. "I was very frightened when he told me that I was to have a baby, a baby conceived not from an earthly father but from the power of the Holy Spirit. He told me that this baby was to be named Jesus.

"I came to understand that this baby was destined to do great things with strength and mercy."

Jesus closed his eyes and shook his head as if he did not want to hear any more. He turned and faced them all.

"What are you saying? I don't understand what any of this means."

Zacharias stepped forward.

"I too was visited by an angel who also gave me charge over you. I have taught you what this all means, Jesus. Your mother has revealed to you your full lineage to the beginning of our world and beyond. Remember the words I had you read to me from the Book of Proverbs?

The Lord brought me forth as the first of his works,
before his deeds of old;
I was formed long ages ago,
at the very beginning, when the world came to be.

The rabbi went on. "Your mother told you how an angel from the Lord announced to her that you were to be given the name 'Jesus.' You also read to me these words from the Book of Isaiah:

Listen to me, you islands;
hear this, you distant nations:
Before I was born the Lord called me;
from my birth he has made mention of my name.

"You were brought to Jerusalem as a baby, Jesus, to be presented to the Lord at the Temple as Anna described. And now we have seen to it that you were brought back for the Feast of the Passover to be presented once again at the Temple, this time to all of Israel.

"And what for?" Zacharias asked him. "Not three days ago you told the priests of the Temple what it all means when you spoke your verse to them. Say the verse again, Jesus, and understand your words."

As if he were hearing it for the first time, Jesus softly repeated his verse,

The Spirit of the Lord God is upon Me
Because the Lord has anointed Me

To preach good tidings to the poor.

He has sent me to bind up the brokenhearted,
To proclaim freedom for the captives
And release from darkness for the prisoners,

To proclaim the year of the Lord's favor
And the day of vengeance of our God,
To comfort all who mourn
And provide for those who grieve in Zion,

To bestow on them a crown of beauty
instead of ashes,
The oil of joy
instead of mourning,
And a garment of praise
instead of a spirit of despair.

Though everyone in the room remained silent as they heard these words from Jesus, they wanted to shout with joy. They had waited years and given their lives for this moment.

"And who are all these words about, Jesus?" Zacharias finally asked.

"They are about the Promised Messiah," Jesus answered. "But Rabbi, I am not the Promised Messiah. It can't be so."

Out of the shadows near the door a hooded figure stepped forward and spoke.

"Yes, it can."

A hand reached up from a long, full sleeve and pulled back his hood. Standing there before a bewildered Jesus was the magician from the market place.

"And even if you think you cannot be the Promised Messiah, there are others who are looking for you right now because they think you are the Promised Messiah and the next King of the Jews."

Balthazar turned to Zacharias.

"Rabbi, when we received your message about the missing boy, we searched throughout Jerusalem. We found that the Sadducees and Roman soldiers, Pharisees, as well as others whom we know not, are talking about seizing him. Fortunately, it was Anna who took him in the Temple for his protection just before the others tried. That's when I sent you the message to meet us here.

"It is critical that you all leave Jerusalem as quickly and quietly as you can," Balthazar warned.

"Thank you, Balthazar," replied Zacharias.

Joseph looked at the light through the window. "The sun will be setting soon. We can leave after dark."

Jesus stood there unable to comprehend it all. A few hours ago, he was the son of a carpenter from Galilee, thrilled to be in the Temple in Jerusalem for the first time and excited to return home to tell his friends what he had seen. Then he had been bound and kidnapped in the Temple on the orders of an ancient prophetess and told by his father and mother that he had no father here. Now this collection of strangers as well as the people he knew best and trusted most had called him the Messiah and even King—and told him he was in danger of being seized by powerful people he did not even know.

A shudder went through his body at the realization that these people around him were not who he had always thought they were, and maybe even he was not who he thought he was. And now, he was in danger inside the walls of the Holy Temple. If he had special powers, he did not feel them. He felt completely helpless.

Jesus slowly fell to his knees. His eyes were closed and his body still. Wild unconnected images started swirling in his head. He saw Rebecca talking to him with a hand gesture he did not understand. Then there was an image of sun glinting off the garrison commander's helmet sitting on the ground next to a blank clay writing tablet, and then the Apostles drinking wine and eating bread and fish. He saw Judas stand up and walk away from them to the entrance to their synagogue where he looked in and out as if he did not know which way to go until the bearded man in the black turban took him under his arm and led him away.

A coldness wrapped itself around Jesus until he imagined the warmth of Maggie with her body close to his and a wine jug in her hand. Suddenly he saw himself under water struggling to breathe when he came to the surface of the Sea of Galilee where he saw the criminal of his recurring nightmare hanging on to his cross floating on the water, calling out to Jesus for help.

Then an image of the scroll of the Torah opened before his eyes. He watched its words shrink down to verses on a piece of parchment. He started to see all the verses that he had memorized flowing through his mind like a rushing brook through the mountains. He could hear himself rapidly reciting the verses, but then he heard his voice start to slow and change. It became deeper and like an echo until it was no longer his own voice that was speaking the verses. Finally he heard the powerful voice speak directly to him.

"You are my beloved son, in whom I am well pleased."

The visions in his head suddenly ceased, and his mind became clear. In that moment, he realized that in the passage he read at the Temple were all the things he had always wanted to do in his short life and would always want to do in the rest of it.

Jesus opened his eyes. Everyone in the room was staring at him, looking anxious and concerned.

"I should be about my Father's business," he said to them calmly.

A puzzled look came to their faces. No one quite understood what or who the statement was about. Joseph walked over to Jesus and kneeled next to him.

"It's time to go home. Our family is waiting for us. Are you all right to go?"

Jesus looked at him and nodded. They stood up together.

Everyone moved into action. Anna told her servants to bring food and water to Mary and to pack for the journey back to Nazareth with them to see that they came to no harm. Joseph went out to ready their donkeys while Zacharias and Balthazar started discussing the best gate through which to leave the city and the route they should take. Balthazar left to check out the Temple and city gates.

The sun started setting a short while later. Joseph and Anna's servants came back into the room once the animals were loaded and ready to go. Balthazar returned next and reported that the Temple guards were examining everyone going through the Temple gates on orders from the High Priest and extra Roman soldiers were posted at each of the gates to the city. Everyone passing in and out was being inspected and questioned closely. Balthazar walked over to Jesus and gave him one of his long hooded cloaks.

"Wear this as you travel with the hood covering your face," he told Jesus. "Do not speak to anyone unless necessary and under no circumstances tell anyone who you are or what you have been doing in Jerusalem."

Jesus tried to give him a look of thanks. But Balthazar could see the edge of fear in his eyes. Balthazar gave Jesus a comforting smile.

"You have great magic, Jesus. Don't ever forget that."

He quickly turned to Joseph and Anna's servants and directed them to exit the Temple and wait with the donkeys by the Royal Bridge. From there they would head for the Mount of Olives.

"We will leave by the Tedi Gate on the north side of the Temple. It is the least used, and the guards will know Anna. Anna will say goodbye to a pregnant woman and a rabbi, and then direct her new servant," Balthazar nodded at Jesus concealed under his new robe, "to see them on their way. With Anna there, they should not be suspicious. But I will follow behind in case there is any trouble from the guards."

They all paused and looked at one another. Each felt some apprehension but also a great sense of exhilaration from the adventure of their changed world. Embraces and blessings were exchanged as they all headed for the Temple gates.

Anna was leaning on Jesus' arm when she approached the Temple gate with an old rabbi and a pregnant woman.

"Bless you both for coming to see me," she said to them standing in front of a Temple guard. She turned to Jesus and told him to see them safely to the main road and then come right back to help her with her prayers and sacrifice.

"The Lord our Father bless and keep you. May His face shine upon you, and give you peace," she called to them after they passed through the gate.

"They must be special people," thought the Temple guard when he saw the tears in Anna's eyes as her friends departed.

"Keep moving, sir," the guard politely ordered an old man with a long white beard who was standing there silently. Balthazar pulled back the hood of his robe and looked wistfully down the street before he reluctantly turned and headed the other direction.

At the end of the Royal Bridge, Joseph and Anna's servants were waiting with the donkeys. Joseph helped Mary onto Jewels who took on the familiar burden with a happy snort. They started moving away from the Temple with the other worshippers who were leaving after the late afternoon sacrifices. Zacharias paused as they started to depart. With a satisfied look on his face, he said a prayer of thanks as he looked one final time at the Holy Place with the last rays of sunset glistening off its gold.

His look quickly turned to one of concern. Ahead of him, he saw the two vinedressers from Nazareth eyeing closely the people passing out of the Temple. Zacharias held out his hand in front of Joseph and stopped them. He called for one of Anna's servants and whispered something in his ear. The servant listened closely, looked over at the two vinedressers and started walking towards them.

"Good friends, can you help me?" the servant said to the vinedressers as he walked up next to them. "I am looking for the Court of Gentiles where the young boy from Nazareth who heals the blind is to appear to do his miracles."

Without answering him, the two vinedressers immediately hurried off in the direction of the entrance to the Temple. Anna's servant looked over at Zacharias with a smile of accomplishment, and once he was sure the vinedressers were out of sight, rejoined the group which began again to move toward the main city gate.

It was almost dark as they approached the gate leading west out of Jerusalem. A half dozen Roman soldiers were busy questioning the last press of travelers who were hurrying to reach the safety inside the city walls before nightfall. As they had planned, Joseph, Mary and Anna's servants went ahead while Zacharias and Jesus fell back a short distance.

One of the soldiers was surprised when he saw four figures and their donkeys approaching to leave the city at dark against the flow of travelers.

"Halt!" ordered the soldier. "Who are you and what is your business?"

"We are pilgrims here for the Feast and are returning home," replied Joseph.

"At this time of night?" the soldier asked suspiciously as he saw that it was a woman sitting on one of the donkeys. Another soldier looked up when he heard Joseph's answer.

"Hold there!" he commanded them. He walked over, looked at the group and peered closely at Joseph. "I know you," he said. Jewels felt Mary tense up on his back. Then a big grin broke over the soldier's face.

"You're the carpenter who works at the garrison. Am I right?"

Joseph smiled weakly. "That's right," he answered. He recognized the soldier as one of the guards who waived him through the garrison gate every morning.

"But why are you heading out for Nazareth at night?" the soldier asked.

Joseph gestured at Mary sitting on the donkey. "My wife is pregnant. It's cooler and more comfortable to keep her out of the heat of the sun. Besides," he smiled at the soldier, "sometimes the toll takers are asleep."

"Well, take care. There are bandits and worse out there," the soldier warned.

"That's why I have my friends traveling with us," Joseph nodded in the direction of Anna's servants. With a wave they moved off down the road.

A moment later, an old man in the robes of a rabbi walked up to the gate followed by a figure covered by a long hooded cloak.

"Good evening, Rabbi," said the soldier as he stopped Zacharias. "A little dark for a stroll isn't it?"

"I am on a mission of mercy, good soldier," answered Zacharias.

"A mission of mercy, is it?" the guard responded. "And who is that under the hood?" he pointed at Jesus.

Zacharias leaned into the soldier and said in a low voice, "He is my friend's son. We have heard there is a Holy Man in the desert who is said to cure lepers."

With a look of revulsion, the soldier quickly stepped back and waived them through.

"Get on with you then," he ordered.

The two of them hurried through the gate and after a safe distance joined the others. The group traveled as rapidly as possible through the night. They took the direct road north through Samaria to speed their return to Nazareth and to avoid the route where bandits or anyone else would likely be looking for Jewish pilgrims returning from Jerusalem.

* * *

The journey back to Nazareth fortunately was uneventful. Traveling as fast as possible without tiring Mary, they kept to themselves for the most part, camping under the stars in the warm air and avoiding contact with others. Nobody spoke much. Each of them was filled with their thoughts about what had happened in Jerusalem. Mary, Joseph and Zacharias knew that life would never be the same, and yet were uncertain about how life would be different. They had reached a critical moment of the Prophecy, but were unsure of what to do at this point in their mission.

None of them knew what Jesus was thinking. He only spoke if someone spoke to him. When they camped, he would go off by himself until they ate and bedded down. Joseph often checked on him and would find him sitting quietly, deep into his thoughts.

Mary watched him closely but left him alone. It was hard for her. She was filled with so many feelings for her son. Her heart burst with pride and excitement at the promise of his future. She had not felt like this since the angel visited her before his birth. Yet she felt a heavy sadness and sense of loss. He was no longer her little boy. He was now the Son of Man and the Son of God. She only knew how to nourish and protect him as a mother and feared that this would no longer be enough.

On the third day of their journey, the sun, as if it were finally tired of standing high in the sky, began leaning towards the hills of Galilee. The weary pilgrims were all gladdened when Nazareth finally came into view. It had been a long journey in so many ways. The place from which they had come seemed much farther than the distance they had traveled.

A great relief came over Jesus. He no longer wanted to think of prophesies, or special powers, or dangers, or unanswerable questions. He just wanted to be home with his family and friends.

Their pace quickened as Nazareth grew nearer until they saw two figures stand up on top of a large boulder next to the road. They hesitated and tensed when the figures jumped off the rock and started running towards them.

Jesus soon recognized Simon sprinting swiftly towards them with his long hair flying out behind. Trailing him was Bartholomew moving as fast as he could with his heavy steps.

"We've been looking for you," said Simon breathlessly as he ran up to Jesus.

"What's wrong?" Jesus asked.

"It's Peter and Maggie," answered Simon. "They are Herod's prisoners in the garrison. Peter's been hurt bad."

Bartholomew stumbled to a stop next to Simon.

"Jesus, we don't know what to do!"

Chapter 20

THE PLOTS

Simon and Bartholomew told the returning pilgrims what they knew of Peter and Maggie. After Peter did not return home, Andrew started searching for his brother. The other Apostles had already learned from the news circulating in the market that a boy and a girl had been arrested by the well for trying to ride Herod's horse. When Maggie's mother appeared at the well looking for her daughter at the same time Andrew showed up asking about Peter, they all soon realized that it was Peter and Maggie who were in trouble.

Andrew went to the garrison. He did not like having anything to do with Roman soldiers, but summoned his courage to walk up to the soldiers in the gatehouse to ask about Peter. They laughed in answer to his question.

"Oh, he's here all right," said one of the guards with a sneer. "But I don't suppose he'll be making it home tonight for supper," the soldier told him. "Do you?" he asked the other guard manning the gate. They broke out laughing once again. He turned back to Andrew.

"I don't think you're going to see him or his girlfriend any time soon. And when you do, *if* you do, he's not going to be looking any too pretty," he warned Andrew. "Now get on with you," he ordered.

There were looks of serious concern on the faces of Jesus, Mary and Zacharias as they heard the two Apostles recount the story. Joseph, however, showed no emotion as he listened closely. When they finished, he gave them short instructions.

"Have all the Apostles come to my home tomorrow just after sunset. Now go quickly to Peter and Maggie's mothers. Tell them that I will be working in the garrison tomorrow and will let them know any news I can find about Peter and Maggie as soon as I can."

The pilgrims then proceeded to Zacharias's home to pick up the children. As Elizabeth prepared some supper, Jesus' brothers and sisters excitedly asked him about the journey, Jerusalem, and the Feast at the Temple. Rebecca's fingers were flying so fast Jesus could not keep up with them as he tried to answer all their questions. Anna's servants marveled at the movements of Rebecca's hands until the two of them were introduced to the children who immediately started asking all about what it was like to live inside the Temple's walls. The questions did not stop until Mary finally scolded them to leave the servants alone so they could eat.

After a short night of troubled sleep, Jesus, Joseph, and Mary were up before dawn so that the two men could get to the garrison early that morning.

"Do you think it's a good idea to have Jesus go with you to the garrison?" Mary questioned. "Don't you think those looking for him will eventually come to Nazareth?"

Joseph struggled with the answer, but tried to sound confident.

"Zacharias and I figure we have three, maybe four days before they can't find him in Jerusalem and show up here to search. We will figure out a plan for him before then. In the meantime, I need his help to assess the situation in the garrison. He knows his way around inside. Besides, no one will be looking at a carpenter's assistant working in a Roman garrison to be the King of the Jews. It's probably as safe a place as we could find in Nazareth," he reassured her.

Entering the gate of the garrison, Joseph nevertheless kept himself carefully between Jesus and the line of sight of the guards in the gatehouse. The sleepy soldiers at the end of their night's watch merely grunted in response to Joseph's wave. Even at that early hour, Joseph noticed the difference in the garrison's normal activity. There were hardly any soldiers to be seen. Instead, Herod's servants in their white tunics were scurrying about to ready the day for the Tetrarch and his officers.

"Joseph!"

He stopped in his tracks with his heart in his throat as he heard his name called out. Turning around warily, he saw, to his relief, Chuza smiling and extending his hand in greeting.

"Chuza, welcome to Nazareth," Joseph replied. They exchanged details about their recent arrivals and briefly talked about some of the plans for Herod's palace in Sepphoris. Joseph decided to use this opportunity.

"I heard there was some trouble with Herod's horse," commented Joseph.

"Yes," answered Chuza. "His Grace was quite upset."

"It was a boy and girl?"

Chuza nodded. "Foolish kids. They had no idea how much trouble they were getting into."

"What's happened to them?"

"The boy is locked up in one of the prisoner cells for interrogation. His Grace is quite taken by the girl. She's being kept with his servants in rooms off the baths."

"Well, I must get to my work," said Joseph picking up his tool box. "Hopefully I'll see you again before you leave."

Joseph headed off for the prisoner cells with Jesus behind him hurrying to keep up. They arrived to see a guard standing outside the door of one of the cells. Joseph set down his tools and pretended to set about a work project. Jesus followed his lead.

"I'll distract the guard," Joseph whispered to him. "When it's safe, check on Peter. Don't take any chances!" Joseph gave Jesus a stern look.

Jesus acted like he was arranging their tools as Joseph walked over and began talking to the guard. Joseph said hello and conversed with the guard for a while until the guard laughed at something Joseph said. Then Joseph pointed with a serious look at the ceiling above the guard and then at the corner where he waved at the guard to look around the turn in the corridor. Once the guard and Joseph were out of sight, Jesus hurried to the door of Peter's cell and kneeled down to look through a small opening in the door next to the floor.

"Peter! Peter, are you there?" Jesus whispered as loudly as he could. In the dim light, he could see a figure lying against the wall on the far side of the cell. There was no sound or movement.

"Peter, can you hear me? It's me. Jesus," he tried again.

Jesus heard a faint choking sound and saw the figure move slightly before lying still once again. He scrambled to his feet as he heard Joseph's voice and footsteps loudly approaching around the corner.

"I can't believe they're making you stand guard here for twelve hours all night," Joseph said ahead of the guard as he slowed at the turn to look for Jesus. "They don't pay you enough for that."

"That's for sure!" answered the guard, appreciative of the unexpected sympathy from someone. "But there are no soldiers in the garrison to divide up the watch until the Legion returns. Herod's men are happy to show up to beat the poor bugger senseless, but then they insist on having a guard and leave me to do the boring work."

Joseph commiserated with a shake of his head. He spoke to Jesus.

"Pack up those tools," he ordered. "We need to go check the baths now. We'll come back here tomorrow."

With a friendly farewell, Joseph assured the guard he would return and moved off down the corridor. He and Jesus walked as quickly as they could toward the baths. As they turned the corner next to the entrance to the baths, they almost collided with some of Herod's servants.

"I'm terribly sorry," Joseph was apologizing when he noticed Jesus staring at the servants.

He glanced over and realized that Jesus was looking directly at Maggie who was being led by the servants in front of her. Afraid that Maggie's response might expose their cover, Joseph and Jesus were relieved when Maggie quickly looked down to the ground. They passed and carried on down the corridor. After a few steps, Jesus and Maggie glanced back at each other. There was a plea for help in her eyes. Jesus nodded to try to let her know they were there to help.

Once they had a sense of the situation, Joseph and Jesus left the garrison. Joseph told Jesus to visit Peter's and Maggie's mothers to let them know Joseph and Jesus had located their children but did not have the opportunity to speak with them.

"Don't give Peter's mother any more details," Joseph told Jesus. "I don't want to worry her when we don't really know how bad he is. I'll be back at the house by sunset to meet with the Apostles."

* * *

Jesus wanted to be alone. Since returning to Nazareth, there had not been a moment to think about anything but the danger to his friends and the reminders of the danger to himself. He finished talking to the mothers of his two friends and was unsure whether the news he brought had made them feel better or worse. All he knew was that he was as worried about the prisoners in the garrison as their mothers.

He walked out past the edge of town to a quiet grove of trees where Joseph and Zacharias often went to talk. There he settled his back against a large rock and in its shade just listened to his breath for a while. Slowly his mind began to focus on the amazing happenings of the last week.

So much had been revealed in Jerusalem that he still did not understand. He repeated over and over in his mind the words that Anna, Joseph, Mary, Zacharias, and the magician had spoken. They still had no real meaning to him. Even if he did believe them, he had no idea from those words what he was to do, how he was to act or what would happen to him.

"Who am I?" he asked himself. The more he tried to answer that question, the more confused he became and uncertain he began to feel.

"I am not the son of a carpenter who lives with his family in Nazareth. I am not who I have always thought I am," he thought with sadness.

"Then who am I?" he wondered again. "Can I really be the Promised Messiah?" he asked doubtfully.

"The Son of God?" He made himself say the words out loud.

He shook his head. This answer could not be possible, he tried to conclude. But that is what the people he loved and trusted most in life had told him. Others had immediately confirmed it. And it made all the unusual things that had happened to him seem to make sense. Yet, it could not be true. It was too much for anyone, let alone a boy from Nazareth, to believe.

"If I am the Son of God, then why can't I even save my friends whose lives are in danger in the garrison? And why isn't my Heavenly Father here to help me?" he mentally argued to himself.

"You can save your friends," a voice spoke behind him.

Jesus leaped to his feet in surprise and spun around. There stood a Roman soldier leaning back against at tree, his hand resting on the hilt of his sheathed sword.

"And I am here to help you," the soldier said to him.

"You're the commander of—you're Flavius!" stammered a confused and frightened Jesus.

"Well, sort of," Flavius answered. "I've been using this body for a while here on earth."

He smiled at Jesus. "I am also your Heavenly Father."

Jesus stood there speechless.

"Don't be surprised. I move in mysterious ways. It makes things much more interesting. And they seem to work out pretty well," Flavius added with a wry smile.

"As for your friends, I am going to help you. But let's talk about you first."

Flavius walked over to a large rock where he sat down.

"Jesus, as for your being the Promised Messiah and my Son, I understand that's a pretty heavy piece of news for a twelve-year-old to receive all at once. It must seem difficult for you to hear and accept what you've been told all of a sudden by your mother, and Joseph and the rabbi in a room in the Temple, and now by a Roman soldier in this grove.

"But I've thought about you and my plan for you for a very long time, even before the earth was created. And while the revelation that you are my child may have seemed sudden, if you think about it, you'll realize that I actually have been revealing this revelation to you a little bit every day of your life.

"So while you are my Son, I am treating you the same way that I treat everyone on earth. And my plan for you will be revealed the same way."

Jesus still did not move, not knowing what to say.

"Come sit with me," said Flavius.

Jesus hesitated. Sitting next to a Roman soldier, sitting for the first time next to someone who says he is your father, sitting next to God—the idea of any of them made him uncomfortable.

"Here, at my right hand," Flavius placed his hand beside him on the rock and gave Jesus a comforting smile.

Jesus walked over and sat down. They sat quietly for a while. Jesus felt a power and warmth that calmed him, the feeling of confidence from sitting in the protection of one's father. He realized that he felt as if he belonged there.

"Show me your hands," Flavius eventually said in a soft voice. When Jesus held out his hands, the soldier turned them over and looked at his palms for a long moment. Then he looked into Jesus' eyes. There was deep sadness in the old soldier's face.

"My plan for you is not going to be easy," he said. "In fact, some of what you will have to do will be the most difficult thing for any man ever."

A feeling of uneasiness returned to Jesus until Flavius stood up and put his hands on Jesus' shoulders.

"But that's why I chose you," he said with a confidant look. "I know you can see it done. You will help the people of this earth. You will change their lives."

Flavius turned and walked over to a tree. As he continued talking, he touched its bark and then its leaves as if he were admiring his creation for the first time.

"However, you must understand that when people here on earth need help, I don't just wave my hand and have it magically appear. I did that for Adam and Eve when I put them in the Garden of Eden, and it didn't work out because they decided they still wanted to sort out matters themselves.

"So after that, I handle things differently on earth. If people are in need, I give someone the ability to help themselves or others, and then it's up to them to sort matters out.

"I didn't simply give Noah an ark, did I? I gave him the plan, the tools and the people to build it. But it was up to him to trust in my help and to believe in himself. If Noah can survive a flood of the whole world that way, I'm pretty sure you should be able to save your friends in the garrison."

He stopped and faced Jesus.

"I'll give you the plan, the tools and the people. Just trust in me and believe in yourself. You will figure things out.

"In fact, I already started a miracle for you and your friends several thousand years ago," he announced with a smile.

"I put a crack into the middle of a boulder that later was hewn into a stone and finally delivered to a stone mason and carpenter in Nazareth named Joseph. So don't worry. I'll stick around and watch closely. You'll all be fine in the end."

Flavius gave Jesus a long loving look. Jesus watched a swirl of dust blowing about his feet. Puzzled by the words he had just heard, he finally found the courage to speak.

"But how will a crack in a boulder—"

When Jesus looked back up, Flavius was gone.

* * *

"What now?" demanded Nicodemus in a perturbed voice. A slave interrupted him with a message as he finally sat down to the sumptuous meal set before him after his arduous journey from Jerusalem following a very frustrating Feast of the Passover.

"It's from Samais, Master," said the slave.

With a grumble, Nicodemus snatched away the parchment and tore open the seal. Samais's message informed Nicodemus that the Pharisees of the Sanhedrin were summoned by Herod to appear before him at the garrison in two days time to provide the identity of the boy from Nazareth whose ambitions with the Romans they had revealed to the Tetrarch. Nicodemus was ordered to meet with Samais at once.

His stomach was still growling as Nicodemus hurried into a large room in Samais's home. The other Pharisees of the Sanhedrin were already there with looks of despair about to turn into panic.

"We are facing a grave situation," Samais announced to them as soon as he saw Nicodemus enter the room. "Either we give Herod the name of a boy from Nazareth in two days, or we could lose everything thing we have."

His face grew pale.

"And maybe even our lives. Nazeera is here with Herod."

Dead silence fell on the room as stark fear filled their hearts at the sound of Nazeera's name.

Nicodemus's thoughts immediately went back to the Temple and the remarkable demonstration of extraordinary knowledge and presence of mind from Zacharias's student. There was nothing that pointed directly to that boy from Nazareth as the Roman's pawn to rule Palestine. But the Pharisees were desperate for any information to take to Herod. Since they started their search, that scene at the Temple was the only indication of any sort which suggested a boy who might be worthy of consideration as the King of the Jews whom the people would follow.

"When are we summoned to meet with Herod?" asked Nicodemus.

"The message said Herod's servant would come for us in the morning on the day after next," answered Samais.

"I cannot promise anything," said Nicodemus, "but I have a suspicion of who the boy might be. And I believe the Rabbi Zacharias may know for sure."

The Pharisees looked at Nicodemus hopefully.

"I will have Zacharias followed and observed constantly tomorrow. If he doesn't lead us to the boy by tomorrow night, I will confront him then and do what I must to persuade him to reveal the boy before we meet with Herod."

"But what do we tell Herod if we don't locate the boy?" asked a nervous Pharisee.

Nicodemus gave them all a confident look.

"We'll make something up," he said as he felt his stomach growl once again.

***

Never before in his life had Herod Antipas experienced anything like this. Never before had he been so disappointingly frustrated and at the same time so thrillingly exhilarated.

Here in his possession and under his control was the most desirable female he had ever laid eyes on. She was a common girl, a horse thief, his prisoner there for the taking. No one dared or could stop him from doing anything he wanted with her. But he was not about to treat this amazing woman like any slave or servant girl. That would be too easy, uninteresting and not as enjoyable. When he took this woman, it would be an achievement as special as her beauty. Herod wanted pleasure from a victory of persuasive seduction, not just physical release from a conquest by force.

The thrill of the hunt now captivated him more than the kill. She was no ordinary prey. She had repulsed his advances, but in a way that avoided angering him. She cleverly made sure that nothing happened by hinting that what could happen would be unbelievable beyond his imagining, but only if it happened as she wanted, not as he demanded. She gave him nothing, and instead of feeling rejected, he was enthralled. He was intrigued by the thought that he no longer knew if he was the hunter or the hunted.

"Tomorrow night in the baths," he decided. He gave Chuza special instructions for the arrangements. "It will be a night," he told Chuza, "that I will never forget."

***

"It will be your moment and your moment alone."

J.B. bowed his head as the Black Turban addressed him. A large group of the Warriors of the Wilderness was gathered in the long room of the nondescript house on the edge of Nazareth. The vinedressers looked at him enviously.

"Herod is housed in the garrison, and the Legion has not yet returned from Jerusalem. Herod's officers will not be on their guard while he is within the garrison walls. And you know the secret entrance to the garrison and the corridors within.

"Lie in wait where you know he will move and strike him when he does."

The Black Turban raised up his arm with a dagger in his fist.

"Strike—him—dead!" he shouted. His followers all thrust their daggers in the air as they clamored their approval.

When they grew quiet, the Black Turban lowered his black eyes and pointed his dagger at J.B. with a final firm order.

"Spare no life to see that he is killed, including—"

"My own." J.B. finished the command.

The Black Turban nodded and gave J.B. a malevolent smile.

"Tomorrow night belongs to you and your dagger, my brother."

* * *

Mary was lighting the last of the lamps from her cooking fire as Lazarus stepped hesitantly through the door just as the day's sun disappeared.

"Good of you to come, Lazarus," said Joseph, waving him to a chair next to the Wine Seller Shikkor and Susanna. Lazarus nodded uncertainly to the big man as he sat down. Joseph closed the door.

All the Apostles except Peter were sitting around the room. Anxious to help Peter and Maggie, they had arrived at the home of Joseph and Mary earlier than instructed. Zacharias stood by the fire.

"We are going to attack the garrison to free Peter and Maggie," Joseph announced.

A variety of looks and emotions responded to his statement. The surprised Apostles felt both eager and helpless, while Simon's jaw was set with determination to lead the charge. The Wine Seller Shikkor gave Joseph a doubtful look. Lazarus was wondering how he could slip unnoticed out of the room at the first chance. Zacharias looked calmly at the fire.

"Now, we cannot attack the garrison like an army," Joseph went on. "But we can attack it with special forces and strategic advantages."

The Wine Seller Shikkor looked over at Bartholomew. "Special forces?" he thought dubiously.

"First, we have important strategic inside information," said Joseph. "I planned and built much of the garrison. Jesus and I know more about its walls, rooms and corridors than even the Romans. Second, we have the element of surprise. The Roman soldiers and Herod's guards in the garrison do not even know that we intend to attack, let alone when."

A nervous rustle moved through the room. There was still more doubt than certainty among the recruits to this new army.

"We will also have the advantage of disguise," Joseph told them. "Herod's servants wear white tunics. When you enter the garrison, you will be dressed in white tunics like the servants. The rabbi's wife Elizabeth, who weaves such cloth, has white fabric that she, my wife and daughters have been sewing into tunics for you to wear.

"We have strength, in power and in numbers. The Wine Seller Shikkor is as strong a man as God creates. And we have strength in our numbers. You Apostles have shown before how you can use your numbers and cleverness to cause diversions and confusion to allow the mission to be executed."

Lazarus was thinking that it would be the Apostles who would get executed instead of their mission, when all of a sudden he heard his name.

"And we have Lazarus," said Joseph. "He can see like a hawk in daylight and like an owl at night. We have the best eyes in Nazareth as our lookout to warn us of danger."

When everyone in the room nodded their agreement and looked confidently at Lazarus, he reluctantly concluded there would be no sneaking out now.

"And we have one final special strength. We believe in our purpose more than the enemy believes in theirs. Our enemy is simply doing a job for pay. We are doing what is necessary to save your friends.

"Now let me tell you the ultimate key to our success, where our attack on the garrison will begin and end—a secret entrance!"

An excited buzz filled the room after Joseph explained how there was an unknown and invisible entrance through a movable stone in the garrison wall. He went on to explain how Peter must be freed first without any noise or alarm so that he could be helped out carefully because of his physical injuries. Once Peter was clear of the garrison, the Apostles then would enter the garrison disguised as servants and do what they could do best: create distractions in other parts of the garrison to cover

Maggie's rescue through the secret entrance. After Joseph gave them the plan, the Apostles suggested some additions and changes that the men in the room had to admit were clever.

"We can get Maggie out with that plan," said Thomas, "But what about Peter? He's locked up in a cell. How do we free him?"

"Leave that to me and the Wine Seller Shikkor," answered Joseph. "And to Bartholomew," he added surprising everyone, especially the Wine Seller Shikkor.

Simon could hardly sit still and spoke up.

"We are ready. When do we attack the garrison?" he asked eagerly.

Joseph looked around the room.

"We will attack tomorrow night after sunset and the change of the guards."

The Apostles cheered. Off to the side of the room, Jesus smiled confidently. He had just seen his Heavenly Father give him the plan, the tools and the people. Now it was up to him to sort things out.

Zacharias, watching by the fire, was worried by another message from God. Dreams never work out as planned or expected.

Chapter 21

SINS

It was already quite dark when the lingering light of the sun hidden behind a layer of clouds faded away. An unusual soft fog was settling in at the garrison as a Roman soldier finished his watch by lighting the last two torches sitting next to each other halfway down the walkway at the top of the back wall. He was tired from the double duty falling on the small contingent of soldiers in the Legion's absence and hurried away eager for his supper and some sleep.

The garrison walls sat empty and silent except for the torches that crackled and hissed in the moist evening air. A dark figure appeared out of nowhere and glided soundlessly up to the wall under the torches. He pressed his back against the stones until he was sure he had not been seen, and then turned to face a foundation stone at the bottom of the wall. Placing his fingers into the gaps barely visible at the top corners of the stone, he pulled hard. Nothing happened at first, but with a second effort, the hollow stone slowly rolled out of the wall until there was a small opening on the side that the man squeezed through. The space where the stone had sat in the wall formed a short tunnel that opened into a corridor.

The light from two torches above the opening in the corridor revealed J.B.'s face as he carefully glanced both directions down the passage to confirm that the coast was clear. He turned back into the tunnel and grasped the handholds at the inside bottom of the hollow stone to pull it back into place. He could feel the stone rolling on the smooth round tree branches on which it sat. After it slid back into place, he headed down the corridor to his right in the direction of the sleeping quarters as Jesus had described to him.

Two servants in their white tunics opened a door and stepped out into the corridor. J.B. barely slipped around a corner without being noticed.

"That's right," one of the servants said to the other. "Herod is dining in the baths tonight."

Are you sure?" the other servant asked. "Why would he be eating in the baths?"

"I have no idea. But it's a fancy supper with the finest wines."

They carried on around a corner and down another corridor. As soon as he was alone again, J.B. headed towards the baths where he found an alcove off the passage in which he could not be seen easily. He leaned up against the wall hidden in the shadows of the nook. Out from under his sleeve J.B. slid his dagger and held it lightly in his palm. He touched the sharp edge of its blade to give him confidence, and readied himself to stand motionless until the moment to strike.

***

While J.B. stood hidden in the shadows inside the garrison, another person approached outside the garrison wall below the torches. This man was not nearly so secretive.

"Alms for the blind. Alms for the blind," he called out, tapping a stick in front of him. When the stick struck the wall and stopped him, he reached out to feel the wall and slid to the ground where he sat with his back up against the stones.

After a few moments when nothing happened, Lazarus looked around him and then up at the top of the wall under the torches above. When he was sure he was alone, he gave a soft hoot like a night owl. Three figures quickly appeared next to him.

"Well done," Lazarus," Joseph said to him. "You have the ram's horn?" he asked as he grabbed the top corners of the secret entrance's hollow stone.

Lazarus reached into his robe and held up the ram's horn that

Zacharias had given him. It was a gift given to Zacharias from some of the Temple priests when he retired. The rabbi was only too happy to part with it for its purpose that night.

"Good. Now if there's trouble, blow the horn as loudly as possible," Joseph reminded him. "The sound of the trumpet blast is the emergency signal for everyone to escape to safety.

"Now stand back, you two," he said to Bartholomew and the Wine Seller Shikkor. As he pulled at the corners of the hollow stone, it rolled out of the wall with little resistance.

"That came out much easier than I expected," thought Joseph. In the dim light, he could not see the tracks from when it had been opened earlier. Joseph picked up his tool box.

"Give me the wineskin," he instructed the Wine Seller Shikkor.

The Wine Seller Shikkor handed Joseph a small bulging wineskin.

"Your finest special wine?" Joseph asked as he put the wineskin into his toolbox.

"Very special," the Wine Seller Shikkor replied with a wink.

"Are you ready, Bartholomew?" asked Joseph.

Bartholomew swallowed and nodded as he smoothed out the front of his white tunic newly sown by Elizabeth. They stepped into the corridor and headed towards the prisoner cells. The Wine Seller Shikkor pushed the hollow stone back into the wall and pressed himself against the wall next to Lazarus, trying unsuccessfully to appear smaller.

As Joseph and Bartholomew reached the passage with the prisoner cells, Joseph had Bartholomew wait around the corner where he could not be seen by the guard watching Peter.

"Stand here until I give the signal to come," Joseph reminded him. "If anyone comes along, just walk away like you are one of Herod's servants and return as soon as you can to this spot."

Joseph started to go and then paused.

"Do you know what a 'little white lie' is?" he asked.

"No, sir," answered Bartholomew.

"Well you may hear me tell one in a moment," Joseph replied.

He gave Bartholomew a confident pat on the shoulder, and turned the corner. The guard standing before the door to Peter's cell looked up immediately and recognized Joseph.

"You're still working too?" the soldier asked. He looked unhappy.

"Unfortunately, yes," answered Joseph. "But I am finishing and you are just starting."

The guard grunted at Joseph's observation. Joseph sat his tool box down on the floor next to the door to Peter's cell and started looking at the ceiling running along the wall to the next corner.

"How can you stand here all night?" Joseph asked. "You are a trained warrior—a man of action. I don't know how you do it," Joseph said shaking his head.

The soldier grunted again, none too happy to be reminded about his unpleasant duty. Joseph reached down and started rummaging through his tool box.

"They don't pay you enough," sympathized Joseph. "In fact, they don't pay me enough either.

"Here—" Joseph held up the wineskin he had pulled out of his tool box. "Let's make up for it a little bit. Go ahead. No one's going to come by here at this hour."

The soldier looked up and down the corridor.

"Why not? No harm done," he concluded and reached over for the wineskin, nodding his helmet at Peter's cell. "After all, he's not going anywhere."

He took a quick pull at the wineskin and gave it back to Joseph. Joseph handed it back to him.

"Go on, have another," urged Joseph. "You've earned it."

The soldier shrugged and took a longer swig.

"You ever think of giving this up?" Joseph asked as he resumed his examination of the top of the wall. "Seems a soldier's life would be hard, far away from home for so long."

"Every day," the guard answered. He had a faraway look for a moment and then took another drink from the wineskin.

"He still in there?" Joseph pointed at Peter's cell. The guard nodded.

"I know his mother," said Joseph. "A fine woman, if you know what I mean." Joseph gave him a wink.

"Mind if I have some of that?" Joseph pointed at the wineskin with a smile. The guard handed it back apologetically. Joseph raised the wineskin as if to drink, but paused as he continued.

"What I wouldn't give to have that woman," he sighed. "I've been trying for months. Her husband fishes in the Sea of Galilee and is never around. But so far, I've had no luck catching anything." He laughed at his own bad joke as he leaned back against the wall and relaxed.

The soldier looked down at the far-from-handsome carpenter. "No wonder," he thought.

"Here, have another," said Joseph as he handed the wineskin back to the soldier without having taken a drink. The guard leaned against the wall next to him and took a healthy swig, and then another after Joseph described in detail the feminine attractions of the prisoner's mother.

"You know, my friend, I have an idea," said Joseph taking back the wineskin. "I have something valuable that you might find extremely useful for getting out of the army and back to Rome.

"I'll never use it, but you could," Joseph added. "And I might get something out of it that I'd like very much." He gestured at Peter's cell with the wineskin and handed it back to the soldier.

"What is it?" the intrigued soldier asked. He took another drink and wiped away some wine dripping from his chin.

"I've got some frankincense and myrrh. The frankincense smells good. They're worth a lot, I'm told," said Joseph.

"What's myrrh?" the soldier asked.

"Well, it's a really expensive spice. I was told it's for making perfume and medicine. But I do know the frankincense smells really good.

"But here's what I'm thinking. What does a carpenter like me do with frankincense and myrrh? I can't really use it. And if I sold it, my wife would just take the money, and I get nothing."

Joseph gave the guard a sly look.

"Now if I gave it to you, you could sell it, and have enough to get back to Rome and live very well for quite a while."

"But what do you get out of it?" the soldier asked. The question came out slightly slurred.

"That's the beauty of it," replied Joseph. "What I get out of it doesn't cost you a thing and likely gives me what I want without my wife knowing."

"What is it?" the guard asked again. He blinked a few times trying to focus his eyes.

"The boy in there," Joseph gestured at the cell door. "If I could return him to his mother, I'm sure she'd be very grateful. You know what I mean?" He gave the soldier a friendly elbow and knowing smile.

The soldier's head weaved about slightly as he acknowledged Joseph's plan with a smile in return. Then the smile was slowly replaced with a serious look and a furrowed brow.

"But what about Herod?" The soldier's words were now badly slurred.

Joseph responded quickly.

"Herod doesn't really care about the boy. He only cares about his horse."

Joseph spoke even more quickly as he saw the soldier's eyes start to grow heavy.

"I'll give you the frankincense and myrrh, and you just let me get him out of here. In the morning you tell Herod's men that the boy died early in the night and you ordered some Jewish workmen to get rid of the body. What do they care about the corpse of a horse thief?

"Think of it. You get a good's night sleep, a good start on your next life, and I—let's just say I'll get what I want eventually."

"I don't know," the soldier hesitated.

"Here it is! See?" said Joseph, as he pulled two small expensively decorated cases from his tool box.

"I don't think so," said the soldier shaking his head sleepily.

"All right," Joseph came back. "How about gold? I'll throw in some gold. Gold, frankincense and myrrh. You can't beat that combination."

"Did you say gold?" The soldier's eyes widened, but then his head started bobbing towards his chest.

"Yes. Yes, I said gold!" Joseph repeated hurriedly. He pulled a pouch of gold coins from his tool box and jingled them in front of the soldier's face. "Now if you just give me the key to the cell, you are a rich man on his way to Rome."

The guard blinked twice and tried to smile as his hand went into his tunic and pulled out a key. When he leaned forward to reach out for the pouch, he kept on falling until he hit the floor and lay there dead still.

Joseph silently thanked the Wine Seller Shikkor for the special wine as he took the key from the soldier's hand. He quickly unlocked the cell door and went in.

Peter was huddled in a corner unconscious. Joseph could tell by the bruises and dried blood that the boy had been badly beaten. He shook Peter gently by the shoulder.

"Peter! Peter, can you hear me?" Joseph turned Peter's head to face him.

Peter's swollen eyes barely opened. When he saw someone before him, his hand came up to cover his face, and he whimpered weakly.

"Peter, you're safe. It's me, Joseph. I'm Jesus' father."

At the sound of Jesus' name, Peter's face flinched and turned away. Joseph stood up and walked out of the cell to his tool box. He took out a hammer and struck the wall twice sending a ringing sound down the corridor. Bartholomew immediately came around the corner and hurried toward Joseph who went back into the cell.

"Come on, Peter. You've got to stand up," Joseph said to Peter as he put Peter's arm around his shoulder. A groan came from deep within the limp body as Joseph pulled Peter to his feet as carefully as possible. Bartholomew came to his side and took Peter's other arm to help him stand up. Peter's eyes opened again and tried to focus on Bartholomew's face. A look of relief came over him and a small tear ran down his cheek.

"Can you hold him?" Joseph asked Bartholomew once they got outside the cell door.

Bartholomew nodded. Joseph stepped over to the guard and propped him up against the wall with the wineskin cradled in his arm. Then Joseph tossed the gold, frankincense and myrrh back into tool box and picked it up.

"Sorry, my friend, but we didn't shake hands on the deal," he said over his shoulder to the comatose soldier as he took Peter's arm and the three of them started moving down the corridor towards the secret entrance.

Peter did his best to walk, but his feet mostly dragged on the ground. Joseph and Bartholomew tried to hurry their pace as they approached the last corner before the corridor to the secret entrance. When they reached the corner, Joseph stopped, took on Peter's full weight from Bartholomew and leaned their backs against the wall hidden from view.

"We'll wait here. Go open the secret entrance so we can take Peter right out to the Wine Seller Shikkor."

Bartholomew hurried to the hollow stone and started pushing. It moved away quickly when the Wine Seller Shikkor started pulling on the stone from the other side as soon as he felt it move.

"You made it!" said the Wine Seller Shikkor as he bent over and started to enter the short tunnel to the corridor.

Suddenly he stumbled backwards as Bartholomew shoved him roughly. Bartholomew started walking away quickly towards one of Herod's servants in a white tunic who had turned into the corridor. Just before they met, Bartholomew called to him.

"What's your name?"

"Nadav," The servant answered and stopped. "Who are you?" he asked with a questioning look at Bartholomew's tunic.

"I'm Bartholomew, a new servant. I'm glad I found you. Herod has been asking for you."

The servant looked surprised.

"For me? Herod?"

"Yeah. Chuza has several of us looking for you."

"But I was just—" he gave Bartholomew a confused look. Bartholomew could see that the servant did not know whether to be pleased or concerned.

"I'd better go," the servant said as he turned around and strode away hastily.

Bartholomew hurried back to the secret entrance.

"Wait here," he said to the Wine Seller Shikkor who did not question Bartholomew's instruction.

Bartholomew walked back to Joseph and Peter where he and Joseph lifted up Peter once again. When they reached the two torches, they got Peter quickly through the short tunnel where the Wine Seller Shikkor scooped him up in his arms.

"Clear, Lazarus?" the Wine Seller Shikkor asked.

"Go!" Lazarus answered, his eyes scanning the darkness around them.

They all heard a sickening snap when the Wine Seller Shikkor stumbled as he turned to head away from the garrison. Only Lazarus's quick move to hold him up kept the Wine Seller Shikkor from tumbling to the ground with Peter. The Wine Seller Shikkor steadied himself and sucked in a deep breath in response to the pain.

"My ankle—I think it's broken."

Without hesitating, Bartholomew stepped up to him and took Peter from his arms. "Put your hand on my shoulder," he ordered the Wine Seller Shikkor. "Can you walk if you use me as a crutch?"

The Wine Seller Shikkor winced as he put weight on his foot.

"I think so," he answered.

"Good," said Bartholomew. "Let's go."

Bartholomew walked steadily in the direction of the barn with Peter semiconscious in his arms and the Wine Seller Shikkor limping along next to him holding onto his shoulder.

"All right, Lazarus," Joseph said to him. Lazarus this time gave two hoots like night owl.

A moment later, Jesus and the Apostles dressed in white tunics like Herod's servants arrived at the entrance.

They were all fully briefed and prepared for their two missions. The first was to locate Maggie. Disguised as servants of Herod, they would follow Jesus along the route of the map they had carefully memorized to the area of the garrison where Herod and his entourage were quartered. Each of them had specific rooms they were to check out to find precisely where Maggie was being kept at that moment. Once they had checked out their assigned rooms, they would head back to the secret entrance where they would report Maggie's position to Joseph and wait for him there while he went for Maggie.

Then they would start their second mission to divert the attention of everyone in the garrison so that Joseph could sneak Maggie out the secret entrance. The diversion was a simple tactic. Once Joseph was in place near Maggie, Jesus would give them the signal to start running through the corridors of the garrison towards the parade ground, shouting and making as much noise as possible. Coming together at the parade ground, they were to keep running right out the gate before any of the surprised guards would know what the disguised servants were up to and how to react. Then they would disperse in the cover of night and make their way back to the barn. During all this distraction, Joseph would slip Maggie out of the secret entrance and with Lazarus return to the barn to meet them.

"Remember," Joseph whispered the last reminder of their instructions, "if you hear Lazarus blow the ram's horn, that means there is serious trouble. If you hear the horn, meet up immediately near the gate house and race through the gate if you can. If you can't get to or through the gate, hide in the storeroom next to where the weapons are kept until I get to you first thing in the morning."

"Is everyone ready?" he asked.

All heads nodded eagerly.

"Let's go!" said Joseph as he pulled on the hollow stone to open the secret entrance.

The Apostles silently followed Jesus down several corridors and turned a corner where they began efficiently opening doors and checking out rooms. When they encountered someone, they simply gave a quick nod and closed the door. Jesus swiftly checked his rooms and was concerned when he did not find Maggie. They were the most likely places where Maggie was expected to be held. Jesus met some of the Apostles and asked if they had located Maggie. Hearing that none of them had seen her, he told them to go report to Joseph and then went to check some other rooms that they had not originally targeted.

As Jesus walked by the entrance to the baths, he heard a voice and stopped. It was Maggie's voice. He was sure of it. He hurried on down the passage and circled around to the back work entrance of the baths next to the wheels that controlled the flow of water. There he carefully cracked open the door and peaked in.

Herod was sitting next to Maggie at a table filled with plates of fruits and sweets and urns of wine. Jesus could not stop his heart from skipping a beat when he saw Maggie beautifully dressed in ivory-colored robes and a delicately embroidered scarf over her thick shiny black hair that cascaded loosely over her shoulders.

"You are a clever girl," Herod said to her as he leaned over Maggie to pluck a large grape off a golden platter mounded with fruit.

"Not nearly as clever as Your Grace's wise and agile mind," she demurred.

He smiled at her and held up the grape in his hand.

"This is a beauty, just like you. Here, you eat it."

Herod pressed the grape against her lips and pushed so that she had to part them to take the grape in her mouth. After the grape disappeared, his forefinger stayed for a moment until he removed it with a sensuous sliding touch along her lips.

"Now, you put one in mine," he playfully ordered.

Maggie took a grape from the platter and put it in Herod's mouth. Her movement was more efficient than sensuous. Herod looked disappointed, but went on undeterred. He filled two golden goblets to the brim from an urn of wine and took a deep drink.

"You must drink," he urged her, setting down his wine and pushing the other goblet into her hands.

As she placed the goblet against her lips and tipped it slightly to sip, Herod reached out, slid the scarf off her head and stroked her hair its entire length over her shoulder and down her body. She quickly set down her goblet and turned her body away from his touch.

"Now don't be a naughty boy!" She tried to sound playful as she scolded him and firmly pushed aside his hand.

"Oh, but I intend to be naughty," he replied reaching once again to stroke her hair.

Just then Jesus heard a voice behind him from someone coming down the corridor. He slipped silently out of the corridor into the back of the baths where he hid by the wheels.

"Are you sure Herod summoned you?"

It was Chuza walking alongside the servant Navad.

"Yes. The new servant Bartholomew told me so and that you sent him to look for me," answered Navad.

"New servant? Bartholomew?" said Chuza. He frowned. Something was not right.

"Come with me!" he ordered and turned into the passage where he entered the door of the main entrance to the baths.

"What is the meaning of this?" demanded Herod. His arms were wrapped around Maggie who was leaning back as far as possible in his grasp.

"Did you summon Navad, Your Grace?" asked Chuza with the servant standing next to him.

"Does it look like I want a servant here right now? Get out!" he ordered furiously.

Chuza angrily grabbed Navad by his tunic and dragged him out into the corridor. As he closed the door and turned back with his hand raised to slap the servant cowering below him, Chuza found himself looking at a boy with dark curly hair whom he did not recognize despite the fact that the boy was wearing a servant's tunic. The boy stopped short in surprise. Chuza heard another noise behind him and looked around. Around the corner ran what appeared to be the same boy dressed in white with identical dark eyes and curly hair.

Both Chuza and Navad looked in amazement at the one boy and then back at the other. James looked around them at John and gave him a smile. John smiled back just before they both bolted at a dead run in opposite directions back down the corridor.

"Nazeera!" yelled Chuza as loudly as he could.

Almost immediately Nazeera's head poked out of the nearby door to his quarters. He gave a puzzled look at Chuza with his servant kneeling below him and then again at the two servants running away at each end of the corridor.

"The garrison's been infiltrated by rebels disguised as servants. We've got to get Herod out of here!" Chuza cried out.

Nadav fell to the floor when Chuza dropped him to push open the door to the baths. Nazeera unsheathed his sword as he and Chuza rushed in.

Herod looked up angrily as Maggie, leaning back, was trying to pry her way out of his arms.

"My Lord, the rebels have invaded the garrison. We have to get you out of here now!" Chuza warned him excitedly.

Herod let go of Maggie who fell to the floor and scrambled to her feet.

Nazeera pointed at the door with his sword.

"This way, Your Gr—"

Herod pushed him aside to rush out the door. Nazeera started to hurry after Herod.

"What about the girl?" Chuza called to him.

Nazeera hesitated and stepped back to Maggie.

"Can you swim?" he asked her.

"No," she answered with a confused look.

With an evil smile, he put his boney hand on Maggie's face and gave her a hard push. Maggie stumbled backward and fell with a splash into the deep bath behind her.

Nazeera and Chuza ran out the door into the corridor. There stood Herod frantically trying to order Navad to go ahead of him down the passage.

"Tell him to do as I say!" Herod said to Nazeera in a hysterical voice.

"Follow me, My Lord," Nazeera said to Herod. "Chuza, go alert the Romans."

"You!" he pointed at Navad. "Go find Herod's guards and have them meet us at the stables."

* * *

J.B. was growing anxious as he heard the echoing sounds of shouts and people running through the corridors. He had been standing in the shadows for some time wondering whether he would have the chance to attack his prey. But something out of the ordinary was happening now. He heard several more shouts nearby and sensed he could no longer wait for the opportunity to come to him. He would have to change his tactics to go after Herod and deal with whatever or whomever was standing between him and his target.

He tensed as he heard footsteps running towards him in the passage. A white tunic of one of Herod's servants shot past the opening to the alcove in which J.B. was hiding and sprinted down the corridor. He started to peek his head into the passage when he jerked back as someone else came around the corner. Another white tunic flew by.

"I have to move and find out what's happening," he thought as he slid out of the shadows and started jogging down the corridor with his dagger pointing in front of him.

Just as he reached the corner, a figure flew around the turn and ran into him. J.B. stabbed with his dagger and struck home. Instinctively he thrust his dagger hard a second time. He heard a moan from the falling body as it collapsed to the ground.

Before he could look down at his victim, J.B. suddenly found himself face to face with two more people running to turn into the passage. Herod and Nazeera skidded to a halt and turned completely white as they were confronted by the sight of J.B., with his wild long hair and black beard, standing with a bloody dagger over a body on the floor. Without hesitating, the two of them turned and ran away, each trying to outrace the other.

J.B. looked down at the body at his feet and saw a red stain spreading rapidly across the white tunic. A horrified look of recognition and realization came over his face. His dagger fell from his hand to the stone floor with a clatter.

"Oh my God! What have I done?"

He kneeled down, picked up the body and hoisted it over his shoulder before heading for the secret entrance with a trail of flowing blood behind him.

Chapter 22

MIRACLES

Maggie snatched a brief choking breath as her head barely broke the surface of the water in the deep Roman bath. The waterlogged robes around her body weighed her down as her flailing arms struggled unsuccessfully to keep her from going under a second time.

Jesus saw the panic in her eyes as he moved to the bath. He laid flat by the edge of the bath and tried to grab her hand even though he knew she was out of reach. His chest was tight with fear, both for Maggie and also from his own horror at being near the deep water. He stood up and backed away to look around for something to use to reach her. Seeing nothing, he looked down helplessly when she managed to fight her way to the air above one more time.

"Jesu—" she gasped as she went under again. She could no longer get her hands above the surface.

He stood there paralyzed with fear, staring at her arms and legs waving and kicking more slowly underneath her robes just below the gently swirling surface. The image came to him of Joseph standing on the bottom of the bath looking pleased as the water filled it for the first time. He looked over at the wheel that controlled the drainage and knew it would be hopeless.

Her long black hair drifted upwards as she started to sink deeper. From his vivid memory, he could feel in his own throat the choking and desperate craving for air that he knew Maggie must be experiencing.

"Oh God, no!" he murmured a desperate plea.

Overwhelmed by the sense that he could not let this happen, Jesus moved despite his fear to edge of the bath. Having no idea of what else to do, he did the thing he knew he must. There was no time left. Taking a deep breath, he closed his eyes, resolved to somehow fight the water, and stepped forward.

His eyes jerked open when he did not feel the water surround and grab him. Instead he felt a slight jarring feeling as if he had stepped off a stair unexpectedly. Looking down, he saw his sandal resting on the surface of the water like it was a mysteriously clear floor through which he could see. Hesitantly, he stepped forward with his other foot. It set down on the water firmly with a small splash.

With only an instant's hesitation, he knelt down and reached a full arm's length into the water where his hand was just able to grasp hold of Maggie's hair. She started to rise as he pulled steadily. When he could, he let go of her locks to grip her robes and kept pulling.

As soon as her face broke the surface, she gasped for air. Jesus grabbed her under her arms and started dragging her backwards through the water until he was able to step up onto the edge of the bath and pull her out. She lay there coughing until she could breathe normally. Jesus looked about the room and was relieved that no one had heard them or come in.

"Come on, Maggie," he urged her as he tried to help her stand. "We have to get out of here!"

Her blue eyes sought his with a grateful look.

"Thank you, Jesus," she said, deeply thankful yet wondering why he was here at all taking this risk.

"Thank you," she thought she heard him reply.

"For what?" she was about to ask him before she realized Jesus was not speaking to her. She looked about the room puzzled. There was no one there.

He led her over to the back door of the baths and glimpsed down the corridor. He heard some commotion, but no one was in sight. Taking her arm, Jesus hurried her down the passageway in the direction of the secret entrance.

***

Lazarus was nervous and knew he had good reason to be. Peter had managed to get out despite the close call with the servant and the Wine Seller Shikkor's broken ankle. Now his role was to stay there in the fog without knowing what was happening and wait for something else to go wrong. He was certain it was only a matter of time before he would encounter Roman soldiers or Herod's guards.

"Something has to be happening by now," he thought. He started to pace a few steps back and forth and then decided to walk farther down the wall to see if he could sense any activity or movement inside the garrison. He was a ways along the wall when he heard a sound behind him. Turning around, he took a few quick steps back towards the secret entrance before he saw that the hollow stone was open. When he reached the entrance and peered in, no one was there. Then he saw blood on the ground and looked back to see a figure with something white slung over his shoulder disappearing into the fog.

Lazarus anxiously touched the ram's horn and stepped into the short tunnel to the inside of the garrison. Just as he peeked in his head, he saw Joseph hurrying around the corner at one end of the corridor and several Apostles in white coming around the corner at the other end.

"Did you find Maggie?" Joseph asked the Apostles when they arrived together at the entrance.

"No," they answered.

"Where are the others? Did you see Jesus?"

They all indicated they did not know where anyone else was.

"Did any of them come out the entrance?" Joseph asked Lazarus.

"I don't know," Lazarus answered. "I moved down the wall to see if anything was happening and then saw someone walking away carrying something."

He was afraid to tell Joseph what he suspected it was. Joseph frowned with indecision.

Their heads jerked up at the sound of someone coming around the corner into the passage. There were Jesus and Maggie with her sopping wet robes leaving a trail of water as they hurried down the corridor. The Apostles ran up to them.

"We've all got to get out," Jesus said to Joseph. "Something's happening back there."

He looked around at the Apostles.

"Where are the others?" Jesus asked.

"We don't know," Joseph answered.

"Here," Jesus gave Maggie's arm to Joseph. "Get Maggie out of here!" he said as he turned and started running back down the corridor.

"Jesus, wait!" Joseph called to him as loudly as he dared. "Wait!"

Jesus turned the corner without stopping.

"You boys take Maggie back to the barn. Go now!" Joseph ordered. "Lazarus, keep the entrance wide open and stand watch," he called over his shoulder as he turned to run after Jesus. "I'll be right back with the others."

The Apostles quickly huddled Maggie through the entrance and hurried off. Lazarus touched his ram's horn again and with a nervous whimper rolled the hollow stone away from the wall.

***

James and John scared each other as they almost collided at a dead run near the parade ground close to the gatehouse. Needless to say, each instantly recognized his brother. They looked around quickly and saw they were safe for the moment.

"Did you hear the ram's horn?" James asked

"No," answered John. "Did you see any of the others?"

James shook his head. As they looked across the parade ground, they saw the man they had encountered by the baths hurrying towards the gatehouse.

"We've got to break for it now!" exclaimed John. James agreed by giving him a push as they started running for the garrison gate.

Two Roman soldiers on guard at the gatehouse looked up in surprise as they saw two of Herod's servants sprint out through the gate.

"That's odd," one of them said. But neither was alarmed at the familiar sight of the servants' white tunics.

Suddenly Chuza rushed in.

"Rebels have infiltrated the garrison!" Chuza blurted out. "They're disguised as Herod's servants!"

The Roman soldier's head whirled around to look out the gate after the two figures that had just run through. He swore under his breath. There were only himself and the other guard at the gate while the garrison was shorthanded.

"Go get Decimus," he gave the order to the other guard.

"Aren't you going to chase them?" demanded Chuza.

"With what? The Legion under my command?" the soldier sarcastically replied.

A few moments later, Decimus arrived and listened to Chuza's story. He immediately gave an order to one of the soldiers.

"Go alert the troops. They're still finishing their supper. Order them to posts armed and resume your guard here immediately with two others."

He turned to the other guard and was glad to see one of his best men.

"Walk the walls outside to check that the perimeter's secure."

The soldier spun on his heel and headed through the gate into the fog. Decimus turned back to Chuza.

"Where's your leader and his guards?" There was little respect in his voice.

"I don't know," Chuza responded with an embarrassed look.

"Go find Nazeera and Herod, and have them meet me here," Decimus instructed him. "Then assemble all your servants on the parade ground."

Chuza scurried out the door.

***

Standing in front of the secret entrance, Lazarus kept looking apprehensively down the wall in both directions and passing the ram's horn nervously from one hand to the other. Now he was hearing occasional shouts from behind the walls.

"Come on, Joseph. Come on!" he urged beneath his breath as he glanced back at the hollow stone and open entrance. His nerves and parched mouth both craved a swallow of wine.

Lazarus froze in place. He squinted hard. A silhouette gathered form as it moved closer along the wall through the thickening fog. His dry mouth fell open in fear as his eyes made out a spear in the hand of the approaching figure. He took a step to run away, but then stopped. From the other direction he heard someone else approaching. Out of the fog came another figure from the dark.

Glancing back and forth, his eyes strained to see through the fog. The figure carrying the spear, as Lazarus feared, was a Roman soldier. Then Lazarus was able to make out the other figure dressed in a black cloak and wearing a black turban. The torchlight above reflected off the blade of a dagger in the man's hand.

Fumbling with the ram's horn, Lazarus tried to bring it to his lips. He missed his mouth when he saw out of the corners of his eyes that the Roman soldier and the man in the black turban had spotted him and picked up their pace in his direction. Finally the ram's horn found its spot on Lazarus's lips. But when he tried to blow the trumpet, his dry lips and flustered breathing produced only a hoarse belching sound that was barely audible. He blew once more. The noise that came out of the ram's horn was so strange that both the soldier and the man with the dagger stopped in their tracks.

The two men stood still momentarily looking at Lazarus from either side, trying to assess the danger from the man and the unrecognizable noise. Lazarus did not know what to do. The Roman and the figure in the black turban each took a step forward. Lazarus dropped his stick, threw the ram's horn over his shoulder and began to run, hoping for a miracle. The ram's horn arched through the air until it hit a spot on the face of the stone above the open secret entrance sending small chards of rock flying. Then Lazarus got his miracle, a miracle that God started a few thousand years earlier.

Before he had even taken a full stride, a loud frightening sound like a sharp thunderclap froze all three men in place. Lazarus whirled around to see a large crack in the stone struck by the ram's horn. Air rushed into the crack as if the stones were inhaling after thousands of years of holding their breath, and the energized crack shot up through the heart of the wall without stopping until the wall was broken in two top to bottom.

A slice of the stone wall around the crack sheared off the stones on either side and slid straight down like an avalanche into the space for hollowed out stone. The avalanche left a momentary breach in the bulwark until the stones of the wall started falling from both sides into the crevice started by the crack.

And so it continued. With a mounting roar, the stones of the garrison walls on either side of the secret entrance crashed inward on the stones that had just fallen before them, steadily imploding and taking down all the fortifications and the inner walls that were attached. In surprisingly short time, the only thing left standing was the archway over the garrison gate. It briefly stood there unmoved until it swayed slightly to the left and back to its right, and then collapsed with a final crash to complete the large ragged circle of broken stones surrounding the open parade ground where soldiers and servants were huddled in terror.

Lazarus, the Roman soldier and the Black Turban completely forgot one another as they stood staring open mouthed at the sudden, devastating demolition. A huge cloud of dust swirled around them when they heard a sound in the scattered broken stones. Then some of the stones in front of them started stirring as if living things. The rocks spread apart as two white figures rose up like ghostly corpses stumbling to their feet out of their graves. Lazarus let out a frightened cry and ran off.

Hearing Lazarus, Joseph and Jesus, covered with the dust of the mortar and stones, looked up to see the Roman soldier with a spear and the Black Turban holding a dagger. The two of them had barely managed to avoid death by diving through the secret entrance just as the wall began to collapse around them. But now Joseph saw that their lives were still in danger.

In desperation, he looked around. His eyes found the ram's horn lying on the ground before him. Instinctively he grabbed and raised it above his head threateningly as a bright red stream of blood started running down his face from a cut on his forehead. Joseph stood there ready to die to defend his son.

To his amazement, the Roman soldier turned and ran, and the Black Turban melted away into the fog. Jesus and Joseph looked at one another with surprise. When they saw each other entirely covered in white dust and looking like unearthly spirits floating in the fog, they laughed out loud with relief. The sound of laughter piercing the fog from out of the devastation spooked the soldier into fleeing even faster.

After a sad glance back at the wreckage that was once his work, Joseph threw aside the ram's horn and hurried away with Jesus towards the barn.

* * *

Nicodemus's servant was out of breath as he gave his report.

"The rabbi left his synagogue and hurried straight to an old barn near—"

"I know where it is," Nicodemus interrupted him.

"Of course," thought Nicodemus. Zacharias was going to the barn where the Wine Seller Shikkor had confronted the boy messengers. Through his mind flashed the fleeting image of wine jugs filled with water. "He is hiding the boy there!"

"Get two other servants and come with me," he ordered as he moved quickly to the door.

* * *

Simon was standing outside the old barn when Joseph and Jesus arrived.

"Jesus, he's not breathing or moving. I think he's dead!" Simon's voice sounded panicked. "What do we do?"

"Who is it?" asked Joseph.

Jesus did not hear the answer as he hurried through the barn door. There was very little light in the shadow filled room. Jesus' eyes took a moment to adjust. The Apostles were standing around silently with scared looks on their faces. He saw Susanna leaning over her father's bandaged ankle and his mother Mary sitting next to Peter lying on some straw, her hand soothing his forehead. Maggie looked up at him from a corner where she was resting. On a makeshift table, another figure completely covered by a blanket lay dead still. Zacharias stood praying next to the shrouded body.

Jesus reeled slightly. His mind was suddenly overwhelmed with his nightmare image of the dirty face of the bleeding rebel fallen before Jesus under the weight of a cross. Jesus inhaled sharply and regained his awareness of the room.

Susanna lit another lamp. Its light fell on Jesus just as Peter's eyes opened to see a hazy ghostly image of Jesus in the white tunic and his face and hair still covered with white dust shining dreamlike in the lamplight.

Zacharias stopped praying and looked at Jesus as he stepped up to the covered body. A figure came out of the shadows of a stall and stood next to Jesus. Zacharias shook his head in disgust and then bowed his head once again to continue praying.

Jesus turned and saw J.B. He looked pale and shaken.

"Jesus, I stabbed him. It was an accident," his voice trembled. "I meant to kill Herod."

"J.B., you—you actually meant to kill someone?" Jesus gave him a look of sadness. J.B.'s head lowered under the weight of his shame. He stared at the ground in silence.

Jesus felt like he staggered backward when he again saw the nightmare's vision before his eyes. The criminal pinned below his cross on the ground implored Jesus, "Save me—Save me!" Jesus was relieved when the vision left as quickly as it came.

Outside the barn, Nicodemus arrived with his servants. Just as he was about to enter, several horses thundered by at a full gallop. Even in the dark, Nicodemus recognized Herod on his black steed ahead of Nazeera and his guard. Once the riders had passed, Nicodemus told his servants to remain there as he slipped through the barn door. He walked over to Zacharias whose hand raised to silence the Pharisee.

No one moved. Jesus' eyes turned to the body on the table. He reached for the blanket covering the body. As his hand touched the edge of the blanket, the inside of the barn disappeared before him. His body tensed in fear as once again he found himself staring into the eyes of the criminal kneeling on the ground under the cross. He watched the criminal's bloody hand leave the cross and reach slowly towards his face. But it was not the face of a three-year-old boy. His mind saw the bloody hand extending towards his face there in the barn.

Jesus pulled back the blanket. His eyes focused on two deep wounds moist with blood. There was no movement, no breathing. The barn was as still as the body before Jesus.

Jesus stood motionless and stared down. Like the body lying before him, he could not breathe. He tried not to think, fearing the nightmare would return again. As if someone else controlled his movements, he watched his hands move towards the body. Each hand firmly touched one of the wounds. Blood oozed over his fingers as they pressed into the cut flesh.

He froze again as his eyes saw the bloody hand of the criminal reaching for him, slowly coming closer and closer to touch his cheek. Jesus ached for the moment when Joseph's hand would grab the criminal's wrist away from his face, and Joseph's arms lift him up to carry him away from this place.

But the saving hand did not appear. Instead Jesus felt the wet touch of the criminal's hand as it slid down his cheek, each finger leaving a bloody line down to his jaw where, without any more strength, the hand fell away. The lines of blood on his cheek turned hot until his skin burned with searing pain.

The face of the criminal and the image of the cross suddenly disappeared as Jesus felt the blood from the wounds under his hands. He sensed the fearful eyes of everyone looking at him helplessly. Everyone's world there in the barn stood still. Jesus swayed above the body as if he were going to faint. He took a deep breath.

Slowly he bent over, looking down into the pale lifeless face before him. It seemed as if he was not moving, until those around him realized that his face had lowered imperceptibly closer and closer until Jesus' lips were almost touching the colorless lips below his.

Jesus paused when his lips could draw no closer without touching.

Then he breathed gently through the unmoving parted lips next to his. When his long breath stopped, a silent eternal second passed before the pale lips below him quivered slightly.

"He's breathing!" cried Simon. The other Apostles crowded around the young body. The deep chest wounds did not bleed as they raised and lowered with each new breath.

"He is the Chosen One," Nicodemus quietly acknowledged to Zacharias with a look of awe. When Zacharias nodded back, Nicodemus felt a comforting, calm acceptance come over him.

Jesus stood up, staring without seeing. J.B. stepped over to Jesus and touched him on the shoulder.

"Jesus," J.B. whispered. Jesus did not move. J.B. could not tell whether Jesus was hearing him or anything else. His eyes filled with tears.

"You—You have taken away my sin."

Jesus turned, looked into J.B.'s eyes and then collapsed into his arms.

Only Mary, Joseph and Zacharias noticed as J.B. lifted Jesus up and carried him to the manger next to Jewels' stall. Everyone else was talking excitedly, expressing their astonishment. The Apostles each tried to get closer to see the breathing body with his own eyes.

"I can't believe he's alive!" cried Thomas, trying to choke back tears of happiness. "Judas, can you hear me? Judas! Judas...."

Chapter 23

THE FIRST SUPPER

Pilate was decidedly drunk. He felt he had earned it. His stay in Jerusalem had gone well with no trouble from the rebels. Although Pilate was disappointed that he had made no progress on his plan to find the boy through whom he would control Palestine, he would resume his search once he returned to Nazareth. With Herod hopefully out of the way through the efforts of the rebels, it would be an easier matter to make the boy Rome's King of the Jews. In the meantime, he would be able to report to Rome that he had kept a million people under control at the Feast in Jerusalem. The Legion would be leaving on the return march to the garrison in the morning, and he was looking forward to a good soak in his baths.

Gathered with his officers, Pilate had just finished a large satisfying meal with fine wine and good stories when a dirty and tired-looking soldier entered the room. It was one of Decimus's best men from the garrison. Pilate prepared himself to look shocked and upset at the news of Herod's untimely death.

Out of breath, the messenger saluted Pilate and blurted out, "Commander, the garrison is lost!"

Not what he was expecting to hear, the words did not completely register in Pilate's wine muddled mind. He smiled and turned to the other officers.

"Well, I'm sure we can find it sooner or later."

They all laughed.

"Sir, the garrison—" the messenger's voice broke with emotion, "the garrison in Nazareth has fallen—two nights ago."

Their laughter stopped abruptly.

"What are you saying, soldier?" asked Pilate, suddenly very serious.

The soldier swallowed hard. "The garrison walls have been destroyed, Commander."

The officers looked at him in disbelief. But the man was a good soldier, and the truth of his message could not be doubted from the despair in his voice. Pilate stood up from the table. The officers' minds were already racing for answers to the questions they knew their commander would ask.

"Who did this? How did it happen?"

They watched the soldier's face go completely white and a frightened look appear in his eyes.

"Two ghosts," he whispered. "They did it with a ram's horn."

"Steady, soldier!" warned Pilate.

"I swear it, Sir! They rose up out of the fallen stones. I saw them with my own eyes. That's why Decimus sent me with the message."

The officers all stood there wanting, but unable, to doubt him. How else could a fortified garrison be destroyed so suddenly and without a large attacking army? Pilate felt a knot of dread tighten in his stomach.

"Did anything happen to Herod Antipas?" he asked the soldier.

"He and his guards immediately fled into the night. His servants lingered for a while not knowing what to do, and then wandered off."

Pilate thought for a moment, and then gave his order.

"Petillius, prepare the troops to return to the garrison at once."

"But Sir, you don't understand," the frustrated messenger interrupted his command. "There is no garrison in Nazareth to return to!"

Pilate gave him a questioning look.

"There is nothing left of the garrison. Most of the troops deserted when they saw what the ghosts had done. Those few that are left are sleeping under their cloaks on the ground and eating rations that Decimus bought from the locals with his own money. There is nothing there but a pile of rocks and rubble."

The exhausted soldier turned his face away hoping that no one would see the tears welling up his eyes. A somber silence filled the room until Pilate finally gave another order.

"Petillius, send a messenger to the garrison commander in Caesarea. Tell him that I will be redeploying the Legion to that garrison. Then send a messenger to Decimus. Tell him to start rebuilding the wooden stockade for replacements that will relieve him shortly."

Petillius walked over to the messenger who slumped with fatigue.

"Come with me, soldier," Petillius ordered in a low voice. He took the soldier's arm and headed for the door.

Pilate sat down and stared at the floor. He remained there unmoving for a long time as the officers around him grew increasingly uncomfortable in the extended silence. They finally filed out of the room without speaking.

A while later, Pilate looked around, surprised to see he was alone. His body felt numb, and his mind still could not grasp what he had just been told. But he knew his life would never be the same.

His eyes fixed on the red plumes and golden bronze of his helmet sitting on a table across the room. His mind flashed on the image of a boy sitting on an awning in the market, holding the helmet. "Welcome to Nazareth," he again heard the boy's voice saying.

Then he remembered the words he heard moments later from another boy. "Please forgive them, for they know not what they do."

White hot wrath flared up inside Pilate.

"There will be no forgiveness!" he thought angrily. "If I could get my hands on that boy from Nazareth now, I would—"

Pilate's eyes came up suddenly and looked again at the helmet. Only in that moment, out of his intense emotion, did he comprehend the extraordinary courage, wisdom and strength in the gesture and words of the boy.

"That boy—from Nazareth. Could *he* be . . . ," wondered Pilate out loud.

***

The Apostles gathered at the barn. They and their friends were celebrating their own Feast paid for from the money they had earned delivering messages.

There was much to celebrate. The Apostles had achieved a great victory over the Romans by freeing Peter and Maggie, destroying the garrison in Nazareth and sending Herod Antipas into the hills like a scared rabbit. After the destruction of the fortification, Pontius Pilate decided that it would not be rebuilt and the Legion of Roman soldiers was gone. Peter and Maggie were now safe. And miraculously, Judas had been returned to them.

Their Feast also would be the last time the Apostles and their friends could be together for a while. Changes were happening. Peter and Andrew as well as James and John were going back to fish the Sea of Galilee with their fathers. Matthew was headed north as well to Capernaum where he was apprenticed to the tax collectors as a money counter. Simon tried to be secretive when he told them he was leaving Nazareth to live in the wilderness, but everyone knew what he was planning. Maggie and her mother were moving back to Magdala to live farther from Herod's attention and secret police. And Bartholomew was no longer going to deliver messages. To everyone's surprise, he had taken a position working in the Wine Seller Shikkor's shop.

The barn was cleaned up for the occasion. The hay stored in the upper loft of the barn was moved out so that a table made out of old boards could be set up to seat them all. Jewels was given a good brushing and extra grain in his stall. James and John brought fishes, Maggie had baked loaves of bread, and Thaddeus and Philip spent message money on lamb, fruits and sweets. Susanna and Bartholomew brought three jugs of wine from the Wine Seller Shikkor along with his thanks for ridding Nazareth of the Roman soldiers.

"Only one cup each!" Susanna warned them with a smile.

The inside of the old barn took on a golden glow when Maggie lit the lamps and called everyone to the table. Peter had his arm around Andrew's shoulder as he tenderly stepped up and took a seat. Under his eyes the bruises were turning from purple to a sickly green, and his lips were still split and swollen. At the other end of the table, Judas looked very tired and sat quietly. Jesus found a seat at the middle of the table as he and the rest of the Apostles crowded in between them.

Before they started eating, Bartholomew rose and told them he had an announcement. The Wine Seller Shikkor and Bartholomew's parents had agreed to his betrothal to Susanna. Bartholomew blushed as the Apostles clapped and whistled when Susanna leaned over and gave him a kiss on the smooth skin of his cheek.

When the cheering started to die down, Jesus stood up.

"My friends, I can't tell you how pleased I am to hear of your betrothal." He gave Bartholomew a wink. "We all look forward to your wedding—because it certainly will have the best wines of any wedding in the history of Palestine."

"Don't you dare touch the wine jugs," called out Thomas. Everyone laughed.

Jesus smiled and then continued, "I too have an announcement."

The Apostles grew quiet.

"I am leaving Nazareth tomorrow. My parents and the Rabbi have decided that this is a good time in my life to take a long journey—to see the world with all of God's wonders."

The Apostles looked at him in surprise.

"Where will you be going, Jesus?" asked Maggie.

"I cannot say," he answered. "But it would be best if I am not in Nazareth for a while."

No one knew what to say. Peter slowly and painfully rose to his feet.

"I remember a verse that the Rabbi taught us from the Prophet Samuel," he said.

> *Go in peace, for we have sworn friendship with each other in the name of the Lord, saying, 'The Lord is witness between you and me, and between your descendants and my descendants forever.'*

Peter raised his cup to salute them.

"You are my true friends and risking your safety for me has proved your friendship. So I say to you now, ask anything of me and it will be given to you; seek me and you will find me; knock on my door and it will be opened to you."

He brought his cup to his tender lips. Everyone raised their cups and drank in a silent toast to their love for one another.

Maggie turned to Jesus.

"Jesus, would you give a blessing for this food?"

He bowed his head and said the simple blessing he had heard Joseph give for his family almost every night of his life.

"Blessed are You, Lord our God, King of the universe, Who brings forth bread from the earth."

"All of you, please eat," Maggie gently ordered.

Bartholomew needed no encouragement. After heaping food on to his plate, he interrupted a swallow of wine to reach into his tunic.

"Oh, I almost forgot, Jesus. I was given this message to deliver to you."

He handed Jesus a folded parchment that was secured by a wax seal.

"Who from?" Jesus asked.

"Some old Roman soldier. He paid me extra." Bartholomew's attention returned to the loaf of bread in front of him. With a smile at Susanna, he tore off a big piece and happily stuffed it into his mouth.

Overcome with curiosity, Jesus pushed aside his plate. He broke the seal on the parchment and carefully unfolded it. The message filled the page perfectly in flawless Aramaic handwriting.

My Son, in Whom I am well pleased,

You have much ahead of You in your time on earth. You will go on great journeys near and far. I am giving these words to You to guide You on your path.

Before the birth of every man and woman, Adam and Eve made a choice. They chose a life for Mankind in which all would have the Knowledge of Good and Evil.

Mankind asked for and received this knowledge. All men and women now know a life that contains evil as well as good.

But now, I give to You the full and true Knowledge of

Good and Evil:

Life is not made up of some things that are good and other things that are evil. Everything in life is at once both good and evil.

In every happiness is a seed of sadness, and in every sadness there is promise of happiness. Triumphs can lead to tragedy, but tragedy can eventually lead to triumph.

How can it happen that sadness will lead to happiness, that tragedy can lead to triumph?

The answer is your message for the world.

Teach all people that sadness becomes happiness and tragedy will lead to triumph only through love, forgiveness and sacrifice for one another.

In the end, life leads to death, but with this knowledge of good and evil, death can give life.

Your delivering this message to all on earth will bring You difficult and painful times. Yet be assured that I am here for You always.

I will forever show You my love, though You may not always understand it. But know this: despite all that happens to You, I will not forsake You.

When You need me in Your life, I will be there. Simply call for me with these words,

"Our Father Who art in heaven, hallowed be Thy name...."

About the Author

Joel Gordonson, before becoming a novelist, has enjoyed a career as an international attorney. He holds law degrees in the United States and from the University of Cambridge.

Gordonson's family tree includes a long line of ministers, including a great-grandfather who emigrated from Europe in 1860 to become a missionary on the American western frontier. It is this lineage that influenced the subject of his first novel, *That Boy from Nazareth*.

ThatBoyFromNazareth.com

JoelGordonson.com

Facebook.com/JoelGordonson

Facebook.com/ThatBoyFromNazareth

Made in the USA
Charleston, SC
11 November 2015